CW01213917

The Beauty of Chell Street

Andrew Dutton

LEAF BY LEAF

Published by Leaf by Leaf
an imprint of Cinnamon Press,
Office 49019, PO Box 15113, Birmingham, B2 2NJ
www.cinnamonpress.com

Print Edition ISBN 978-1-78864-942-1

British Library Cataloguing in Publication Data. A CIP record for this book can be obtained from the British Library.

Designed and typeset in Adobe Jenson by Cinnamon Press.
Cover design by Adam Craig © Adam Craig.
Cinnamon Press is represented by Inpress.

Acknowledgements

Scripture quotations are from the World English Bible or the American Standard Version of the Bible, both in the public domain.

For a Sweet, Gentle Grandmother
and in memory of a Mad Aunt

The Beauty of Chell Street

The Beauty of Chell Street

1967

'When I was a girl they called me The Beauty of Chell Street. I had long brown hair, so long I could sit on it, and the loveliest brightest blue eyes any man ever beheld. "If a woman have long hair it is a glory to her". Saint Paul said that. I know my Bible; and unlike certain other people I could mention, I read, understood and obeyed the book. And I was so glorious then. They would look at me; the men from the factory, the delivery boys, the Tommies going to and from the war, even the older men; there was a time I turned every head. Some even called out, right saucy things they'd say too; they all noticed and they all wanted me. I could of had any man I chose. They offered to take me dancing and buy me presents. I could of been a rich man's wife.'

Nora Wilson's voice faded and in its place came a clicking from her throat, as if a cough was trying to emerge but dying before it could reach her mouth. She dragged smoke out of her cigarette and blew it towards the chair opposite. Sometimes there was somebody in that chair, sometimes there wasn't; it didn't matter anymore. She told her story anyway. She sat close to the gas fire; her chair, an old friend to her, but every day she struggled a little more to get out of it. She could push herself up, for her arms were still strong enough to hold children, push mops and brooms and manage heavy, sodden washing, but the problem was her useless legs. To manage the few feet to the kitchen door she had to crawl along the wall like a spider, holding to the mantelpiece all the way, all the time feeling something pulling her down, her head going light as she shuffled along step-by-sideways-step. One day that dizziness would overcome her and she would fall as if from a cliff face, her skull would crack on the cold, bare tiles of the scullery floor and that would be the end.

The only sound in the near-silent room was the clock ticking, like the heartbeat of a tiny animal. Too fast, Nora thought, too fast, you're leaving me behind. The clock was on a small table by her side, next to her ashtray, cigarettes and matches, an empty tea cup, three packets of pills and her pension book, signed and ready. Also there was a circular mirror; she could see her face, at an angle, in its smeary surface. She saw the lines that scored her skin as if it were clay worked mercilessly with a wooden knife. She saw how the wrinkles pointed towards her mouth, as if radiating from it, or worse pulling her face down, to where her looks would be consumed and lost forever. She seized hold of the mirror and turned it sharply so it was edge-on to her.

She looked for comfort to a photograph on the mantelpiece, the one she kept in pride of place, always.

'I could of had any of em, I could of. And who did I get?' she asked the empty air. 'Sam bloody Wilson, that's who.'

2011

'Stop making excuses young lady!'

'But it's late and I'm *cold*,' whinged Francine Latimer.

'You've had all day to do this. You've been dragging your

feet. You've got less than a week to hand this work in; I'll not have you panicking at the last minute again. Get on with it!'

Her mother's voice was a shove in the back that propelled Francine to the garage. It was gloomy inside, the electric bulb feeble, and what little natural light there was had to crawl through the obstructive greenery of a bush grown over the back window. Further protest was pointless, and so Francine complied resentfully. She didn't want to do this. History was boring. Family history was *mega* boring.

She found the old trunk easily; it was covered with a dirty sheet and piled high with paint pots, discarded toys, broken garden tools and empty, soggy cardboard boxes that took ages to clear. The lid only opened after huge exertion and it surrendered with a rasp, crack and groan, suggesting that something was now broken forever.

The contents of the trunk were unimpressive; yellowed papers, a few fetid, horrid-smelling books, albums of photographs that hung apart at their spines, other pictures stuffed higgledy-piggledy in plastic bags. A past buried in haste, without thought for posterity—there was not much essay material, Francine mused, as she shuffled through the faded documentation of the lives of people she had never known. Her interest flared as she found two photos still in their frames. She didn't know why, but they seemed special.

The first must have been a hundred years old: the time-drained image touched the youngster's wonder; it was like looking at a person preserved behind an amber mirror. The girl she was looking at was no more than sixteen; she possessed a still, unsmiling loveliness and with her perfect features and elegantly-dressed hair the photograph looked to Francine like the first publicity still of a movie goddess. The face, although young, had a loving, motherly gentleness about it as well as a sort of playfulness; the serious expression was forced, as if it had been demanded by the photographer but was threatened with ruination at any moment by a sunrise of smiles and a carillon of girlish giggles. Fascination grew within Francine as the face in the picture drew her closer, it was so familiar, surely it was her Mum, no, her Gran, no, it was her Aunty Eileen, no: it was Francine herself.

The second picture was joined to that of the girl, quite accidentally, by an ancient but still sticky piece of tape; the two frames were really quite hard to separate, this old thin thread held on tenaciously as Francine pulled at it. The man in this frame was surely not much older than the beautiful girl, and yet his dark hair appeared to be streaked with white. It made him look stern and mature beyond his years, and he gazed out at her with a self-possession that made Francine believe he must have been a soldier, a man accustomed to command. Unlike the young woman, there was no silly smile flickering on the edge of his pursed lips.

1967

'It reminds me of that song, "You Always Hurt The One You Love", oh it's so true.'

The smoke from her cigarette made Nora's eyes water as

she as she looked across at the visitor's chair. Who was there—one of her children perhaps, ungrateful mares every one, or maybe Mona Welkins from across the road? She couldn't see, and for a moment couldn't remember either.

'So true. I don't know what he saw in her. She was a skinny, pinch-faced cow you know, five years older than him and her husband not long in his grave. She dressed as if she made her clothes out of blackout curtains. She read books and newspapers. And he said he just wanted to talk about her. Talk! I told him "bumholes", yes I did.'

The little clock ticked frantically.

'It was a kind of breakdown, the doctors told me, something in his mind that just snapped. They showed me a picture, like an x-ray, this broken line it was. They said what he did to me was discussting, just discussting.'

Ash fell from her cigarette, but she didn't notice. Her eyes were on the photograph.

'Are you all right Nonna?' asked a child's voice.

'I'm dying,' she whispered.

2011

Now Francine knew who it was. The family still spoke of her; Nonna Nora, who'd died of a broken heart every day for nearly fifty years.

1944

The Royal Oak was alive with voices and wreathed in a slow-moving tobacco fog. Tucked into a corner of the bar,

George Shenton was entertaining Jack Carthmain with his favourite reminiscence of palmy youth.

'So I got me hand up there, fingers right on er clout—eh?'

Jack shushed him and nodded his head towards a figure at the door.

'Clean up the language and put the clothes back on the women,' advised Jack. 'His Holiness has come to visit the sinners.'

Sam Wilson entered wearing what the Oak's regulars called his 'I've only come in from the rain' look, and nodded curtly to the men at the bar.

'Ey up Sammy, ow at?' Jack grinned, larding his accent for Sam's benefit.

'Ow's your lady?' George joined in. 'Up the stick again yet?'

Sam ordered a half without replying; he was used to their double-act.

He sat with Jack and George and soon they were discussing the progress of the war in earnest tones. Twenty minutes later Sam bade them good evening and walked out into the cool night air.

Jack shook his head. 'Trouble with Sammy there is he's stuck up.'

George pondered before adding, 'And the trouble for his wife is he's stuck up Mirabelle Ellis.'

Out in the street, Sam heard their easy, dirty laughter and winced.

The Place of Lost Stories

2011

Write a short essay about a member of your family who lived in the last century. Explain why you chose them, their relationship to you and important events from their life.

You may use a computer for research, but otherwise use pen and ink.

Optional: start a family tree, tracing it back to your chosen relative.

I have chose *(an 'n' was added in red ink)* to write about Nonna Nora, who was my great-grandmother. Everyone thought that she was born in 1900 but when they found her berth citificate (*'birth certificate'* the teacher corrected) it said 1899, no one knows why.

Her family was from Lackashire *(Lancashire)* and she had three sisters and three brothers. She was ten years younger than the nearest of them because her mum and dad lived apart for a long time even though they did not disvorce. *(divorce)* They had split *(separated)* because Nonna's dad had been a coachman, actual coaches and horses, as it was the very old days, for some kind of lord or aristocrac *(think about how to improve how you say all this)* but when the motor car was invented he refused to drive it and he lost his job. He set up as something called a rag and bone man, again with a horse but with only a cart and not a posh coach. Nonna's mum thought this was terrible because she thought they were a posh family and posh people weren't rag and bone men and she would have nothing to do with it. But even after all them *(those)* years they came back to eachother *(still officially two words)* and the family story is that Nonna Nora *(just say 'Nora' or 'my great-grandmother')* was a sort of reunion gift they gave each other. *(see above)* Funny but that's how it was for my mum too, she says they were interrupted families. *(think about how to express yourself more clearly)*

Nonna Nora married into a family called Wilson and moved here. *(to our town)* She married in 1920 when she was 20 *(you probably don't need to put her age here)* and had eight kids. *(children)* Three of them died before they could grow up, two of them from the same thing, a disease called memigitis *(meningitis?)* people had lots of kids in those days because they expected them to die, I find this hard to imagine. Another one of the kids almost died from the same thing but she was saved because there was this brand new drug as saved her *(don't write as you might speak)* but my gran*(dmother)* says that both Nonna and Sam thought that she would die and they weren't as upset as they were over the others. *(You make them sound very cold—were they?)* None of their kids are alive now except for my gran*(dmother)* and she is dead old. *(don't show her your work this time, perhaps?)*

Grampa Sam *('my great grandfather')* left Nonna Nora after the Second World War. She never got over it and she always talked about him. She called him 'that bloody man'*(???!!!)* and said he'd gone mad. She said she was ill but no one knew what with *(re-word this passage)* and she was nearly ninety when she died, and no one knew why she did, even the doctors said it was like she had just given up.

Apart from Grampa Sam leaving her the worst thing in Nonna Nora's life was her children dying. She couldn't help the ones that died of the disease but it must of *(have)* been worse when her only son died. Nonna Nora had insisted on the whole family moving house because they lived right near a big park which had a big, deep pond in it and she was afraid that Alex would fall in it and get drownded *(you're writing slang again!)* so they moved house to a place where my gran*(dmother)* still lives and Alex was killed there when he touched an electric fire and he couldn't be saved. Gran *(my grandmother)* says that Nonna Nora always had tears in her eyes when she talked about Alex and the others, and she'd sing a song that Alex always sang when he was playing outside which went 'Run bugger run bugger run run run'. *(perhaps a little too much information here!)* Although Nonna always cried when she mentioned the ones who died, my gran*(dmother)* says Grampa Sam never so much as spoke of them, and he shut Nonna up when she tried.

My gran*(dmother)* says that Nonna Nora was very beautiful and you could see that even when she was a very old lady, but she *(Nora/my great-grandmother)* never looked at another man again and never got married again.

Soon there will be no one who remembers Nonna Nora, not properly, and I think that's well sad. *(think about rewording here, and can you expand by saying why you think it's sad?)*

'That's a good start Francine,' the teacher handed her book back, looking pleased, 'subject to more work on your spelling, grammar and tendency towards verbal chaos, you have the beginnings of a very worthwhile little project here. Has doing this made you interested in finding out more of the story?'

Wedding Bands

1981

MONDAY	TUESDAY
WEDNESDAY	THURSDAY
FRIDAY	SATURDAY
SUNDAY	

I count time by the packet of pills on the table, not that nagging little clock. I'm supposed to know which pill to take because I know what day it is, but to tell the truth I only know what day it is from the pill I'm taking. I expect I slipped up long ago, missed a day or took two doses in one day, then I kept on slipping up until my time became meaningless, measured only by the rustle and pop of another little metallic packet.

I expect the pills to make me well, but they never seem to make any bally difference. I ask the doctor what they're supposed to do and he answers as if he's talking to a bloody child and it all sounds like fairy tales, told to keep this gaga old fool quiet. He can't even explain what's wrong with me, so how can he cure it? I'd change doctors but the buggers are all the same and I don't trust these young doctors that are coming in now, what can they know? After a lifetime of illness I know more than they do. And I wouldn't want their hands on me, you never know what's on their minds, especially the foreign ones, the packies and the blackies Mona Welkins calls them. Sam Wilson, Sammy, he never trusted darkies neither, not till one saved his bloody life anyway, then he changed his tune the miserable hypocrite: they were never dreamed of as our doctors when they were just colonials in the old days, the good old days when we had the empire. In them days I was something worth having too, I wasn't stuck here in this chair, sickening ever more and waiting for the end; I really could just sit here until I die. They'll find me here eventually, cold I'll be for they come so rarely now. I could be gone a twelvemonth before they come looking. So much do they care when I gave so much of my life—all of my life—to them. They never want to listen, 'Not your woes again, Mum!' they cry, and they tell me to stop brooding on the past, why don't I think about what life could give me even now, why don't I think of the children and the grandchildren, the way I used to play with the little ones, why can't I do that, get out of this chair and be what I was once again?

Because I'm not bloody Lazarus, that's why, and me getting up to play football or cricket with the kiddies again would be a miracle beyond even Our Lord. I'm sick, I'm a cripple, and no one seems to understand that. I know they all think I'm play-acting, that I'm doing this out of spite: they should suffer like I do and then they'd know it for the truth, and how would they like that? If I could walk then I would walk, it's common sense, and the fact I don't walk surely speaks for itself, have they no common savvy? Everyone thinks I'm soft in the head, my own children treat me as if I'm the damn village idiot, I'm a little deaf and people these days do mumble and gabble so, but I'm no silly arse, my brain's as good as theirs, as good as anyone's so it is, *it's* not crippled but they see me sut here and they think my brain's as athrititic as my legs.

'It's not "athritis" mother, it's "arthritis", the prissy madams correct me time after time. It's athritis to me, what's in the way that you say a word; it doesn't change the pain I suffer. They lord it over me, if I can't say the damn word I can't have the damn illness, that's what they seem to think, and so I'm just a daft old woman in a chair making believe she's sick and can't even choose a sickness that she can get her dentured jaws around—silly old stoat. Silly; silly. Old; old.

I never wanted to be old, to look and feel this way, I'd as soon be dead. Why else is it I can only ever think about that fact, that I'd be better off dead? I'm dying bit by bit anyway, but probably not quickly enough for the tastes of *some* people. I never asked to be this way, I never asked to be here, all alone and broken. I was different once, I wasn't ignored and put upon, no, the centre of attention I was, the girl everyone desired, that was me, the Beauty of Chell Street. I wasn't just pretty, I was truly beautiful, I knew it for the truth, I knew it sure as I knew my heart was beating, same as I knew how to draw one breath after another, and I felt it too, yes I did, deep in my bones and down in my soul. All the stares, all the compliments and attention I got, just confirmed it. It was a sort of power, a gift from nature that made people come to me, wanting to be with me, it made them want to please me and to work hard to make me smile. A wonderful feeling. And oh, I knew what was in the mind of many a man, but that felt wonderful too, and that power it flowed even stronger inside me when I sensed their longing.

You hear girls complaining about men undressing them with their eyes, but I knew what that felt like many and many a time, even in the days when men knew a little shame and weren't so open about displaying their lusts. I understood what they were doing inside their heads, but it made me feel the stronger. These days they talk about free love, everyone seems to be in and out of everyone else's bed without a blush, nobody cares anymore. Imagine what I could have had if things had been that way when I was young; I could of had any man, I know that much. I could of taken lovers, a thousand, all the handsomest in the land, I could of picked and chosen and walked away with every beautiful man I saw. I could of bin anything I bloody well wanted.

'Don't say "could of bin", mother, say "could have been".' That's what my girls would say if they were here, always putting me right as if I was some stupid schoolgirl. Their father was forever doing it. 'Nora, you set such a bad example to the girls with your sloppy diction and all those nonsense words and slang! You know the children will emulate you!' I took him to mean that what the monkey hears the monkey will repeat, why did he have to talk that way? But they never did 'emulate' me, they *copied* him. Oh they are his wretched seed right enough. Faint dead away they would if they paid attention to what I was saying instead of how I said it. But they never do listen to me.

I could of bin a Queen, laying in the bed of a King. I would never've had to worry about where my next meal was coming from, how I could afford my next dress or put a roof over my head, it would of all been provided by my eager beaus, each and every one of em craving the favours of the Beauty. I would of bin known as the most beautiful woman in the world. Yes, in the world, not just in one small street or tiny town. My picture would be everywhere, just like them film stars now, and everyone would want me, everyone.

I wish I'd been painted in the nude. There'd be no shame in that, it wouldn't be like them girls in them magazines now, showing theirselves off like tarts, it would of bin a work of art, I think I should of bin painted in oils, there's something about oil paintings that's better than anything else, truer, more alive. Yes, I wish I'd been painted naked, I had a lovely body, slender and yet goodly curvy, with beautiful bubbies not too big, not too small, a flat belly that never needed corsets and legs that deserved to be seen and not bundled up in thick clumsy stockings or wrapped in heavy curtains of skirts. I'd be painted lying down I think, like a rich and noble lady resting on her day-bed perhaps, eyes looking out bold at the world, aware of its envy of her. I would be able to look at that picture now and see myself, *that* beautiful, forever.

Or perhaps I should of been standing, bathed in streams of morning light, standing at a window and opening the curtain to let the sun caress and know me. My back would be partly turned and the dawn's rays would touch my body like a man's gentle fingers, exploring me, naked at the window, one neat breast catching the light and my petite rear hiding coyly in shadow, half-visible but showing its perfect shape.

I should of bin seen naked ('Mother, don't use such *sloppy diction!*') as for only Sammy Wilson ever to have seen me that way is a crying shame. It's as if he possessed that portrait but hoarded it away, shut it up in some dark and dusty attic only he knew about, visiting the neglected treasure less and less until it was forgotten altogether. I wish I had such a painting, I would show it to this day, proud I'd be, show it to anyone who stepped in here—I'd hang it over the fireplace in the living room, in place of that damn mirror where an old and shrivelled woman confronts me every time I go in there. I hate that mirror. I have always hated it. Far better that it should be replaced with beauty, timeless beauty, the real Nora Wilson, not that hag that floats into the silvered glass.

Beauty of face and body stayed with me for many a long year; it didn't creep and seep away leaving me old at thirty, not like the other women in this Avenue. Mona Welkins and her ilk looked dried-up, shadow-faced and tired even before their kiddies had gone to the Secondary Modern, but still I was unchanged. Oh how the soldiers used to call out to me in the Great War and how my mother was scandalised, but our dad said it was good for the lads' morale, they'd beat the Bosche for love of me. I didn't tell anyone about how it made me feel—warm inside. And I was still being called out to even in the last war: 1943 it was, and I was walking down the Avenue when a great truck came down, full of lads, they must have taken a wrong turning looking for the barracks three miles away. I heard them and at first I started, I thought they were angry, voices raised because they were arguing, but then the hubbub of shouts became clear even above the rumbling growl of the truck's engine.

'Look at the wiggle on that!'

'Never mind the wiggle, look at the *tits* on that!'

'Show us them tits, lovely!'

'Show us yer cunt!'

'E's probably at work, mate!'

There was a loud volley of booming bass laughter from out of the canvas-covered back of that truck and they were gone. I looked around rather nervously but there was still no one else to be seen in the Avenue; all was quiet again and nobody had heard. I tossed my head and walked on, but I felt that tingling warmth again, just like when the Tommies called to me years back, a feeling in my belly and my loins like the one that came when I rubbed myself. 'Look at the tits on that!'—I was forty-three years old and I had given birth to eight children but still the British soldier called out to me, I was helping them to beat Ole Hickler as sure as I did my bit against Kaiser Bill. Stick *that* in your pipe and smoke it, Mirabelle Ellis. And it's one in the eye for you Sam Wilson, you civvy-street coward you, for by that time I was nothing more to you than the creature that had borne your brood, an obstruction in your bed, no more did you come to me for your hot, dirty pleasures after you'd done with your prayers; but others would of.

Oh god, I imagined, I saw myself, allowing myself to be dragged up on to the back of that truck, lying on its hard floor as it rattled off to base, those boys with their rough hands on me, their barely-shaven faces all over me, against my skin, my hands feeling the hardness of each of them and letting them do it, do it, do whatever they wanted, oh *Christ* how I miss the feeling of a man inside me. Damn you Sammy Wilson, for I swore to love you till I die and I always keep my word: you have crippled me Sammy Wilson, you have killed me. We never did just make babies together, it was no cold process of production, you sweated and gasped, your breath coming in short piglike snorts, for you would rather kiss than gulp for air, and you ground hard into me, against me, oh we were alive with our passion. What turned you cold? That cheerless church and some filthy guilt lurking in your cheating soul, that's what Sam Wilson, that's what.

That I only ever had one man was a source of pride for me at the time, for I was a good girl and a good wife who had never thought about straying, but it's no cause for self-congratulation, not now. I bitterly regret chaining myself to you, Sammy Wilson, and I regret being in such a hurry to wed you and give you babes. Jesus hates you, Sammy Wilson, he's hated you from the moment you abandoned love for me and turned your attention to that raddled bag of bones, that bitch as stole you away, and then that empty sack of a woman you married just to fill the days of your old age. You are a liar and a cheat, Sammy Wilson, how could you do what you did, leaving your wife and children for some whore? How could you betray your marriage vows, the ones you took in the church that you held to be so holy? I never forgot my vows, no, I stuck to them then and ever since—and unlike you, I'll be true to them until death. So the common sinner proves to be better than the preacher, truer to what she swore than was the man who read out God's word from that silly old lectern. Jesus hates liars, Sammy Wilson, he abhors deceivers and fornicators; the Day of Judgement will come for you, and what then will you see but the fires of hell? The faithless husband, the man who abandoned his children, who married again with foul lies in his mouth even at the altar—oh don't ever believe I'm ignorant of what you did, denying your own flesh and bone, disclaiming its very existence, evil sinner that you are, you tried to make a fool of God and now God hates you too, there's no forgiveness in the whole heart of heaven for you Sammy Wilson, and I shall look upon your torment without pity, I shan't even give you a second thought. How many times would you have denied me as you took your poisoned wedding-vows; three times before the crowing of the cock, perhaps? Jesus will show no mercy to you, he knows the difference between true righteousness and mere self-righteousness. That's what folks called you, self-righteous, and for so many years it grieved me to hear it said: but it was true, oh so true. Even your own 'flock' despised you Sammy Wilson, each and every one of them.

I wasn't short of men who would of taken me—to wed or bed—even when you were gone Sammy Wilson, but I turned away every one, spurned them when I should of had them, had them all in turn, just to spite you and just to feel the presence of a man again, to taste and touch someone who was not *you*. Why did I keep my vows when you couldn't be bothered? That troubles me still. Your infidelity was a needle of pain in my veins, a pain that grew and grew until it stopped my legs and bent my back and turned my stomach sour; your falsity made me what I am, but you only ever broke my body, not my mind. And God saw you do it to me. God abominates you, Sammy Wilson.

I thought my body belonged to you, my husband and lover, and now it seems that in the most horrible way possible that this was so and remains so, I am still joined to you as your corruptions seep into me and take their toll upon my frame. I used to wince and grimace and take any pain that would give you pleasure, and the Lord knows I felt pleasure too, it was love, the purest and best love. And here I still am, waiting to hear your footfall on the path; if I hear steps coming to the door I think it could be you, I think it even now—today, tomorrow and every day until I cease to be. That is yet another curse I must live with.

I think about you and your new wife, the one you lied to God for, and I see you in your home and your beds—yes, separate beds, that's what I see, with perfect covers and starchy unstained sheets where no sweat of passion was ever shed, for you used up all the love you were capable of, you left it here with me and my memories, you have married again but only because you must, because you think it makes you respectable, because your adopted church would look upon you with suspicion if you were not a husband. But is there any life there within your new marriage? No, you are dead inside, Sammy Wilson, your life was here with your real wife and with your children, and you walked away from us all: if you hadn't of done that, I know how happy we could of been. You could still come to me, old age be damned, so eager and excited, and I would still do anything for you. But I bet *she* lives like a virgin, that she washes right away any spot of her body that ever feels your touch, purging it with disinfectant and shards of glass. You used to draw blood from me and I gave it willingly, yes oh god I prized every moment, I groaned and swore and writhed for you and it was love, love, love, true skin-touching love. I bet she hasn't even tasted your mouth, she would rather die and be buried than take your tongue and drink down your spit like I did, the cold, loveless, sexless frostbitten spinster of the parish that she is, yes, a spinster still, she won't have shed a drop of blood for you or for any other man. She doesn't want you as a man, Sammy Wilson, she wants you as a prop, a crutch, so nobody can pity her to her face or talk behind her back saying she will die alone and unused. You think you're the comfort of each other's old age, but it's a false, empty comfort because you belong elsewhere, I know.

There are red pills, yellow pills, white pills, pink pills. Sometimes I think that they give the dratted things to me just to keep me busy during the day, that these things are candy drops and pieces of chalk that have no healing power at all. Red pills for the sunrise, yellow for the noon, white for the day's clouds and pink for the sunset. With these I count out the short remainder of my days. I know that the day has come to an end when it is time for the pink pill, time for some tea and then to sit in front of the television to see the evening off. What do you do Sammy Wilson? Talk earnestly to your ill-gotten wife about your religion, read to her from the Bible in your so-clean and so-cheerless parlour? At least I sit before a good warming fire with a cup of tea and the comforts of an unstained conscience.

The room in which I spend my empty evenings is the same one where we were supposed to spend our old age, sitting quietly, receiving visits from our loving and loyal children; our room. It used to be your room alone, you shut out everyone, even me, and even now I shudder when I come to take possession of it in the evening, fearing that your spirit is still there, forbidding visitors, driving away the little ones, and confining me to the kitchen. It was your room until you were ready for your beer and cigarette at that dratted pub with your dratted cronies. You're still master of this house; how many years have you been gone? I wonder what power you wield now, in that igloo you inhabit. Does that frigid cow obey your every word, or does she give you no peace, dictating every waking moment of your life? We belonged together Sammy Wilson, we still do; you don't belong over there with her, it is against nature and you know it. If I had you now I wouldn't need any of these silly pills, not one of them, my body would work again, old age and illness would melt away, the world would be in the shape it was meant to be.

Another pink pill then, the dying glow of another day, smoke from my cigarette, steam from the tea cup. I'll have some buttered toast later, if I can bear the palaver of getting to the kitchen and back. And I have friends. The people in the plays on television keep me company. I bet you don't even look in at the television do you Sammy Wilson, for fear of seeing or hearing something that may upset you or your prim, praying, false wife; something about adulterers perhaps, Sammy Wilson? You could write the script for such a thing, couldn't you, you swine, you hypocrite, you *bastard* you? I imagine you in your beds, you and her, marble figures on a tomb, side by side but never touching, hands folded in two-faced supplication to the Lord. Cold and dead. I bet you don't have a fire in that chilly chapel of sin in which you cling to existence. How can you live with your lies, Sammy Wilson, how can you go on in the sure knowledge of what is coming to you now that you have walked away from the only thing that could ever redeem you? I'd have died for you Sammy Wilson, I would have suffered your death and accepted your torment in eternity too, and I would still have been glad you were delivered to safety. But not now; don't you even begin to hope for that.

You made this a cold room, even when I had set a fire—and what a job that used to be—you could draw the heat out of any four walls. She's like you, you're two icicles together, what a pair. I used to want us to make love in front of this fire, for you to undress me as you kissed me, my breath coming sharp as I smelt the coals and felt their heat upon my bare skin, your warmth as you held me, then your weight as it shifted up and down upon me. We could lie on our thick rug and there would be no light but the flickering yellow of the fire, shadows bobbing on the wall, the shapes of the two of us joined as one. I'd of let you have me in firelight any time, and if you walked in now and lay down I'd lie with you, no matter the gap of years, what does that matter when there's love? I can see your face in the fire sometimes. We could have toasted crumpets over these coals, wrapped in blankets and clinging close as the sheen of love glowed on our skins. The children would be abed and there would be no danger of their disturbing us, for they would know never to come in here; but in my dream that would not be through fear of you but out of love, love and respect for their parents, from knowing that this was our space, our time, our room, where we cultivated the love that kept us alive and young.

Would not this house have been better as one of love than one of fear? It would surely have been better for the children's games to have been played in their riotous fullness than to have them silenced, brought to sudden end by an angry roar from your den? I think always about our happy house, the place it could of bin. Could have been. It wouldn't have mattered then that the walls were so dark and the rooms so chilly, we could have supplied the light and heat, weathered the war, watched our children grow and loved and loved and loved. If you were still here, the family would come readily enough, our daughters and their husbands bringing the little ones to see Nonna and Grampa, and every day would be full again with the joyful noise of infants' play, and there would be no heartbreaking waits for short duty-visits from those hard-faced girls, no lectures as if I were a dratted half-wit, no speaking to me as if my old brain had dried up and blown away on the wind. It is the fact that you are missing, that you are in the wrong place, that is the cause of all of this.

I used to imagine dying with you inside me: when we were so afire in our marital bed, I sometimes thought I would. Women often didn't see out their allotted span in those days, especially when they'd borne child after child and life was hard; I imagined my life ending as you came, and I would of bin content to die that way. So even then, in a way, I knew you would be my death, but I was too foolish, too lovestruck, to see that it would be in *this* way, not in passion's heat but in fading slowly, my body breaking down bit by bit as I wait endlessly, hopelessly for you.

Sam Wilson, I will live just long enough to see you buried and then I shall die contented, serene even, secure knowing that I shall look down from God's right hand and see your fate.

The Place of Lost Stories

2012

'Francine, I'm going to see Aunty Peggy, do you want to come?'

Kara Latimer made this as a throwaway remark, and her daughter's dull eyes confirmed her presupposition, along with the apathetic voice that couldn't even add a 'wh' to 'oo'.

'Aunty Peggy, you know! I'm taking your Gran to see her, she's very old and it may be our last chance before she—Aunty Peggy, I mean. Gran wants to see her. She's in a home now.'

'Uh.'

'Don't you remember me telling you about her? When she was a young girl she lived next door to Nonna Nora.'

'Oh. Not a real aunty at all then.'

'Well no, they called her that because they were fond of her. People used to do that.' Kara couldn't help sounding peeved, bloody surly child. 'Just thought you might take an interest. Your essay—you know.'

'That was *years* ago!'

Why was it that teenagers regarded events that occurred more than eighteen months ago as ancient history? Kara decided she didn't want the discussion.

'You can stay here I suppose. You're old enough not to do anything too daft: but keep your mobile on and if anything's wrong, anything at all, go straight to Aunty Eileen's.'

Good, thought Francine, a chance to be on my own; there's homework skulking around somewhere I can kill off, and if Mum doesn't say anything annoying before she goes I might even do that tidying-up she keeps on pestering about. And then—alone! I'll watch whatever I want on the machine, think about stuff, be free!

When Kara pulled the car out of the narrow driveway, she was mildly astonished to see her daughter standing there, washed, changed and ready to leave. She didn't like herself very much for suspecting instantly that Francine was about to do something calculated to ruin her plans for the day. Tough, girlie, she thought, I will not let my mother down no matter what.

'Decided to go to Eileen's?'

'Decided to come with you.'

'It's a long drive to Wales—an hour and a half each way.' I wanted her to come and now I'm trying to put her off; Kara wondered at herself.

'I've got my music box.' Francine patted the neat white-trimmed square at her belt.

'No moaning.'

'Course not.'

'No boring declarations of boredom.'

'*No!*'

Rules made, journey agreed, they set off to collect Flora Latimer.

Kissing the bristly, papery cheek of an old lady, *ugghhhh*; but Francine swallowed her disgust and did it, as it seemed to be expected. Aunty Peggy was a tiny white-haired doll propped up in a chair, her legs wrapped in blankets and her body looking wispily frail, as if she should have been kept in a glass case; she was a near-ghost, the trace of a memory about to be lost. The place smelt of hospital; Francine hated hospitals.

'Well how nice!' the old woman's voice creaked and piped, as if powered by an intermittent, failing battery, but Francine heard a brightness of tone she found attractive, while Kara, sitting next to her, heard the voice of the kindly middle-aged farmer's wife forever baking and passing round treats for the little ones; Flora Wilson strained to discern through Peggy's almost musical wheezing the brassy tones of a one-time tomboy who could swim, race, climb trees and knock down the toughest boy in the village.

'I'm so pleased,' continued Aunty Peggy, and her glittering, still-alive eyes came to rest on Francine. 'And your Mam and your Nyn brought you too! Now I haven't laid eyes on you girl, not since you were small enough for your Mam to wash you in the kitchen sink.'

'Nyn' or 'Nine', that was how she'd said it, in a voice filled with gentle inflections like soft shadows, stresses that fell in all the wrong places as if she were getting by in a foreign language: Francine found the lilt comforting and beautiful.

Conversing with the elderly was hard: discussion of the here and now stuttered and stopped, and here it was made worse by the fact that all four women in the room were keenly aware of the presence of death; they could not examine the present too closely and so by tacit consent their chatter slid gently, comfortably to the past.

'Oh but won't this be boring for...' Aunty Peggy said slightly helplessly as she and Flora exchanged memories of far-off childhood. Francine thought Peggy was wonderful for that.

'Not at all,' said Kara firmly, I think in many ways that's why she's come. Francine is the family's budding historian. She'd like to hear what you've got to say, especially about Nonna.'

Francine was none too flattered by the label 'budding historian', but let it go.

'You want to hear about your great-gran? That's unusual, young kiddies these days never seem to be interested in such things.'

I'm not such a 'kiddie' either, thought the teenager, but then again everyone in the room must have seemed a kiddie to Peggy. Kara explained about the essay and the discovery of the photograph. 'It piqued her curiosity. Now her teacher wants her to turn it into a complete research project.'

'Research project?' Aunty Peggy repeated, smiling, and spiky Francine suspected she was being made fun of until the old lady continued clearly impressed and thoughtful. 'Lovely. Better than in my day, there at school all day sitting in rows, terrified of the teacher, chanting our times-tables parrot-fashion… we learned nothing, you know, nothing at all…' Her mind seemed to wander a few moments but then that life-loving eye of hers fixed on Francine. 'It's an interesting subject you've chosen, young lady.'

Aunty Peggy's face was delicate, little more than a skull with a tight-stretched covering; she was barely able to turn her head to look at Francine and her breathing was shallow and uneven, but still those eyes transmitted life and intelligence.

'S'pose everybody tells you, but you're very like Nora, you and your Mam especially. To look at, I mean.' Aunty

Peggy added the qualification hastily, as if she had just delivered an unintended insult.

'How did you know her?' Francine's question salved the awkwardness. 'Mum says you were neighbours.'

'Yes-yes we were: not neighbours in that on-top-of-you way you have nowadays, the family lived some distance away. Our Mam and Dad had a smallholding on the edge of the next village; I remember Mr. Wilson insisted on calling it an allotment, that didn't half irritate our Dad, he used to refer to Mr. Wilson as "that English idiot". Mam told him not to say things like that in front of me, but he said I had to find out about the English at some point, sooner the better.'

Peggy laughed, a rustle and a whisper of memory, another breath spent.

'Our Mam met Nora at the market one day; they had children of similar ages and they got on well, so she began to come to see us for tea, bringing her little ones. She wasn't typical English, not Nora, she made no judgements on us, didn't try to belittle us; she tried hard to fit in here.'

'She always said that she was happiest in Wales.' Flora's memories lapped across Peggy's, her voice rueful. 'She talked about it so much, said she'd love to come back just once before she died. Once I told her I'd learn to drive, buy a car specially for that one journey and bring her back to see the old village again. But I never did. Sometimes I feel guilty about that.'

'Well you should *not*!' Aunty Peggy snapped—in a shocking change, the frail, reedy-voiced old woman became more like the fierce old-time schoolmistress she had feared so much. 'Don't be sentimental Flora, you know what your mother was like! It was one of her games, that's all: if you'd bought that car, bought it special and it was made of gold, she still wouldn't have come with you! You were not much more than a babe in arms when your family lived here my dear, so you couldn't know it, but Nora was never happy here, for my money I don't believe she was ever truly happy *anywhere.*'

Kara and Flora nodded as Peggy caught her breath, exhausted by her vehemence but determined to continue. 'When I was still quite a little one, Nora would sit with me and tell me all about Morecambe, the most beautiful place in the world she said, far better than Wales, far better than any old place in the world, and she always said how she wished she'd never left. I remember walking on the beach with her, Prestatyn was it, and she'd tell me how the water was so much lovelier where she came from. Now to me it was just the same old sea, but she was so serious and so sad that I believed her and *I* wanted to go with her to her old home and live there forever. I was *very* young.' Peggy finished in a struggle for breath, but she moistened her lips and rallied again.

The three younger women maintained a respectful, attentive silence as the flow of reminiscence became Aunty Peggy and she it. 'It wasn't as if she hated Wales and she certainly didn't look down on us, no, not like you-know-who. She was a lovely girl at heart, and did try hard to be a good friend and neighbour. She could never master the language but picked up little phrases she never forgot. I went to see her years later and I remember her warning the children not to pinch stale bread she'd cut up for the birds; "*Ach Y Fi*," she meant to say, *that's disgusting*, but she'd been away too long and the words had lumped together into "Acky Vee". I found to my amusement she also still said "Look you", but that too had melted into one lumpy new word, "Lewkya". Nora had moved about the country so much in her married life, picking up so many half-remembered little local phrases it was sometimes as if she had her own language.

'Don't mistake me now, I loved Nora, she was young and loving and yes, like a second mother to me. She could never have displaced my own dear Mam in my affections and nor would she have wanted to, but I did love her and she loved us—I mean the children, all the children. I recall how she would play with us, look after us, dry our tears, heal our cuts and stings, oh we trusted her utterly. She always had a new game for us to play, kept us interested, making sure nobody was ever left out; sometimes she seemed more absorbed in the games than we were. She was *alive* when she was around kiddies, she was herself. I always thought that when she was surrounded by children she was with... her equals. Oh dear, did that sound awful? It wasn't meant badly.'

'What about Grampa Sam... Mr. Wilson?' Francine prompted, after a lingering silence.

'I don't recall him half as well as I do Nora, not from those times at least, isn't that funny? I'm not sure I was even allowed to be in the same room as him when I was small. Except one time—I was at their house quite late one evening, in the big old kitchen they had, all we children playing—bar you, Flora, you were probably already abed—and Mr. Wilson came in from his room, his den like, and he just *looked* at his daughters, not a word did he have to say, and they all fell silent sure as he'd cut out their tongues. All he then had to do was to move his eyes slightly, still not a word, just an "up" movement, and they put up their toys and went straight to bed without looking at me—or him. I was left standing next to Nora, and I just wanted to flee, or to hide in her skirts, as Mr. Wilson stared at me, then Nora.

'"What's this?" he asked in a horrid, stony voice. "Are we opening a blessed orphanage now?"

'Nora didn't answer him back, she just took me into the scullery, helped me on with my coat and then walked me all the way back to my Mam.'

Francine found herself enraptured by the rising, falling music of Aunty Peggy's sigh of a voice as it broadcast news from the past. Her mother and gran were the same, nobody seemed at all minded to stem the flow of her recall, as if they knew that once it had ceased, it might never be recovered.

'I still saw them, lots of times, after they'd left Wales; Nora was always very good at inviting me to come and see her—you may remember some of this now Flora, you were a bit older—and when I was a teenager I'd sometimes babysit, to let Nora and Mr. Wilson go out. The older sisters, no, they were never interested in such a thing, they had their own plans and wouldn't be put off them unless their father raised his voice. And that's how I became Aunty Peggy—and you were the Bisto Kids, remember now Flora?'

Francine saw her gran flush a happy, sunrise red. 'Anty Piggy!' she squeaked in a babyish falsetto, 'Tan the bisto tids tum down?'

Peggy's throat pulsed with a chuckle.

'I'll tell you now my love, whenever I did let you "tum down" from your beds, I was as scared as you were of your father coming back unexpectedly and raising Cain. But he never did.' The last words were addressed to Francine, to reassure her that the nocturnal conspiracy had been a success.

'Was everyone frightened of Grampa Sam?' Francine ventured to her mother and gran, as Peggy seemed in need of a rest.

Flora nodded.

Kara thought deeply and said, 'I was. Terrified.' Her voice was so quiet you would have thought the old man was lurking nearby. After taking a gulp of water with Flora's help, Peggy took up the story again.

'I loved going to see the Wilsons, wherever they'd landed in their travels, but yes, I was afraid of him too. He lived and breathed fire and brimstone as far as I could tell, and never relented, not in my sight or hearing.'

'I wonder if he was quite so stern with Mrs. Ellis?' said Flora, a naughty-girl glint in her eye was caught and amplified by Peggy.

'I've no idea I'm sure, but I tell you what, I saw them meet outside the church many a time—"Good morning Mr. Wilson," she'd say, "Good morning Mrs. Ellis," he'd reply, all grave and correct, but even then I knew in my bones there was more than the occasional good-morning going on between those two. I was but fifteen and knew nothing of the ways of the world, but I just knew. And yet the first time I saw them pair, Mr. Wilson had just read the lesson—St Paul's letter to the Corinthians, the passage about love—and he'd read it so well I'd been convinced he believed every word of it and wanted *us* to believe it too and to follow its teachings. He was at his most tender in church, his gentlest, as if the words needed to be handled with care and respect; he left the admonitions and the threats of hell to the vicar, at least within those four walls.' Peggy paused; it wasn't clear if she was collecting her thoughts or wool-gathering, until the playful beam returned to that thin, lined face.

'One thing I do know, Mr. Wilson didn't go after that woman for her looks. I think she was short-sighted, too vain to wear her glasses in public; her eyes always fixed upon the end of her own nose, as if she were terrified of bumping into things—a ship in a fog, that's how I always thought of her. She was some sort of academic or librarian, if memory serves, clever so folks said, and it was that I think attracted Mr. Wilson. Nora was so beautiful, so good to us all, but oooooh, I don't want to be unkind, but she was, what, flibbertigibbet, she had a butterfly mind, she simply couldn't concentrate sufficiently to do and say the things adults normally did and said, and I remember that always annoyed Mr. Wilson something terrible.'

Another pause was followed by a deepened wheezing from Peggy's frail chest. Flora helped Peggy to more water and asked if they should leave, but the old lady seized her wrist and insisted, perhaps begged, they stay. 'I remember when we were but small girls and Nora told us all about the war, and how "Ole Hickler was trying to invade England, but that he would be beaten in the end." She had no doubt, it was all like a story to her, as if we were living out nothing more than a morality play where Good would prevail over

Evil, as it always did. That gave me confidence: I used to have nightmares, bad ones, about Hitler breaking into our house, looking for me, but Nora helped those dreams go away. She knew the mind of a child, she knew how to soothe those fears: it's a pity, mind you, no one ever understood *her* so well. I don't think Mr. Wilson did. Bad for each other those two were, in many ways. We all knew it. Not least because he was a man who'd found out what it was like to be worshipped. And that was no good for his soul.'

'Did Nora ever tell you how she felt about the goings-on between my father and Mrs. Ellis?' Flora asked gently.

Peggy screwed her face up. 'She never said a word to me, not till he'd finally upped and gone. Then she warned me not to go near "that bloody man" ever again, said he'd got a "roving eye" and no girl was safe from him. I wasn't at all sure what she meant, and I pictured one of his eyes leaping out of his head and rolling about on its own. But I do know what his leaving did to her: it killed love for her, stone dead. I remember a few years later when I went to tell her I was to be married; thrilled I was, head over heels, and I wanted Nora to be my Matron of Honour. I recollect telling her, babbling half-Welsh half-English, but Nora understood me full well and I was waiting for her to leap up from her chair, to hug and kiss me, to say yes, but she just sat there, lit a cigarette and said, "That's lovely for you, but I shall be dead by then."'

Aunty Peggy's eyes fluttered and her light head fell back a little, making extra puckered dents in the pillow that supported her. Her eyes closed once more and remained so for a long moment, then she directed a watery look at

Flora.

'I'm so sorry, but suddenly I feel so tired. I would dearly love to go on, I could do so all day my love,' she turned to Francine, 'but I am so, so tired.'

Francine, her mother and grandmother stirred from the hypnotic trance of the storytelling and, all of them reassuring Aunty Peggy it was quite all right and they understood perfectly, levered themselves out of their seats and put their coats on.

'So lovely to see you Peggy.' Flora smiled, leaning to kiss her cheek; Francine saw her mum follow suit and so felt compelled to do the same. She felt that warm, hairy parchment under her lips again, but she contained her shudders.

'Such a long way to come to hear some old crock ramble on about things so long ago and far away,' Peggy whispered to her, smiling, 'but I have enjoyed it, it's been so nice to have you all here, I'd love it if you all came back; I have more stories for you, young lady, if that will help to fetch you back!'

'We'll come,' Francine pledged instantly, without looking at the others for approval.

'Nos Da,' whispered Peggy faintly as her visitors waved goodbye, walking slowly out of the room.

Francine, even above the music she was pumping into her head, could hear the skirling of the phone and then Mum putting on her posh telephone voice; she overheard the dignified 'Hello' become a friendlier 'Hi!' and then an ambiguous 'Oh' before the conversation dropped out of earshot. Mum came back after a short time, gesturing 'off' at the music box; reading her face at once Francine complied without question.

'A little bit of bad news,' announced Mum in a brittle voice, and Francine felt a frisson of fear, followed by numerous selfish worries about what could be wrong—was their holiday cancelled, were her friends not coming round as they had promised?

'I'm afraid Aunty Peggy passed away last night.' Mum looked drawn, as if she somehow felt responsible and expected to be punished. 'I suppose it was to be expected, but...'

Francine felt and showed no emotion for a moment: an old woman she barely knew had died, what was that to her? But as she pondered the news she became more reflective; something had been lost, something important, with which she had enjoyed only the most fleeting acquaintance. She felt sorry for Mum and Gran—Nyn, as that fluting voice had called her—for they had lost far more, and she recalled the frail figure in the chair, recounting her memories of the people who had gone before her. If only they could have had one more visit, just a little longer with Peggy and her tales from the vanishing past. Anyway; Mum looked as if she needed a hug.

2018

History was boring. Family history was mega-boring.

Francine snorted quietly to herself: what a stupid kid she used to be; now what would that kid have said if she'd known what would come of her little project? She thought about that in-a-trice decision to join her mother visiting Peggy; at the time, she'd have described it as a whim, but in retrospect there was something fizzing within, a desire to be told the tales of the family's past, to listen to anyone, anyone at all, who could tell her something new. Boring old history had won her over and she was viscerally fascinated. At first, Francine did not have the words to describe the feeling, to epitomise her curiosity and the urge to save history from extinction, to rescue family photographs and papers, and most importantly gather the voices of people before they died away to irretrievable silence. The words came to her much, much later: she wanted to save Nonna Nora and Grampa Sam from The Place of Lost Stories.

It was waking from a deep sleep, that impossible, sticky process, which had brought the phrase to her. She would often awake with music lingering in her head as if, in the addictive last slumbers before the intrusion of the daylight and the explosion of the alarm clock, someone was by her side, picking at sweet, light notes on silvery strings. It had always happened to her, and when she was small she had thought it must be her mother or father coming to her bedroom, urging her in the gentlest manner to part from the night, and that the muffled strumming was an antidote to sleep, a sort of reverse-lullaby: but no one was ever there when she opened her eyes, and in any case there were no musical instruments in the house and no players to be found for them. As she grew older, Francine realised the music existed only in her head: she sometimes wondered if she concentrated hard enough whether she could coax the sounds back into the waking world and write that soft music down—but she hadn't the ability, didn't know the notation, and anyway the wispy staves were always gone the moment she parted her eyelids.

One morning after the news of Aunty Peggy's death, the ending of sleep brought not fragile music but words, an idea, and this survived the transition into the light. *The Place of Lost Stories*. It was the home of histories untold, half-told, unfinished and overlooked: narratives that had, untimely, been separated from their tellers by forgetfulness, distraction, sickness, death. It was a place where truths large and small came to die, or live on only as shades and vapours, with vanishingly small hopes of returning to the light. It was a limbo for stilled voices, an impersonal, abstract store-room of undocumented tales, incomplete thoughts, lost diaries, autobiographies that had never seen print, a paltry few of which had perhaps even seen desultory starts before being choked off and even fewer near-complete works that wanted but a few pen-strokes. There were jokes that had tailed off before their punch-lines, speeches and declarations killed by nerves or apathy, rotting, yellowed papers filled with scribbles, corrupted and deleted digital information, every untold tale there ever had been. The Place contained matters both important and unimportant, much buried trivia that belonged in obscurity but also resonant and vital truths that had failed to be told: what had really happened, who really did it, lost dénouements, lost whos, lost wheres, lost whys.

The Place was not peopled, oh no, it was not *for* people. Francine believed that after death men and women went on to another and better life, but that just as they could be shriven of their sins as they departed their flesh, they were also separated from their stories; a soul cannot go on, cannot be fully redeemed if it is dragging with it the weight of past existence. To start again, you have to be free of it all. But someone who was still in this world could take charge of those stories, saving them from the emptiness that was the Place. Aunty Peggy was gone, and what she may have told on future visits was in the Place; Nonna Nora was long gone, Grampa Sam too, and yet there were still people who could help her to rescue their near-extinct stories.

Nonna Nora had once threatened to 'tell the truth'. Mum had told Francine about it; 'You girls, you and your father, how terribly you've treated me! One day I shall tell the truth about all the wicked things you've done to me! All those vile, wicked things!' Mum and Gran portrayed Nonna as a serial moaner, a burdensome bore with her constant woes, but privately Francine felt she shared her great-grandmother's driving compulsion. By telling the truth, Nonna had meant she wanted to tell her own story; how Francine would have loved to hear it from her. Everyone had the right to do that before they and their history were lost. She understood why people kept diaries and journals, why they filled the virtual world with the trivia of their petty day-by-days: somewhere in there were secret truths that would outlive the tellers and everyone who was told about. Every sundown and sun-up is unique and deserves its record. There should be no lost stories, not ever again.

Francine had come to know she was something of a collector, a completist; once she had started something, it was in her nature not to rest until she had finished it entirely and neatly, without fuzzy edges or cut corners. Years back, she had collected little plastic flags of the nations—they were still around here—somewhere—and then she had collected free CDs and popstar posters from that little girls' magazine, and she had only given up when the free gifts dribbled dry, and there had been lots of other little crazes, all executed to thorough, detailed perfection, never abandoned halfway or left to moulder. Told of her home habits, one of her teachers had sighed and begged her mother to prevail on her to apply the same attitude to her school work; but it wasn't the same, why didn't they understand that?

Mum and Gran had been keen enough to retell the lives of Sam and Nora, but Francine had ceased to accept their assumption that her great-grandmother was nothing more than a loveable but silly woman. She had grown, over the years, to wish that she had known Nora, to have been able to sit where her mother sat and hear Nonna's 'truth' for herself. And, she told herself, she would not have undervalued them or dismissed them as the petty madness of a lonely, monomaniacal old woman. All the stories were of value, they were *all* important—every one.

2013

'You're completely serious about this, aren't you?'

Even as she said it, Aunty Eileen had a wary look, as if she half-suspected she was the victim of a prank. Her discomfort with Francine was odd, as the two of them were usually easy in one another's company, they would talk for hours and neither was afraid of speaking plainly. The serious look on Eileen's face brought Francine to mind of the photograph, and of her aunt's resemblance to Nonna Nora. But much as she loved Eileen, Francine could see that she was not now and had never been the ethereal beauty Nora once was. Eileen's neck was too fat, for one thing, it spoiled the perfection of her face, over softening it and making it weak; Francine resolved never to let her own face be affected in that way, she would watch her weight, preserve her looks, she would... Eileen was waiting patiently; Francine shook these silly thoughts away.

'Are you recording this or taking notes? Ahemokay, here goes. I have a queer sort of advantage over your mum in remembering Nonna Nora; not that I necessarily remember her better, just *differently*. Partly it was a question of our ages; I was born eight years before your mum, and so for a long time she saw Nonna as a child does, simply I mean, taking everything as it appeared on the surface, whereas I had grown up a little bit and could... well, I started to *read* Nonna's behaviour, I didn't just listen to what she said, I realised what it was she meant, I became alive to nuances—not that that's what I would have called them at the time—and it was often very odd, to hear her speak and find so many meanings in apparently simple words.

'There was a special link between Nonna and me that probably helped. My mother and dad had split up when I was little, it caused me the most terrible distress, and then later, having barely spoken to me about it, they got together again—and before I'd truly taken *that* on board they'd given me a sister. Well, I was mixed up, in shock, overwhelmed first by loss and then by a rush of new things, new people. Other families weren't like that, why were we? I used to wonder why we were different, what was wrong with us. No other adult, not even my own parents, understood how I felt, none except Nonna. I suppose that was because we were both children of interrupted families, in our different ways. She knew how much I'd missed my Dad and how desperately I'd wanted him back but then again how hurt I was by getting only a half-answered prayer, how cruel and perverse I felt fate was, that things weren't as they were supposed to be. I suppose in return I understood how much she missed Grampa Sam—well, it all helped me to understand it a *bit*.

'So we were simpatico, and it wasn't long before I stopped thinking of her as a grandmother and more as—what—a slightly older cousin, maybe? Nonna didn't seem like a granny: grannies in those days were old and cold and distant, shrill pickled creatures who'd shriek at you whether or not you'd misbehaved, they looked like Queen Victoria, dark clothing and sour faces. My dad's mother was like that anyway, she neither liked nor understood children. She hated me being in her home, she'd forbid me to do anything or go anywhere, I wasn't allowed to explore her house, as if the door of each room was a portal to hell, I wasn't allowed to touch anything for fear I would break or steal it, she never fed me a scrap and only ever gave me cold water to drink, never lemonade or anything nice. She snapped at me to sit down and stay still, but I was never allowed to choose my own chair, *she* would pick the most uncomfortable place and then spread newspaper on it "in case she wets", even when I was years out of nappies! She was a creature from another world, in my little point of view.

'Now Nonna wasn't like that, not a bit. She was so beautiful and looked so young, and she didn't behave and talk like someone from another place and time. She was generous and indulgent, sometimes in silly ways, reckless ways even, as if she too was a child and possessed no adult judgement. I remember one day she was peeling potatoes, hands plunged in cold water, a small and sharp knife in her grip; I was about five, yes-yes, five, and I wanted to help, I *so* much wanted to help, but not to put the spuds in the pot as she suggested, no, I wanted to do the peeling, I craved to handle the knife, it looked so easy when Nonna did it. Now, where my Mum would have told me no, don't be silly, Nonna brought in a hard chair and stood me over the sink, keeping me steady and putting the handle of the knife in my palm. She told me what to do, but I didn't listen, I was in such haste to copy her, and of course I was over-eager and ham-fisted and lasted about two strokes of that knife before there was blood in the water. For a moment I thought it looked beautiful, creeping out in little ribbons as it did, a striking maroon against the stark white of the old sink, then I felt the slit I'd made in my finger and it stung as more blood seeped out and I realised it was coming from me and wasn't going to stop and I felt sick and faint and frightened. Nonna lifted me down, took my hand, and cleaned the wound and gently patted it dry, but then I heard a voice that just said "*Oh Mum!*" in the exasperated tone, that oh-no-not-again sound, and my mother was there, taking charge, stemming the blood and binding the cut while scolding me *and* Nonna. And despite my panic, I didn't feel sorry for myself, I was always getting told off, it was my lot; no, I felt badly for Nonna. I wanted to plead with my mum and tell her it was my fault, all my fault: I didn't want Nonna to be upset and cry.

'We were always at Nonna's on a Saturday; the family would arrive just in time for lunch and there'd be fried eggs and baked beans, cooked cheese, bacon, sausages, oatcakes and fritters, all with bread and butter, salt and pepper, red and brown sauce and big thick chunky homemade pickle, too. You could spend as long seasoning your dinner as you did eating it. Nonna would make tea that was always this amazing bold red-brown colour, it seemed to achieve that strength as soon as the water hit the leaves and it never stewed no matter how long it stood. You always got milk and sugar whether you wanted them or not as Nonna always forgot who took what, but nobody complained, you always found you liked it; it was the right time and place for such powerful, sweet stuff. You would always step away from the table thinking you'd never want to eat again because you were so full, but within perhaps two hours there would be cake—home-made, of course—and biscuits, Nonna loved milk-chocolate digestives, and gallons more of that tea. And you found you wanted it all, you didn't want to stop.

'Then we'd all go to the front room while Nonna washed up—she never wanted help. "I'll not have a crowd in my kitchen, get gone!' The telly would go on and we'd watch the sport, and eventually Nonna would come in for a rest, and when the wrestling came on she'd laugh and catcall at the fighters, "You bunch of hairy jessies!" and then she'd fall asleep in her old chair, her head tilted gently over her breast; sometimes she'd still be holding her tea-cup, but if you tried to take it from her she'd fight for it, slap your hand away, tighten her grip on her cup, clutch it to her heart, and all without waking up.

'As I got older, I realised she was an adolescent in some ways; I suppose I can tell you this... she was amazingly sexual. I mean even as an old lady. I recall being absolutely crazy about the Beatles...'

'The who?'

'No, The Beatles: never mind, it's an old joke. They were a 1960s group who'd recently ditched a loveable, well-groomed image and grown their hair very long, sprouted scruffy beards, started sporting kaftans and beads and whatever other hippy have-you. Anyway, I had bought a picture of them, and because I loved them so much I showed it to Nonna. She studied it closely, her eyes lingered on it for a long time, and then she handed it back and announced, "I'd never sleep with *any* of them!" Well, I was amazed, it was so unexpected. I've often wondered if "sleep with" meant something else to her, but no, she meant sex, it was her first thought, her main concern, her overwhelming priority in assessing them as men. It was a fundamental lesson in the truth of who Nonna was.'

2012

'Why was Grampa Sam the way he was?' asked Francine, childishly wide-eyed and faintly self-conscious at having slipped easily into a habit of referring to a dead man from a near-lost past by such a familiar name. But sometimes she felt less like a dedicated researcher from the future and more a direct participant in events, albeit one who had somehow turned amnesiac and had to have the story—to the tiniest, fragmented detail—recapitulated to piece together a jigsaw of memories.

Asked about her father, Flora shook her head, as if she too was desperately fathoming out an insoluble puzzle for the millionth time. 'It is so, so hard to say; that remote, stern, religiosity of his—but I'd hazard a guess it had a lot to do with his childhood. I rarely had much close contact with his side of the family, but you're aware of course that children were treated very, very differently in those days—"children should be seen and not heard". How many times did we hear that old saw! I've always thought that Dad—Grampa Sam—gave his own brood a hard time, but I've a notion it was nothing compared to what happened to him. I was truly scared of our Dad, but the few times I met her I was much more frightened of his Aunt Laura. She brought him up you see, his parents gave him up to her as he was the oldest...'

'That's horrible, gross!' Francine appealed, however inarticulately, on behalf of the stolen child.

'It was done in those days, especially when there was a big family, and believe me, his parents continued to stack em up, even though not many of the children survived infancy. But they couldn't possibly have looked after them all.'

The teenage interviewer felt that Gran's dismissal of the boy Sam's distressing abandonment was cool to the point of callousness.

'I'll tell you a story about Aunt Laura, one from when I was a very little girl. She lived in the country, near woods, a magical fairy-tale forest it was to me, somewhere you could equally easily meet pixies, men or monsters. I never dared go too far in, it was forbidden anyway and one didn't cross our Dad on matters like that, but I used to play in a little clearing that was surrounded, besieged by the most beautiful flowers, deep blue blooms shot through with purple and white, that's how I picture them now, and one day I decided to pick some and take them to Aunt Laura. I knew she loved flowers and I was sure she would adore these just as much as I did. I carried a big bunch all the way to the house, all the time thinking about how lovely they would look in the tall green vase standing in the kitchen window, oh I can see them even now in that big, bright window with the sun streaming through...' Gran's voice faded into a sigh and she gazed ahead silently, before recovering herself.

'Anyway, Aunt Laura was there in the kitchen when I got back and she even smiled at me a little as I came through the door, and this emboldened me to offer up my home-made bouquet: within an instant I was surrounded by scattered petals as she slapped the things out of my hands, yelling, "Weeds, weeds, filthy weeds! What are you doing bringing these things into my house you stupid child?" She boxed my ears—that sounds funny but it wasn't, I can tell you—and then marched me round to pick up every shred of those ruined plants, and stood over me as I threw them away. When we got back to the kitchen she was still in an unholy fury and bellowed at my dad, who was hovering around in the far doorway, he must have seen and heard it all.

'"Samuel, Samuel, did you see what this *wretched child* did? Did you see how she attempted to pollute my home? Stupid girl!"

'Dad stood still and silent. I *knew* he had witnessed it all and prayed he would leap to my defence, I appealed to him with my water-filled eyes, surely he knew my good intentions, could tell this screeching old hag I had only childishly, innocently wanted to please her? But he cut me dead with a look—he was devilish good at that sort of thing—and the only words he spoke were a dull, obedient echo of his aunt; "Stupid girl. You should know better." Now I felt hollowed out—"gutted" you would say nowadays—by this. Dad was perfectly placed to restrain that poisonous spite and wrath of hers, but instead he chose to abandon me and let her loose on me. I was too young to realise that such small, callous betrayals were my father's stock-in-trade. It was a salutary lesson.

'I was distraught, but it didn't do to sob and weep in front of those two furies, it would only have maddened them further, and so I begged to go to my room and only when I was there could I let loose and bawl until I could barely breathe. Now don't take on Francine my love, it was all a long time ago, what a sense of injustice you do have! In any case, I have something more to tell you: my tears were dried up as soon as my little brain came to realise something. It was perfectly true my father had witnessed the entire set-to between me and that dratted woman, I had caught a glimpse of his face as she began to screech like heaven's vengeance, and recalled in that instant that he had *flinched*, his eyes had closed tight and his body went rigid just for a moment, as if all the rage, all the scolding and violence was about to be heaped on *his* head. He was a big, sturdy man who had been reduced in a fraction of a second to a small boy, braced for a beating. And at that moment I no longer felt betrayed by him, I felt the deepest sympathy and sorrow for that little boy and what he'd been through.

I was overwhelmed with pity, and this time I cried for him, not myself.' Flora let free a long and loud huff of sad breath. 'But the feeling didn't last for long,' she confessed ruefully.

'But you remember that feeling,' marvelled Francine. 'You've carried it with you and you remember it after all these years...' She gathered in the story gratefully.

'Oh yes, for all that it was short-lived, I remember—and vividly too, as if I was living every second all over again. Short-lived and rare was that sprig of sympathy, and all the more precious for that. I really cannot recall having many tender thoughts towards that man. Nobody could get near him, see, he simply wouldn't let you. I don't even recollect that my dad had many—any—friends. He spent his days at work of course, and went to the pub regular as clockwork, but he was never there long. We never heard him speak either of workmates or drinking pals, not names, not details, not the slightest, silliest anecdote or borrowed joke. I truly think he was too much of a snob to get to know anybody in the neighbourhood wherever we lived; he was utterly convinced he was better than everyone else and that by allowing the lower classes near him he would contaminate himself in some way. "The Wilsons are one of the finest families in this county—in the whole of England, never forget that!" he used to say to us, and that was a legacy of that god-bothering harridan aunt too, the conviction that he was tantamount to royalty. His voice but her words, her faithful echo once again.

'Even when he was at home he would not spend much time with us; he shut himself up in the front room, reading the newspaper, listening to the radio, goodness knows what he did, just avoiding people, I think. It's a matter of eternal regret to me: we were his girls, we were in awe of him, but we could have been his companions and his pals, if he'd suffered us to be near, his own children. He had a surviving brother and sister, but kept his distance from them too, refused to see his brother at all because he was "one of those".'

'Was he?' Francine prompted.

'I never met James Wilson, but Mother always said that although he was a little effeminate and a bit of a show-off, he wasn't anything more: you could always be sure of Nonna's instincts. But Dad would have none of it, to him homosexuals weren't people, they were no part of God's creation and that was flat. You may scowl Francine Latimer, but he was after all a man of his times and there was nothing unusual about that point of view, not then. Funnily enough, Sam looked up to his sister Jane, inasmuch as he thought well of anyone, and he was completely and utterly blind to the fact that she never married and lived quite cosily with a widowed lady from her village—and I mean *cosily*. Everyone knew, but they all behaved the same as our Dad, they dismissed the entire matter because women didn't do that sort of thing, did they?'

'Or because women didn't matter?' Francine growled.

Gran shrugged. 'I suppose so, yes. Don't be too much of a modern-miss about it love, it was another time, almost another world.

'Anyway, I must stop this prattling, I've things to do. "You've got too much of what the cat licks its bottom with!' That's what our dad would say.' She coloured and looked furtive for a moment, as if again suspecting that the old man was listening from a hidden nook as she gave away his secrets. After all these years, thought Francine, Grampa Sam still commands awe. And fear too.

1967

When I grow too old to dream
I'll have you to remember
When I grow too old to dream
Your kiss will be here in my heart
So kiss me again and let us part
And when I grow too old to dream
Your kiss will still be in my heart.

The child sat entranced and yet discomfited by the voice, a high, wistfully beautiful sound forever on the brink of cracking with sadness. Every song it sang ran with a cold current of lament. The old woman sang with her head tilted up, her eyes shut tight as if she were wishing or dreaming. Kara looked closely at that face as the mournful undertone came to dominate the song, and she wondered if tears were about to flow. She felt a stab of alarm—perhaps Nonna was not wishing, not dreaming—perhaps she was remembering.

'I love to see Nonna, but I don't like some of her songs,' said Kara out of nowhere, earnest and frowning. Flora, who had been bouncing the girl on her knee moments before, became still and busied herself tidying her daughter's hair, studying her little face as they spoke.

'Her songs?' Flora prompted gently as the child lapsed back into sober, serious reflection.

'Yes, the songs. I like it when she sings *Chick-chick-chick-chick-chicken lay a little egg for me,* but I don't like the sad songs. It's no wonder Nonna's not happy, remembering all those things.'

'What things, baby?'

'Well, she sings about Bobby Shaftoe going to sea, and he never comes back, you just know he never comes back. And she sings *Oh dear what can the matter be* about Johnny who's gone to the fair to buy ribbons for her, but just like Bobby Shaftoe you know he's not going to get those ribbons and he's not coming back. You know that long before she's finished singing.'

'How do you know, Kara?'

'You can tell from her voice, you know they're gone forever. It's so sad and I don't like it. Have people always gone away from Nonna? And why did they do it?'

Flora frequently found herself struggling to explain the world to her little girl, and she had to take a deep breath before attempting to unravel this especially aggravated aspect of it; whatever went on in the poor child's mind when she listened to her grandmother?

'Now if she sings songs they're not about her you know darling. They're just like… stories. Think about the chick-chick-chicken, there isn't one there is there? So there's no Bobby Shaftoe, no Johnny, not really. See?'

'I s'pose not.' But the reply was slow and reluctant, and the frown on that perfect brow deepened, Kara was still thinking. 'But it *seems* like it,' she concluded firmly.

'And so it did!' protested Kara, sitting opposite her mother and her own daughter, 'The songs really seemed to be about her, every one of them! Old Bobby Shaftoe...'

'Bobby Shaftoe's gone to sea/silver buckles on his knee/he'll come home and marry me/Bonny Bobby Shaftoe,' sang Flora, to give Francine its flavour. Kara looked at her mother with a jolt of surprise; if she closed her eyes she could truly believe it was Nonna Nora sitting there singing in that thin, fragile voice.

'When I'd stopped being distracted by odd images like someone having silver buckles on his knee, which sounded painful, I really, really did have the conviction that Bobby Shaftoe wasn't coming back—not to her,' Kara mused. Then she herself began to sing a snatch of a half-remembered tune.

'Oh dear what can the matter be
Oh dear what can the matter be
Oh dear what can the matter be
Johnny has gone to the fair.
He promised to buy me a bunch of blue ribbons
He promised to buy me a bunch of blue ribbons
He promised to buy me a bunch of blue ribbons
To tie up my bonny brown hair.'

Kara stopped, and she looked at the others with the eyes of a serious child.

'I heard that song so many, many times, and each time the emphasis grew on those words, *he promised, he promised, he promised*—he lied. Sometimes I used to make up excuses to get out of the room when Nonna sang that.

It made me angry and broke my heart.'

'The songs weren't *about* her!' Flora interceded, as urgently as if four decades had not gone by and she was still trying to dislodge the misconception from her little girl's mind, and Kara replied in kind, still thinking dreamily of that old, sad voice. 'Hmmm, but it always seemed that way to me. All of the songs. All of them.'

2020

Stories of Nonna, stories of Sam, of their family and the people around them, the lives and deaths of them all; Francine now knew those tales by heart and was glad, for most of their tellers were gone, and the many offshoots of the fecund Wilson marriage were so scattered and dispersed it would be impossible to track them down. It had been an effort to get this far, an obsession perhaps, but it had been worth it even if the rescue attempts had sometimes been like pulling teeth. Francine laughed to herself: people didn't know the value of their stories and they were incontinent and wasteful of them. They would pile them up in far corners of their minds as if they were rubbish, loose them wantonly like small coins of no account, bury them in holes and forget their burial-places, piss them up the wall when cross-eyed drunk, and tangle up precious memories with by-the-ways and silly, irrelevant details. No disrespect or anything, but people just couldn't be trusted with the past, they knew nothing of its value, couldn't distinguish between treasure and turds. If their stories had been pressed into books, the mould and worms would have had them by now. But Francine vowed to retrieve that of Sam and Nora Wilson, and she had been true to that vow.

1966

Kara was feeling so sleepy; she lay in Nonna's lap, curled tight like a ball of wool, the old lady's arms wound protectively around her. Kara felt warm and safe, she wished she could stay there forever. Nonna was singing again, and as she sang she rocked gently forward, back, forward, back, and this sloshed the sleepiness around the infant's small body. Kara didn't really understand the song; it was about someone who was with their true love 'on top of old smokey', and she wondered fuzzily if this might be one of the tall, thin brick chimneys that dotted the borderline of the town. If it was, that was a very queer place to go, hundreds of feet up on a factory stack, for the purpose of courting and kissing. But surely nobody would... how could they... wouldn't they be scared up there... She lost interest in such petty objections and slid into sleep, still rocked gently, still secure and happy, listening to the steady thump of her grandmother's heart as it accompanied her song.

Now courtin's a pleasure
And partin's a grief
But a cold-hearted lover
Is worse than a thief

The Trappers

1970

'He was Sam if you knew him, Samuel or Mr. Wilson if you did not.' Nora reminisced, a half-smile on her lips. 'Never "Sammy"—except to me. He let me call him names he never allowed anyone else to overhear—I mean pet names, lovers' names, bedroom names. What we had was special. But otherwise he insisted on respect, on his dignity. He always carried himself well: proud, erect. I remember the first day we met; he was so handsome, so grand, I could barely dare to look at him, I thought he was the most beautiful man that I had ever seen. I should have listened to my mother, "That one's a good deal too fond of hisself," she said, and she was right. "Sammy Wilson always did think he was the bee's knees."'

1940

Jack Carthmain had not thought the news that funny, but George Shenton clearly did. At the moment he was told, he had just taken a mouthful of mild and bitter, and this he sniggered out of his nose in a brown fountain-stream onto the bar. His mouth free, he loosed a laugh that sounded to Jack as if it belonged in the jungle background of a Tarzan film. George recovered himself sufficiently to speak briefly before he relapsed into woohoo haha monkey whoops. 'A lay preacher! Sammy Wilson's a lay preacher! Oh but that man, he's a treat, a real sodding caution, and if I had my lifetime over to explain it to him he could never be made to understand why! Oh thank you God, thank you, we thank thee for thy gift of Sammy Wilson!'

Jack sipped his pint and waited patiently for the hysteria to abate as the barman stepped over, towel in hand, glowering at George.

'Yew dirty bugga!' he grumbled.

George paid no heed as he stood before all assembled with hand on heart and glass raised in salute. 'Gentlemen, we honour the achievement of Brother Samuel! Join me please in the appropriate toast!' He gestured Jack to join, and a few other drinkers' arms also rose, albeit hesitantly. 'To Sammy and his preaching!' boomed Shenton, adding 'Up, Jenkins!' before collapsing in gusts of helpless laughter and this time spilling his beer over his shirt.

1941

Jack Carthmain topped six feet and was broad and powerful of body; hair sprouted promiscuously from wherever the eye could see, his chief glory being a huge beard and an ill-disciplined mane that gave him the aspect of an unkempt yet magnificent lion. He was a successful man of business and acknowledged as twice as canny as any man in the village, but to the uninitiated he seemed more like the Wild Man of Borneo. He was valued at the local, not just as a stalwart at the bar and a heart of oak, but also because there was rarely any bother, even from the most fractious of drunks, while Jack was there—no one dared to disturb his peace.

By contrast, George Shenton was a little wire brush of

a man who stood under five feet six in his socks, looking old and withered before his time as a testament to a life of hard work and its legacy of lingering sickness; he was always to be seen in a tweedy jacket that looked even older and more crumpled than its wearer, as if his outfit had spent an even longer career down the local pit. His crinkled features lent him an air of perpetual sardonic amusement, accentuated by his dark and humorous eyes. He had always worked with his hands and never rated himself as any kind of a brain, he deferred to Jack in that department, but he was nevertheless talented and prodigiously creative—at least insofar as teasing Sammy Wilson.

When Jack had first met the old feller, he had taken one look at the dishevelled character at the bar and come to the Sherlock Holmes conclusion, 'here is a man whose wife does not love him.' And as his acquaintance with George burgeoned, it became clear that this deduction had been accurate, the Shenton marriage was a mere observance of form.

'Separate beds, aye, not that I care, who wants er gruntin and fartin nex to me all bloody nate? She'd ave separate rooms if only we could afford a bigger place, separate ouses altogether if she didn't think the shame would kill er mother. *Nothin* could kill er bloody mother.'

'Was there ever a time,' enquired Jack, 'when you adored her, desired her, thought she was beautiful and couldn't live without her?'

'I saw er an decided she were as good as I could ever do, and that me time ad come.'

'You make it sound like death.'

'Likely I do. Only the lucky get what you ad, Jack. She

may be gone, bless er soul, but you was lucky with Peg.'

'Marriage is a rightful state between a man and a woman, they say,' Jack parried.

'A right old state, you mean,' the old man grumbled.

The Trappers were deep in conference, preparing the next snare for their prey, but also, as trappers do especially when they're half-cut, yarning about past triumphs and the minutiae of their craft.

'I watch his eyebrows.' Jack was absorbed in the discussion of fine technique. 'They seem to take off like Lancasters off the runway, rumbling slowly up and then—zoom!—into the sky as we score a hit. I reckon he believes he's not showing a thing, poker-faced like, but I can always spot the eyebrows, an then I know we've riled him!'

George too was aglow with the glories of the hunt. 'I got im a good un t'other night when I told im old Churchill was in the next room, lookin for his advice on ow to win the bloody war! He took a step so he did, a half-step at least, towards the door, and e had to convert that into a trip to the bar, just to save face!'

'Ahh true, that was good, that was good.' Jack sighed as his beer went down, and he savoured the memories as much as the drink. 'Mind you, the simplest ones, sometimes the silliest, are the best, the times when e doesn't know where to put imself. Remember a couple of weeks ago when you spotted him coming in and just yelled, "Ey up Sammy yer daft owd ferret!" Those eyebrows never came down again the whole time he was here.'

'Oh yesss, e likes to maintain is dignity does Sammy, that's plain enough. He hasn't gone doolally at us yet but we can always hope.'

'Thing is with a pub, George, you should leave your dignity and gravity or whatever on the hat-stand, that's one of the best things about coming in, but Sammy doesn't seem to grasp that at all. We're different from him, he's different from us, I understand that, but the point is that in here you should be able to set aside those differences; but he stays buttoned up like an army greatcoat, he don't relax. And when he sips a half of mild you'd think he was bibbing communion wine.'

'Or sipping the nectar from Mirabelle Ellis's…'

'Ey now, don't lower the tone owd!'

'Thought your dignity was on the atstand,' grumbled George. He was getting more than a bit kaylied.

Jack drifted into a still more thoughtful state, sipping contemplatively at his pint, flecks of foam lingering on the lush grey hairs of his upper lip, as if fertilising and feeding the growth.

'What does he come here for George?' he asked gently. 'What does Sammy Wilson *want?*'

'A pint an a half o dark mild, that an no more, for an hour or so, twice a week.'

Jack clacked his glass down and turned to remonstrate with his drinking pal, but he drew the words back along with his breath when he saw George's good-natured grin.

'Unlike us,' George was determined to finish his thought, 'What we want is two quarts o Netta's bestest, thrice or five times a week!'

Jack took his cue to resume his musings.

'I mean why does he come, why *here?* He isn't a pub man. He doesn't like you, doesn't like me, he only registers the presence of anyone else with a tip of his hat and a bob of his head: he's not one of us, he don't *belong* here. You could more easily see him taking a sweet sherreh with his leddeh wafe back at the manor hice.'

George cackled at Jack's ability to combine a gormless aristocratic cadence with a nastily accurate mimicry of Sam's clipped, authoritative tones.

'He gives you a bit o respect at least, Jack. You were the coal merchant whereas I was just one o the daft buggers who brung it up to the surface, e don't want to know me an I resent that. I may be just a broken-down old dataller but I'm not *thick* like e thinks I am, I'm not *worthless*. And what makes im so important anyway, e's just a fuckin pen-pusher in some office isnee?'

'True; but I think that job of his is important enough to keep im out of the war...'

'If e weren't too old anyway.'

'I thank fuck I'm too old, mate,' said Jack feelingly. 'But all in all, no, I don't see why his lordship think he's a cut above us.'

'And that, Jack, is why it's our sacred duty to take im down a peg or two.'

'I'll drink to that, ole lad.'

'Netta likes im.' George nodded in the direction of the landlady as she served pints at the bar. 'Says e's a gent. Unlike us.'

'Netta knows nowt.' Jack scowled, with unexpected sourness. 'Oh Sammy knows how *t'behave* like a gent, I imagine he's got posh table manners and all, but he's not a real gent any more than he's one of us. So what is he, what's e want and why does he come here?'

'To get away from the wife?' George hazarded, then

answered himself without hesitation, 'Mebbe. But, tell you what, I wouldn't mind goin home to *that* wife!'

Responding to a silent but nevertheless profound admonition from his companion, Mr. Shenton wiped the dream-soaked look off his face and returned his attention to the discussion. 'Ow's about the kids, mebbe it's the two dozen screaming kids e's avoiding.'

'Two dozen? Gerroff, y'daft bugger. They're not all kiddies neither, oldest would be old enough to drink in here but that she's serving with the WAAF.'

George uttered a thin, wondering whistle.

'That old? Then that wife of Sammy's *is* looking well, she must be forty year and then some, and she's still...'

'Oh yes,' agreed Jack firmly. 'Still. Very. Now forget about her for crying out loud!'

They continued to ponder after refreshing their drinks.

'Maybe God sent im,' suggested George.

'Eh, what, to save our souls?'

'Sammy saves arse'oles, ha, ha, ha!'

'What *are* you on about man?'

'Awrate, ere's the idea: from The Book Of Sammy, Chapter One, Verse One.

'And the Lord sayeth "Sammy, go thou forth to the Oak for a bit twice a week, so that thou mighst mither some other bugger an give me a fuckin rest from thy prayin and pratin an holy hullabaloo!"'

Jack could not hold back a guilt-tinged laugh. 'Aye, seems about right. But you'll burn in hell for blasphemy our George!'

The mystique of their prey continued to occupy the Trappers' thoughts and Jack spoke again after a long, thoughtful pause.

'There has to be *something* up with that pretty wife of his for Sammy to be so keen to dirty the seat of his posh pants sitting in the Oak with the likes of us. Not to mention for him to behave like a common sinner with dear Mirabelle Ellis...'

'Any road Jack, you can ask im in person—ere e is!'

'What? Jesus wept, I'm not ready, he's caught us napping owd, it'll have to be up to you George!'

'Eh? But it's your turn!'

'Gerron with it an tweak im before e can order is pint, you know the rules of the game!'

'You let im sneak up; on us and it's your turn—so you do it!'

Sam Wilson was quietly pleased. The customary puerile sniggering that accompanied his every entrance to the bar was absent, Carthmain and Shenton were instead embroiled in an animated discussion; perhaps he would get some proper sense out of them tonight. To have an adult conversation would be more intoxicating than any ale. He was further gratified when he received an appropriate greeting.

'Evening Samuel!' called Carthmain with a welcoming smile and a flourish of his pint glass. Sam nodded politely, doffing his hat.

'Would you care to join George and me?'

'George and *I*,' Sam corrected him automatically, hanging up his hat and coat and making for the bar. George Shenton jerked with spasmodic but silent mirth while Carthmain's smile grew as broad as any mine-host's could ever aspire to be.

'Sammy Wilson, guardian of the King's English,' muttered Jack to his co-conspirator. 'Let's ave some fun.'

The Trappers' prey was disposed to taciturnity this night and at first the pickings seemed poor, but after laying a trail of grammatical howlers and solecisms to tempt the man's pedantic appetite, Jack turned to Sam. Jack Carthmain could speak perfectly if he so chose, but his local accent returned powerfully in three situations—in drink, under stress and in the company of Sammy Wilson.

'Nah then Sammy; hast seen any good flicks lately?'

'Flicks?' enquired Wilson with curt distaste, as if the word fouled his mouth. George hid his grin in his pint.

'Flicks Sammy man, the pickchoors, cinema, fillums!'

'I do not go along. I never have the time.' The victim made a lame attempt to fend off his tormentors as they closed in.

'Oooh, I like a good fillum meself,' Jack took good care to breathe beery fumes over Wilson, 'why me an George were down the Bug Ut just t'other dee…'

'George and *I*.' Sammy just couldn't help it, this was so easy. A pause.

'Bug Ut?' he repeated, puzzled.

'Aaaah, y'know, the Bug Ut, the Pickcher Palass! Yer walk in—but yer ride out!' Jack's specially-thickened brew of a voice was enhancing Sammy's suffering something wonderful. Realising the comedian was in need of a feed line, George asked, straight as a die, what Jack meant.

'Bug Ut, flea pit o course!' Jack was eager to offer enlightenment. 'D'yer know why there are so many fleas in there? Well, there's no jakes in there see, and some of the little kiddies can't—y'know—hold it in like, they go an piddle down the back o the seats and it all runs down the rake into the old orchestra pit an the little biting buggers breed down there. Word o advice Sammy, if yer find the time to pay a visit, sit at the back eh?'

Wilson's eyebrows were aloft like kites in a southerly, and it looked as if he could scarcely stomach another sip of his beer; for an entirely unprepared hunt, it was going exceedingly well.

'Any road, George an me...'

'George and *I*,' Wilson cut in with the asperity of a man forced to parley with simpletons.

'Was you there too then Sammy?' This intervention earned George a vexed glare from his prey. Jack resumed swiftly.

'George and *I*, we went along an saw one o them Yank musical comedies. Load o nonsense o course, but we enjoyed it an came out singin and dancin...'

'And scratchin,' added George, attacking imaginary invaders in his clothing.

'Aye, and scratchin, but it were worth it. Well, George and *I*, we thought so didn't us?'

Wilson's mouth moved as if to chew over Jack's error-strewn utterances, but an access of common sense struck him dumb and his lips closed. For a moment, thought George, he looked like a landed fish.

'Any'ow, yer should come with us next time out Sammy, you'd enjoy it!' Jack was all smiles and sincerity.

'Thank you so much gentlemen, but I truly don't believe I shall have the time.' It was a foggy November morning of a reply. The Trappers were thrilled to note Sam's hand straying to scratch nervously behind his ear.

When Wilson's hat and coat were back on and the bar door closed reluctantly behind him as if it was slipping slowly from an invisible grip, George was barking and quacking with laughter and his face turned ruby-puce-purple: fortunately, this time he had not just taken a mouthful of beer.

'Magnificent! Bravo!' He slapped Jack on the back and then gestured to Netta to set up their celebration drinks. 'Brilliance under pressure; cometh the hour cometh the man! That was subtle Jack, such subtlety as gladdens my heart!'

Jack too abandoned all restraint and the Trappers howled out their triumph together. He and me. He and I. We two. Us.

1940

'Ey Jack; d'you get the feelin that new feller over there is from summat of a higher social class than us—or at least that e fancies e does?'

'Hum.' Jack sipped his pint thoughtfully, 'hadn't thought on it George, I barely know the bloke.'

'But...' George fished determinedly, unsatisfied with such wishy-washy prevarication.

'But... yes. A bit of a toff.'

George nodded assent, but his face then twisted with a sour anger. 'That there is the kind o man who thinks as coal appears by magic, ready in the sack for your boys to drop it at his back door, as if e'd never credit that there were men crawlin in the earth for the fetchin of it.'

'Is that what he said?' Jack was ribbing George, but the old miner grew increasingly serious.

'Good as, Jack, good as. He's got nowt to say to me, but I eard im juss now, holdin forth about working men knowing their place, as if we want more than our deserts and we just spend our days loafin off like dogs in the sunshine!'

'There is a war on, George, everyone has to make sacrifices...'

'That inna what he's sayin, and besides my boys are doin *their* bit, them young lads and even the bloody half-dead ole timers are doin their bit and then some, with some o them pits bigger death traps than any bloody battlefield!'

'Steady on George—at least you don't have to go down there anymore!'

'That ent what matters, Jack! Alphonse there thinks e's better than the workin man: bloke like that shouldden be comin in ere and puttin on airs!'

'Maybe you've just got off on the wrong foot with him George. Give the man a chance, after all you and I became firm friends no matter what our differences.'

'True, but you've no side to you Jack, you can talk our lingo an you dunna snub a man jus cos he's got blue dust under is skin. *And* though yer sound more schooled than me, yer dunna talk like yer at the bloody Royal Garden Party!'

'Tell you what, let's buy the man a drink and bid him welcome. And see if he mends a bit.'

While Jack tried to spread tolerance and forbearance, George shared his doubts with his glass. The old man had felt ill at ease from the moment the stranger walked into the Royal Oak. He was tall and slender, his face serious and self-important, and this was echoed in how he carried himself and his manner—upright and lofty in all ways. Standing at the bar, George had been introduced to the 'new customer' by Netta, and instantly found that his sincere efforts to be friendly were received with a slighting stiffness. While Jack Carthmain got along with Mr. Samuel Wilson, it appeared that George Shenton simply couldn't do right for doing wrong.

'Are you new to Woolsend?' Jack asked Wilson, one man lounging with his elbow on the bar, the other standing up ramrod as if his RSM was due in the room at any moment.

'Yes. We moved less than two weeks ago.'

'What brings you here tonight?'

'I had some business at the church, I was talking to the vicar, introducing myself.'

George observed that where Jack was chatting friendly-like, Wilson made snappy pronouncements, a boss-man talking to an underling, not wasting words or encouraging familiarity.

'Church? Oh, St Mag's, just here?' Jack smiled. The church was four doors away.

'St Anselm's, as a matter of fact.'

Now Jack froze slightly, noticing that the newcomer had not simply replied, but was correcting him, and sharply too, like an old-fashioned schoolmaster. There was no call for that; there were a dozen cheery ways to put him straight.

'I came for a short stroll, then felt rather dry, and so...'

Wilson raised his glass both in demonstration of his point and in half-hearted salute, perhaps realising he had sounded unnecessarily testy. In spite of the severity of his qualms, George felt obliged to join the conversation as an old stager of the Royal Oak. Besides, if he didn't register his presence he could be cut out of the conversation altogether and wasn't about to have that happen on account of some jumped-up new boy.

'Ah well mate, glad yer found us, and yer didn't ave to come very far eh? Where there's a church there's always a pub, that's what they say.'

As George was later to explain to Jack, 'It were as if I'd just towd im God were a bloody toper! You saw it, e fixed me with is gimlet eye an just said "Quite", no more'n that, but I felt I were shut outta doors in mid-winter wi no trizers on. And I knew I was ruined forever in is eyes.'

'Ahhh, don't take on so George, he's just a bit of a cold fish, time will put matters right.'

'I onner so sure. I don't want im invading my drinking-space with is cold eyes and frosty churchyard vapours. I dunner like the man, e makes no *effort* to be liked!'

'Give it time, George, let's see how we like him in time.'

'How I like him?' grumbled the retired miner. 'What's me choice—fried or boiled?'

It took some time for Sam Wilson to realise somehow he had become a figure of fun. In all fairness nobody could have blamed him for this, as his own behaviour never changed and by his own lights he never said or did anything that should attract mockery. The changes came in the mien of his fellow-drinkers as they sought ways to deal with his habitual lofty disdain, with being corrected on their ABC as if they were recalcitrant infants and with hearing the opinions of S. Wilson Esq. stated as incontrovertible fact. Sam's inelastic consistency of behaviour, his almost nonexistent humour and stiff-necked pertinacity in coming to the Oak when Jack and George had begun their hunt and were openly sniggering and teasing made him the ideal target. Sam's rigid dignity became the prime quarry of the Trappers.

George Shenton shed his awe of Sam Wilson in one special moment. He encountered the man on the street in the company of his wife. Safely back at the bar of the Oak, the old man recounted the meeting to Jack Carthmain.

'I seed em comin but they didn't see me, leastways Sammy didn't otherwise e'd ave shot off down another road, any ol bloody road. So I were on top of em before e noticed me an when our eyes finally met, a look like ruddy death crossed is face, I reckon e'd rather ave met Ole Nick imself on that street. Well, I could see e were minded to cut me dead, but is Missus was lookin right at me an he couldn't stop er, so I chanced me arm. Bright as you like I pipes up, "Ow do Sammy!"—and e *winced*, Jack, sick as a pig e was! And worse, he glares at me as if to say, "Oo let *you* out of yer cage?" Well: didn't that just make me all the more determined to sneap the bugger, so I sings out, "Now then Sammy, introduce me to yer young lady why don't yer?" She liked that, smiled and tucked her chin down she did, modest-like, but well pleased.'

'"Mr. George Shenton—my wife Nora," e says, brittle and reluctant, then e touches is at and e's gone. His Missus though, she lingered and smiled at me for a moment, then trotted off an caught is arm. I tell you Jack, that man was barely civil, only she were prepared to make an effort of any sort. Well I'll pay "Samuel" Wilson back, I'll pay im back a treat. E used to put the wind up me, I thought he was icy, reminded me of my Dad more'n I'm comfortable with, but now I dunna think of im as icy. I think of im as a great wet snowdrift what wants trampling.' George lit a Woodbine to calm himself as Jack beckoned to Netta for 'more of Mr. Shenton's nerve tonic.'

'P'raps you shouldn't have called him "Sammy", owd. I reckon he dunna like it.'

George grinned through his agitation. 'That were a bit o devilment I admit, but he were goin to snub me utterly, if I'da stood there choosin me words e'd ave swept by an made me look a fool. So I decided to be a bugger. Glad I did; I shan't fret about im comin in no more. E's no better an me, and I've more right in ere than e does.'

As their recharged drinks arrived, devil-George smiled with refreshed wickedness.

'Mind you I see now why e's got five kids.'

'Six,' gently corrected Jack.

'Six kiddies, bloody ell. You wouldn't know it, slim as a bluebell she is. Now *there's* a woman, Jack, there's a beautiful, shining, warm woman!'

'How's *Mrs.* Shenton?' asked Jack, but George ignored his mild reproof.

'A woman like that—with Sammy Wilson! With her belly full of his pups! There's no bloody justice in this world, Jack.'

'Thou shalt not covet thy neighbour's wife.'

'Oooo, let me do it a bit Father Jack, just a bit, I've so few pleasures left in life.'

'Take your beer, take your fags and be satisfied, owd.'

'Oh I would if I'd not seen her! She's made me feel somethin I've not felt in nigh on twenty year.'

'Erm, don't feel it in front of me, eh George?'

'By: what a *woman*!'

The Beauty of Chell Street

2012

Three generations of women sat talking, their discussions presided by Nora's photograph, long liberated from its mouldy oubliette and transferred to a new frame complementing its autumnal sepia and better emphasising the still sweetness of the girl it embraced, the coming woman who had sat for her portrait nearly a century before.

'It's hard to imagine her as a grandmother.' Francine adjusted the frame's stand, as if making a guest more comfortable.

'I find it hard to imagine her as anything else,' Kara replied. 'It's difficult to believe that old people have a past, at least when you're a child, you think they have always been that way.'

'Charming! Thank *you* missy!' Flora took the remark playfully amiss and pouted; all three women laughed. 'But of course I always think of her as Mum, I somehow ignore the changed woman who came later, what I hold in my heart is the young, beautiful woman always singing. We all have her trapped in our memories as we first knew her.'

Francine thought deeply. 'If she was here, how would she see herself? I mean as a young woman or a mother, a grandmother? What happened as she changed and grew older? When did "Nora" become "Nonna"?'

'A good historian's question.' Flora nodded appreciatively. 'I've no doubt she would see herself as she was in this photo. Even at age ninety she still saw herself as the Beauty of Chell Street. Oh she was keen enough to take on the roles of wife and mother, but I think for her life was all downhill from there. She came alive when she became desirable, when she realised the power she had over men. She regarded the transition from nubile to lover to bride to mother to grandmother as a slow degradation. At least you'd have thought so from the way she went on in later life; and indeed from her behaviour when Helen, her eldest, fell pregnant.'

'Ah,' Kara chipped in. 'The story of Aunty Helen's miracle baby!'

'But it wasn't Helen's, *ahem*, suspect timing that upset Mother. It was the fact of it. You'd call it denial nowadays. "She's just running fat!" she insisted. She blamed Helen for stopping smoking, blamed her brother-in-law who worked at a sweet factory for giving her bag after bag of broken bonbons, scrabbled about for any face-saving excuse. She was bitterly unhappy that any daughter of hers should have a baby so soon, it was a form of betrayal to her, one of the many cruel things we did to her over the years. Mind you she changed her tune when the little one made its debut, changed it radically, and she went on and on about that little bundle to the extent that anyone listening would've sworn it was her own.

'But even then she was not to be openly spoken of as a grandmother, nor yet a grandma, gramma, granny, nan or nanna. She forbade all such names, and after a period during which she probably thought of little else, announced that the kiddies should know her as Nonna. No other grandmother was a Nonna; it was a title of her making. it protected her vanity and made her unique. And I suppose eventually it became who she was—Nonna Nora. The Beauty of Chell Street was forgotten by everyone except her.'

1969

'I'll choke on these things one day!' complained Nora. 'Pills, pills, damn rubbish!'

'Why are you going on like that Mum?' Helen countered. Superior little smarty-pants she was, always answered back. 'You've maintained for years that you're ill; well now you've a fine spread of pills to prove it, shouldn't you be happy?'

'Pah!' Nora pulled a face and gestured at the little bottles and packs. 'Sugar candy for a baby. They don't believe I'm ill, practically said as much to me face when I had all them tests in the hosspickle.'

'*Hospital,* mother.'

'Shuttup, clever clogs! All I'm saying is they've given me these just to keep me quiet!'

'If that was their plan, it isn't working is it?'

'Bum'ole! You girls, the lot o you, you got no respeck for me since I got sick. I don't know how I came to this. I'd be better off dead so I would.'

'Oh mother!'

'Folk had respeck for me once, paid attention to what I said, but now that's gone. Time and sickness and Sammy Wilson, have took it all away from me.'

'*Taken.*'

'Bum'ole!'

1965

The girls probably believed they had been thoughtful; they had bought her a little clock, a companion for her moments, to fit neatly on the table beside her chair so she wouldn't have to struggle up to look at the old time-totter on the mantelpiece. But all it did was measure the ever-widening gaps between one face and another appearing at her door. Faster than heartbeats it hastened the days, later, later, tomorrow, later, later, *rickersnick rickersnack*, carrying her towards her meeting with the Dark Angel. Have they bought this just to make mock of me? I have time counting in my head, always counting, time elapsed, days added upon days since my husband went away, why add yet more ticking, why remind me, why rub it in?

2012

'To me, Nonna Nora was a small toy-like creature, a little like a talking doll,' Kara began to tell. 'She was always loving, but sad and frail too. She had a "hairy" voice, that's how I thought of it, hoarse and rasping compared to someone like my Mum. I suppose it was old age, that and the cigarettes, that made her sound that way, but I was too young to think about such things. She seemed to me to be darker-skinned than anyone else I had seen, and she had these fascinating vivid stains on her fingers—the fags again. She smelt—and remember this is me as a little girl, the thoughts that went through my head—like she'd been kept in a cupboard for a long time and had only just come out, musty but with that shut-away odour overlaid with a strong perfume. She seemed smaller every time I saw her, a little more immobile and helpless. I wondered if she was vanishing bit by bit: it occurred to me this was perhaps how people died, diminishing until there was nothing left. Death was a mystery, I was just too little to understand.

'One or two very old relatives had done this vanishing-act, there one day and gone the next, and I was told that they had "passed away" and little else. I thought for a time I had discovered the secret of death. And Nonna Nora talked about *that* often enough, I can tell you.

'"I shall go up and sit on the Lord's right hand," she'd say, and I would wonder how he would then use his hand, unless she consented to move. "And then I shall look down upon my family and look after them from above." But then her voice would grow hairier, grumbling and low, filled with tremors of gleeful anticipation. "Yes I shall look right down on the Earth and then right down *there,* and I shall see what has become of Sammy Wilson. I shall see his eternal punishment and I shall be happy, because that will be justice."

'Both Nonna and Grampa Sam talked about God a great deal. But I fancy they wanted very different things from him...'

The Articles

1941

'Why does a man like that have children?' Jack Carthmain was minded to wax philosophical, but George was in one of those moods again and he had a clever-dick reply at the ready.

'To sell in ter slavery? A constant supply of fresh food?'

'Shurrup yer daft a'porth! No, *look* at him George, have you ever seen Sammy out and about with his family?'

'Yerrrsss, but me eyes stay on his wife.'

'Apply yourself for pity's sake owd, think what they look like, that family of his, specially if you've seen em going off to church on a Sunday?'

George grew a little more serious. 'All in a row, single file following their leader. Ducks. No, a food queue, no, *soldiers!*'

'Precisely, ole fellah. Soldiers, drilled, disciplined—and *scared* George, that's the key, scared witless of their CO.'

'I thought mine were a cunt,' muttered George with bitter reminiscence.

'Stick to the point!' commanded Jack. 'Now come on man, what is it that you need most of all to succeed in having kids?'

'A good rifle that don't shoot blanks.' The last brown beer dribbled down George's throat.

'Jesus wept an well he might, I swear I'd rather talk to Sammy sometimes! Look George, what I'm sayin is that any bugger can do the business, get a girl up the duff, but if you're going to be a good father you've got to *like* children, have you not?'

'S'pose so.'

'And do you contend that Sammy likes *his* children? It doesn't look that way to me. Have y'heard how he bellows at em if they start to straggle on their way to prayers? "Come along article number one, article number two, hop to it!"'

'Article?'

'*Article.* Articles with numbers, one to eight or however many Sammy and Mrs. W have got this week. And that's him bein nice. I tell you George, my ol man used some harsh words to me, but he never treated me as a thing, a burden like. But that's what those girls are to Sammy. There's no love in that man.'

'I think... that in is way e loves em, but from what I seen, hmmm, how to put it; Sammy's as scared of them as they are o him!'

'Ye Gods, George Shenton finally makes sense! Yes mate—amen! He's cold and he's vile and he's stroppy with em—and yes, he's afeared! But I've no sympathy for the man. I'll tell you, I was passing his gate the other day—literally passing, I'd never dare darken his door...'

'Unless he were out,' interrupted George, grinning lasciviously.

Jack would not be diverted. 'Tell you what owd, I saw him and I heard him, bawling like a sarn't major at some poor little lads playing in his garden with the youngest of his brood. Birks's boys they were, and a better pair of little lads from a more respectable family I've never met, but e pitched them boys off his property with growls and curses, as if they were lepers or fifth columnists or something. Know why?'

'Sammy don't suffer little children to come unto him,' George burped.

'True for you Mr. Shenton, but I know why. Jim Birks is a good man and decent, but e's a bus driver for Motor Traction, and the Lord o'the Manor, he won't entertain the children of the lower classes! "Haven't you got a home to go to?" he yells. "Get back where you came from, what d'you think his is, Doctor Barnardo's?" I know the man is a prize arse and a snob, but really...'

'I bet e'd call hissen old-fashioned, Jack.'

'You know what I think of "old fashioned", mate...'

'Aye, I do. An I was brought up with a firm hand too.'

'I'm no lily-liver George, but there's no call to go terrorizing bairns. The boys took to their heels, and Sammy turned on his own mob, scoldin em for "associating with such low creatures"—and I quote.'

'Jesus wept.'

'Aye, George, aye. And it's not just the little uns neither, just watch that column of press-ganged worshippers trudging to church, you'll see it in their faces one and all, young and old. They quake at the sound of his voice, I'm sorry in me heart for em. It's not right, George.'

'S'pose he's right to teach em the fear of God...' George was generous enough to venture.

'Of God, George? Is that who he's making them afraid of?'

Silence prevailed, and was broken by George, who had gone misty-eyed with thought—or drink.

'Articles; one, two, three.'

'You what?'

'Articles—one, two, three. Probably what ole Sammy says as his Missus casts off her unmentionables, off they come, articles one, two, three...' George went a queer colour, as he often did thinking of things he oughtn't.

'Give it a rest old son. She's got enough to put up with in her bloody husband,' said Jack wearily.

1936

Flora's hands were perfect, thought Nora. She was no longer a baby and those hands were growing slim and strong, but retained the babyish delicacy that had held Nora and the other women in the neighbourhood spellbound, examining the newborn's tiny fingers and sighing with admiration as if handling an exquisite work of living art. And yes, you still wanted to hold and caress those hands and spend timeless time admiring those small, unblemished pink nails.

Flora was four now, and sat with her sisters squeezed around the dinner table. Sam naturally sat at the head of the family, with Helen and Minnie nearest, then Phyllida and Petra, and Flora, on a big cushion, with her mother close. All the family together; a rare event. Nora felt a tickling, pricking sensation in her eyes, stirred by the sight of the children before her and the thought of those who should have been: Jocelyn, Vanessa, there is still room for you at this table.

Sam said grace; he prayed with the same fervency as he did in church, but here he had his eyes screwed tightly and hands raised, palms-upright, as if he were a pagan priest conjuring an ineffable power, or feeling for rain. Nora kept her own eyes open, a fact that would have caused Sam immense irritation had he become aware, but it was the better to keep watch over the children, from oldest to youngest. Helen was slipping into a doze, or a religious trance. Phyllida mimicked Sam, moving her lips soundlessly in echoed piety. Petra by contrast was tight-lipped, her face pained as if the prayer irked her. Flora too was copying Daddy, eyes closed so tight there were lines on her sweet little face, and she clasped her hands firm against her chin; praying or begging?

As usual it was Minnie as had to be different. She had tilted her head downwards, but her eyes were narrow slits that shot out surreptitious spying-expeditions left and right before her hand shot out and snatched a morsel from the cracked tureen with no lid, all before God had been properly thanked. Minnie could never wait; and as ever she would affect indifference to her father's rage should he catch her. You may think you can get away with murder, Nora warned her with a look, but your father is in charge he won't make a favourite of you if you make a mockery of the Lord. You may be twelve years old and think yourself quite grown up, but if you behave like an infant he will treat you accordingly.

But Minnie was Sam's pet girl, oh wasn't that the truth. She shared his colouring, his cast of face, his dark brows and habitual disdainful look. She had also inherited his steely gaze, his air of authoritative self-certainty and sandpaper tongue. Like her father, Minnie could not bear the company of fools, and neither was slow to make their views known. From time to time the precocious madam would assume Sam's entire mantle of thundering mastery, as if she were trying out a hand-me-down from a dressing-up box, but she was far too young to carry it off. Instead she appeared rebellious, truculent, wilful and plain disobedient. In short, Minnie Wilson would never be *told*. Once she had made her mind on something, anything, she was immovable, rigid. Her disobedience took many forms: she had never cared for schooling and was forever in trouble. Not many days before, she had proudly worn a brand-new overcoat, presented to her by her father, and because there were no pegs available to hang it up, her teacher had instructed her to fold it and put it under her chair, just as the other children had. Minnie refused vehemently. 'That coat cost good money and that floor is filthy-dirty!' Unafraid of her teacher or any other adult, she had been sent home; as they awaited for their father to return from work, the other girls attempted to comfort Minnie, for surely he would part her from her breath when he heard the news. But Minnie pushed away their loving arms and damned their welling tears.

Sam Wilson had received the intelligence in stony silence and then summoned his daughter to his den, from which she emerged dry-eyed and curl-lipped a short time later. 'He's going to see my teacher, now. And he's going to tell her that I'm in the right.' Not one of the sisters could believe it—and yet whatever else she was, Minnie was no fibber. Sam's indulgence of Minnie was an oddity, an aberration, and the more outrageous her rebelliousness the greater his unspoken admiration for her. So—you are a favourite, miss, but your father won't protect you if you mock his God.

'Amen,' finished Sam.

'Amen,' responded his family, apart from Flora, who distinctly said 'Our Men.' The child would learn: the words had precious little meaning for her yet. Sam carved and Nora dished up the vegetables. The girls waited, even Minnie, hands folded on their laps, for their father to begin eating, and then there was a clack-clack of cutlery on crockery and light metallic scrapes of forks against teeth.

God had been praised for his bounty and yet Minnie looked anything other than grateful. She scowled at the evidently meagre pickings as if she were a Ladyship dining amongst peasants. Eat what is put before you madam, there's plenty out there who'd be thankful for half of what you've got, and it is going to be many a long year before you are served with the royal feast you seem to think is your right.

Yes, Flora had perfect little hands. One lifted, curved and cupped, covering the side of her mouth as she leaned to her right to whisper to her sister in the next seat. The family jumped as sharply as did the dinner-plates as Sam slapped his hand palm-down on to the table's dark, polished surface.

'No talking at the table! Let your meat stop your mouth!' he commanded.

The little girl looked momentarily woebegone and tearful, but subsided slowly towards her meal, shoulders hunched, abashed and frightened. Sam glared from seat to seat, child to child, but all was at peace again. Nora followed his searchlight gaze with her own, to ameliorate it with a warm and reassuring look of love.

Petra pushed a lump of turnip around her plate as if

wishing it could drop off the side and so be forgotten. She hated turnip, but there it was and she should take it, there was no choice. And she would eat it tonight or her father would insist it be served cold as her breakfast and for every meal thereafter until she forced it down. Waste not want not Sam Wilson preached, for reasons of thrift as well as his unswerving demand to be obeyed.

Flora was eating heartily, soon there would be nothing on her plate although she was plainly still hungry. She was growing, but would have to learn to make do. Nora would sometimes pass the child something from her plate, but it had to be done swiftly and without Sam seeing, or that voice of his would roar once again. Flora drew her knife through the last of her gravy, making lazy little patterns, but Nora tapped her on the wrist and hissed to her to finish properly.

Phyllida was staring in wordless accusation at Sam's plate, which was still half-full as he sat upright, chewing carefully. The girl's own plate was so clean it might never have borne a scrap of food, but she too was clearly still ravenous. Positively outgrowing her strength, and yet her father still received bigger servings than she, or anyone else in the family. Nora saw the question etched on her brow and burning in her eyes, 'Why? Why?' Because that is the prerogative of the head of the household, never presume to argue. And I cannot pass morsels to a thirteen year old, my love; that really wouldn't do. Unlike Minnie, however, there was not the remotest danger of Phyllida making a fuss. She was the only one of the girls who never, regardless of the circumstances, openly questioned her father's judgement or came secretly to her mother seeking an angel to soften his heart. Quiet and close that one, almost mute of malice. In private, Sam evinced some admiration of his second-born, 'Stoic, uncomplaining.' It grieved Nora that their children should ever have a thing to complain about.

Timid and retiring but with those unlovely, aggrieved eyes. Nora feared what was lurking in the lightning-flashes of resentment that were Phyllida's stock in trade. But she would have to slice the child in two with a carving-knife if she was ever to hunt out her secret.

Helen ate slowly, mouth always working, ruminating. The enforced silence at the table suited her; Nora was convinced she would never have talked even if such a thing had been permitted. And she hadn't that much to say even when her mouth wasn't full, always drifting away on her own thoughts that one, how could that ever be good for her? Nora fretted that Helen was becoming a pallid, bookish, unmarriageable creature. She needed feeding up and taking out of herself, but she was only with them for a day or two and then she would be back in the grip of that holy terror of an aunt of Sammy's. Why had he ever consented to allow that church-poisoned old wraith to raise their daughter? Nora nursed the uncharitable hope that one day soon Aunt Laura Wilson would be called to her maker and Helen restored to her true family. Then her mother could bring her back to life, help her to be a proper young woman and not some closeted, worm-riddled nun.

Helen rarely smiled and that spoiled her lovely face: she was too sober, too serious, too much her father and too much her great-aunt, too much a pure bloody Wilson. At least she seemed satisfied with her meal—no doubt it was glorious provender compared with her usual fare, which consisted of cold water and bitter prayer, beyond a doubt.

Nora invariably finished her meal last of all, forever shushing a child when she saw the urge to chatter dawn in its eyes or helping little Flora to cope with tough meat, spilled peas and gravy, wiping faces, ensuring everyone was eating and attending to their table-manners as religiously as their father demanded. Flora, bored now, squirmed for release, but Sam stifled her with a shake of his head, and the little girl sat still and stiff on her cushion.

'Elbows off the table!' Sam ordered as the meal came to its end and concentration grew lax. 'This is not one of your common households!' He shot out a glare encompassing everyone, and several guilty pairs of elbows slipped quickly down to their owners' sides. Petra leaned forward and pressed her hands on her belly; she was probably getting her funny tummy again, a distressing, inexplicable sensation that often gripped her after meals. It was no sort of indigestion or heartburn, Petra was a careful, even fastidious eater, and yet sometimes she would writhe in her mother's arms as Nora tried to administer Kaolin and Morphine, pleading with Sam to excuse her from the table, 'She's not play-acting Sammy, I know she's not!' When the pains subsided Nora would put the child to bed and sit with her until sure she was comfortable. The doctor had never found anything wrong, but Nora suspected the man was a humbug. She could not restrain occasional morbid speculation: two of my children are gone, and if I am to lose another to the Dark Angel then Petra is she. At the very least I fancy I shall see out my days tending to her needs, for she is so delicate she will never leave her mother. At first, Nora had thought Flora would be the one to remain at her side, she had barely survived her first year and been sickly a long time, but now she was blooming and it was her sister whose pale face and poorly looks concerned Nora.

The meal was done. Sam took himself to his room and closed the door on his family. The girls cleared the table and then squabbled over the washing and drying. At Sam's insistence and order, Nora sat at rest, stroking her own belly not in appreciation of her dinner but to offer caresses to the child growing in there. It was a boy, she knew it was a boy, she had consulted the gypsy and the gypsy had confirmed it. She did not dare tell Sam this; to him, the gypsy spoke for the devil and all demons, he would have been incensed. But on a day not long to be postponed, Sam Wilson would see for himself that he had a son, and in that knowledge he would be happy; and, as the gypsy had also foretold, their troubles would be at an end, all would be well within the Wilson family forever more.

The Book Of Fire

1948

I don't want to go in there, I don't *have* to go in there; and if I don't want to do something then I won't do it. That is the one good thing about being alone, the opportunity to make your own decisions. I don't want to go in there. I do not *need* to go in there. Through that church door there is nothing for me, through that door is the place they met, the place that stood by while he was stolen away by *her*. Thou shalt not commit adultery! Empty words! He didn't listen, she didn't listen: are *any* of them paying a scrap of attention to what's said in there? I did everything they told me, everything they preached, and still they did nothing to stop her taking him.

How could they let him read out all that holy rot, knowing he was disregarding every Commandment? Well, the one that matters. Just because he had an impressive speaking voice, those pompous, sonorous, self-assured tones that filled old rafters with such a rumble of righteous thunder? Weren't those words rendered meaningless declaimed by a man in such a state of sin? Wasn't it irreligious, blasphemous? If they didn't think so then their piety, their bent-knee worship, their Sunday best and smiles of goodwill were all equally false. Liars. Traitors. Hypocrites. I have turned your book inside out, shaken the words from it, and not one syllable supports their deeds. The opposite!

Should she not be cast out as a whatsit, a Jezebel or

whoever it was? She came to no good fate I recall. Should those churchgoing people not have been coming to my door to offer their sympathies and tell me how sin shall be found out and repaid? Where were they then? Looking the other way and saying nothing. *Thou shalt not covet thy neighbour's husband.* And may she take one of yours next, you Sunday-pious bitches, how many kiddies will she make fatherless before you realise what she is? I hope it is you next, and you and you and you, and I hope it *hurts.* How can you face your God when you stood aside and let me suffer? I'm sure they say somewhere that doing nothing is just as much a sin as doing evil. Yes, I'm sure that's what they say.

Nora had always seen the church door as a barrier. Even on bright Sunday mornings, arm in arm with her Sam, the children following them in a crocodile, all dressed up neat and silent, all blinking the warm sunlight out of their eyes, even then the church door was not a welcoming portal but an obstruction. Tall solid double doors of aged oak studded with black metal points as if shot through with an enemy's arrows in some ancient siege, two enormous cold metal rings for handles: there should have been a portcullis and a moat, for it was a fortress door for soldiers, not a gate of light to Heaven. For Nora to step through the gap in those doors was to know she could never have shifted the weight of even one of them on her own, to imagine those great slabs of timber falling from their hinges and crushing her flat as she tried to shepherd her children out of danger.

And what was within when she got there? An oppressive hush, holy silence, or organ notes so melancholy she fancied there was a funeral perpetually in progress rather than acts of praise, stained glass that made a cold claim to beauty but adulterated the good light from outside, unforgiving stone, bare wood, a place where living breath would mist and it seemed a frost could fall any moment even when the streets without were sweltering and everything shimmered in a heat haze. And the poor children; they were supposed to be there for the good of their souls but instead were offered nightmares by the robed man in the pulpit with his threats of doom, they were dragooned to Sunday School, kept from their mother and introduced recklessly to the terror of death. And there was nowhere comfortable for them to sit, nowhere to play, indeed no conception whatsoever of play within those walls, nowhere even to take the poor little things when their bladders were bursting. Nora resented having to smuggle them out of a side door and watch over them as they piddled, humiliated and afraid, crouched by a huge stone buttress, half in sight of a comfortless timber cross that stood sentinel over the nearby crossroads.

Through those doors was a harsh place that offered nothing but the bone-chill that prepared you for the tomb. That and the floating grey mist of incense that snaked under the nose and tickled, aromatic, thick, revolting, *ach y fi*, like that blue-nosed bitch's cigarette smoke.

1943

That which you love is that of which you are afraid. That which loves you is that which will punish you, in order to redeem you. Love and fear stood inextricable. Sam Wilson had learnt this lesson long ago. Aunt Laura used to terrify him, but it was a cleansing terror, a thing that had made him strong. He should have seen the church door as welcoming, Earth's representation of the gates of Paradise that would one day open unto the saved, but as he loved the church so he feared it. What punishments would he have to endure to receive its love?

'God knows what's in your mind Samuel Wilson.' Aunt Laura would brandish the Bible in his face. 'God knows all. Obey him through this book. This book is a book of fire!'

Every time he walked towards those guardian doors, Sam feared they would fly together and shut him out.

He dearly loved to read to the congregation; as he spoke them, the words truly meant something, he felt he had found his true path, believed that all he had to do was to overcome his mortal weaknesses and he would be freed from a tyranny of Hell. Each step up to the lectern was one towards being a better man, the man he knew he could be, and to declare before all those immortal words was to perfect himself. But every step away from those words, every step back down to the ground, carried him to the compromised, condemned soul he yearned to leave behind. To be the man he desired to be, he would have to dwell forever within the church's confines, not outside of them. His soul craved sanctuary, but if he was ever to achieve the tranquillity and rest he needed, many things had to change, he had to shut out the fearful child who still quailed within, and someone else must be shut out too, someone who always listened raptly to him, listened closely, too closely, every Sunday as he turned the quarto pages on the decorated lectern, adoring him where she should adore something higher, making a graven image out of him.

Love is patient and is kind; love doesn't envy. Love doesn't brag, is not proud,..

'You've been seeing that woman!' Nora's voice was verging on hysterical, she had probably thought of nothing else since he had stepped out of the door, she had whipped herself up in this fine state of nerves. Sam looked at her reddened features with injured innocence and cold anger: he had only been for his customary drink at the Royal Oak, that was that; she was a false accuser. How distorted her face was when she screeched, her mouth stretching like a ravening animal's, her skin creased and aged, tears winking in her eyes like glass shards, dark stains trailing down her cheeks. This, he shuddered, was a woman who flattered herself that she was beautiful.

'You've been walking out with her—that or worse—I know you have!' Nora turned away and sobbed. Sam toyed stupidly with the idea of challenging her to question Carthmain and Shenton about where he had been, what time he had arrived and left, what he'd imbibed, but he knew it would not matter. Nora had made up her mind and, fantasy or not, would have it so. The time he'd left; perhaps that should not be mentioned. To Sam's chagrin, a weight of guilt sank down on his chest and he made no further attempt to defend himself.

It was true he'd had no assignation with 'that woman', yet on his way home from the pub he had taken the longer route that took him near to Mirabelle Ellis's house. This had meant negotiating an uneven, unlit and potholed back entry, and braving these hazards had cost Sam a shoe full of water and a ricked ankle, but it meant that his diversion would not be witnessed. Standing in deep shadow across the way from Mrs. Ellis's tiny terraced house, Sam gazed up at her bedroom window; the blackout curtains were in place but hanging slightly loose, as if they were exhausted by their duties, and a sliver of light shone through. Sam could not knock on the door and warn her about it at that time of night, for someone might notice and people might talk. He hoped to spot a movement, her body, briefly as she passed, but nothing happened and eventually the light was snuffed out. Sam stirred, straining to see his watch, and realised he had been standing there for over half an hour.

Love doesn't seek its own way, is not provoked, takes no account of evil;

So hard, so hard to cleave to this injunction: Sam found himself unable to forget the catalogue of petty and great irritations that was his marriage to Nora. He cast his mind back to the outbreak of the horrifying slaughter convulsing the globe, the day he sat reading his daily paper in silent horror. As usual, Nora would not give him the peace he needed to absorb the enormity of what was in prospect, she was fluttering about, reading over his shoulder and then darting in front of him, impatient for him to explain the unfathomable workings of the world.

'War?' gasped his wife in the thin, shocked tones of a child faced with a broken promise, 'Why war? I thought the newspapers said...'

Sam writhed in his chair, mind and body tortured by his rising impatience.

'The newspapers were wrong, Nora. They are often wrong.'

But she continued to protest, 'I saw in the newspaper, heard on the wireless, Mr. Chamberlain said it was peace, that Mr. Hickler had agreed...'

'Mr. *Hitler* has made a laughing-stock of this country my dear. Mr. Chamberlain is a damn fool and so are...' Sam was appalled by what he was about to say to her, held his tongue and looked up at his wife, trying to summon some fondness and comfort for her; yet he knew that all she saw from him was a cold glare. When he spoke again he did so as softly as he was able, 'I wish my dear,' he heard an unintended condescending note in his voice, but he could neither desist nor resist it, 'that sometimes you would read the full story in the paper and not just the dratted headline. Then you would stand a chance of knowing why it is war now and not peace.'

Mirabelle Ellis would have read and thoroughly understood the news reports, she would have known that war was coming and if things were different he could have spent the evening with her discussing and dissecting the events that had led to this dreadful pass. Mirabelle Ellis would not have resembled a frightened animal, uncomprehending and vulnerable. Sam looked up at the window once more, imagined himself within, with her, talking in soft voices, talking, perhaps through the night. With a suppressed gasp he made a supreme effort, tore his eyes away and turned for home.

Love bears all things, believes all things, hopes all things, endures all things. Love never fails...

Sam had the devil of a struggle with his back door key, but finally managed to open up without making any noise. Mindful of the need to keep the house tidy he shed his dirty shoes in the scullery before padding towards the back kitchen. He could tell someone was there, just out of sight, he could smell the fresh, exciting aroma of a cigarette newly lit, when the smoke was blue and clear, not like the grey fug in the Royal Oak. Strange: Nora did not smoke, who could it be at this hour—surely it must be *her!* The feeling of imminently stepping into her presence sent an electric flutter across Sam's guts and erotic, heated, guilt-laden thoughts packed into one tiny moment and then... but what was she doing here? How could she get in? And was she not above the common habit of neighbouring, dropping in for chatter, empty gossip with those harsh-voiced women who peopled the avenue? Was she here to confront Nora, to demand that she give up her husband? Or to perform an act of contrition before the woman whom she had wronged, confessing all and begging forgiveness? Would the two of them combine and turn on him, denounce him before the parish for his sins? The electric twinge crossed his insides again, but this time as a sick shot of fear.

He stepped into the room braced for any fate, to find Nora standing at the window, the greying smoke snaking from her hand and unravelling in the air as she kept her back to him. There was only a dim light within the room but Nora herself illuminated everything; she was dressed up, as if to celebrate the victory that still seemed so far away, and she looked slim, desirable, touchable. When she turned to face him Sam saw that she had made up her face with exacting care, she might almost have been the girl he had encountered before the end of the last war, a presence of purest, seductive light. Nora took a long draw on her cigarette and puffed the smoke out from between coral-coloured lips; oh, the way her mouth worked, her eyes closing in pleasure, her tongue flicking out slightly, reminding him of the nights long ago when she... She drew near, slithered her arms around his neck, nuzzled his nose, touched her lips to his, sneaked her tongue into his mouth. Sam did not resist.

'I can do anything she can.' Nora breathed into his ear, thrusting herself against him, guiding his hands down her sides and on to her buttocks.

'You don't need her. I can do anything. Anything.'

She kissed him again, mouth now wide agape, and at that moment Sam Wilson realised just how repulsive a scent could arise from the combination of tobacco smoke and cheap, sweet scent.

Nora too was sniffing deeply. 'You've got the smell on you, the smell of bitch. How can you come back to me when I can tell, the children can tell, everyone can tell?' She paused to suck at his lips, thrust her tongue once again inside his unresisting mouth. 'But I forgive you,' she hissed, 'I forgive you and you can come to me again. Come to me.' They were lost in the next kiss; Sam was a column of ecstatic fire. Her hand closed upon his pegger, he wanted to tell her to stop, what if one of the children walked in, but his mouth was too busy to trifle with words.

Moments later they had parted, Nora's eyes were full of tears. 'You've been seeing that woman!'

But now remain faith, hope, and love: these three. The greatest of these is love.

Angels of Light

1917

Sam felt constricted. His neck, chest and stomach were held in a tight vice of clothing and his hat squeezed the sweat out of his head. The presence of his Aunt Laura by his side as they promenaded provided an equivalent constraint on his speech and manners; he could not forget himself in the tiniest way in front of her and kept his peace as they stepped out carefully down the road, walking as if their strides were being measured and judged. He was ever afraid of this fierce, stern woman and it made precious little difference that he was now a strong and fit seventeen year old, head and shoulders taller than her, rather than the cowed little boy who had been given to her like a votive offering and subsequently steeped in the unique, austere culture of her personal universe. In her company he was forever the child who had learned to feel the presence of God as an ache in his head and a pain in the pit of his stomach, one whose deepest soul yearned for peace, for freedom from his restraints, but who obeyed the ingrained demands of his upbringing and remained silent and uncomplaining.

'Oh... bother.' Aunt Laura's piqued voice was almost inaudible. She stopped dead, and Sam halted obediently and glanced at her, seeing her habitual expression of lofty, purse-lipped disapproval deepen and harden as she screwed up her eyes to examine the two figures that were approaching them. Sam fancied he could see his aunt cast an almost desperate glance across the busy road in the direction of the railway station, as if she were contemplating risking a fatal dash under the wheels and heavy hooves in preference to the imminent encounter; but then her features settled into pained resignation and finally a rictus smile. Sam realised that Aunt Laura was obeying her own rules, no hypocrite, her inner desires had to be sacrificed to public politeness and forbearance.

'Good afternoon Mrs. Payne, how are you today?' Sam concealed a smile as he recognised his aunt's 'mixing' tone, the fluting voice she employed to disguise her distaste at meeting anyone whose presence she felt demeaned her. She was shrill and snide whenever she tortured her voice and nature this way, but not one person ever betrayed anything other than delight at her manner. The stifling demands of courtesy applied to one and all.

'And Nora my dear, you look so pretty. This, by the way, is my nephew Sam.'

The young man swept his hat off and was then left twiddling nervously with the horrid, oppressive thing as the three women proceeded to ignore him utterly.

The sun was almost directly behind the newcomers and it took a drawn-out moment for Sam to adjust his eyes and to descry their faces. His discomfort deepened as he realised he knew the older woman from his childhood trips to this seaside town in the company of his aunt. Mrs. Payne was what Aunt Laura referred to cuttingly as an 'accidental acquaintance' who simply could not be shaken off, notwithstanding that the two old women loathed one another. He recalled an account of a previous encounter with 'the Payne woman', one awash with vitriol.

'That woman is the most egregious snob imaginable—and her high opinion of herself is based upon quite *what*, I ask? Her people, she says, were landowners: the most generous possible interpretation of that claim is that she comes from farming stock. But strict truth, I think, would read "peasants". She married Darius Payne because he was the coach driver for a baronet—and a very minor one to be sure—but our Mr. Payne was a horseman through and through and he would have none of these motor-cars when they made their first unwelcome appearance. Sadly his nobody of a master was all agog for any novelty engine, wheel and piston-crazed they say, smitten from the first moment and so on his estate the horse and cart began to die a terrible death. To be fair to the good gentleman, he tried hard to persuade Payne to see reason and learn to handle the new carriages, but unless he could see horses' rears before his eyes the poor thing was quite lost. He took some lowly job—I'm bothered if I can remember what—and that dished *her* for a good while—I'm told you can still see the bald spots on la Payne's head from where she tore her hair out. That's a story she has kept dark for many a long year. And yet still she fancies she's one of the upper crust!'

On the sea front in the declining sun, Sam was for once glad of the presence of his formidable aunt: she was the only known antidote to the onslaught of the skeletal creature that was Mrs. Payne, always swaddled in all-over black and pinched in viciously at the waist. She reminded Sam irresistibly of a rolled-up old umbrella, abandoned on a hat-stand. This effect was enhanced by the way in which old age had begun to push her shoulders down and her head forward, and pulled spitefully at her already pointed nose. In spite of the assault of the years on her body, the despised woman still affected the air of an aristocrat. The girl was unknown to Sam, a pretty thing it had to be said; so pretty surely she could not be *that* creature's daughter? The two old women closed in on one another and exchanged electrically-charged insincerities.

'Ah, dear Miss Wilson, if only I had known you were here, I should have invited you both to tea!'

'Thank you so much dear Mrs. Payne. Perhaps another time?'

The sinking sun turned the two old ladies into stark silhouettes: Sam let his eyes rest for a moment on the girl Nora, who stood apart from them, her head lowered demurely but with a delighted childlike smile on her face as loud agreement was reached and compliments offered on her striking good looks. She was dressed, mercifully, more brightly than her mother, and her rather gay bonnet, decorated with a small sprig of flowers, complemented her abundant brown hair, which although it had been pinned and trained to stay in place, was bursting free in small flowing streams down her neck, over her eyes and across her cheeks. Nora angled her chin a little, aware that she was being admired and like an obliging work of art she was allowing her public a better perspective on her crafted beauty. A moment later she raised her eyes in Sam's direction and her smile became markedly more mature, less shy, but before its boldness could come into full bloom the expression closed off as her mother spoke her name.

Aunt Laura and Mrs. Payne were black, featureless

two-dimensional figures that cast the shadows of giants, but the girl Nora was bathed in light. Sam realised, his attention moving reluctantly from the lily perfection of her face, that although her dress was blessedly brighter than her mother's it was a fussy and fulsome thing that would only have been in fashion years before the current war; he suspected old Mrs. Payne of trying to stifle her beautiful daughter and tie her to a dead but unburied history. Aunt Laura would doubtlessly take it as a hint that the Paynes were not just peasants but paupers. The momentary speculation fled Sam's mind as he became dazzled by the growing contrasts of light and shadow as the sun dipped lower still; the old women were plunged into a twilight that threatened night, half-dead, but the girl was the promise of the dawn and life just becoming.

Nora's gaze now stayed cast primly on the ground while Sam's danced around her, darting a direct glance at that sweet face whenever he dared. Moments later he found himself locked into her eyes—she too was chancing surreptitious looks, but she was perhaps better at concealing her efforts—and she smiled again, radiating yet more light, bright and sensuous, yes, she *wants* to be looked at, *wants* me to admire that beauty of hers, for all her simpering whenever they mention her name she cares nothing for the facile compliments of those two hateful old hags, what matters to her is that she has claimed my attention.

The girl was somehow blending with the light, she became at once translucent and reflective; the sun's rays fell upon and around her like a corona, so different to the old women who continued to fend one another off in a hell of deep shadow. Now the caressing, intimate sunbeams seemed to emphasise Nora's body, in a moment the beauteous light would penetrate those garments as if they were no longer there, showing the truth of the girl as clearly as if she had stepped free from her ghastly outfit. With a rising inner confusion, Sam forced himself to tear away his eyes, and when he dared to look at her again her aspect was again demure, her gaze evasive, and the dance began afresh. Sam's face flushed with heat and he ceased swapping his hat from hand to hand, lowering it as gently and discreetly as he could, held firm, to cover his crotch.

'Come along Samuel, we *must* catch our train now.' Aunt Laura took his arm stiffly after good-evenings had been exchanged, and Sam allowed himself to be guided away, finding that there were lights still dancing in his head as if he had been staring directly at the sun.

1918

When they first kissed, a passionate and un-witnessed kiss rather than a formal brush of pursed lips on the cheek, Sam was astonished, excited, appalled. Nora moved to him with such speed, such athleticism, she turned her body so swiftly, twisted and tilted her neck in an impossible direction as if it was part of some circus trick, and then her lips smack-sucked onto his with a hot, adhesive impact. Her mouth, warm and moist, stole his breath as if she were a succubus from the damnable depths sent to leech his vitality. Then her tongue flickered to his mouth; in, out, shallow then deep, she sank her slight weight against him and slid that exploring tongue about, then before he could react, protest or seize hold of her and crush her to him, their mouths parted and she was patting her hair down, looking around nervously to ensure they had remained unseen.

'I love you Sammy.' Her eyes caught the light, that light again, as if she was the source of all radiance. 'I love you and I want to kiss you all the time, all day, all night. I want you to kiss me.'

His lips were still wet and his mouth still full of the taste of her. Sam Wilson's mind was splintered by a competition of imperatives, all arriving simultaneously and fighting for dominance. The desire to cry out. The desire to wipe his mouth, to let the taste and smell of her linger on his startled face. To harrumph and recover his dignity by pretending nothing had happened. To remonstrate with her. To demand more, seize hold of her and take what he wanted. To denounce her for tempting him to an act that was wrong, immoral, insanitary. Oh God what would that boiling mouth feel like pressed against the rest of his body? Oh Lord, were we seen? She was good at that, frighteningly so: has she done such a thing with another man?

Nora pushed her face close to him and hissed lustfully, angrily, 'I love you Sammy. And when we're married we'll kiss all the time.'

He straightened his tie.

1936

Before he vanished into his room, Sam had given Nora the strictest instructions; 'I do not wish to hear children's voices. Not one peep.' Children were to be seen and not heard in the course of any ordinary day, but at a time such as this Nora knew Sam's injunction was as holy writ.

Sam slumped into his favourite chair, where on any other day he might enjoy the warmth of the fire, read the newspaper or listen to the radio. Every member of the family, Nora included, was forbidden to enter that room when Sam claimed it. The interior was sparsely furnished and the firelight made shadows slide up and down the plain walls like playful ghosts. The yellow light of the flames reflected from the glass-fronted cabinets Nora had filled with family portraits and fussy ornaments. Sam was normally indifferent to these cabinets, but tonight he could scarcely keep them out of his unquiet mind; they seemed to him like museum cases filled with pickled specimens and undead stirrings. He left the radio dial untouched and the newspaper lay by the hearth ready for Nora to roll it into fire-starting balls the next morning. He felt no need for other people's bad tidings. He listened for footsteps, voices, but the house and avenue outside were silent. He was gripped by an irrational and near-overwhelming desire to remain forever within that room in eternal peace, to seal himself within. An unwelcome tear steered a hot-cold, unimpeded course down his face and for a moment after it had rolled away it seemed to have taken the whole of his eyesight with it, for he could see only a spectral haze and shadow forms.

To lose a child: 'lose', a strange word, it implied that her imprudent parents had turned their attention from the poor mite, to find her gone when they deigned to call her back to mind. But no, they had watched her every moment and failed to preserve her life. They had watched as enforced onlookers as she complained of feeling queer, then as the rash came, that which did not fade, and then the fever, the one that did not break. They had watched her worsen, watched her die. Had it taken moments or did she linger for days? He couldn't remember, time and recall were crushed and mangled. And what was most grotesque, most painful, was that they had been made to witness the same thing just three years before as little Jocelyn took sick and died just as Vanessa now had. Death had touched the family twice, and in such a short time, and with the same poisoned fingers. Dr. Dyedd had been with them: he lived only two streets away and had rushed to be there, but even as he spoke of help, of hospitals, hope drained from his voice and the girl faded too.

'I'm sorry. There's no cure,' Dyedd whispered, but Sam and Nora knew the truth already. There had been no relief for little Jocelyn either. It had only taken the slightest brush from the wings of the angel of death to carry their girls away.

Sam was relieved that Nora had at last fallen silent; taking charge of the children, bewildered as they were, had concentrated her mind and put an end to her irritating, noisy grieving. What was the point of all that bawling, the hysterical imprecations to God, when He had already acted, decisively and irrevocably? Now was the time for quiet and purposeful reflection on the meaning of the children's deaths, of their place in the Almighty's plan. But Sam found himself floundering: his gentle Jesus was in abeyance, and instead two competing, primitive theologies battled within his mind. Nora, her muddled head a breeding-ground for every superstition that ever sought a haven, had convinced herself the family was the prey of a rebellious and vindictive dark angel that sought to torment her by making off with her loved ones before it finally came to claim her. A loving God and divine providence were gone from her scheme, and she could not be dissuaded from this heresy.

In bitter combat with this hopeless, godless conception was the ferocious, arctic piety with which he had been brought up; had Aunt Laura been present, even at this time of mourning, she would have preached her cold catechism—the destruction of these infants was no less than a blow against the sins of their parents. Sam's face burned and stomach boiled and heaved as the cruel thought sank into his body, enervating and stinging. It was Nora's punishment, no, *theirs,* that these young lives had been snatched, payment for her—no, *their*—savage, degenerate enjoyment of the getting of them.

'Oh God let there be another way, let there be another reason.' Sam Wilson was no longer reading from any book of fire. His own faith was in turmoil and he could not accept the alternatives that lay before him. There had to be another way, and he needed to be reassured and guided anew.

1940

Sam sought the truth in solitude within the church. He recalled the pain of the loss of his two girls, but this suffering was revisited one thousandfold now that their brother too was gone. He had been uplifted by eternal hands to join his sisters in Heaven, so Nora had told the rest of the children—O Lord let it be so! But why take him my God, why?—within a short time the children's need for constant story-book repetition of this consolation and Nora's damnable habit of gilding and embroidering the story on each retelling had finally raised an unquenchable fury within Sam's monkish core and he had fled the house for his only possible place of refuge. The stricken man shared no words with the vicar; there would be little comfort and certainly no answers forthcoming from that holy fool. Sam seated himself in a pew three rows back, his head bowed as if he were taking part in a communion of the lost. He prayed, tried to meditate upon the past and his sins, and yet nothing entered his soul that was balm for the twisted, barbed distress that writhed therein and would not rest for a moment. The empty pews echoed with a breathless, choking, gasping that Sam realised was his own; he was unable to contain his sobs any longer. Somewhere deep within he was amazed to hear how angry, how enraged those sobs were, the sounds of a many-layered and complicated mourning.

Sam only became aware of someone sitting next to him when he smelt her; at first the odour mingled with the lingering musk of incense in the church air, but then he realised that there was a fresher smell, something clean and floral, scarcely detectable unless the woman was sitting close by. He was scarcely acquainted with her, he knew her name, knew she lived in Lion Street and was widowed, that she was in steadfast attendance at the church but that was practically all. And yet at this moment it seemed correct and appropriate, even God-sent, that she was there by his side and that he should speak to her without preamble or formality, confident she would know all that troubled his mind.

'I have searched and searched, there has to be a reason, but…' His voice, normally so muscular and resonant in this place, leached impotently into the indifferent stone walls.

'God is good,' was all she said, and her voice, thin and high, was attenuated still further in the cold, open space, and yet Sam found it comforting, a whisper from the beyond.

'God is good,' he concurred in a hot exhalation, tears pricking at his eyes.

'He did it to save them, perhaps to spare them from what is to come.' That voice pierced the veil again. Yes, to save them from the bullets and the bombs, from the coming invasion, from mistreatment and brute violence at the hands of barbarians, was that not utterly believable?

'God is good.'

'They are with the angels now, all of them. They *are* angels now.' Mrs. Ellis laid her hand on Sam's cuff in a chaste gesture of comfort, her body angled away from him as if she were afraid of more intimate contact here in the sight of the Almighty.

'They *are* angels now,' Sam repeated in a prayerful response. Coming from this woman the words expressed a simple and perfect truth. His companion stroked his forearm as if it was a living creature in its own right. Sam's eyes welled with tears at her sweet thought; his boy, his little girls, they were gloriously transformed in eternity and they could be hurt no more. He held fast to the idea, closing his eyes tight and letting the water run down his cheeks in a warm stream he feared would never end. He stifled an urge to seize his handkerchief and mop his face, or better to cover it entirely and shroud himself until his emotions had run their course: anyway, the woman's hand remained on his arm and he could not simply shake her off, that would have been both ungrateful and ungentlemanly. For the moment he let his tears flow; it was better to be unmanly than impolite. The air of the church was filled with the blended scent of those lingering streams of incense and the close odour of honest, godly womanhood and Sam breathed deeply of this blessed air, his chest slowly steadying and the sensation behind his eyes abating as a tremulous calm took possession of his soul: God is good.

Mrs. Ellis had not moved from Sam's side during his timeless meditation and her hand still rested lightly on his sleeve; Sam turned his head to look at her and she smiled shyly, her fingers slithering slowly from his cuff as if reluctant to leave their station. Mirabelle Ellis was, at a guess, forty-seven years old; she had been widowed before the war and now she lived alone in the small terraced house she and her husband had kept since their marriage. Her hair was black but spun with nascent white threads and her face was thin, her nose a little sharp and hawkish, her cheekbones pronounced and her upper teeth jutted out a little way. The skeletal aspect of the woman was heightened by the strange light within the church, which seemed to penetrate her skin and reveal how horrifyingly close the bones of her skull were to the surface; Sam could see the orbits of her eyes and he wondered at the miracle of creation that had filled those enormous holes with living tissue, he could trace her jaw-line as if it were fleshless and it all made her a living *memento mori*, as if such a thing were needed at this time. Mirabelle Ellis was tall and thin and she spoke with an adenoidal twang Sam, for a moment, compared unfavourably with the warm, sensuous tones of the woman he had married, that musical voice, always singing away to the children. Now his thoughts turned to the full and firm body of the girl who had emitted light, who had an affinity with radiance and was not stripped by it, an eternal mother who smelt perpetually of infants, even now the youngest were growing up Nora still emitted a sweet powder fragrance underscored with an earthiness that attracted little ones to her. Sam also felt that smell was meant for him, a forewarning that yet another little one was perhaps now growing in her belly.

Mirabelle Ellis radiated no such aroma. Nora masked her natural scent with heavy-handed libations of cheap perfume, seeming to believe that to retain her Sam's amour she had to saturate her skin with these reeking love-philtres. Mirabelle Ellis was of a more modest, less brazenly overstated womanhood, and nowhere amongst the subtle odours Sam inhaled as he sat beside her was there the cloying smell of child-at-breast or child-to-come. The Ellises had been childless, but Sam did not know whether such a state was their own choice or by God's decree.

Notwithstanding that they barely knew one another, had barely spoken and never spent a second alone together, Sam felt drawn to this widow-woman. 'God is good,' she had said, that and not much more, and then she had allowed silence to carry her words aloft. She spoke with precision, economy and, Sam felt, an understanding of his grief and his need to ease the unbearable pain. The few words he had had from her made Sam feel that here was a woman of intellect, levelling common sense and above all religiosity: she thought first and foremost not of man's affairs but of God, she knew Him and trusted in Him and she could see that divine plans, though unknowable to human minds, supervened their petty lives. She had seen death and knew that it was God's to deal out as He was minded, and we could never know the fullness of that mind. Her quiet acceptance had helped to calm Sam, and he plucked his handkerchief from his pocket and ran it slowly over his face. God is good. His children were in good hands, better by far than those of any earthly parent. Samuel Wilson smiled at Mirabelle Ellis, a mourner's broken smile, but one that showed he had found a long sought peace and comfort with her help. She may, momentarily, have appeared skeletal, but she was the ministering angel of an epiphany; not the dark angel, but its life-giving antithesis.

'Thank you,' he whispered as she returned his smile, her thin face filled with a delicate spiritual generosity. She bowed her head in prayer and Sam gazed for a long moment at the nape of her neck before realising that he should emulate her. He hung his head and gave thanks to his redeemer, and when he opened his eyes once more he realised that he wanted Mirabelle Ellis's hand to return to him, he desired to be blessed by her touch.

1976

'Holy Knickers, that's what I used to call her! That old crow, scavenging other folks's husbands when she wasn't haunting that damn church! She hung around that place like a bad smell, it was unnatural the amount of time she spent there. "Doing the flowers," she told people, "Helping out". And praying, praying—praying indeed! She spent so long dallying there her husband died from neglect, that's the real reason he took his gun and... And there's no point in your praying, lady, you'll never be clean of sin, you done what you done to me so how can praying help? What were y'doing, apologising to God and then going off to pleasure Sammy Wilson just a little more? I bet they met in that church, had their pleasures in there—no, I'm saying it as I think it's true. If a man and a woman don't care to hold to their church's teaching, what would they care for violating its walls? Sammy Wilson had access to that ole tomb and that's where he took her says I, but he could hide his guilt so ill he may as well ave taken her on the altar in full view of the Sunday congregation!'

'Mother, that's enough!'

'Unholy sinner. There's no mercy in heaven for him.'

The Beauty of Chell Street

1965

'Mum? Mum? What are you doing down there? You looking for something?'

'Can't get up.' Nora's voice was reedy, too feeble to be heard. The kitchen floor was a chessboard of lino, only a fraction warmer than the quarry tiles below. Face down on that floor, Nora could feel the cold, but not in her legs, hips, trunk and hands where they touched the floor, not anywhere but in her right cheekbone as it rested on the greasy surface. There, an intense icy spot was drawing the heat, the lifeforce of her body, out through her face. She had wondered if her blood's warmth would seep irrevocably and leave only a trace of what was once Nora Wilson as her stiff corpse lay awaiting discovery.

'Mum!'—this cry came in a stop-this-nonsense tone Nora had noticed her daughters were adopting increasingly; they were addressing her in the same manner they did their children. But within the authoritative bark of that monosyllable there had also been an undercurrent, an eddy of worry rising to fear, in her visitor's tone.

'Mum, for goodness' sake...'

'Can't get up. Fell down. Can't get up.' Face frozen, it was incredibly difficult to speak.

'Mum, how did you *get* there?'

Flora was squatting over her mother, mauling at her shoulders as if considering yanking her free, but the hands lifted off after a moment, a reconsideration of the would-be rescuer's tactics was clearly necessary.

'Fell down.' Nora managed to repeat.

Flora hovered, perplexed and frightened. Nora was lying almost flat-out, her body thrust beneath the kitchen table and, into the bargain, she was stuck head and shoulders between the legs of one of the chairs, her arms entangled, as if she was a child who had come to grief in the course of a dangerous game. She seemed quite tightly jammed in.

'You *can't* fall down and land like this.' Flora grumbled and clucked, still working out how best to extract soft limbs from stiff wood, 'What were you doing crawling under there? Were you cleaning or chasing a mouse or something?'

'Can't remember. I fell.'

'What on earth were you up to?' Her daughter sounded pettish now, frustrated she could not solve the puzzle. 'Should I call the doctor?'

'Doctors, they know nothing.'

'Are you hurt?'

'I'm cold.'

'How long have you been there?'

'Don't know—the clock, I can hear it but I can't see it. I can always hear it, it goes so fast...'

Flora shook her head.

After a little more consideration and gentle pulling and lifting, Flora extricated Nora from the tangle, eased her to her feet and then escorted her safely back to her chair. Wrapped in a blanket, Nora slipped into a peaceful doze, but a worry insinuated its way into her daughter's mind, worming and insisting: was falling asleep supposed to be a good thing, wasn't it a bad sign when someone had hurt their head?

'Mum?'

No reply.

'Mum? *Mum!* If you don't talk to me I'm going to call the doctor out!'

No reply.

Doctor Speakman was a tiny china doll of a man, painted and glazed by a perfectionist with an eye for detail and a predilection for glossy, rounded shapes. He was as precise and cool in his manner and speech as in his flawless dress, and exhaled an astringent antiseptic. His slight burr, the way he would for instance render the word 'iron' as 'eye-ron', and the cold starshine flash from his neat, round glasses added to his air of great, slightly impatient, disinterested learning and lofty, impersonal disdain. He began to pack away his stethoscope and as he did so he sighed heavily, his waste-of-time sigh, a thing Flora and her sisters had come to know well.

'I can find absolutely nothing wrong with her.'

'I'm sorry doctor…' Flora was interrupted by another, sharper sigh.

'Mrs. Latimer, I think you'll agree we have been here before. In recent months I've seen your mother for chest pains, heart palpitations, breathing problems, and now this. There is never anything wrong with her. You may imagine it is taxing my patience somewhat.'

All Flora could think to do was to say 'I'm sorry' again,

and the sleek little man did not look appeased.

'I have to tell you Mrs. Latimer, I am giving serious consideration to striking your mother off my panel, and frankly I cannot see another doctor in the area being willing to take her on. There have been too many of these, ahhhh, *phantom* illnesses. It has to stop.'

'I'm sorry I called you out, but I was worried.'

'It's not your fault.' The words, although offered in reassurance, sounded brittle, like something snapping, and his eyes left Flora and his glasses caught the light again as his gaze came to rest on her mother, settled in her chair and sleeping lightly again. Dr. Speakman left, taking a chillier draught than the one soughing through the door as Flora held it open for him.

Flora returned to the back kitchen and turned the gas up a little, then resettled the blanket over Nora gently, silently patting it down over her shoulders and neck to leave no gaps for the cold air to penetrate. Quietness continued to hold sway for a few more moments, there was only the warm hiss of the gas fire and the over-excited metallic clicking of the little clock on Nora's table.

'That man,' said a quiet but angry voice. 'That man is the most hated man in all the towns and villages around here.' Her small head sticking out of the swaddling folds, Nora's eyes were wide and alive with the fury of the humiliated, but this flare drew all the strength out of her increasingly frail face, making her age visibly.

'Mum? How on earth would you know that?'

'I know it cos a woman on the bus told me.'

'When have you been on a bus lately? These days you'll

barely leave the house.'

'I just *know* that he is,' grumbled Nora, looking away and closing her eyes once more.

A few days later, Nora was seated in her favourite chair with a serious-faced Kara opposite her, listening closely as Nora told of her 'collapse'.

'And Nonna couldn't get up, and the silly old doctor didn't know what was wrong and they had to send for the ambulance to take Nonna to the hosspickle!'

The sound of the child's shocked intake of breath was followed by the disapproving click of a tongue as Flora stepped into the room, a wet cloth in her hand. 'Mum, that's not true and you know it isn't! You mustn't romance like that to the little ones, they'll never know what to believe!'

Kara looked wide-eyed first to her mother and then to Nonna, than she closed her arms around Nonna's neck and hugged her hard, to show how glad she was that her ordeal was all over now, whatever had happened.

Flora stepped back into the scullery, straight to the firing-line of a puzzled scowl from her oldest sister.

'What's she doing?' Helen barely bothered to keep her voice down as she and Flora stood close to the boiling kettle, she no longer cared if Nora could hear her complaints. 'What's she doing? Not so long ago she'd be racing that child round the garden, tossing her in the air and rolling round. Now she's just… stopped. She's plopped in that chair, drawn a blanket over her knees and declared herself a damn cripple. Why, Flo, why?' Helen didn't await an answer, and carried on talking as her sister scalded the pot, 'It's as if she's done it all deliberately like a child flopping down in a fit of pique, she's going limp and just... rotting!'

Flora nodded in agreement; Nora's response to old age was, apparently, fervently to embrace the process and to do all in her power to speed it up. She complained endlessly of the heavy, leaden feeling in her arms, the pains that stabbed up her back and through her guts, the invisible chains that shackled her ankles and passed a paralysing, metallic chill through her legs. And she welcomed these things, dragged the limits of her world close in around her in order to accommodate them. Not long ago she had been able to shoot up and down the hill to do her own shopping, she had scorned help in maintaining the house, she outran her grandsons in every and any game you liked: now her circumscribed world was two rooms in that big house, her elderly armchair, the small table with her pills, her tea, a glass of water and the little carriage clock that ticked away so wildly as if trying vainly to inject some excitement into this dulled, sedate world, defying its atmosphere of exhausted sickroom surrender.

'Nonna come and play now!' rang out Kara's voice.

'Oh I can't sweetheart, you know Nonna's too pooly-bad. It's time to go; I'm cashing in me cheques.'

'Mum, stop it!' shouted Flora, crossly.

'What is she *doing*?' Helen fretted, shaking her head and worrying at a fingernail. Flora didn't even try to reply; she spooned the fine brown tea into the pot and listened to the smooth hiss of the water as it swamped the leaves.

The Book Of Fire

1940

'Sammy Wilson is nowt but a whited sepulchre.'

'A what?'

'Cum on now Jack, do ye not remember yer Sundee Skew?'

'Sunday *School* George, please do not abuse the language with your slang and poor enunciation: my, how our Mr. Wilson would scold you!'

'From the Book of Matthew it is, yer must know it, *Ye are like unto whited sepulchres,* Jesus said it... y'do know oo e was now don't yer Jack?'

'Bloody hell George, are you makin a bid to challenge Sammy Wilson for the post of bar-room holy man?'

'Gerroff—when did I last set foot in church?'

'But you seem to know your texts.'

'Well if you don't recall your Sunday School,' George paused briefly to let Jack admire his rounded and correct pronunciation, 'then I sure as eck do. Drummed into me it were, and with a bloody big stick too. That's why it jams in my craw, Sammy and is holy-joe nonsense, specially when I know what I know now.'

'What's that then George?'

'I hear tell—and from someone with every reason to know the facts—that our sainted friend is sinning away with a woman who inna his wife.'

'Really now? Hey, you're not usually one for gossip;

George, you always tell Netta to shurrup whenever she's spreading tittle-tattle!'

'Aye well, but this is different, on account of it's about Sammy.'

'Well come on man, don't keep me waiting now you've started!'

'Dost know of Mirabelle Ellis?'

'That name rings a...'

'A *church* bell Jack. She is one of yer faithful but not very bloody joyful, mate, a long thin streak and, not to beat about th bush, a snobby old cow. The War Office uses her stony bloody stare to bring down German bombers, an her nose to puncture zeppelins. Lives a stone's throw from Sammy she does, up Lion Street. Y'know, the one who's husband went...' George mimed a gun at his temple.

'Well I reckon that colourful little portrait places her right enough,' Jack interposed mildly, but his drinking mucker's excitement was growing and he was eager to tell the rest of the news.

'She an Sammy, they bin seen around and about, supposedly on parish business, but they parade like they're the bally King an Queen, and word is that's not all they've bin doin neither.'

'What about Wilson's wife?'

'She knows, so folks reckon, and she's sneaped beyond all sayin, but what can she do with all them bairns on her hands, and all of em relying on Sammy for their daily bread?'

'And what about the church?'

George shrugged. 'Would't be the first time there'd bin funny business amongst the cong'gation, and it wouldn't be the first time that vicar's turned a blind eye, specially when the sinners in question arf-ways keep his wretched church goin.'

Jack grunted in cynical agreement. 'An it wouldn't be the first time there'd been things going on even at the Manse itself—it must be something in the holy water.'

George however was still shaking his hoary head in vexed, overheated fascination over the behaviour of the Trappers' straying prey.

'Y'know mate, I can rub along quite nicely with all manner of men, I'll even grant some of em occupy higher places in this world than meself, but I conner bear an ypocrite. I can smell out an ypocrite a mile off, owever far that may be in cubits, and Sammy Wilson is the patron saint o the bally lot.'

Silence fell for a time, but thoughts remained ecclesiastical when Jack spoke again. 'Never thought of being in the church yourself then old son, seeing as you seem to know the words well enough?'

'I were born and bred for underground, that's my fate, Jack. There's no windows in the pit, never mind stained glass uns.' George pulled at his beer as if refreshing himself after a long shift. 'As fer yer texts, yes, you name it, I reckon I can trot it out, like I say, I were taught by rote, and the rod. Aye, I can rattle it away but it don't mean much to me: it were just easier to learn it than to take another beatin.'

'So are you a believer at all, our George?'

'Oh I believe well enough, just not in the God that *they* taught about, the cold-hearted ole cusses. I believe in a loving father above who sent his only son to save us. And likewise I dunna believe in His Holiness's God neither, the one what says, "Thou shalt not commit adultery unless thy name appens to be Sammy Wilson". Chuff that.'

George adopted a faraway thoughtful look that could also have been a precursor of glassy drunkenness, and then smiled, a half-insane crumpling of his face and a flash of his dirty old teeth. 'Ave you ever thought o goin to see Sammy?'

'Where?' Jack was baffled.

'On Sundees like—preachin, spreadin the good Word!'

'No more than I'd trouble to see a performing monkey, George. I'll stick with a man who knows his texts and has never breached them.'

'Not for want o tryin!' George bared those teeth again and the two men laughed, but George then slipped back into a brown study.

'Pride comes before a fall—that's what Sammy needs to bear in mind.'

'Where's that actually from, old mate?'

'Book o' Proverbs, *Pride goeth before destruction. And an haughty spirit before a fall.* Sometimes I think that book were written wi Sammy in mind. Just not in the way he thinks.'

1910

'This is a book of fire, boy!' Aunt Laura brandished the heavy, dark Bible as if she intended to strike her nephew with it and dash his brains. 'If there is an ounce of evil in you this book will find it out: touch it boy! If there be sin in your heart then your flesh will sear and blacken—touch it now! Let me see your hand!'

The white-faced evangelist seemed dissatisfied at Sam's

pink-white fingers and soft palm, and would clearly have been more pleased to witness blackened skin hanging from charred bones. Sam was sickened and terrified, his heart hammered, one day the burning would happen to him, it could only be the grace of God that had saved him, he was being given another chance, but oh one day soon he knew he would burn, knew what wickedness lurked within his soul, he was bitterly aware of it every day.

'You were one who needed special attention; I could see right away.' Aunt Laura was fond of this lecture, the text familiar to Sam as any gospel verse: 'On the day of your baptism you were calm, seraphic, I was thinking, but the moment the pure waters of Our Lord touched your head you screamed as if you were burning alive, screamed and kept on screaming till we despaired of your ever ceasing. It found you out did that holy water, revealed the evil within you; but though I knew fine well it was there, that wickedness, I was sure that I could drive it out and save you. But oh, you were a job of work, and so you remain!'

One day soon, thought Sam as he examined his pristine palm, one day Aunt Laura will be triumphant and I shall burn.

Left alone with that Bible, Sam Wilson sought inspiration and comfort, not a book that would scald and scorch. He sought in those pages a God of loving forgiveness, not one of jealousy, vengefulness and condign punishment. The Samuel of the temple heard God call out to him in the night: Sam Wilson heard no such direct call, and yet he was sure of the presence of the God that he sought, sure and certain.

'Consider the fates of the cities of the plain! Consider

the fate of Onan—young boys should especially think on *that*—consider what happened to any man or woman who disobeyed the word of the Lord!'

Aunt Laura preached with the relish of a destroying angel. Sam struggled within his head to work out how a man could be upheld as good and free of sin when he offered his daughter up to the mob, albeit to preserve the sanctity of visiting ambassadors of Heaven: was that man simply obedient because he was afraid, and not actually *good* in his actions? Sam could not abide thinking of the way in which other, essentially good, men were struck down by the Lord for offences that seemed trivial and profoundly obscure. It didn't seem to make sense, and yet there was no one available to him who could reconcile the bothersome problems. He certainly could not ask his Aunt; nor question the local vicar, nor any teacher, not one of them would tolerate any cavilling about the best of books. He had no one to help navigate the book of fire to find its peaceful inner reaches, and so his confusion remained, wrapped in guilty, secret silence. So: if the good and holy men faced such bitter trials and pains in pursuit of their faith, if some of them were destroyed in the process, what chance of redemption did Samuel Wilson stand, a small boy who already bore a terrible burden of inborn sin? Sam Wilson's merciful God understood human failings; He was slow to chide and swift to bless. As he grew older, Sam examined his Bible again and again looking for that God; his escape route from the damnation he had been promised from the cradle.

1941

An unlovely tome it was, heavy in the hand and oppressive to the eye, emitting a musty stink as if it were a long-dead creature, rotting slowly in its shadow-populated alcove. Why did Sam hide it as if it was something to be ashamed of, or some strong poison, to be kept out of the wrong hands? But ah, this thing was not salted away for any such reason, no, Sam Wilson had hidden away his holy book because, as was his habit and custom, he did not want to share it with anyone, not even the family of his bosom. Oh, the family had its own Bible, the one that the children were encouraged—nay, commanded—to touch, read and learn, but of this grand, glowering volume, Sam demanded exclusive possession. It was his nature.

The hard cover was more for the fingers than the eyes; it was black, hopelessly and almost satanically black, and apart from its title picked out in spindly gilded letters that were fading rapidly, there was almost nothing else to see on its surface. Nora ran her fingers over the cover, feeling its indented swirls and ridges, but as far as she could tell they formed no pictures, spelt out no words. She wondered if in some past time the book had been decorated, the fingers-only design swathed in bright colours to entice the senses and encourage the eager believer to immerse herself in this book of rainbow light. Pah, knowing its owner that was but a faint hope! No, no, this book had always been black: un-pretty black layered on black, sombre to the point of morbidity. It eschewed colour and celebrated darkness, and with the secret eyeless language of the esoteric patterns on its surface it seemed more a book of wicked spells than the source of all that is good and hallowed. Was there perhaps some incantation within that the old witch up the road had used to take away his wits?

Nora had not come to this book for guidance, nor was she seeking comfort: she had come to the book, *this* copy, no other would do, for evidence. She had come to find the passages that would prove her husband the fraud and charlatan she knew him to be; she had come to find his shame and to cast it in words he could not so easily dismiss with his clever, sharp tongue. She aspired further to discover phrases to break the enchantment and summon him back, to help him find his redemption in her, for Nora had always believed sin could be redeemed. She set aside her revulsion for the book and set to work flicking pages, hunting.

Shall we begin with a reading from Ephesians V, verses 25 and 28—*Husbands, love your wives, even as Christ also loved the church, and gave himself up for it; … Even so ought husbands also to love their own wives as their own bodies. He that loveth his own wife loveth himself.*

I was ready to do that for you; for Jesus and the church, but chiefly for you, Sam Wilson.

Perhaps we can turn to Hebrews XIII, verse 4—*Let marriage be had in honor among all, and let the bed be undefiled: for fornicators and adulterers God will judge.*

So; the words are here. I shall ransack your precious book for the words that will condemn you, I'll look out the incantation that will reawaken your conscience and call you back to me. I have proof positive that you defy the very book you claim to venerate, the very words you declaim so proudly come the Sabbath day. You think me such a fool that this task is beyond me, but I have read your hidden book and in it I see your damnation. Got you, Sam Wilson, trapped you, chapter and verse.

Over months of secret, episodic reading Nora had progressed from picking surreptitiously and hopefully at phrases and snatches of gospel, seeking chance encounters with verses that would vindicate her thoughts, to a committed and systematic scouring of its content in her quest for what she wanted. In her eagerness for an ally, she also acknowledged some fear: this was a book of violence, destruction and terror, mass killing sanctified by an unrecognisable God of blood. If this was so, could there not also be some passage or other that would defeat her purpose by justifying Sam Wilson and his misdeeds, some hostile formation of phrases that would absolve him of blame? But ah no—time and again she found quite the opposite.

Now to Leviticus XV—could you claim that you cast me aside because you found some uncleanliness in me? What might that be? There is none, Sammy Wilson, I am clean, cleaner than that she-devil anyway, and should not be put away as if I had wronged *you*. And your sins have not rebounded on you, Sam Wilson, not yet, but here it says plain that if you disobey and abhor the judgements of the Lord then you shall be sent plagues and punishments, *And I will send the beast of the field among you, which shall rob you of your children, and destroy your cattle, … and your ways shall become desolate.* Sam Wilson has paid no price, but now I see why three tiny lives are already forfeit, two taken by fevers and the third by another sort of burning, all for one man's defiance of holy laws. And look further—*the tent of the wicked shall be no more.... For he knoweth false men: He seeth iniquity also.* How can you attempt to shelter from your God, Sam Wilson? How vain shall your efforts prove to hide from Him within the confines of His own house?

In the course of what she privately, jokingly called her Bible study, Nora surprised herself with her assiduous scholarliness: I don't need you, my preaching husband, to understand this book. Among the other humiliations that you heap on my head, you tell me I shall never properly comprehend these holy words, not without your help, and yet here's your book, Sammy Wilson, opening up to me and surrendering its secrets, exposing what you have concealed from me, granting me power over you at last.

Can you even bear to let your eyes rest on the Proverbs, Sam Wilson? *To keep thee from the evil woman, ... Lust not after her beauty in thy heart;* ('beauty' be blowed!)... *He that committeth adultery with a woman is void of understanding: He doeth it who would destroy his own soul..*

Is this the book from which you claim to draw your strength? Well I have uncovered your weakness in it. Read here the moral virtues and their contrary vices: look me in the eye and tell me, of the two of us, who is the virtuous one and who is steeped in vices? Gaze upon the praise and properties of a good wife and see a mirror of me, just as every condemnation of unfaithfulness should be marked with your unhappy name.

Even your Bible has deserted you: how friendless can a man be? But Sam, Sammy, husband, love, there is always hope of mercy to the penitent; can you, should you be offered this? Will you repent and make everything well again, will you return to God and to me? Or, when you are judged, with your earnest eyes and silver tongue, will you beg and crawl and get away with what you have done, will God cheat me as his church has done?

1944

I must be tired, thought Sam Wilson as he rubbed his eyes: harder, harder, before resettling his gaze upon the page. But still the feeling remained: this book is resisting me, it is shutting me out and it will not say what I want, what I *need* it to say to me. He lifted it up in his hands and it pulled like a dog on a chain, fighting against him still. The volume had been gifted on him by Aunt Laura when he was a small boy, and now it seemed to be yearning for a return to the time when he was unable to lift it properly, when its strength was greater than his. The front cover was coming away from the binding, swinging from two remaining hinges of thread like a broken gate in the wind. Sam had for what seemed an eternity been intending to repair it and he felt a nagging guilt at his failure to attend to the job. How that formidable woman who had thrust it in his feeble hands all those years ago would upbraid him for his laxity.

Such a dark book when what he sought was light. So imposing and moody a thing when his desire was peaceful inspiration. He needed his Bible and the hope therein to be fresh and eternally renewed, not time-worn and stained. When he mauled at the pages and turned to any passage he found wrath, warnings, burnings and punishments, nothing else. It was as if Aunt Laura had imposed upon this holy tome her own storm-cloud interpretations of the scriptures, banishing the light.

And yet there remained the hope of salvation. The passion that he felt for Mirabelle Ellis was pure, it was a higher love. They were joined in the adoration and, crucially, the understanding of God and all his greatness. There was no sin in their love, nothing dirty whatsoever: she sought to serve the same Lord as he, she knew the good book and to her it was no book of fire, no catalogue of impossible-to-avoid traps, but a lamp that cast a gentle and yet penetrating illumination over a stark and unforgiving world, it broke through the surrounding darkness and made sense of life, a balm for those wounded by the painful, unpredictable process that was mortal existence. Oh why had he not married such a woman in the first place? Why had not fortune brought him such a woman—*this* woman—all those years ago and spared him from the lure of the false light and a union based upon nothing but carnal lust? But Sam knew that he must be humble, grateful that it had been decreed that she should come to him now. He should not question the Lord's plan. 'God is good,' Mirabelle had said to him at the very time he had sorely needed to hear those words, he had to cling to that simple wisdom, God is good and there is a purpose and a meaning to everything he sends us, whether those things be pleasurable or painful. Armed now with a higher love, Sam Wilson felt himself capable of anything.

His love for Mirabelle Ellis was not a temptation, no poisoned offering from below to make him stray from his duties as a husband and father, no, her coming to him was a reward for his steadfast faith and an intimation of the happiness to come; your God wants you to have this joy, the message was plain, stronger and louder than anything he had ever felt from the bosom of the Almighty. Aunt Laura's fanatic curses were defeated at last.

1941

I shall mine this book for your ruin, Sammy Wilson. The Old Testament condemns you from the ancient deserts, crags and mountains; may you find respite in the New? No sir, you may not.

Every one that looketh on a woman to lust after her hath committed adultery with her already in his heart.. From this cause shall a man leave his father and mother, and shall cleave to his wife; and the two shall become one flesh: so that they are no more two, but one flesh. What therefore God hath joined together, let not man put asunder..

In the Book of John, Jesus delivers the woman taken in adultery. His words make me smile, thinking of the two of you. 'Go, ... sin no more.' Could I ever say such a thing to Mirabelle Ellis? I look forward to the day.

There, both of you—squashed flat by your own gloomy book.

Wedding Bands

1954

I kept my wedding ring here on my finger where it belongs. What did you do with yours Sam Wilson? Have you hidden it, sold it, pawned it; tossed it into the gutter, perhaps? What then did you do with the mark on your finger, the indentation left by over twenty years of gold against flesh? Did you wrap a bandage around it and claim you'd had an accident, hoping to keep that band of tight, compressed skin out of sight long enough for it to recover, puff out and remove the wound inflicted by marriage? The wedding ring leaves a weal, a scar. It is a holy mark.

I've not forgotten you, not a moment or a word of you, not one touch, in all these years. Nor have I forgotten what we were to one another, all those vows, you with your face so serious and me so nervous I was giggly as if drunk. I said the words breathlessly, gravely, no giggling then, oh I meant them. And I'm still here. Faithful till death.

Have you forgotten that little Commandment, Sam Wilson?

2012

At Eileen Wilson's flat, three storytellers and a story-collector were in earnest conference.

'None of the Wilson women has ever had much luck with men,' Flora mused, submitting happily to further interrogation. 'I suppose it's a sort of legacy handed down by Nora and Sam. The family curse, perhaps.'

'How d'you mean?' probed Francine.

'Well let's see, closest to home first, I rushed off and married a complete and utter…'

'Mother!' warned Kara, semi-seriously.

'…scoundrel.' The old woman flashed a naughty smile, but then she became degrees more serious as unhappy recall darkened her face. 'Yes, a lying, cheating scoundrel who I threw out after three miserable years, with my little girl my only compensation. And then what did I do? Folly upon folly—I let the same man convince me with his protestations that he had seen the light and improved, remarried him and then carried on hoping against empty hope he wasn't lying yet again, right until the day I drove him out for the last time, with another little walking talking compensation to warm my heart and make me feel at least some of it had been the right thing to do.

'And Nonna was definitely a very strong factor in my decision to get married to that… I knew that Trevor Latimer was no star catch by any stretch, but he was pretty much my only prospect and it seemed better to give up my life to look after him than to do the same for a woman who had schemed for years to keep one of her girls to herself as her nursemaid and who, when she got any sort of care or attention, became patently more grasping and demanding, inventing new illnesses and crises. Nonna fought hard to keep me at home with her, God did she, but that just meant I pulled even harder to get away. I knew Trevor's unattractive qualities as well as I knew his good points—of which he had some, at least at first—I was never blind, but told myself any problems were surmountable. Vain, deluded child that I was!' She looked at Kara, whose own face had become scarred with sadness. 'At least, darling, you chose a good man.'

Kara said nothing; Flora held her hand for a few moments. All four of them knew this part of the family's history too well. Flora may have walked unblinking into the arms of a brute and a bastard, but Kara and her Brian had been so right for one another, sharing ten years of deep love and finally being rewarded with their adored baby girl. This event had even spurred them into talk of marriage, 'Going legit,' as Brian called it, but in the end gentle, funny Brian proved unable to hang on to life, his heart gave out, cheating him of his wedding day and the chance to see his daughter grow up. Francine knew that the extended Wilson clan had treated her mother badly over the whole business, first haranguing her for 'living in sin' and then behaving as if she had been at fault for selecting a lover who had proved such a weakling.

Flora picked up the thread of family disapproval. 'My sisters found it hard to pontificate too much about my broken marriage, pot-kettle and all, but they never forgave me for not changing my name back to Wilson on my divorce. But I'd ceased to be a Wilson and I had no desire to revert to that state. Shallow and petty, on the part of all of us, to have long-running rows about such things: they couldn't keep their noses out of my life, and I refused to recognise that you can't change your heritage just by changing your name. Ah—and they disapproved of me for having only the two children. Apparently they were offended because it was *the family tradition* to have at least five.' Flora rolled her eyes in mock, mocking despair.

'And so you can just imagine what they made of it when I not only refused to marry but then refused to have kids even *out* of wedlock!' Aunty Eileen laughed, but the sound was thin and sad to Francine's ear. 'Against nature, never mind bloody family tradition, that was me! Inevitably there were whispers, sometimes shouts, that there was "another Aunt Jane" disgracing the line! I loved my aunties, course I did, but I could never explain to them that I'd made my choices precisely *because* of the family's history and its damned traditions! I'd seen what had happened to Nonna, what happened to *them*, and made up my mind to stay on my own and just… escape it all.

'The family and its traditions and its respect for "proper" marriage!' Kara continued as Eileen's voice trailed away, as if drained of energy, her own voice alive with scorn and asperity, 'None of them were exactly paragons of stable, respectable marriage!'

'Ah yes,' Flora took up her cue, 'but some of them liked it so much they just kept on doing it!'

'Mo-ther!' Eileen scolded playfully.

'Oh come along, it's true. Wilson husbands, parade, shun!' The word 'parade' was drawn out.

'Mum, you're terrible!' The three older women collapsed in laughter and it cost Francine some effort to marshal them back to the telling of the past.

'There was but one of us sisters who chose her man and then stuck with him and him alone; that was Helen, the oldest, but even she, the most conventional, religious and downright *straight* of the whole bunch, even she didn't do it quite right…'

'How d'you mean, Gran?'

'She married in white but also in a bit of a rush if you see what I mean, dear. We had to fib a little concerning dates, to stop people talking.' Flora blushed, girlishly coy, as if this family secret still tickled at her breast.

'As for Minnie, well, absolutely everything in her life was over-complicated, dramatic and traumatic, she just couldn't help it somehow. She suffered her first broken heart during the war, but she recovered...'

'Well, she didn't recover quite that much, as we were to find out...' Kara interrupted, but Flora waved away that tale for now; Francine quietly resolved to pursue it—later.

'Then, towards the end of the war, she met an army driver called Tom Edge, they had a bit of an innocent fling, but when it turned serious Nonna stepped in and threatened never to speak to Minnie again if she married him. She said he was "a toper and a no-good, just like his father had bin!", and of course that was all it took to put the tin hat on it for Minnie, she was dead set on him from that moment. Stupid, stubborn wench.'

'Oh yes Mum, fancy marrying someone just because Nonna didn't want you to!' Eileen teased.

'Hush up sharp-shins. Anyway, Tom Edge went back to war and Minnie swore that if he came back she'd marry him—no matter what.'

'And he came back?' Francine ventured, imagining a tragic payoff to the tale, a man cut to pieces in body and mind, broken and bearing never-healing scars.

'Yes, he came back, and Minnie wed him, both to keep her solemn word and spite her mother.'

'And?' Francine demanded impatiently.

'And he turned out to be a toper and a no-good, just like

his father had been. It took her twenty years, six children and three beatings a week before she'd break with him: we had to pledge Nonna to silence but she just couldn't conceal her told-you-so smugness. Minnie would get spitting mad just at the sight of her face.'

'Did Minnie marry again?'

'Oh darling she was a trouper, she stuck at it. The next collector's item she dragged home ran a pub, told dirty jokes and helped himself from the till. This time Nonna liked the beast and she wouldn't hear a word against him, not anyway until he started telling his jokes to her grandchildren. But before she could vent her fury over that he was gone, made off with everything he could carry from the pub plus our Minnie's savings. He fled town with a hundred angry creditors on his tail, and Minnie had hell trying to persuade them to leave her alone once he'd done a bunk. Took her even longer to unearth Eddie Barnes and wring a divorce out of him. She swore she'd never marry again.'

'Aunty Minnie's oaths—ten a penny!' snorted Eileen.

'You'll gather, Francine, that she didn't keep her word; but at least it was third time lucky. Jeff Clayton was—no, *is*, he survived her and he's still with us—one of the best and most sensible men on this Earth, one of the most patient too and Lord knows that's what he needed to stick our Minnie. Nothing she said ever upset him, no matter how outrageous, oh and trust me, she was. In front of the whole blasted family she once blurted that the thieving piss-artist Eddie Barnes had been "the love of my life". Well, Jeff just tipped back his head and laughed, roared he did, and then offered to clear off and find the man for her, bring him back home, "I could do with someone else getting the earache for once!"'

Kara set a cup of tea in front of her mother, but Flora was enraptured in the retelling of the past and she didn't even notice it.

'Now our Phyl, Phyllida, she only managed two hubbies, and we made the most terrible fun of her, called her the Gold Digger because she married a man twenty years older than her, and when he turned up his toes she married another still older! We told each other she'd insured their hides and then killed em off, we giggled and said the rozzers would be on her tail any time now...' Flora blew out a heavy breath as if tiring of an old game. 'Thinking back, after all this time, I think the real reason she married such old men was as simple and sad as any truth can be—she wanted a father who would be kind to her, someone who would give her the love and approval our own dad found so hard to give. We all suffered from our dad's loveless, biting, sarcastic nature, but Phylly most of all, I think.

'Nothing any of us ever did was good enough, and our Phyl was quite an artist at one time—until, that was, she showed some of her work to Mr. Samuel Wilson. Nobody knows what he said, but he crushed her, utterly. I found her paints and brushes in the rubbish soon after. And he seemed to victimise Phylly, almost as much as he made a favourite of Minnie: her schoolwork, hair, handiwork, speech, table manners, God knows what, he taxed her with no end of tiny failings, and unlike the rest of us she never learned to take it in her stride. So I'm not surprised she looked for softness and indulgence elsewhere—not so sure she ever got it though. She always said that Percy, her first husband, was a gem, but to me his only resemblance to a gem was that he had any number of faces, all with a cold, hard sheen. Bernard was a better man, loving in his own way, but he was a silly old ass, a smiler who exuded warmth and charm but hadn't a penno'rth of brain. My sister was clever and deserved an equal, someone to encourage her and grow with her.'

Flora inhaled deeply now, a long refreshing breath as she emerged from the melancholy currents of events long gone. 'Our Phyl deserved better—from all of them.' She discovered her tea, warmed herself on it and her spirits' revival was manifest in a wicked wink at her daughters.

'And who's last but not least?'

'The man-eater!' cackled Eileen, while Kara mimed a beast gnashing and clawing the air. Francine was for a moment a child left stranded, bemused as she was left out of the joke, but her grandmother explained, smiling.

'I'm talking about the real surprise package of the bunch, Petra, the silent sister, the one who survived life with her parents and siblings by turning invisible, becoming a shadow. She didn't argue, didn't demand, she made Phylly look boisterous, never said boo to a goose throughout her childhood. But oh, when she grew up! *Four* husbands she got through, and she brought up ten children too, largely without male help as she was the boss, and the moment one of those poor so-and-sos stepped out of line she savaged him a treat! And when they upset her seriously, out on the street they'd be, with their shirts, shoes and smalls raining down on them from the bedroom window!'

'Aunty Petra died a long time before you were born,'

Kara told her daughter, 'but I reckon you'd have *loved* her! She wasn't afraid of Grampa Sam, I think, she was *studying* him! And she was far more terrifying—exclusively to men. She was my heroine. And almost as soon as the old man was safely out of the way she started her...'

'Collection,' offered a helpful Eileen. 'Then when she found fault with one of em she packed him off where he came from, like duff goods from a store! And she never repined, never looked back. Fierce she was. I adored her too.'

'The younger generation—your cousins, girls—seem to have done a little better with their men.' Flora's optimism set Kara shaking her head.

'I don't know, there's enough break-ups and divorces brewing up out there; there's at least one marriage that's only rattling on because neither partner has the gumption to put an end to it, and one or two murders in the making when certain wives find out what their husbands are doing in their spare time—all good old fashioned Curse of Wilson stuff.'

'Oh well; perhaps our girls will do better—choose better—in the future.' Flora remained hopeful. There was silence for a time, and Francine felt her mother's eyes upon her, judging and assessing; was she tainted with the curse? Francine found herself brushing at herself with flapping hands as if trying to unstick something malevolent from her skin.

'Leave her alone Kara!' Eileen had read the scene with perspicacity, her voice warm and song-like. 'She'll turn out fine—the best of all.' Francine hugged her aunt in gratitude.

Happy laughter changed the atmosphere, but not for Flora; the events of the past had not done with her yet.

'Nonna believed there was a curse. She called it Sam Wilson's Blood: "You all carry it!" she warned us. And whenever that curse struck, as another marriage went west, though she shared our tears and gave us comforting words, that's what she was thinking about. And there was a kind of satisfaction in her too, a childish one that said that if she couldn't have happiness then nor should we.'

1949

I told Peggy she looked beautiful, you should always tell the bride that on her wedding day. But I told her nothing else of what was in my thoughts, though I was minded to, minded strong. I sometimes think these girls would be best warned: marriage, it's a pretence see, love a sham; even the wedding is just a damn show, insincerity on parade in its best bib and tucker. Families making a sickly pretence that they can stand the sight of one another, a couple desperately hoping they're doing the right thing, each half-afraid the other won't turn up at the altar and half-afraid they will, a snowstorm of false good wishes, counterfeit shows of joy, all concealing envy, unhappiness, gloating predictions of disaster made behind the hand. Fancy dress and fol-de-rol, a day of fulsome, forced togetherness and then a lifetime of drudgery and workaday heartbreak. I think of the bride and I wonder if she knows that her fine wedding dress will soon be swapped for a stained housecoat, her veil for a dusty headscarf, her soft virgin hands chapped and calloused from hard work, her back sore from unending discomfort and her insides worn out with the never-ending factory business of the bearing of children.

And for all the efforts to create a perfect day, even the small things are wrong. Oh, I saw and heard nothing amiss at my wedding, blind and dazed I must have been, but wisdom has come to me with the years. Even when waiting for the bride we have to endure the hack-work of some sausage-fingered so-and-so at the organ as he does sheer violence to the holy music, my girls could play better than any church organist I've ever heard, do they choose these people out of pity, knowing that for all their piety they couldn't wring a decent tune out of a washboard?

I can scarcely hold my peace as the poor young things exchange fragile vows and debased metal bands: beware of his vows, he has no care for them and will break them oh so soon, no intention has he of keeping his word! Marriage simply makes it lawful for a man to do what he would have done anyway, law or no law, and it saves his whelps from being bastards but that is all. And there is nothing there, nothing at all, for the woman. My husband-to-so-soon-be stood close by me as the vicar read out his words: he spoke of marriage, Sam Wilson, how it should not be entered into lightly or selfishly, were you listening Sam Wilson? It should be reverent and responsible—were you listening, Sam Wilson? Joined together in heart, body and mind, joyful commitment to the end of their lives—*were you listening, Sam Wilson?*

And soon after this flummery will come the rain of confetti, and just like the hollow promises that have just been made it is hurled into the air carelessly, is pulled in an instant to the ground, then trampled on and left to rot.

1962

They were not joined. They did not declare the impediment. In natural law, in the law of their own wretched church, they were not joined. He is still my husband.

1942

'Tell yer somethin for nothin old son—Sammy Wilson's marriage is headed up the Swannee.' Jack showed his pint who was master, and summoned up the next contender. George nodded distractedly, as his thoughts had carried him off to a place where faint but lewd grins were all the rage.

'Quit daydreamin about *her*,' commanded mind-reader Carthmain. 'Listen to me, and none of yer sordid daydreaming! Use yer noddle, can't y'see it, y'see them out and about together as man and wife, but never does Sammy talk of his Missus when he's here, not one word. A man who was proud of his lady, who loved her, would speak of her at any opportunity, and speak well too.'

'True for you Jack; you still mention Peg—bless er soul—with a gleam in yer eye and a lover's sigh in yer voice. Whereas I...'

'Never mind what you say about your ole lady, eh? No, Sammy and Mrs. Sammy, one look at em and you know it's not right. There's nothing... nothing there. E fancies himself a brain, she fancies herself a beauty and... there's nowt between em, there's nothing joins em.'

'Correction if I may Jack ole mate—she *is* a beauty, an *e's* kiddin imself.'

1955

'Floozyanna, that's my name for her. A tart in lady's clothing she, no better than a common prostitute.' Nora's voice was bitter-toned with fresh, raw hurt. Petra, sitting next to her, took her mother's hand and looked into her eyes with dour concern.

'Mum, there's no sense in you doing this, surely. It was ten years ago, why rake it all up over and over again?'

'Painted herself as a Christian so she did, a churchgoer; and yet she took away my husband. Sammy Wilson's Bible warned against the Whore Of Babylon. Clearly he didn't read that bit.'

'Mum, we've been through all this so many times before, it does you no good. Why let it prey on your mind so?'

'What else can there ever be in my mind until she gives me back my dratted husband?'

'Mum, she never took him, she never left with him, remember?' Petra drew her hand across her mother's brow as if mopping away the sweats of a fever.

'Do you know what Mona Welkins told me about that woman, heard it from Marjorie Batten she did…'

'Mum, please!'

'Praps he'll come back… for those things she can't give him. *Won't* give him, more like.'

'Mother, that's an appalling thing to say!'

Petra's outrage only served to amuse Nora.

'Well, she won't. Dry-fannied old hag that she is! And don't you purse your lips at me Miss Prim, it's not as if you've never done such things, as Landwell Woods would witness if they could talk! Like your sister, you had no right to marry in white...'

'Mum, *please*...'

But Nora was not listening.

1960

'Be sure your sin will find you out.'

No one had spoken and yet there had been a voice. Sam closed his eyes, pinched the bridge of his nose and shook his head as if expelling something from within it. But there *had* been a voice. He sat still in the pew, Yvette beside him: she was still thrilling from the reading of their banns, 'Between Samuel Wilson, bachelor of this parish, and Yvette Parson, spinster of this parish...' the priest's voice was like the smoke from the censer, it seemed thick and slow to carry, but it rode the air deliberately and thoroughly, finding its sure way to all those there gathered.

'Be sure your sin will find you out.'

Again, words with no speaker. If there truly was a voice then it was not of one person alone, it was more a blend of two; the flat certainty of his long-dead aunt and the brooding vengefulness of Nora. Had they somehow joined to seek the satisfaction of their differing predictions of his doom? How could they be here, where were they? Sam Wilson feared momentarily for his wits. Calming himself, he decided he was anxious, and with good cause. But to everyone here he was just what he presented, a respectable man, a respectable *single* man who had at long last met the partner of his heart. It had never been his habit to wear his wedding ring, out of Nora's sight at least. He had always kept the thing in his pocket however, it had seemed important to do this. Nora had worn hers proudly and ostentatiously, advertising and boasting her unavailability with a relish Sam always found distasteful. Shallow and vain creature that she was, she revelled in the attentions of other men even as she enjoyed their disappointment at the glint of gold on her finger, she seemed to take pleasure in their frustration. Oh yes there had always been something of the coquette about Nora, and more than a hint of the whore.

1940

For a whore is a deep ditch; and a strange woman is a narrow pit. She also lieth in wait as for a prey, and increaseth the transgressors among men. Stick that up your weskit, Sammy Wilson!

1960

Sam attempted to turn his attention to the Mass, and to abandon the spiral of half-insanity that had snared him, and yet his thoughts remained with that cruel, dark zealot of his youngest days; what would she say if she knew his current situation? No doubt she would indulge her gluttonous appetite for the denunciation of sinners—'bachelor of this parish' indeed! Yes, he had allowed that falsehood to be published; he had allowed the priest to believe it, allowed the congregation to believe it too and, most heinous, allowed Yvette to believe it. But what he had done was for a better end, the best; surely forgiveness awaited him?

1940

The wife of thy youth, against whom thou hast dealt treacherously. Now does that ring any bells, my husband?

1960

Yvette shifted slightly next to Sam in the pew, and a moment later came her sweet odour of talcum powder and good soap. If anyone had asked him for a single word to describe Yvette he would have selected the adjective *clean*. It was the first impression he had of her, the first thing anyone of judgement would say of her—clean, neat, fastidious even. She was also not a woman who was too easily drawn into excesses of emotion, thank God; even this quiet, undemonstrative happiness at their coming union represented his fiancée at her most excitable.

On the appointed day, Yvette's friends and family would fill this place, sufficiently, he hoped, to compensate for the fact that the groom's side of the church would be almost empty. He would take that overspill and be glad of it—after all, who was there he could call upon to witness his vows? Anyone from his former life would surely bring ruin to his new one, just imagine if one of his children happened into the church or, worse in some ways, one of those sottish vaudevillians from the Royal Oak, what if they found him out by some freakish hap? He had been reduced to asking a ridiculously pleased Platt from the office to be his best man, this when they had barely a year's acquaintance, but at least the stalwart, vapid Platt knew nothing that could harm Sam's hard-won happiness. There would be one or two other friendly souls from work in attendance and fellow-spirits from the church itself, but not one person who knew him well. This was sad, mused Sam, but necessary; some things had to remain discreetly veiled.

He could scarcely wait for the wedding, for it to be over. As with the disembodied voice at the service, he was becoming coldly terrified by visions of the varied sorts of disastrous end—terrible, pathetic, humiliating—that the happy day could come to. Sickening shadows of shame and exposure threatened him—he saw himself and Yvette trapped at the altar, confronted by Nora and every one of their children and grandchildren, teeming generations of witnesses to the lie, the *necessary* lie that he had propagated. The phantoms plagued him without let.

1940

The day cometh that shall burn as an oven; and all the proud, yea and all that do wickedly, shall be stubble.

1960

He had not lied to Yvette. Not completely. After they had become engaged he had told her of Nora and of the fact they had children, but, cautiously, he had only named

Helen and Phyllida, the oldest of the girls. He would tell her, gently, of the others, but after the ceremony, when his mind would at last be at peace. Yvette was a wonderful woman, understanding, loyally discreet, unswerving in her devotion to him and to the Lord of them both. Even when she knew everything, even when he had confessed every one of his sins, she would never pack up her traps and leave, she would stand by him; he was confident. Yvette would not see him excluded from Communion as a divorcee in a permanent state of sin; she wanted and needed him by her side as she took the Flesh and the Blood. The banns were to be read one more time: soon it would be done. Their unifying desire was to be husband and wife, it was just and right that they be so.

1960

One last chance Lord, strike him down!

I don't understand your God, Sam Wilson, the heartless idol you worship. But you are his creation, right enough.

1945

If only they would listen to me I could tell those girls of mine the future, the future of each and every one of em. Oh, not some made-up nonsense from the bottom of a teacup, chattered over by some daft old woman, but a true foretelling of their ordained, inescapable fate. Each will marry a man who seems like a prince, a godling, she will rush into his arms and wait for happiness, but then she'll find it's backbreak and heartbreak that awaits, work and dirt, not dances and dresses and happy laughter. Their future will be no different from my past, my present; produce that man's babies and then woman and child one and all will be cast aside on to the rubbish heap with not a care for whether they live or die.

Be born—breathe—breed—grieve—try again—die. What sort of a life is that? A woman's future; always has been, always will be.

1960

Lord, strike him down, strike him down! Now! Lord?

1924

Nora had been fretting and fussing over this, that and the other frippery for days now, she was disproportionately and melodramatically upset by untidiness, dusty corners, children with muddy clothes or grazed knees, the aches and pains of her pregnancy, any silly, flyaway thing. Sam composed himself for patience and waited for her to cease prevaricating and address her true grievance. Nora was an odd creature at such a time, she was as shaped, and as ripe, as some exotic fruit, the new baby might make his appearance at any time; in this fact lay the real reason for her husband's forbearance, for he knew that the greater she became with child, the more infantile she herself became. Right now she was sulking and playing the martyr, lower lip thrust out and eyes moist, sitting uncomfortably in a kitchen chair but refusing any other 'For the sake of my poor back.' At last the moment had arrived, and she levelled a minatory stare at Sam.

'Sammy, don't take my baby away.' She clutched at her great belly as if she suspected him of planning some obscene pagan rite.

'She is not a baby; she is nearly four years of age.'

'That's still a baby,' smouldered Nora into her own breast. She had known about the proposition for some time, and fought against it in a ragged and indirect way from the beginning.

'It's wrong to make me give up my baby.'

'For crying out loud woman, you make it sound as if she is to be exposed on a mountainside! We are allowing Helen to go to her aunt—for her own good and for ours too.'

'*Great* Aunt,' Nora corrected him, as if this point clinched the argument for her.

'She is to go to her *Great* Aunt Laura the better for you to take care of yourself, of Phyllida, and of course, of our new little companion.'

'There won't be a little companion to Helen if you have your way.'

'Helen is to go away and live with Aunt Laura, it is not as if we shall never see her again, she will of course come back to us for occasional weekends, holidays...' Sam was making a sterling effort to keep his voice even and filled with a tone of unflappable good sense, yet still Nora remained truculent and tearful.

'It should be the other way round,' she riposted.

'Helen is to go to Aunt Laura. It is a done thing.'

'It is a wrong thing.'

'It is done; it *shall* be done.' Sam couldn't help it; he had raised his voice.

'It's still wrong.'

'That. Is. Enough.' Sam now tried his church-house boom, but his wife was still in a temper to fight.

'We never did such things in *my* family.'

'It is a tradition in *good* families. Helen would have gone to the care of my parents, had the Lord graced them with longer lives, but now it is Aunt Laura who is to take her in hand. What happened in your family is neither here nor there.'

'She doesn't like me,' Nora began to whine, 'and she'll school my little girl to scorn me too. It's nothing but child-stealing.'

Sam made a cold and formal defence of his aunt and, sensing a lack of conviction on his part, Nora pressed her case.

'She treats me like a damn child…'

'She has a right to!'

'She's a flint-hearted splinter of church wall Sammy, you know that's the truth, she doesn't care for children, she doesn't know them, she doesn't understand what goes on in their little heads, she's no *love* for them! And don't you try and tell me that she made you the man you are, that will be no argument, none at all, for only someone whose soul has nothing but ice in it would hold to that, you may never speak of it but I know fine well what that woman did to you when you were but a boy! You think me a fool, she thinks me a fool, but I know what she did to you, and she'll serve our girl the same, you must know that in your heart, I'm begging you!'

Sam was now upright in his chair, bristling with

uncontainable rage. 'Aunt Laura will take care of Helen, we can be sure that the child will be brought up in good Christian ways. You can pose no objection to that, I am sure.'

'It's cruel,' Nora began to keen.

'It is done. Helen leaves tomorrow.'

Sam took the girl alone on the train; Nora was in no fit state to travel. Keen to escape any hysterical farewells that may have upset Helen, he forbade his wife and daughters from any such show and escorted her away in silence. He looked at the child's face as she sat opposite him in the carriage: sober, sensible Helen, an old head on very young shoulders, she spoke not a word, shed not a tear.

By the time Sam returned, the house once again had three children. The new arrival was not a boy.

1940

The sound of the squealing reminded Nora horribly of the times she spent at her Uncle Herman's farm when they were taking the pigs away for slaughter; that dragging, throat-tearing high pitch screech that mixed incomprehension with nascent realisation and overwhelming fear.

Alex screamed, expelling all his breath as he struggled vainly to fight off his father's unbreakable grip and flee to his mother. He seemed to believe in his puerile confusion that if he could escape to the haven of her arms then punishment would not fall upon him, not this time at least. Nora followed the two as Sam dragged the boy along; Alex was no weight at all but he managed to cause the maximum inconvenience to his captor by flopping against his legs, kicking, struggling, squealing, still squealing, as Nora held out her arms to him, imploring him to come to her, impotently promising the protection he sought while seeking to soothe the furious glower from her husband's face, beseeching him to leave hold of the little boy, bleating ineffectually 'Sammy, Sammy, he's a good boy, a good boy, he doesn't mean it, please let him be!' It was a hopeless, purely token action, for Sam's wrath was never so easily diverted or slaked, and did she but know it her efforts made matters worse, her husband was more enraged by her twittering intercessions and feeble defiance of his authority than he was by the infant and his piffling transgressions. Sam got a better grip on the squirming child and hoisted him bodily into the front room, slamming the door with a rifle's report. Nora halted outside; Alex was in Sam's absolute possession now, in a place she had not the least power to aid him. Sam Wilson was at work shaping the character of his son and was not to be interfered with.

Nora stayed in place, head slightly bowed, listening to the cacophony within and sharing her little one's pain as Sam administered the boy's deserts with whooping swishes of his belt. That belt, she hated it as much as the children, she should hide it so Sam could never find it again but then what would he use? Something else, something worse? She sometimes upbraided him about his ferocity with his offspring but he was immovable, proof against pleading, seduction or tears, for he believed that foolishness was bound in the heart of the child, and that only the rod of correction could drive it out. He would pontificate on the matter to the point at which Nora could barely restrain herself from shouting, 'There speaks that blasted woman who raised you, not you, not my love but the monster that hated little children so!' Oh, Sammy Wilson had never uttered a word about what that God-mithering old crone had extracted from his hide, but Jane Wilson had told her everything, and armed with that knowledge she would sometimes stare at his naked back and buttocks and wonder if any of those marks that she could see, those old raised weals, were the dead remnants of that long-ago savagery.

She stayed by the door, never stepping away, her nose almost pressed against the gloomily-painted wood, but even when she felt exhausted by her vigil she never leaned forward, not even to rest her aching forehead for a moment, she feared that this would somehow be a transgression and that it would be all the worse for the boy should Sam detect it. The door sprang open at last and Sam ushered Alex out: the red-eyed child fell into Nora's embrace, but he only began to bawl out louder when the kitchen door had safely shut behind them. Both later tried to punish Sam with their eyes, gazing at him with deep reproof as he presided over another frostily silent family meal, but as ever he was indifferent to such childish ploys.

1968

'He wasn't fated to stay long in this world,' Nora told her daughter as renewed tears trickled down her cheeks at the thought of her dead boy. 'They never do stay long in this world, the angels don't, heaven calls them back, God always wants the best of them by his side.'

Flora bit back hard on the world-weary and spiteful retort that swirled in her head; if she so much as moved her tongue, the words would come spitting out, 'So he's an angel because he's dead; and if he'd survived the accident you would have drivelled on about *guardian* angels—Mother, it's all just so much sentimental tosh! Why go on and on about it, why not let the poor child lie still in his grave? It's nearly thirty years on and you… you're still mourning, and what's more you are revelling in it!'

It would have been so easy, far, far too easy to succumb to the temptation to crush Nora in this way, but Flora beat back the temptation. To indulge in such a thing was her father's way, not her own.

2013

'Poor Alex. It was no lure of Heaven that threatened to carry him out of this life, it was more the competition between his mother's suffocating over-attentiveness and the liberal application of his father's belt. Poor Alex, so beloved and fought over by his parents, yet neither of them ever got to know him or understand him. Long before his death he ceased to be a child and became… a dratted icon.'

'Golden haired cupid Alex, the apple-cheeked cherub, a special case, that child, an exception to the family's usual rules of selfishness and spite. Everybody loved him and we all competed for his attention, we all wanted to make him laugh, to hear him sing: the baby of the family, his mother's poppet, the summit of his father's ambitions. Oh he was so pretty, the little ringletted godhead who bore so many hopes on his shoulders he couldn't possibly be expected to bear their weight.' Flora halted, brushing in amazement at her face. 'Good God, tears.' she said mildly, 'And there was me forever scolding our Mum for turning on the waterworks at the very mention of his name.'

'Why did Nonna and Sam make such favourites and play such games?' asked Francine with a rising anger, 'Why couldn't they love all their children as... as individuals?'

'Oh child of another age, another planet!' Flora mocked gently, 'Very much like you, young lady, Nonna and Sam were people who found it very hard to conceal their passions. Nonna could never control her emotions, not on any matter and not at any time, and our dear Samuel didn't possess a scintilla of the lofty self-mastery he fancied he displayed. They drew battle-lines with the children—Sam's favourites were the black-haired ones, his colour before he went grey so young, and Nonna made pets of the ones who favoured her colour. They used us as proxies in their own war, when they weren't battling over control of Alex.'

'What about you?'

'Me? I favoured Nonna in looks, but I had mousy, no-shade hair, neither of them wanted me especially. Our Dad never liked me, never, and he didn't take much trouble concealing it either. When I came along he told mother that was the end of their baby-making—"No more of the little so-and-sos!"—although of course he managed to erm, slip just once more. But no, he never liked me, and he favoured me with the strap more often than with a smile. He had a queer old way of showing his love.'

Francine was speechless, impotent in the face of the cruelties of history.

'I used to hide under the bed when our Dad was angry, angry about anyone or anything, which was much of the time. I'd hide myself and wait for him to go away; sometimes I wished he'd go away forever. We were taught to worship and fear a temperamental and vengeful God: I used to imagine that he looked just like our Dad.'

1932

Flora Jean Wilson was born late into the night of the tenth of October, and Nora's first thought on looking upon the wizened, rat-like creature she had borne was that on the old farm the runt of the litter was usually left to die, unless one of the farmer's family took pity and raised it as a pet. The baby was more noise than flesh, a stretch-skinned thing like a grotesque sausage with slowly-flailing stick-limbs. From the moment the girl-child had seen light she squalled and yelled, her crying unstoppable, so powerful it seemed forever on the verge of exhausting the few sparks of divine energy that animated the tiny body. None of the other children had been so patently unhappy at their arrival in this life. Here was a child who would always be sickly, always need her mother and would never stray far from home. She nestled Flora in her arms and gave suck, gave warmth, gave comfort, but still the scrawny thing screamed in protest and could not be placated.

The new child's arrival caused a predictable upsurge of excitement amongst the girls, but then excitement gave way to the long, hard chore of daily living as at all hours and opportunities those eyes screwed up and the mouth gaped and she howled fit to shake every window in the house. Sam had even less truck with the newcomer than he'd had with her sisters; he was reluctant to hold her, even for a few moments, he refused to be present when she was put to bed, and forbade her presence at mealtimes. The screams drove him to his room but even in this inner sanctum they pierced his skull and he would rush out to the kitchen where Nora was trying hard to soothe away the enervating noise.

'Shut that kid up!' He added his own scream to the din before slamming the door and retreating to the relative peace of his den.

1937

Vile, hateful man, does it make him happy to be so horrid and make us so miserable? I must stop sobbing and catch my breath and lie doggo or he'll find me out, I don't want him to find me, I don't want to see him, I'd be happy if I slid from under here and found he'd gone, up and left us and taken his stormy-dark Bible, then we could all be happy, sleep abed on Sunday mornings and play games and laugh and shout, we could go to bed when we pleased, eat when hungry, drink when thirsty, even put our elbows on the table if we wanted. Let him live in that freezing cold church with its rotting-book air, let him preach to the empty pews and tinselly hangings and never bother us again, he takes the fun and joy out of everything, makes it all a sin, a crime; I'd rather stay here like a jerry-pot than emerge again while that ogre sits at the head of our table, I'm sure Mother must have been different before she knew him, as beautiful as she is now but full-coloured with a happy smile, not pale-faced and cry-eyed; I bet she sang better then too, that same lovely voice but happy songs, not those sad notes she sighs out when she thinks no one's about, she would pipe so prettily if it wasn't for him. I hate him, I hate him, why must he be with us, why must he be; he talks about his family as if we are so special, the best of people, everyone around us he scorns as gypsies and tramps, but even though he says we're better he never treats us as if we are, he's always so disappointed with us, cross, angry, shouty, we're filthy little arabs, street urchins, articles, that's what we are to him, horrid man, scowling monster. He should have married some dry old stick of a woman full of Bible words and psalms, Mother should have married a good man, a common man, the sort *he* sneers at, a factory hand, a miner, a sagger-maker from the potbanks, someone from the lower classes that *he* so hates, a daddy who would smile and joke and play with us, shouting hellos to the people we meet and not looking away with a mouth like a pillar-box and a wrinkled brow, if Mother or my sisters would pad up here and slip my dinners under the bed and then sneak the plate away when I'm done then I could stay here very well, maybe with a book to read, but not that beastly Bible, let that stay on the shelf and pull dust on to itself until it's utterly buried and never seen again. Oh don't let him find me here and drag me out with his cold hands and swish that belt of his! I hate him, I hate him, let me stay here till I grow so much I'm stuck fast, till he goes, till he goes and never comes back!

1944

Nora stood with her back to the shelf as if defying her husband to proceed further, insisting he should not violate this sanctuary, protecting her children whose sweet faces shone from their three small picture frames: happy, innocent faces, innocent of everything, including their own coming deaths. The photograph of Jocelyn was taken when she was five, the last year of her life, and it was blurred and fading, as if both she and the memory of her were melting away. Vanessa beamed a life-loving smile and her image, crisp and clear, seemed determined to retain its last hold on this world; she had fought on longer than her sister, but the Dark Angel had been far too strong for her. She had been such a beautiful girl, if she had been spared she would have blossomed into a young woman and sat for the portrait man as her mother had, then perhaps even The Beauty of Chell Street herself may have been eclipsed. Alex was not just smiling, he was cackling, it was that naughty-boy laugh of his when he was readying to sing another of his cheeky songs as he skipped and ran in the back yard. So alive he was, he could so easily have stepped out of that flat frame and carried on living the life of which he had been cruelly robbed.

Sam scowled, and it seemed to Nora he was bracing to lay his hands on her and hurl her bodily out of his way.

'Nora. This is not a church, and shrines to the dead do not belong in a room for living.'

'But they're our children Sammy, they deserve to be remembered. I put them here so they could be with their sisters. With their mother and father.'

'And we do remember them Nora, we all do, the whole time. But remove these photographs from here; they were children; they shall not become graven images.'

'Sam please...'

'I am adamant. I am going out now, and I do not expect these pictures to be here when I return.'

'Where are you going?' Nora blurted the words, half-shrieked them, wracked by a twist in her insides, a keen blade of jealousy.

'That is my business.'

'Stay here.' She had meant to demand, but she knew she was pleading.

'I have already had enough unnecessary fuss and disruption. The discussion is at an end.'

He was gone. Nora gathered her lost children to her breast and bore them away.

2012

Aunty Eileen's voice was interestingly different from Mum's, it had a slightly strained sound, as if her words were always fighting their way past taut violin strings, picking up random snatches of harmony and discord on the way.

'Your Mum suggested I tell you this tale as she was so little at the time she didn't really know what was going on. Mum—our Mum—had decided for some reason she owed it to Grampa Sam to take his grandchildren to see him. Given what you know about Sam and children you might wonder what she imagined she was up to, but she's often had fits of conscience about Sam and Nonna, she worried she didn't treat them properly, worries about it even to this day. So, for whatever her reasons, she dressed us up in the stiffest Sunday best we had—indeed my overall impression of the trip was that it was like going to church—and off to see Grampa and dear Yvette we went.'

'You didn't like "dear" Yvette?' Francine enquired archly.

'A child never takes to someone who makes no effort to be liked. She never looked at either of us, not in the eye, and gave us not a single smile. She didn't know where to put herself with us and plainly wished we'd never come. She gave us tea and rather nasty little coconut cakes, and was completely on edge the whole time, terrified we'd wet ourselves or spill tea on her sofa or, horror of horrors, that we'd let a crumb of cake fall on her carpet! I got the feeling that we should have been put into some kind of quarantine chamber; she may have been satisfied then.

'So I was as tense as could be and aching not to be there. Kara was too little to read the air like I could, but she too was restless, we had been forbidden to get up and run about, we weren't to touch anything, and we weren't to speak unless Grampa Sam spoke to us first. No chance of that! He and Yvette spoke to your Gran to find out our names, our ages, if we wanted tea, everything, as if we were little animals or aliens. Well eventually the atmosphere became so pressured that Grampa Sam himself offered relief, "I expect the girls would like a breath of fresh air," he suggested, and told Mum to let us out into the back garden. Didn't do anything himself mind, didn't budge from his chair, but Mum got up and naturally we followed her fast as we could go. I was momentarily grateful to Sam for realising we needed to get out of there, but later I realised it wasn't our needs he was responding to—he knew his old lady had had enough and wanted us out of the way.

'Anyway, the garden was almost as boring as the indoors, there was nothing in that place, nothing for kiddies, and we stood around like lemons trying to think of a game. The garden was too cramped for us to run around much and we were far too intimidated to make noise, and within a short time we were as uncomfortable there was we had been in the house, with the added bugger of not even being able to sit. Anyway, we hunted for anything, anything at all, to amuse ourselves, and by the garden shed I found some garden canes, you know, the sort of thing you support plants with, barring the fact there were no bloody plants in that desert for them to support. Odd thing that, it was a neat and trim garden, but barren. Anyway, I grabbed a couple of these canes, Kara wanted to play sword fights but I knew what would happen if we did *that*, so we just stood there on this pocket-handkerchief lawn trying to work out a use for these damned sticks! Now I don't know if the devil got in us because we were just bored out of our little skulls, or if somewhere in our minds we'd decided to take a little revenge on behalf of Nonna Nora, but before we could be stopped we were jabbing those canes into the lawn, making little holes, then making patterns out of the holes, seeing who could jab hardest and go deepest.'

'Ooops!' Francine laughed.

'Ooops is right!' Eileen joined in the laugh, 'We'd been at it about three minutes when we heard this great bull-roar from the kitchen and Grampa Sam called Mum to, "Come and deal with these brats, these vandals!"

'Well, we were scared shitless, Mum was standing over us taking the canes off us and apologising to her dad as he emerged to survey the damage, but although she was scolding us she was protecting us from him as he stood there telling her precisely what he thought about her brace of ill-brought-up little horrors. Kara and I had heard stories of that belt of his and we were just getting knock-kneed with fear when there was an interruption: there was a voice, friendly but rather jeering, it boomed over the fence and shut the old man up as he turned to see what was going on. It was Grampa's next-door neighbour, a grizzled old thing who must have lived outdoors all year long; he must have seen the whole business.

'"Now then Wilson," he said all sing-song voiced, "don't be so arsh on em, that lawn o yours needs aeratin, told yo bout it before but you don't look after it proper, an that's all the little uns ave done. Saved you a packet they ave, I reckon you oughtter give em somethin for their trouble."'

'Did he pay up?'

'No fear, girl! But the old man's intervention took the wind out of Sam's sails and he stomped off indoors to Yvette. I recall the old neighbour leaning over the fence and winking at me, I think he rather enjoyed taking Grampa down a peg or two.'

'Was that the end of the visit?'

'Ra-ther! I don't remember, but Mum says we were out of there in record time, no sad goodbyes! And strangely enough Mum's conscience never forced her to take us there again!'

'Did Nonna hear about this?'

'Ah yes. Delighted she was, as if we really had been

operating under her orders. She made us Madeira cake and gave us half a crown each. Thrilled to bits. Guaranteed to make her laugh was the slightest reference to that caper, right up to the day she died.'

The Dark Angel

1952

The Dark Angel is making sport with me: I would welcome death but the foul creature just mocks me with that blessed release, he dangles it before me and then snatches it away like some spiteful brat at play with a helpless infant. Many's the time I can think of nothing but the end, yet still it does not come and I am left contemplating the guilt, the terrible, terrible guilt that death has not come for me and instead I have to stand helplessly while it steals my babies. Mocking me, mocking me it is, that cheating sprite. I fear I am doomed to outlive each and every one of my own children, I shall be forced to bear witness as they fall prey to sickness or grow old and feeble: how long shall I be forced to live against my will, how many generations must I see buried? To be trapped in this life and denied my true reward, that's the fate I fear the most. Come down, come down, stop your cruel torments and come down!

2014

St Anselm's did not have a graveyard of its own; the church stood too close to the old turnpike road, now the main thoroughfare to town, to have anything except a small garden at its rear, and no sensible worshipper either then or now would consent to the bones of their dead lying restless under the rattle of coach wheels or the ever-increasing traffic of the modern day. The church instead shared some of the abundant land belonging to St Margaret's, some half a mile away. The graveyard was a sprawling ocean of long grass that eventually gave way to an increasingly violent slope that swept down towards the broad flat terrain where once stood the winding gear of Woolsend Colliery. It was almost possible to imagine the supernumerary dead of the crowded cemetery were tumbled down some subsurface chute to populate the abandoned galleries of the sleeping deep mine. The Wilson family had bought plots in the graveyard not long after their arrival in town, and it had become another of Nonna Nora's familiar themes, rehearsed to all of her visitors, 'I have my place. I know where I shall go. It's a comfort to be certain of something, even just that one little thing.' On the street outside the church, the wind had been playful, tugging hems and ruffling hair, but on the exposed hillside it played rough, pushing and shoving people bodily and making the unkempt grass of the graveyard rush and ripple. The path close to the church was flagged with ancient gravestones, their dates and dedications eaten away by time, and recent rain had made everything treacherously slippery until visitors could reach the safety of the cinder pathway some yards down the hill. Kara did an inelegant variation of the splits on the slimy surface and could only recover herself with help, and moments later she strained her back catching her mother as the old woman's feet slithered from under her as if they had been roped together and pulled hard by some invisible, mysterious force. Francine took charge of the two small bunches of flowers that her grandmother had been carrying and she steadied

Flora's arm as they inched cautiously down the tricky slope.

The matter had not been discussed, but the three women went to Nora first by unspoken consent. Although the grave had been made over twenty years previously, it was still well-defined and its stone relatively unstained. Francine read the name and dates, simple statements for the woman that she had never met but who now fascinated her so much. Flora knelt awkwardly, Kara hovering over her, to remove a bunch of old, dead flowers and to take the new bunch from Francine and put them into place.

'Do you ever talk to her?' asked Francine.

'Just a little, dear, but I certainly don't blame those who have a good old chat to the ones they've lost. The least I can do for mum is to come up here whenever I can, keep the plot tidy and offer a few words. She'd be pleased to know she's not forgotten.'

'She's far from forgotten,' said Francine, her quiet words whipped away by the wild air.

Kara's hair was being tossed around as if the clawed wind were raking through it for treasures or secrets buried in the thick tresses. Flora's eyes were watering and Francine shivered, a deep, body-trembling shudder almost as if she felt the presence of phantoms all around. Kara glanced at her. 'You should have come in...'

'A thicker coat, yes Mum, thanks so much eh?'

Kara smiled tolerantly and Francine turned to look down the slope: Nonna's last resting place lay not far from where the ground started to shelve away; there were other, newer graves further on, but after them the slope grew too sheer and the grass ran downhill uninterrupted. Francine could see half-demolished buildings, the remains of the colliery and the steelworks in the dirty valley below, a dead space that had once teemed with activity above and below the surface. The angry wind struck at Francine's hat and threw it to the ground; turning around to retrieve it she found her mother and grandmother still staring at the gravestone.

'There she is, in the place she was wishing herself into from as far back as I can remember.' Kara's voice was thrown to Francine by a keen gust. All three then stood in silence, their thoughts concentrating on this one woman, ignoring the attention-seeking wind as it shoved and barged at them.

The walk back up the path was a battle against the swirling bully wind as it gusted hard in revenge for their scorning its power, and they took a little time to locate Sam's grave. Francine noticed that although her grandmother had brought posies of exactly the same size for each of her parents, there were small give-away signs of favour and disfavour nonetheless—just as they did not go to him straight away, Sam was the more neglected, his resting place less clear-cut and more weed-run than Nora's. The three generations of Wilson women were silent once again as Flora arranged Sam's flowers, until Kara let out a stuttering sound Francine realised was a snigger; she saw her mother's face pulled to and fro by contradictory tics of wicked fun and furtive shame.

'I'm sorry.' Kara waved a deprecating hand, 'I've just remembered the most terrible thing. It was Grampa Sam's funeral, I was standing over there.' She pointed to a position six long strides away, under a tree. 'I was standing well back to be honest, keeping clear, as they lowered the coffin in the grave and it was a really-really serious, solemn moment…' She sniggered again and Flora looked as if she was about to slap her with the pair of leather gloves that she had just pulled out of her pocket to relieve her reddening hands.

'Pull yourself together girl!' she commanded; no slap. Kara apologised, and with a lift up and drop of her shoulders she took a snatch of the fast air and announced that her remembrance wasn't really appropriate for this place, this time. 'I'll finish later,' she promised, and as they left the graveyard she seemed to be finding it hard to suppress a fit of the giggles.

'Aunty Minnie and Aunty Helen and their children were gathered at the grave, but I stood well back because Aunty Minnie was hamming it up a bit, overdoing the tears. Even when I'm not terribly upset I always end up blubbing when someone else does. So, from where I stood I could see Minnie and the others on the far side of the grave, and all around it stood the funeral director's men who'd acted as pall-bearers and had lowered the coffin into the ground too. They were standing upright, heads bowed in respect and their hands folded in front of them at waist-level…' Kara lost her words in another naughty-girl chuckle—she simply didn't seem able to control herself. Patient Francine let it happen; she could wait for more words.

'I'm sorry dear, but it's so absurd. And, erm, disrespectful too. You see, I could only see the backs of the lads on my side of the grave, their hands closed in front of them, and in one awful moment I realised that they all looked as if they were pi… *urinating* into the hole!'

She couldn't bear it any longer and she hooted with wild, loud laughter and slapped hard at her thighs. 'Oh god, oh god it's terrible but they really, *really* looked like they were... One moment I was trying not to be tricked into letting loose false tears and the next I was biting my lip to stop another sort if hysterics!' She lost the words again and found laughter in their stead. 'I'm sorry, so sorry, but I was behaving like a teenager, my head suddenly so full of bloody sick ideas. This is why I couldn't tell you this in front of your Gran, or in front of... I suppose it just shows the lack of feeling in my heart for Grampa Sam. I sobbed my way through Nonna Nora's funeral and I've never felt so sad as when I saw her go into the ground, but for Grampa I felt detached at best and then those funeral men... I know you shouldn't speak ill of the dead but Grampa Sam, he... well, he wanted so much to be respected and feared, but people made fun of him you know, and far more often than you might expect...'

So this was not exactly the sort of story that Francine had expected to collect, but it still told her a great deal. It had its place.

'Gran, d'you mind if I ask you something?'

'My love?'

'At Nonna's grave just now, I couldn't hear when you were talking to her; d'you mind telling me what you said?'

Flora smiled, bashfully. 'Oh trivial stuff, "Here's fresh flowers for you Mum, you know you always liked flowers and they're your favourite colour..." I find myself bossing and cajoling her even now, "Now you *know* you like them Mum!" Just as if she were sitting there in her back kitchen moaning and groaning and finding nothing to please her.

Oh dear oh dear.'

'Did you say anything at Grampa Sam's grave?'

'No. Nothing. Hmmm, I never did know what to say to your great-grandfather. And I never said anything worthwhile anyway as far as he was concerned. And I can't even find any words now, not even when he can't come back and crush me with one of his nasty sarcastic remarks.'

Flora let out a breath; her eyes were on something that wasn't quite in the room. 'Queer isn't it, I'm having the same sort of conversation—or lack of it—with my parents in death as I did in life? Exactly the same.'

1980

'Mum, you've simply got to stop going on and on about dying! It can't be good for you and it confuses the kiddies; it frightens them, it *frightens* them Mum!'

'Threescore years and ten, that's all any of us has got! They need to know that and you're not telling em. Y'should always tell children the truth.'

'Threescore years an… Mum, you're eighty for goodness sake, you're living disproof of all that nonsense!'

'Used up me time haven't I? I'm overstaying me welcome, I could be taken up at any time. Sooner the better.' Nora's throat click-click-clicked.

'Oh Mother, you're fitter than some sixty year olds—if you'd just realise it! You could live to a hundred and something, you could see in a new century, what about that?'

'And why should I want to do *that?* Should of gone long since, I should. Before long it will be forty years, forty years since I was left all alone. Then fifty, sixty, seventy… why should I want to live through that?'

Gathering the Family

1977

'It's discussting how they never come round to see me. Shame on them.' Nora lifted the corner of the net curtain on the kitchen window and peered out for a moment, screwing up her eyes as if blinded by overwhelming light even though it was a dull old day, then she shuffled resignedly back to her chair. There was no one coming. She lit another cigarette—the packet was nearly empty, it was her next to last one; one of the girls had to come soon, she needed bits of shopping, not just the cigs, and she was in no fit state to drag herself up the slope to the shops. With a click-click-click at the back of her throat she started to speak again, watching the smoke spread into the empty air. 'Shame, yes. Of all things I'd of thought my girls would've grown up with a sense of *family*.'

2012

For Francine, her grandmother's home had always cried out a bright welcome to one and all, it was a light-loving and airy house, with that warm and open aspect perhaps underscored by a certain loneliness, the knowledge that only one person now lived there where once there had been many. For Flora to occupy that big house alone was perfectly normal for Francine; it was a part of nature for one part of the house to be vibrantly active and the other rooms to slumber in silence.

She had, from time to time, heard her Mum, Eileen and Gran in conversation about 'Getting somewhere smaller', always with the younger women urging and cajoling, and the older refusing, arguing, defending herself, both gently and robustly. 'I don't know why I want to stay,' Francine overheard her grandmother say, 'I know this has hardly ever been a happy house, but… there you have it. I shall stay until I can't manage any longer, and that's flat. Don't pester me out of my home darling, just leave me to it. It's my nature; when I'm attached to something I find it hard to let go.'

But today the house was shedding its lonely atmosphere, there would be people and life and noise again. It was Gran's eightieth birthday, and she was throwing a party: a celebration that was to bring the extended family together for the first time since Francine was tiny.

Gran tried to insist that *she* should contribute, either by cash means or at least by making some of the food, but her daughters insisted, 'Mum it's your birthday, your party, for once we want you to relax.' Gran told Francine that they were bullies, but she was smiling. 'It's an experience when everyone gets together,' she confided to her granddaughter, 'and I tell you what, it'll be an ideal platform for *your* researches. Make the most of it my love; it may be the last time for some of em. D'you know this is only the second time anyone has even attempted to get the family together since Nonna Nora died?'

'Why?' asked Francine, and instead of replying right away, Gran seemed on the verge of crying, although it soon became clear she was in truth suppressing little liquid slivers of laughter.

'Everyone's afraid of a repeat of last time, in one way or another; you were too little to remember it, it was at Aunty Minnie's eightieth birthday party. If you want to know what I'm talking about, imagine the sight of two elderly ladies—my dear sisters—fighting like teenagers at a disco! I remember thinking all that evening that there was something in the air, but the party went on and nothing seemed to come of it, the younger people started to make their excuses and drift away and yet the sisters remained, way past their bedtimes, and then it happened. My sisters Minnie and Phyllida, octogenarians both, having to be held back by a squad of grown adults, but they were still nearly dragging their captors over and spitting like cats, ready to rearrange one another's faces!'

'What for?'

Gran was laughing too much to answer now; wet eyes, crinkled skin, teeth bared.

2004

'I've waited over sixty years to put you in your place! You ruined my life, destroyed my one chance of happiness you jealous bitch! And everything went wrong for me after what you did, *everything*!'

The music had been turned down at the request of the remaining guests and the dance floor was empty. Flora was helping to clear glasses, dirty plates and the remnants of burst balloons when the voices of Minnie and Phyllida snatched her attention from these end-of-the-night duties. Aunty Phyl was frail these days, white-haired, thin and sunken-cheeked, and she looked ten years rather than one year older than her sister, who stood leaning aggressively towards her, one hand on a trestle table for extra balance as she waved a poker-stiff finger in short, angry beats. But although Minnie was mobile, robust and filled with a well-matured rage, Aunty Phyl was not to be intimidated and answered with a biting, if slightly quivering voice; practically nobody else in the room knew what was going on, but Phyllida knew precisely what Minnie was referring to, and she was not wasting time on protestations to the contrary.

'So,' Phyllida curled her lip as she made a curt and cruel summary of her sister's life, 'I was the one who made all the idiotic choices throughout your life, was I? I made you marry two alcoholics on the trot, did I? It was I who forced you to fall out with all your sisters in turn and then with every friend and neighbour you ever had? And then in my infinite wickedness, I stood over you and demanded you spent every penny you ever got before it could get cold in your purse? *Then* I persuaded you to be jealous of your family because they'd put money away in the bank and you were stony broke because you couldn't clap your eyes on any old useless trinket without being greedy for it? Must-Have Minnie I always called you. You always were soft in the head our Minnie, you never needed *any* help to be foolish, girl!'

Her righteous rage suitably stoked, Minnie surged forward, fists bunched, and she had to be restrained by two of her sons.

'I would of bin all right if *you* hadn't interfered!'

Flora exchanged alarmed looks with Phyllida's

daughters, who had been idling by the door waiting for the aunties to ask to be driven home. Minnie, taking advantage of the half-hearted grip of her own astonished sons, dragged herself and them far enough forward for her to be able to raise her fist in her sister's face, and at that moment two of Phyllida's three girls stepped forward slowly, confused and embarrassed, as they realised that any moment now they really may have to prevent a no-holds-barred fight.

'You need to know the terrible things you've done to me! Everyone here should know the terrible things that you've done to me!' screeched Minnie, struggling still as her sons, cheeks burning with mortification and muttering apologies to whoever stood nearby, hauled her away.

1943

'I'm worried about our Minnie,' fretted Nora to Phyllida in a confidential tone as they sat knitting in the back kitchen at Woolsend Avenue.

'What's the matter Mum?'

'Ohhh, it's that Yank, her and that Yank. I'm sure it's not right, people in the Avenue are starting to talk; what will become of her? Look at all those girls these soldiers promise the earth to and then leave behind...'

'*He* seems alright Mum.'

'He's "alright" in front of us, oh yes, he's a charmer. But what's going on when we're not about, eh? I think he only wants one thing...'

'Oh you say that about *all* men, Mum, I'm tired of hearing it.'

'I should know, my girl. And I've heard talk—Marjorie Batten saw them walking towards Landwell Woods last Saturday.'

'Lots of people go there!'

'And some girls who go there are never the same again, that's my whole point!'

'Mum, if that's all you're worried about, Minnie can look after herself, she's nineteen years old! If any girl can look after herself she can, what d'you call her, Wildcat! The only way he'll get a baby on her is when she's got a ring safely on her finger, and if he tries anything before that he'll rue it! And anyway, don't you listen to him when he talks, Mum? His family's very religious, he believes in the sanctity of marriage.'

'Anyone can say their halleluiahs,' snorted Nora. 'Doesn't mean there's not a black soul deep down inside.'

'Well I'm sure he's a good man, and I'm just as sure that he's going to ask her to marry him.'

'But don't you see what that means?' Nora's voice was hoarse and raw, her eyes filling with tears. 'He'll take her away, we shall never see her again!'

'He'd be taking her to America, mother, you make it sound like he'd be dragging her to hell! She could have a much better life there, I don't think his family's short of a bob or two.'

'She's being selfish darling, can't you see? Just thinking of herself, what about us, what about her family, her mother? Oh you'll all be gone one day soon and I'll be all alone…' her appeal trailed off to a whine.

'The rest of us aren't going anywhere Mum—and you'll have Dad…' Phyllida regretted adding that, she knew well about the disharmony between her parents, but Nora ignored her discomfiture, she had other fish to fry.

'You *will* go. If she goes you'll all want to, you'll all leave me, and who will look after me then?'

'I won't leave you, Mum.'

Nora shook her head as if that pledge, no matter how heartfelt, was simply not sufficient. 'No my girl, we have to stop her before it's too late. It's for her own good, because we love her, you can see that can't you?'

'But you can't just tell her to stop seeing him, you know what Minnie's like, if she knows you want it stopped she'll want him all the more, she'll elope or something!'

Nora shook her head, then pinched tears out of her eyes. 'He's not what he seems: there are at least three others he's making the same promises to; that's what these Yanks are like.'

'Do you *know* that?'

'Can you doubt it? You have to protect your sister, protect your family, if you love her, if you love me.'

'But Mum, how?'

2012

'The story goes that Aunty Phyl wrote a letter to the American, warning him about Minnie, saying she would never make him a good wife, that she was headstrong and wilful, that she would always disobey him, that she was impulsive and would soon regret marrying him, and that she would just get bored and run away back to England. I think there may also have been something in there hinting that she'd, er, been about a bit as well, that he wasn't exactly the first. I never knew if that was true…' Kara had now taken over the story from her mother.

'Did they split up because of the letter?' asked Francine.

'Well, Aunty Minnie never heard from him again—but it was in the middle of the war, so anything could have happened to him. Nonna always told Minnie that if the Yank was worth anything he'd find some way to get in touch with her. When he didn't, Minnie was heartbroken, but then she decided that what Nonna said was true, he wasn't worth bothering about. Aunty married Tom Edge not so long after.'

'Didn't she know about the letter?'

'Not then, not for years after. And she only ever knew that Aunty Phyl wrote it, not that Nonna told her what to say.'

2004

As if she were a police suspect, Minnie was being gently but firmly pushed into the back of a car, struggling breathlessly still to have at her sister, yet still able to find a spare lungful of air to bellow back into the hall, 'I would of bin happy with him!'

'You'd never be happy with anyone! It's not your way!' was the ear-burstingly shrill riposte that stabbed out into the night from a shadow-figure in the doorway emitting streamers of yellow-white light.

The old ladies were finally removed, with difficulty, to their separate cars, Minnie white-hot and angry, Phyllida shocked and shaking. Flora continued to clear up and spoke to no one, wondering silently at her family's ability to nurse poisonous, undying grudges.

1966

January 14th

My dearest Phyllida,

I have just had a long chat to our Minnie about something that has been troubling her for many years, and I am shocked to learn what happened. This goes right back to the War, and to my amazement she has been suffering this terrible hurt all this time.

I gather from what she says that her American officer did not just disappear off as we had all thought, but that he stopped seeing her after you wrote him a very nasty letter telling him to have nothing more to do with her. I find it hard to understand how you could have done something like this to your sister. I know you were single at the time and not cheerful about it, but Minnie and her American could have been happy, and it was wholly wrong of you to interfere.

I can scarcely believe that you could have been such a bitch, I can only assume it was jealousy and your youth and inexperience that caused you to be so, and so I will say nothing of the matter to the family and nor will Minnie, so that we may all get over this more quickly. I will do my best to seek your sister's forgiveness on your behalf, and she has promised that there shall be no bitterness between the two of you.

With love always,

Mum

Parties could be interesting. Family parties could be *mega* interesting. On the day of Flora's eightieth birthday, Francine made a fuss of her Gran, ate a good deal, sneaked a glass or two of wine, although she had been forbidden by her mother, she chattered and charmed, but above all she attended to her labour of love; it was a unique opportunity for rescuing many small scattered histories from the brink of the Place of Lost Stories. The people and the tales they brought with them had not gathered in one place for years, and they would probably never again. As the family gathered, Flora, Kara and Eileen worked the crowd like seasoned politicians and the atmosphere was one of jollity and goodwill; and yet Francine ached to detect the ripples of ancient Wilson conflicts spreading out from old generations to new.

At times she felt she was almost cold-blooded in her behaviour; she loved to meet people and make merry, but underneath what she wanted was the contents of their memories, and she carefully extricated herself from conversations with relatives who proved too distant, or those, like her, too young. She homed in on those who possessed direct knowledge of Sam and Nora, and became excited, agitated almost, at the prospect of meeting anyone who had known them in their prime.

'Now let's see,' Gran had said as they all pitched into prepare for the festivities, 'let's see if my old memory is working right. I'll tell you who's turning up and where they fit in… it's a bit of a task, all the surviving in-laws, grandchildren and great-grandchildren add up to, oooh, a fair number. But I

think I'm up to the job.'

'You'll need pen and paper,' commented Kara, attempting to joke but sounding somewhat sour instead, 'Or a computer. A bloody great powerful one.'

So many people—and so many of them were women! Such an outpouring of daughters of daughters of daughters, a cascade of femininity flowing from the joining of Nora and Sam; how would he have felt about this, Francine wondered, the man who had ceased his relentless building of a family only once he had sired a son?

Again and again the features of Nonna Nora and Grampa Sam appeared among the gathering, but altered in large and small ways, by a squarer jaw in this branch of the family, deeper and larger eyes in that, longer noses, buck teeth: diluted looks, intruding alien features. There were also present some of the men who had introduced these changes to the Wilson template, altering it as the price of its continued survival; several were as handsome in their way as had been Grampa Sam, and some of their sons and grandsons were still more handsome. And yet not one of the women there present was remotely as beautiful as Nonna Nora, not a single one. Francine left her Mum, Aunty Eileen and Gran out of that reckoning; herself too. Deep within herself she was certain nobody in that room, nobody in the entire world was as beautiful as Nora Wilson once was, or Francine Latimer was destined to be.

'Well, we don't need to ask any questions—*you're* a Wilson right enough!' was the stock comment to the teenager, and one or two people who had been at the booze table a few times too many did not seem to mean terribly well by it. One woman, a distant second-third cousin who never even gave her name, practically dragged Francine over to stand by a picture of Nonna, which stood on the polished sideboard, then shouted to her husband and daughters to come and see, as if she were the barker at a freak show.

'To the life!' she gasped in wonderment.

'To the life,' agreed her husband, but with considerably more interest in the girl than in the photograph, so Francine reckoned. It jangled her nerves a little that she was a dead woman 'to the life', but she soon forgot this qualm as the fuss about the resemblance took its effect, spreading out across the room and, at last, putting people in mind of the past. The anecdotes flowed, too quickly and in too great abundance for Francine to chase and net them all.

As the afternoon gave way to evening Francine was increasingly uninhibited in seeking stories, it would soon be too late. She felt a pang of guilt again at valuing her fellow guests, her family, less for their humanity than their value as purveyors of histories. But that did not stop her.

'Minnie now, she had four children, all by her first husband. The second was too soused to be capable, and by the time she met Jeff Clayton she was too old, more's the pity. Jeff would have made a wonderful dad. Terry, Minnie's eldest, he's coming, lovely lad Terry, he always was.'

'Lad?' objected Kara. 'He must be sixty by now, and he's got five kids of his own!'

'So he has,' Flora mused, momentarily lost, 'I don't think that Paul or Ralph, his brothers, will be coming along. Last I heard they weren't speaking to the family, can't remember the reason why and there probably isn't one. Minnie never needed

a reason for her goings-on and they seem to take after her. They were such lovely little boys Paul and Ralphie, I really don't know what's got in to them.'

'But Jeff will be there,' Kara promised her daughter, 'now you'll like Jeff a lot.'

'It all seems a bit silly now,' the grey-haired and yet still boyish Terry admitted with a minute flash of a smile. 'These bloody family squabbles, they were nothing to do with us kids and yet we kept on getting dragged into em. I remember when I was about ten year old, we stopped going to see Aunty Helen for over a year because Mum felt slighted in some way. Never made it clear what it was about, she didn't, just said her sister was "hoity-toit" and "above herself". She took against Nonna too, in the days after old Sam came to live in our house, started telling anyone who'd listen that all the stories about Grampa were stuff and nonsense, that he was a wonderful man and Nonna had poisoned our minds against him. And *that* led to a row with Aunty Flora, who got sick of our Mum singing hymns to the old sod: Flora she says, "Oh, you think by going on like this you're going to get the silver teapot?" Well our mum had six fits over this, spitting mad she was. I hadn't a clue what it all meant. Still haven't. Not that I worry about it overly.

'Now I'd never really known Grampa Sam until he came to live with us, and, I'll be honest with you—sorry our Mum—I thought he was a self-centred old crab. Mum idolised him right enough, but I reckon she had no choice—worship him blindly, hear no evil and all that, or throw the old bugger on the streets. Jeff, that's him over there, he saw through Sam right away. When he moved in, the old feller tried to claim our living room for himself, telly and all, really resented any of us going in when he'd settled for the evening, but Jeff was havin none of it. "Supposed to play sardines in the kitchen, the rest of us, are we Sambo? Yeah, that's what he called him, not very PC or whachacallit, but it drove the old man nuts and Jeff just couldn't resist having a bit of fun at his expense. He's sensible Jeff, kept Mum's feet on the ground: he saw there was a difference between tolerating the old git and worshipping at his feet.'

'And the most fecund of them all was Phyllida—stop sniggering you idiot girls, I said fecund. *Eleven children, nine of them girls, and all of them by her first husband.'*

'Fecund Phyl and Potent Percy!'

'And what *a potent Percy!'*

Eileen and Kara were still laughing, leaving Francine more than a little embarrassed. Flora patted her head and smiled at her as if to give permission for her to be a latecomer to the joke.

'Oh, it was true enough. Percy may have come late to the marriage bed but he didn't half make up for lost time! After Phyl died, I'm sorry to say her sons and daughters fell out terribly, most scattered around the world now, in long-term, continent-striding Wilson sulks. Three sisters are all that remain to us—triplets no less. They will be here later and, you watch, they'll arrive together, sit together and leave together. They live miles apart, have their own lives entirely, but when they get together they revert to girlhood, there's no separating them. Linked like train-cars they'll be, but you should get and talk to them—an artist, a vicar and a college lecturer. They did well for themselves.'

'A vicar, now I remember!' chortled Eileen. 'The old man

would have had six fits and died in the first!'

'I see the Three Witches are here,' said an unpleasant, carping female voice close to Francine, but she could not tell whose. Her grandmother was guiding her to Phyllida's daughters who, as predicted, sat close and seemed disinclined to break their formation. Francine saw three red-haired ageing women with thin, nervous faces and lemur eyes who seemed to regard the gathering with timidity and not a little awe.

'Now then: Irene, Olga, Margaret, I want you to meet...'

'Francine,' said one of the three lookalikes. 'Oh we know about you, please come and sit down!'

Flora was gone, swept away by well-wishers, and Francine found herself eagerly admitted to the enclave of the three sisters. Within a short time she had changed her view of these women, turned it upside down. She was not talking to a triangle of frightened creatures nor a trio of 'witches,' but three distinct individuals who by an accident of birth happened to wear the same mask. At first the older women plied Francine with questions, but with some effort she persuaded them to speak of themselves, and then finally of the past. She found their stories, at least of Nonna. All three refused to say anything much of Sam. 'I'll tell you one thing, he helped me to reach an understanding of God,' said Irene, 'but not in the way he might have intended.'

'As for the rest of what we might say, perhaps charity demands we leave it unsaid,' added Margaret.

'Our Mum taught us not to speak ill of the dead,' finished Olga.

Very honourable, highly admirable, but no bloody help to me, thought Francine the historian.

She was far luckier on the subject of Nonna. The three girls had all adored their grandmother, and because of the size of their family and the closeness of their home to hers, had spent a great deal of their time with her.

'Practically lived with her we did, but we weren't dragged away to her like they did in the old days, we loved going there and being with her.' Olga grinned.

'She was so lovely, lively and loving,' said Irene nostalgically. 'We three being born in 1951, we knew her best when she was relatively youthful and beautiful, we feel we had the best of her. As the other grandchildren grew up the clouds were forming and the moaning and the illnesses took over, and some of the younger ones only ever knew Nonna when she was glued to that wretched chair, with sad songs, talk of death and pills and pills and pills all over the place.'

'But she was so good to us and our Mum, who couldn't have done without the help, especially when our Dad got ill and incapable. I sometimes feel guilty; it wasn't just that we had the best of Nonna, I, *we*, sometimes fear we wore her out. We worry we made her old.'

'I don't share that, sister.' Margaret shook her head at Olga, 'Nonna let her own life force go, it was her choice, just as she eventually chose to give up the ghost altogether. Nobody wore her out except herself and...' Margaret silenced herself, for her mother's sake.

'We outgrew Nonna, it has to be said, or rather as we grew up she spent more and more time with the smaller children and had less for us.'

'I take the view that we grew up but she didn't grow up with us.'

'We felt a little abandoned by her, but we never stopped loving her, we went to see her, together or separately, as often as we could. But life was calling us, all off in different directions, and we all three heeded that call. A lesson we learned from Nonna, but from her suffering and not her wisdom.'

'We never, ever fell out with her—but we had a fight on our hands when each of us decided to go to University. It wasn't done in the Wilson family, we were the first, and it certainly wasn't done by Wilson women.'

'University, what's that? A posh word for *school*. I shall never ask you how you're doing at *university*, I'll ask you "How's school?" Just so you get no funny ideas!' Irene became Nonna for a spellbinding moment.

'In my day you got to Standard Three and if you did that you was a good scholar!' griped Margaret, the next to take her grandmother's mantle. 'I can count and read and write good as any of you, so don't you put on no airs in front of *me*. "University" indeed!

'Anyway, you lot these days stay at damn school too long, educated till you're daft, that's what you are!' Olga quavered as Nonna.

A triangle of throaty laughter followed; witches' cackling, perhaps?

'There's one branch of the family that bore no fruit at all; you won't be meeting any of Petra's children, not today and not any day.' Flora reported gloomily. 'She raised those tne kids of hers with tigress fierceness, every one of them survived infancy and they all seemed to be tough, determined fighters just like

her. And yet she lived long enough to see all of them taken to the churchyard rather than the altar, the last of them just a year before her own heart gave out. You know, our Petra, more than any of us, had a right to feel abandoned by God and failed by every good angel, but she said nothing, she just wept. And I'm sorry to say that Nonna behaved appallingly over every last one of those losses, she wailed and she howled and she told everyone that the family was cursed, persecuted by that damned dark angel of hers. She wouldn't let it go, just kept on and on even though we all got angry with her. Oh she had every right to be distressed, but she should've been Petra's support, her rock, and instead she robbed her of her tragedy and turned it into her own melodrama. She could be so bad like that and yet she could never see she'd done anything wrong. Her and that overworked dark angel...'

'Are any of Aunty Helen's lot coming?' Kara was stealing chocolate chips from a cake; Flora slapped her hand.

'Ah Helen, Holy Helen of the virgin birth...'

'Mo-ther!' Eileen scolded to encourage.

'Weeell, we all know it was a close thing... but let's be fair, Helen was the most fiercely religious of all us sisters.'

*'*We *sisters.' Kara snapped, grinning evilly. Flora threw a chocolate chip at her.*

'...Of we sisters, but barring her one little slip she practised what she preached. Unlike you-know-who. Anyway, her oldest, Rachel, is coming along...'

'Oh God!' Eileen rolled her eyes. 'The Laughter Doctor!'

At first glance, Rachel was bookish and serious, and her half-moon glasses and untidy hair furthered the impression of academic gravity, but she beamed, smiled, laughed, found jokes and puns hiding everywhere.

Francine took to Rachel at once, and liked her even more when it was clear that she was not the least reluctant to be led to the past.

'Oh I always got along famously with Nonna, I was the only one to have the same fun with her as an adult as I did when I was a kiddie. I pulled her leg and made her laugh, it was what she needed, it took her out of herself. Nobody else ever thought to try it; everyone either indulged her morbid fantasies or just treated her like an irritating half-wit. They never really tried to reach out to her, not like I did. She'd made herself a stranger to laughter, it was such a shame, a tragedy. A good old giggle changed her, brought her back to life. But goodness me, I'll admit it was hard work!'

'And after the sunshine you'll get the rain—Rachel's sister Nina will be there too.'

'God, it's years since I've seen her!' said Kara, 'Eth Glum, that's what we called her! None of Rachel's chuckle-medicine ever worked on her!'

'Oh don't be horrid darling, she can't help it!'

Nina was a shadow compared to her sister; quiet, undemonstrative and disinclined to smile at all. But she was, in her fashion, friendly, and willing to talk.

'Everyone says I was a gloomy old thing even as a child, but I changed whenever I went to see Nonna. There was something about her, a magic, I don't know, there was nothing truly wrong with my childhood, with my parents or with my home, but I was only truly happy when I was with her. I always hoped that my mum and dad would send me off to live with Nonna, like they used to do to the kiddies in the old days, I thought that if they did that then everything would be alright, but…' Nina thought deeply, and her face and voice redoubled their ruefulness. 'And when Nonna lost that magic, the talent to give joy, that was the end of joy for me. Isn't that queer?'

Francine was lost for words.

Francine threaded to and fro, making herself useful to her mum, aunt and gran by fetching them plates of food and topping up their drinks as they concentrated on their diplomatic duties. Gran often protested that when too many people were talking at once, she couldn't hear individual voices, just 'one great roar', but Francine's hearing was acute and discriminating, and as she passed by bodies she picked up voices. Like the Wilson faces, these were changed by intruding outside elements, hints of accents and inflections from any number of places; someone even sounded American, though Francine couldn't tell if this was the real thing or a TV-influenced affectation. What mattered, in any case, were the words, snatches of conversation she picked up and sifted as she passed by.

'And the Lord sayeth that when two or more Wilsons are gathered in one place, Lo shall there be a bloody great fight.'

'I dunno, it all seems fairly peaceful here.'

'It's early yet.'

'Have y'seen the teeny in the red dress over there? She'll be hot stuff in a year or two, eh?'

'Don't be disgusting, she can't yet be fourteen!'

'That's what I'm *saying*…'

'See all the grey hairs in the Wilsons? That's from old Sam that is, he was white-headed by the time he was twenty-five.'

'Is it true, d'you know, that he used to cover up his grey hairs with shoe polish?'

'Oh go on, that was just one of the old lady's stories she'd tell the kids!'

'Nice to see yer—but didn't you swear by Almighty God you'd never set foot in this house again?'

'Shut up then! That was a long time ago, I overreacted...'

'Good God, a member of this family capable of admitting she's wrong! Whatever next?'

'The Wilson clan all gathered together in one place. I say lock the doors, start a fire and do the bloody world a favour.'

'I even hear that Cousin Jeanette is going to make an appearance.'

'Oh... superduper, that'll cheer everyone up...'

Cousin Jeanette did not appear old, thought Francine; well not *that* old anyway, older than Mum but nowhere near Gran's age, but she had the sour, weary look of someone who had seen too much of life. She sat alone in the least comfortable chair in the living room, radiating discontent almost as if she had attended the party solely to destroy it from within. Jeanette was Minnie's youngest daughter, and had achieved that same mirror-catch of her mother's looks that Francine had with Nonna's. 'To the life,' thought the fascinated youngster, mentally comparing the face before her with what she had seen in Gran's collection of photographs.

Francine sat on a stool at Cousin Jeanette's feet, looking up at her with no little awe, as if she were a new attendant to some liverish queen. Jeanette spent a moment studying the girl's face, a look of heavy displeasure momentarily deepening and enriching her habitual frown of disapproval.

'No need to say it is there? I've heard everyone else going on about you. Much as you might favour her, you'd best pray that her looks are all that your great-gran has passed on to you.' Her examination of Francine's features became still more myopically intense, and then she smiled a thin, self-satisfied smile. 'Are you surprised at what I say? Shocked?' she demanded peevishly. Francine shook her head, but it was impossible to tell whether or not that was the response required by this odd, unsettling woman.

'Oh I've sat here and heard them all wittering—this that and the other about *Nonna Nora*, oh she was so good with children, so loving, so caring, blah-de-blah, all spouting happy, happy memories, and all because they're too stupid or too frit to speak ill of the dead, even the long-dead. If you'll hearken to me, girl, I'll tell you something.'

Francine supplied a sharp nod as if she were bidding at auction. This woman both frightened and attracted her; she had a fierce, wildcat look with her sparkling eyes and narrow, steeply-arched brows, pointy teeth and painted red nails curved like talons. Her body was bulky and disinclined to move from her chair and yet Francine somehow envisaged Jeanette, should she be inclined, pouncing and pinioning her young audience with those long claws, holding her fast until she had been told Cousin Jeanette's version of the truth.

'Everyone says the old lady was so wonderful. Well...' for a moment Jeanette's voice wandered away as if her inner self was consulting a note or checking facts in a book; her eyes dimmed and her voice took on a slight slur as she came to and began to speak again. 'Not sssooo wonderful,' she restarted as if she had been wound up like a gramophone from Nonna's time. 'Not as far as I was concerned. I tell you she made trouble, I tell you true that trouble was her pleasure and she wasn't content until she'd stirred up everyone into a complete ferment, stirred up the ants. Ants…' she wound down again, looking about herself as if wondering where she was and how she had come there.

Her older brother passed by and handed her a drink. As if reassured by his presence she renewed her assault. 'Sssstirring, yess, sstirring. That's all she did, I can remember her plain. Our da… our dad, he refused to see her ever again after what she did… tried to spread tales about him that he was a drunk…'

'Come on now Jeannie, he *was* a drunk.' Terry stood over her, laughing lightly and catching Francine's gaze; he was dismissed with an imperious wave of the red-tipped hand.

'She made trouble. She told lies about Grampa, blackened the character of a good man. And she wasn't done making trouble when she was dead. This house…' Cousin Jeanette opened her palms, wrists pressed, as if to accept a gift, 'this house, see, she willed it to Aunt Flora, but that wasn't for love of Flora, *that* was to make trouble too.

'Aunt Flora was no better than the rest of the family, she did nothing to merit being treated like a damned favourite. My mother had a perfect right to this house but *grandmother* kept us out of it, for spite. Any of the family had right to it, or to a share, come to that, but she made sure only Flora got it. And *she* wasn't honourable enough to sell it and share the money out, she was just as bad as that old cow. As bad as her mother. As bad as her trouble-making bloody mother... And you'll be the same, I can see it in your face. Flesh and soul you're old Nora come to life, born again to plague us all...'

'Well, enough of all our yesterdays, time we were taking you home then, lady!' Terry interrupted in a jocular but firm tone, standing behind Jeanette once again with his hands placed firmly upon her shoulders as if showing his intention to silence her with his bare hands if she didn't shut up at once. Cousin Jeanette allowed herself to be removed all unprotesting: as she stepped away Francine saw the long-stewed anger melt from her face, replaced by a lost, panic that only relented when her brother placed her coat over her shoulders and steered her away.

'Well, Story'un, what sort of a day have you had?' Flora sat catching her breath almost as if she had run a marathon. Kara and Eileen were passing back and forth tidying after the surprisingly late departure of the last of the guests.

'Interesting.' Francine grinned. 'Interesting.'

Sipping on a late-night cup of tea, Flora listened to her granddaughter's encounters with the family's living ghosts. She barked with laughter at Jeanette's outbursts. 'I shouldn't laugh, she's got a point bless her. I think the business over the house was one of Nonna's games, she was deliberately setting the family at each other's throats. Her way of paying us all back for "all those terrible things you did to me". I never asked her to will me the house, I certainly can't say I did anything special for her and I most decidedly didn't devote my life to looking after her, which is what she was always angling for. But the will was her decision and that was that. I didn't see that anyone else had a stronger claim, it freed me from an awkward situation over my old marital home and I wasn't going to sell this place and share the money like they all wanted. They could have come here and enjoyed the place, it could have been the centre of the family as it was in Nonna's day, but they chose to take umbrage and stay away. Oh they came round at first, but those visits struck me as reconnaissance missions, they were measuring the rooms, putting price-tags on furniture, working out their share of the profits. Well I wasn't having that; this was the family's home, and I wanted it kept that way.'

Francine was surprised by her grandmother's resolute, steely tone. Was Cousin Jeanette right; was Gran just as selfish and manipulative as Nonna had been? And was she herself destined to be the same?

'Who were your favourites then?' Eileen flopped next to Francine, keen to dispel the scent of bitter old family battles.

'Oh you know already—you were right, it was Jeff and Uncle Barry.'

'It was all worth it for them, alone eh? They're quite a team, aren't they?'

Barry Fenton was heading for ninety; his hair was snowy-white and his face thin, pale in places and alarmingly ruddy in others, with occasional empty bags where once there had been full flesh that may, time was, have borne his high colour well. He couldn't get up without help and his physical frailty was accompanied by an air of uncertainty that increased whenever his daughters descended on him to 'check if dad's all right'. He was significantly livelier, Francine noted, when they were not there; she bided her time to seek out his recall.

Her task was made easier by the arrival at Barry's side of Jeff Clayton. Jeff was younger than Barry by some way, but there was an uplifting camaraderie between them that enlivened the older man the moment his pal took a seat. Barry's hesitancy dropped away, he took a drink proffered by Jeff and the two of them looked straight at Francine, drawing her from the edge of the room to their smiling, kindly presence.

'Miss Latimer.' Jeff raised his glass to her. 'We've been dying to meet you! We hear you're looking for the dirt on old Sambo Wilson and his straying ways—well, we're your men, we've got the goods! Siddown and pin back your ears girlie, you're in for a treat...'

The Beauty of Chell Street

1962

Nora felt a twinge in her back, but she decided to ignore it and play on; the boys would be so disappointed if she gave up now. Besides, she had put a fair old bit of work into this game; Minnie had dropped her sons off in something of a hurry and they were left with no toys, no bats or balls or anything to distract or amuse them except what Nora could whip up by applying her wits. Within moments, the boys had announced with the serious finality of little ones that they wanted to play cricket; Nora had attempted to divert them to another activity but they rapidly became fractious and so she set to work, digging out a balding tennis ball from the garden shed and, having failed to find a piece of wood of suitable size, improvising a bat by strapping two sturdy garden stakes with twine, before chalking a wicket on to the stained reddish brick of the tall garden wall.

Nonna bowled, the boys took it in turns batting. Paul, aged six, was fiercely competitive and he was far more practiced and coordinated than Ralph, not yet five years old. Ralfie was becoming competitive too, and he cried and protested when Nonna accidentally bowled him out; Nora had a job on to persuade Paul to 'let him have another go', the older boy only giving way reluctantly and sulkily when he realised there would be no game at all if his little brother was just left sitting there on the grass, bawling. Paul himself showed an almost alarming cunning; he flailed at one of Nonna's gentle under-arm pitches and the ball bobbled past the bat and on to the chalked wicket.

'Out!' cried Nonna, and Ralfie threw his arms up in celebration.

'Not out,' pronounced Paul with chutzpah to rival W. G. Grace. 'The bails have to fall off to make it proper.'

Nora gave the little smart-alec a quelling glare, but it was too late; Ralph was in tears again, squealing, 'Cheater, cheater!' It was another age before they would settle and play nicely. Paul hit the bowling far more often than did his little sibling, and cleverly pushed the ball through the air towards the small boy in the confident knowledge his brother could not catch or stop it properly; he marked his runs up on an invisible scoreboard with a wet finger, grinning as he watched Ralph clap his hands uselessly at empty air as the ball passed straight through his clumsy efforts and rolled to the edge of the small lawn.

But finally he was too clever for his own good: he patted the ball off the centre of the bat, on which the twine was beginning to unravel, intending to tease his brother with being rubbish for dropping another 'dolly,' but his aim was skewiff—the ball arced neatly in Nora's direction, she stuck out her left hand in a snap, instinctive gesture and much to her surprise it fell into the cup of her palm and her fingers closed around it. Paul looked stunned and pained as Ralph danced in triumph. The bat came apart as Paul flung it down in disgust, but Nora decided not to scold him for his pique, using that gesture as the appropriate moment to end the game. 'Do cricket champions drink lemonade?' she asked brightly—yes, cricket champions did, and they ate cake too, and the boys hurried ahead of her into the kitchen, only half-heartedly arguing over who was the *real* champion.

1969

'You haven't had a respeckful word for me since I fell ill,' Nora snapped at Minnie. 'When I came too ill to sit your kids for nowt.'

'You can't say that Mother!' Minnie was hotly outraged, but Nora remained haughtily calm.

'I say it as it's true.'

'Come on Mum,' Flora intervened. 'You've sat all our kids over the years and we've been grateful, no need to fall out over it now.'

'Funny way you lot of got of showing gratitude.' Nora was now casting herself as a tragic heroine, and her performance was too much for Minnie.

'You *wanted* the children, mother, you *asked* to have them, and you did plenty of pestering to get them too, so don't come it with me.'

'What's brought this on all of a sudden, Mum?' Flora determined that as peace was impossible, she may as well have reasons.

'I'm cashin in me cheques.' Nora announced, 'And before I go I'm going to tell the truth. About *everything*.' Satisfied with her threat, Nora let it hang in the air.

She didn't notice her daughters rolling their eyes at one another. 'Here she goes again.'

1970

'The doctor told me that for all the medicines in this world, there's nothing better than a drop of sherry. A drop of sherry does you no harm, warms you up and settles your tummy. Be a good girl and fetch me a drop will you?'

Kara hesitated; she had never handled drink before. Nonna seemed to understand.

'Get one of them little tumblers.' She pointed to the kitchen cupboard. 'And the sherry's in the front room, in the cabinet by the door. There's a good girl.'

Kara saw no reason to disobey Nonna, but as she placed the glass of brown liquid on her grandmother's small side table she couldn't help thinking her Mum would tell her off for this for some reason.

'Good girl.' Nonna smiled with a wink that told the child plainly not to say a word of this to her mother. They *were* doing something wrong.

'We only used to take sherry at Christmas.' Nonna was starting her stories again, Kara realised. 'Only at Christmas. Old Sam Wilson was too much of a skinflint to buy it any other time. Mean ole man he was.'

Kara's attention began to wander.

1979

'Mum, where's that cough medicine I bought for you last week? I put it in the cupboard here.'

Nora cleared her throat and wheezed a little. 'I've got it here—I need it. I'm not well, you know?'

'Have you got a cough now?'

'I've always got a cough.'

'You seem fine to me.'

'So much do you know.' Nora lit a cigarette and spluttered heavily. 'See?' she huffed, with a watery-eyed look at her daughter.

'That's the smoke, not a proper cough.' Helen scolded; Nora ignored her. 'I'll put the medicine away.' Helen swooped on Nora's side table, seizing the bottle and grimacing at its stickiness.

'Mother, half of this is gone.'

'Is it?' Nora sounded like one of her own grandchildren, caught in some naughtiness.

'How *bad* is that cough of yours?'

'I'm sick.' It was all Nora would say.

'I'm putting this out of your reach, Mum. If you need some, I'll give it to you.'

'Put it back here!' Nora's voice cracked in anger and then appeal.

'No Mum. I don't know what's going on but I'll deal this stuff out from now on. And I'll tell the other girls about this too.'

'What if I need it and no one's here? I won't be able to get it, I might die!'

'Nobody dies from not having cough medicine.' This madam always was too clever, and too bloody proud of herself for it too.

'Bugger up the back!' Nora scowled over her cigarette. 'You don't understand how you hurt me, you and your sisters, the way you treat me! You'll be sorry when I'm dead.'

Helen fussed around in the kitchen for a few more

minutes and asked if Nora wanted a cup of tea before she left, then swept out with a final, accusing glare at the top cupboard where she had placed the linctus. Nora pondered; she could try to make her way over, stand on a tall chair and stretch up there, perhaps just reach the bottle, she needed it. But she had heard the thing thump against the back of the cupboard, even if she could balance on the chair she could never get her hand far enough in there, Helen had made sure of that. The little cow. Bugger up the back. You could tell whose daughter *she* was. Nora stubbed out her cigarette, feeling a wave of weariness take possession of her.

'Holy knickers,' she muttered as she acquiesced to sleep. 'Two faced god-botherer.' The last of the smoke from her cigarette crept up into the air and fanned out, dissipating slowly in a blue incense trail.

The Trappers

1942

War has its privations, and for Jack and George these came in the ugly form of beer shortages. The Royal Oak had failed to open its doors for several days and the two old stagers had tried to outlast the drought without transferring their affections to any other alehouse: they were loyal to the Oak, and unlike other drinkers they were not to be found paying the local lads to scout the area to see where the drays were delivering the fags and beer.

'We're a pair o ole soaks,' pronounced George over a welcome glass of the best at his now-reopened spiritual home, 'but we're *onnerable* with it!'

'Aye,' agreed Jack. 'We only drank at the Potters Arms an the Duke o'Bridgewater.'

'But we were the last ter leave these doors an we didn't *stay* away Jack. That's what counts.'

'I'll drink to that.'

'Hey now, we anna seen Sammy for days, George. Let's make tonight a treat.'

'Sammy o'course! I got news, I got news o Sammy the preacher man! Fancy dress!'

'Beg pardon owd?'

'Fancy dress, man!' George was beaming all over his crinkly face and almost dancing a jig, as if he had been gifted a fortune and was making ready to desert his ramshackle two-up-two-down home for the country mansion that was his by right. He was the picture of delight; what on earth, wondered Jack Carthmain, was the old bugger jabbering about now?

'Fancy dress!' the old man repeated unhelpfully, stressing the 'fan' and falling heavily on the 'cy', while raising his arms as if attempting to enfold the still-uncomprehending Jack in the joke.

'I hate to be slow-witted owd, but I still haven't the foggiest...'

'Sammy Jack, Sammy! When e does is bit o readin on a Sundee! E conna do it like an ordinary bloke, no not im, as to be special dunt ee? E dresses up, Jack, Mary Peachman told me just three hour ago, e dresses up an e looks the part better than that useless wazzock o a fuckin vicar!'

'You however would never pass for a vicar ole feller, the way you cuss...'

George waved aside the compliment: he was too keen to capitalise on what he had learned about their prey and his Sabbath-day vestments.

'C'mon Jack, we got about a quarter-hour to make ready for im...'

And when Samuel Wilson, lay reader at the Parish Church of St Anselm, Woolsend, made his stiff-backed way through the pub's portals, the Trappers were fully prepared. Sam nodded curtly to all there gathered, as was his way, and summoned up his half of mild from Netta with polite words and a tight smile.

'Evenin Sammy.' Jack was affability itself.

'Carthmain.' Sam nodded.

'Yer Reverence,' muttered George.

'Mr. Shenton.' Wilson appeared not to have noticed anything out of the ordinary and he condescended to settle at the Trappers' table, where after a few minutes of inconsequential chatter he realised that Shenton was paying inordinate attention to his clothing.

'Art comfy Sammy?' enquired the old miner solicitously.

'Quite comfortable thank you.'

'You sure? I mean yer shirt fits aright and all that does it?'

'Yes.' Sam shot a quizzical look at George, as if finally convinced he had taken leave of his senses.

'That collar not botherin yer?'

'No. Should it?'

'Well, I were only wonderin, seein as it's not what yer accustomed to...'

'It is the kind of thing I wear every day. A collar is a collar, surely?' Sam's tone betrayed his conviction that the old man should be wheeled away to Bedlam, post-haste.

'Well, in the general manner o things yes, but ain't that thing a bit, well, *sharp* for yer Sammy? Not yer more usual *rounded* sort o shape?'

'This is nonsense.' Sam was fully on his guard by now.

'And what about yer at?' George pressed on, 'The mitre or whatever they call it...'

'Did he say "mitre"?' the mystified Sam appealed to Jack.

'Might'a done.' Jack began to splutter.

'And the crook Sammy, you'd look well with a crook...'

'Mr. Shenton, I...'

'Could they give thee one o them bishop pricks?'

Wilson gulped at his beer and glanced anxiously at his coat on the hat-stand.

'Sammy tell me honest now, what really happens in that there vestry?'

'I'll bid you good night.'

'No, Sammy mate, wait! Before yer go, couldst elp us with the next bloody shortage—couldst wave thee hand over a gallon o'water an turn it into best bitter?'

'Good night, gentlemen,' said Wilson with wintry dignity as he stood.

'Cost get elected Pope?' bellowed George at his departing figure. Jack had his face on the table, sobbing with laughter.

'The Bishop o Bath An Wells as gone wom.' George Shenton announced to one and all. 'Probably felt e was surplice to requirements.'

The Trappers hooted: the night's hunting had been good.

Wedding Bands

1949

Three women stood a half-pace back from the window, all with serious, sombre faces set as if watching the progress of a funeral cortege. The yellowing net curtain that swathed the broad bay window made them practically invisible, but the people they were watching knew that they were there, for the couple in question had only left the Wilsons' doorstep a few moments before. Six eyes tracked the teenage girl and her swain, who was older but barely yet one-and-twenty, as they strolled arm-in-arm along the neat, quiet avenue.

Nora clicked her tongue loudly; the sound was a heavy, gloomy precursor of evil.

'Seventeen.' she pronounced leadenly. 'Only seventeen. She knows nothing. But she'll soon find out.'

'Find out what Mum?' Petra knew Nora's meaning, but she also knew that it was the right thing to do to ask the question.

'She'll find out what men are like.' Nora, accepting her cue, continued, 'See that raincoat he's carrying? Always got that coat has Terry Cauldon, whatever the weather.'

The two figures were diminishing, and the gauzy curtain's intervention made it seem as if they were disappearing into a mist, but the coat was still plain to see, folded over the young lad's free arm. Nora shook her head slowly but then stopped; she didn't like the feeling of loose, rippling flesh in her face and neck.

'I know what he's like, all men are the same, but some of em can at least *wait*. That girl will find out that he's one as can't, and she'll find it out in Landwell Woods or somewhere of the ilk, a place where there'll be no help for her. Mary Piggott says that boy kissed her once, meant to be a polite peck it was, just to say goodbye, but he kissed her with an open mouth, that's what she said. That's the sort of man he is. Acky vee.'

Her throat clicked urgently, as if she was having trouble swallowing. Petra and Phyllida throat-clicked their own disapprobation, but they also shared a glance: Mrs. Piggott was Mona Welkins' mother, a gossip and a malicious one too, a dusty and lined seventy year old with overly-aware, prying eyes and the breath of old communion wine—surely no man would *ever*... not their men anyway, so they comforted themselves.

1920

Sam could barely contain himself; he *had* to see her naked body. It had all gone on so long—the wedding ceremony, the speeches, the glad-handing, the advice, it had all dragged on so long it was as if it was a conspiracy to deprive him of his prize. And when at last the moment came, Sam felt as if he were in a trap: he had everything he desired, everything he had yearned for but now he felt alone and inept—what to do and how to do it? Nora, by contrast, was absorbed in the business, she had waited just as impatiently and now she was indecently keen, so much so Sam couldn't help but wonder if she had done this thing before. It began, this thing he had waited for, and his heart shook his ribs and made him miss alternate breaths. Nora at first made light moanings, then she turned her head to one side with a broad smile illuminating her features, she was a gourmand at a feast. Then there came shorter, stronger, coarser grunts, and a frenzy of abandoned profanity. Where, he wondered as he thrust into her, had she learned such words?

'Fuck me Sammy, fuck me hard, hard, harder, oh Jesus Christ oh God, fuck me, God-Jesus-fuck me Sammy!'

This angel of light had the mouth of an irreligious harlot.

He had at her instigation already put his pegger into her mouth and she had manipulated it and sucked on it until he could hold back no more, and then she had drunk down his seed, declaring it to be sweeter than the finest of wines. And then she had kissed and caressed him, licking and sucking at him until he was again at full stand, then she had mounted him as if she were the man, thrusting her breasts in his face and kissing, kissing. He was being consumed by joy, by lust.

'Fuck me Sammy, oh God, *fuck!* Oh Lord this is good!'

Sam at first was too embarrassed to utter a sound, but he felt like crying out in pleasure and triumph. Nora's lips were hot and her mouth was wet, she was sweating, her breasts heaved and bounced as she ground herself hard against his body; he grasped at her hips, jamming her even tighter to himself. The heat and the pleasure went on, and yet within his soul Sam Wilson experienced a cold wave of guilt: this was wrong, wicked, could such a thing happen even between man and wife and still be anything other than sinful? These thoughts were swept away again by the thumping of hearts and twining of bodies, Nora cried out all the more and Sam found his voice as he came again, he called her vile names that made her squirm and laugh, she resorted to factory-girl filth yet again and Sam's consciousness near enough left his body, a momentary fainting as he released his burden into her. And then it was over and there was the sweaty weight of woman on him, her head resting on his chest.

'Do it to me again Sammy,' whispered the naked angel that lay upon him, sliding her hand along his thigh and then caressing his private parts, which responded though he had thought himself drained and spent. 'Do it to me again. Do it to me *forever*.'

1927

After the birth of their first child Sam had expected, almost hoped, that Nora's appetites would be curbed a little, and that her energies would be directed to the baby and her desires tamed, but if anything she became more fiercely passionate and physically abandoned. She was overwhelming, she could hold him helpless with her physical presence, transfix him, persuade him to lose himself in her and do things from which his soul should have shrunk. She had invented a language of passion and lust, she tempted, forced him again and again to use language that should not be heard outside of a barrack-room; in her burning, fleshly presence such words were not dirty and shameful, they were *right*. And more, still more of the little ones came to the world through their joining, yet Nora did not tire, nor her ardour fade.

Sam lay by his wife's side as she slept lightly, looking at her naked back. Was this what Adam saw at the dawn of time, was this shape the true and sole cause of the fall of man; was the serpent a merely incidental interloper? Oh God, but when they made love he felt such frightening emotions, his heart's boom still shook his frame and his pegger pulled him forward, bound him to her, his hands eager to touch-caress-squeeze-grab, he wanted to possess her, he wanted her so badly and she was yielding, warm and eager beneath his hands and lips, yes, it was she, the woman, who created temptation within man, she who led him to shame and destruction. It was the power she wielded over him, the way she brought him down. The woman was the destroyer of paradise.

She had even wanted him to commit the sin of Sodom: he held her, excited and fearful as he was, as she slithered against him, breathing in tight packets of gasps, pulling his foreskin up and down, urging him to do it to her, she loved him and he could do anything he wanted to her. She kissed him, moistened his hard pegger with a spitty kiss and then braced herself for the act. For a broken fragment of a second Sam wondered once again if this creature had not been sent to him by the devil of the wilderness. She groaned and then buried her head in the pillow as he pushed into her; Sam felt the grotesque pleasure of this tight encounter and the desert demon broke loose within his soul. He pushed harder and harder as he gained in confidence while Nora wailed obscene encouragement into her pillow.

Afterwards, she lay breathing softly in the semi-darkness. He could only see her profile; she appeared to be drifting off to sleep. Sam examined himself and then her, running a hand over her bare rear and, in a voice disturbingly unlike his own in its scarred huskiness, he whispered, 'You are a whore.'

Nora smiled happily; she was unmoving and her eyes stayed closed. Perhaps she believed that he was still trading in bedroom names.

For her own part, Nora had been amazed at the reality of physical love. Her mother had told her pitiably little, and the girls at the munitions works had told her a great deal too much: when a man comes off inside you, they said, the stuff is red-hot like shrapnel, and you can do naught but scream in agony. Men's privates were like tomcats', covered in tiny spikes that hook tight to your insides and they tear your flesh as they pull out, you'll yowl like a queen-cat in an alley every time. Even when she had outgrown this nonsense and learned the truth for herself, she listened with curiosity, amusement and no little self-satisfaction as neighbour-women, gathered for a cup of tea and gossip, complained how their husbands 'used' them, talking as if the whole beautiful process was a brutal, painful and unnecessary waste of their time. Nora could then only marvel at the specialness of her Sam; if he made her insides burn then it was with pleasure and not with some mythical scalding splash, and she never, never felt 'used'. If anyone was used it was him by her; there were times she had to tempt his appetite, but happily there were none too many of them.

'The sole reason I ever regret bearing your children is the time when you can't be inside me,' she would whisper to him as she fingered and tongued his earlobe. He would hush her and she would laugh. The children could not overhear them, they were downstairs and knew better than to disturb their father during his Sunday afternoon lie-downs. Sam and Nora played out this scene time after time—lustful whisper, *shhhhhh*, laughter, she would kiss him, he would breathe her in, they would be joined and reach ecstasy again. And perhaps at the end of it all another Article would then be gifted to them by their love.

2015

Kara sat at her bedroom mirror, tidying her hair with excessively violent brush strokes, pulls and twirls that should have had her wincing with pain, but she was too intent on her own angry and frightened thoughts to register the torture she was inflicting on herself. She stared hard, but her gaze bored through the mirror, drove through the solid matter of the dividing wall and into the adjoining room where her daughter was seated sculpting her own hair, probably with rather gentler hands, and certainly with an easier mind. Francine's joyful anticipation was Kara's poisonous fear, and as one sang and chirruped to herself, the other brooded and scowled.

For Christ's sake girl—no matter that you can practically reach out and touch your sixteenth birthday, you don't leave school for another year and so a girl you still are—have you any idea of what you look like? Have you any conception of the messages you're sending out about yourself, to every randy young sod, every dirty old man, every middle-aged roué out there? If you step out of the door looking like that they'll spot easy prey, the moment they set eyes on you…

'Penny for them?' the lower part of Flora appeared in the mirror behind Kara.

'Oh leave off, Mum,' was the sulky rejoinder.

'And that is what she will say to you, should you try to meddle. It's what you said to me.'

'What d'you mean?'

'Come on, you're not the first mother to go through this. She's off on a date and I know what's going through your mind—the same thoughts that went through mine those years ago when I saw you doll up for your first serious date.'

Kara, deflated, gave up on her hair and turned mournful eyes to her mother. 'How did you know?'

'Experience.' Flora sat on the edge of Kara's bed, smiling gently.

'Oh god Mum, what do I do? I want to just walk in there and lay the law down, forbid her to go. Is that terrible?'

'She'll think it is.' Flora answered evenly. 'Tell me sweetheart, have you by any chance been cooking up a fake emergency or a sudden illness to stop her going? Go on, be honest and tell me—mother to mother.'

'It crossed my mind.' Kara tried to hide her face but the mirror betrayed her and bounced the image of her shamed face over to her mother.

'There's no need to blush so; I was the same, you know. I think all of us are. Her dad would be having kittens if he were here.'

'Mum, she's so young...' Kara twisted in her dressing-chair to make a direct appeal.

'She'll be fine.'

'Girls her age are so easily bullied by boys into... you

know... and they're convinced you can't get pregnant if it's your first time...' Kara was gabbling, but Flora maintained her calm demeanour.

'Did you have no silly ideas at her age, were you told no daft tales by other girls? I cringe to think of the codswallop I believed when I was fifteen.'

'But the *clothes*, Mum, the clothes! Girls these days are wearing as little as possible below the waist, I've been fighting a running battle with her to wear something halfways decent! The way they all look, it's practically an invitation to...'

'Calm down, she's not so bad. It's all just stupid fashion, it'll pass. A while back girls seemed to be determined to reveal as much of their midriffs as possible, and what a sight they were but they thought they were *it*. I remember following three teenagers in a winter gale, they were displaying nothing more attractive than acres of wobbling flab studded with goose-pimples, but they clearly thought they were god's gift and wouldn't have been seen out of doors in any other outfits! It's all just fads, it means nothing. In my day a trim ankle was the thing to show off. It all changes, yet it's all the same.'

'How can you be so philosophical?'

'I've had the advantage of time, and I'm not in the front line this time. And I have one other thing, a gift from your grandmother—inadvertently.'

'What?'

'I had all the same thoughts as you as I watched you grow up, time after time I was tempted to grab your tail, fence you in, to forbid this, forbid that, keep you close to me by saying I was ill, or insisting *you* were ill and had to stay at home, anything to bind you to me… well, I stopped myself by thinking about Nonna.'

'Is that what she used to do?'

'It was her forte, she tried her games with each one of us. I asked myself why did she do it, was it to protect her girls and keep the family together as she always claimed, or to spoil our fun—as we thought? Tell me darling, what's your real bottom-of-the-heart reason for not wanting Francine to put on her favourite clothes and go out with her young lad?'

'I…'

'Think carefully. Nonna never did; she just followed her instincts, put her plans into action and tried to ruin everything we did. And her girls pulled away from her one by one—the more she tried to snare them, the further they fled.'

'Mum, it's so difficult…'

'I know.'

1953

No living soul could say 'ah yes' in quite the manner of which Ella Cauldon was capable. It was her response to 'good morning', her reply to 'how are you', her farewell, her retort to sharp words, her nod of understanding and her sigh of regret. Had she been a character on the Light Programme, half the listening public would be eagerly repeating her catch-phrase. It was all in all her shield against the everyday world, her sole claim to have comprehended what was said to her, even when she was patently not listening. It so happened that much, quite possibly all of the time, Ella Cauldon was not listening. Ah yes.

To Nora, those two words always soughed out of Ella's painted mouth like the groaning of a cold wind through a rickety window; the words were the distant whisper of a mind quite detached from this world, but positively uninvolved with other, higher thoughts. Ella Cauldon was a scatterbrains who owned nothing but a wilderness within her small head. On any other day this would perhaps not have troubled Nora, but today she had an urgent message to convey to the dratted woman, one that required tact and delicacy—and subtle, undivided attention. She felt like a carthorse labouring uphill dragging an intolerable burden.

'Our Flora's a frail girl; she always was.' Nora spoke loudly, as if to an idiot, and Ella nodded and smiled, a bad sign. These words had to go home, could she not settle her flighty thoughts for one split second?

'Months she's been in that place, months,' Nora pressed on. 'The doctors say she may be home in some weeks—a small miracle to be sure, for we truly thought we had lost her.'

'Ah yes,' said Ella Cauldon with such sudden gravity Nora ventured to press her case. And yet Nora feared that the wretched fool would have wheezed out those words had Nora been reporting her daughter's full recovery, or even talking of the preparations for her funeral.

'I shall have her room ready; in point of fact it is ready now.'

'Ah yes.'

'And I suppose I shall be looking after her a good while to come: it will be like having her as a little child again. I had thought she would be my comfort in old age, but now it seems I shall be attending to a cripple for the rest of my days.'

'Ah yes.'

'It is what a mother must do, no matter the sacrifice.'

'Ah yes.'

Nora had reached the crucial moment. She silently implored empty-headed Ella to listen and comprehend.

'I have to say she'll not be much of a bet for poor Terry now. It's been for the best he's stayed away from that awful sanatorium, it isn't right for a young man to be exposed to such a place, so distressing. And I'm thinking... of the future. A good strong lad like him needs a sturdy wife, I mean a robust one, a girl who can look after him *and* his children, should God bless them. The doctors say it would kill Flora if she ever tried to bear a child.'

Was Ella listening?

'Your Terry is a good lad. He deserves the best.' Nora put her thrust home.

'Ah. Yes.' Ella Cauldon's cloudy eyes were clear, if only for a moment.

And in spite of their dwelling in separate and unbridgeable worlds, the two women understood one another.

2016

Shayla's room always smelt of a heady, slightly overpowering perfume, a scent that could make you sneeze if you breathed in too deeply and got hold of too much in one go. Francine was surprised the room—big, light and airy—should retain its citric sweetness: if only a fraction of Shayla's claims were true this space should have reeked of tobacco and wine and boys' sweat and spunk, nothing sweet or innocent. Shayla was smoking, lying on her back with all but the top of her head on her bed, her long black hair spilling away and fanning on the floor. She handed the ciggie to Francine while squeezing a thoughtful stream of smoke from her dark, much-kissed lips. Francine puffed hard and tried to direct her smoke to the open window; Shayla always seemed to get away with this, but to be sure and safe she had an electric fan on full pelt and the window tilted at the widest angle to expel the fumes.

Francine and Shayla had grown up together; their mothers met at the maternity clinic and the girls had always been in one another's company. Their friendship was deep-rooted, easy and enduring; it was common for them to share secrets over a clandestine smoke. Francine knew she could turn to Shayla about anything, tell her anything no matter how shocking or embarrassing, and vice versa. It was good to have. They rarely fell out and rows never lasted in excess of a few days, but Francine felt something brewing, something new for which neither had a word, but each knew was present.

'You still doing that history thing, the one about the old people?' Shayla asked languidly as she took the fag back, almost biting at it, its red tip flaring excitedly.

'The family thing? Yeah.'

'You been doing that for years now.' That sounded almost like a complaint. 'And you been hanging around old people again, I can smell em on you.'

'It's research. You have to talk to people.'

'Research makes you smelly.'

'What, and these don't?' Francine pulled out the ciggie and waved it about.

'You can cover that, you can do it with most smells. But not with the smell of old people. My granny smelt. She was in a home for oldies and I had to go with the school choir and sing for these biddies. There was this total ronk of antiseptic and poo and piss and old blankets... and there was something else lingering, something I could never identify but I reckon it was... gangrene.'

'I smell like *that*? Ju want me to go?'

Shayla laughed as Francine made a big play of leaving in a huff.

'I'm sensitive to smells that's all, you know that. Freshly-lit ciggies, that's my favourite, that and perfume and the way boys smell close-up. You should spend more time with boys and less with biddies, you'd smell better and have more fun.'

Francine felt that unnamed, unnameable something tug at her insides and she faked a coy smile. 'Who's to say I haven't been spending time with boys?'

'Like who?' Shayla took the bait; she rolled and bounced on to her front and looked down at Francine, lying prone on the floor trying to compose a cool facial expression.

'Like Mart Payton f'rinstance. Went out with him the other day, walked up to Landwell Woods.'

Shayla's eyes flared with lascivious fire. 'What ju do there? Ju do anything? You let him...' She sighed as Francine shook. 'You should of, he's buff. Oh c'mon, so what *did* you do?'

'Snogged him, let him see a bit, have a few handfuls.'

'That *all?*'

'Sucked him off.'

'Spit or swallow?'

'Neither. I pointed it away and let him clean up his own mess.'

'You should swallow, it's good and they like it. You don't know what you're missing. You should even put some of it on your skin, spunk's good for it, gets rid of spots.'

'When have you ever had spots? And anyway, maybe I'm not missing out.' Francine couldn't say that without cracking a grin.

'God you like to be mysterious sometimes. C'mon, tell all, we always tell each other… you haven't even told me if you're still a virgin, are you? C'mon, c'mon, you're sixteen for fuck's sake.'

Francine frustrated her with a smirk as she dragged on a new cigarette.

'If you go to Landwell Woods with a boy, you're no better than you ought to be. That's what my Gran was told by her mother.'

'So are you no better than you oughtta—what's that mean, anyway?'

'It means someone like you.'

'Get out!'

'Oh c'mon, think about what you do just to say *hello* to a bloke!'

'Shuttup then!'

'Ju ever get worried about that?' Francine was reflective after a long pause. 'I mean about what people will say, about being called a slapper?'

Either the question or the smoke caught in Shayla's throat and she coughed violently, sitting up sharply but waving away help. She recovered from choking, reconsidered the question and tumbled into laughter.

'Naaaaah!' she was cheerily confident. 'If I done something with a boy I tell emif they try to drag my name through the mud I'll tell their girlfriends what they get up to—works every time. Now c'mon, are you going to see Mart Payton again?'

'Dunno.'

'Ju like him?'

'Yeah, but…' they both let the thought die.

'Would you ever get married?'

'What the fuck? How've we come to that?'

If you got pregnant or something, would you marry the bloke?'

'I'm never gonna get married,' Francine was done with teasing and games. 'I'm never gonna have children.'

'Why not?' Shayla was surprised at the undertones of anger in her friend's voice. 'Me, I'm gonna have fun then find the right bloke and away we go.'

Francine shook her head, as if that would properly arrange her pattern of thoughts.

'My great-gran got married at nineteen had eight kids.'

'How old would she be now? God, she'd *stink!*'

'Oy, does that mean you think my Gran stinks? I thought you liked her?'

'Nah, she's no stinker. She's a sort of *young* gran, she's not given up like some of em do.'

'My great-gran did.'

'After eight fucking kids who wouldn't? I'm not doin

that, I'm gonna have a sensible number.'

'No-no, she gave up after her husband left. Lived to the age of ninety but she was never happy again. Half her life. That's why I'll never get married, never have kids. I couldn't go through that.'

'It don't always happen like that.' Shayla sought to reassure, almost as if Francine was already struggling with her first broken heart.

'Gimme three examples from our friends or families where it hasn't.'

'Fair enuff. But it'll be different for you—and for me. I'll find the right guy and it'll be forever. And I'll marry in white.'

'White—with little yellow stains all up it?'

'Fuck off Francine—the Landwell Woods cocksucker!'

The serious mood broke down into a play-fight, but when order was restored Francine was solemn again, seated side-by-side with Shayla, leaning against the bed.

'Ju think you mum ever knows what you get up to?' Shayla didn't look at Francine, she sent the question off the wall.

'Don't think so. You?'

'No way—I always plan and I always cover up. She'd go spare. She thinks there's a *real* white wedding in the offing some time.'

1939

'Landwell Woods?' hissed Nora, 'What about Landwell Woods? You went there?'

Helen nodded. 'He said there were the prettiest flowers

there, all hidden away where no one goes. He knows about flowers and things like that, and the stars and engines and everything about the...' Helen shrieked as Nora's open palm caught her hard across her left cheek.

'You dirty little arab! I know what goes on in Landwell Woods!' Nora was quivering, her eyes streaming with tears of humiliation.

Shocked and stung, Helen bleated, 'But Mum I only went there to see the flowers, that's all I—all we did, he never asked me to do anything else, he even gave me a bunch of...' She screamed again as a harder blow shook her skull nearly off her neck.

'You stupid slut! And you the oldest and supposedly cleverest of my girls, the one who was brought up on the Bible! Just *going* there is enough, if anyone saw you then it's all up with you, with all of us! If Marjorie Batten or one of them others saw you and starts to whisper it about...' The storm of Nora's rage broke and she collapsed into a chair, wailing with self-pity. 'My daughter will have the name of a whore and I shan't ever be able to show my face in the Avenue, not ever again! Why are you girls so cruel to me?'

2016

'What *would* your Mum do if she knew? Drum you out the family?' Shayla asked lazily.

Francine thought. 'I reckon my Gran would be more understanding than my Mum. They'd both be upset, but Gran wouldn't be as bad. Mum must surely have had her own...'

'Landwell Woods adventures?'

'Well, yeah, but it'd be like that didn't count, she'd still half-die of shame if she knew about me. But I s'pose I'd get forgiven, eventually. Not like in my great-gran's time.'

'Did they even *have* sex then?' Shayla's lopsided mouth signalled she wasn't serious.

1944

Barry Fenton felt cold and lonely; he could stay on his feet all day at the workbench without trouble, but he now felt his legs wobbling and aching as if he had just run to the middle of town and back. Mr. Wilson sat in a big, comfortless armchair and although Barry was standing by its spindly twin, his prospective father-in-law had not indicated that he was permitted to sit. He was almost overwhelmed with a fear of falling, a dizzy nausea that competed in his aching head and drumming chest with the instinct to run; he was sure his bandy legs would serve him if only he could flee.

Helen's father had a reputation in Woolsend; those who spoke well of him called him stern, and those who spoke of him worst gave him the character of the devil, one with a cruel barbed-wire tongue. Barry could not work out how old Mr. Wilson must be; Helen was twenty-three, and so the man must have been in his middle forties at least, but were it not for the silver-white sheen of his hair this handsome, brooding, commanding man could have been any reasonable adult age, his aspect shifted from young to old almost before Barry's eyes, the only constancy among this unending change being the deep and self-regarding seriousness of his expression.

At last Wilson spoke, looking up at his visitor with an evangelist's undisguised disapproval. 'Mr. Fenton, Helen has told me about you.' One would hope she had, said a bold voice in the head of the frightened young man, but he doused that silliness with despatch. 'Tell me, what do you do to earn your living? Sit you down, by the way, sit you down.'

Barry wobbled into the chair and sank too quickly, jolting himself almost bouncing his suffering body back up to attention even though the chair was hard and springless. 'I am a toolmaker, sir, working at Rastons.'

'Rastons? Is that the factory out at Tilegate?'

'Yes sir. We make some of the parts that'll help our boys to win the…' Barry ran out of courage rather than words or breath, his interlocutor did not look impressed; did Wilson think that the youngster had just blurted out some state secret? He certainly had the look of the hanging judge. There would be no dignity, and yet no shame, in bounding up and making away, a coward tone replaced the brave voice in his head, even now; but he thought of his Helen and held his ground.

'Have you been there throughout the war?' Wilson asked, with an alarming, even pleasantness.

'No sir, I have only been there for the last year or so. Before that I was—' he hesitated.

'Army? Navy? Air Force?' Wilson offered these options as if they were cigarettes.

'The mines, sir, I was in the mines.'

The room was chill and cheerless regardless of the guttering runt of a fire, which was too far away to be of any benefit to Barry and in any case even if the house were ablaze its fury would have been doused by the cold wave of hostility that emanated from Samuel Wilson.

'A Bevin Boy?' he almost snarled. 'You were a Bevin Boy?'

'Yes sir, we was chosen,' the tortured man stammered.

'*Were* chosen,' Wilson interposed to Barry's alarm and amazement. 'We *were* chosen.'

'Yes sir, like you say, we didn't have no choice...'

'If you "didn't have no choice" then you had a choice.' Wilson cut across him again, and Barry's nerves were in tatters; he would have been unable to run for it now even if Helen had appeared, hurling the door open and begging him to save himself.

'We had no-no choice,' stammered the former Bevin Boy, 'government told us where we'd go, I'd've taken the Air Force if I'd been able to choose, 'cos of the engines, see, I like the engines, I'm interested...'

Wilson waved him to silence; somehow he seemed to be satisfied by the explanation, or perhaps his satisfaction arose from having disconcerted and routed his man in so uncompromising a fashion; that was part of old Wilson's reputation too. 'My daughter has kept you as something of a secret—from me at least—until recently, is there any reason for that?'

'No, sir, I can't think of any, other than she's very thoughtful and very cautious, she might only have mentioned me when she knew she was serious bout me rather then when we were just walking out...'

'Where did you "walk out" with her? I never heard a word about the two of you.'

'We like going out walking sir, both of us like to stretch

our legs, notwithstanding she gets a bit breathless, so we walk along the old tow paths, sometimes out to Tinsley, sometimes up in Landwell.'

'Landwell Woods?' the crystalline hostility had returned to Wilson's voice.

'Amongst other places sir, we both enjoy the sights of nature.' Wilson harrumphed, as if he were hearing the most disgusting confession. And then seemed to lose interest in where his daughter had been walking. He asked some cursory, almost desultory questions about Barry's prospects and ambitions, where he lived, and almost nothing, to the young man's surprise, about his family, and by then it seemed Mr. Wilson had, for good or ill, heard enough. Barry's judge let out a long, deep sigh and lapsed into silence, looking at the low fire and breathing with the rhythm of a man dozing off.

A prisoner on trial, a soldier at court-martial, a coward awaiting the rising sun and the steely burning of the firing-squad's bullets could not have been more frightened than Barry Fenton during the arctic silence that ensued as Sam Wilson considered the situation. Once or twice there was a sharp intake of breath as if a verdict was nigh, but then silence reclaimed the room. Eventually Wilson shook his head and stared hard at the youngster.

'I am sorry, Mr. Fenton, but I can see no merit in your marrying my daughter. Your background is scarcely what I would have hoped for in a husband for my oldest child, your war service we shall omit from mention, your current job grazes the boundaries of respectability but offers her, as far as I can see, few prospects. You may be better searching for a wife amongst the wenches at the pot banks and factories, there is certainly nothing for you here. Good day, Mr. Fenton.'

'But…'

Wilson's neck nearly broke, so quickly did he snap his head back up to stare in amazement at the young man who had seen fit to cavil at his dismissal. 'You have something more to say to me?'

'Mr. Wilson sir, I have to marry your daughter, I love her so much, you and I haven't even spoken of that…'

'I'm sure she is admired by many a young man, your ardour is irrelevant to me.' Wilson responded as if he had swallowed a bloody dictionary, but he was waxing angry, a crimson hue crowning his cheekbones. Astonished at his own audacity, Barry held the man's gaze and, shocking himself further, raised his voice and gabbled desperately, 'I have to marry your daughter sir, I love her, she loves me just as much: and in any event, she is expecting.'

Barry emerged from Sam's front room lair reeling like a toper from the tap bar on a Friday midnight and made his unsteady way to the back kitchen; he opened the door just a little, slithered round it as if he was a thief afraid of detection and found himself looking into Helen's anxious eyes.

'What happened, what did he say, I heard raised voices!' Barry, unused to any loss of composure in his clever, level-headed girl, took her by the hand and sat her down at the kitchen table, loosed a long breath and mopped his brow with the back of his hand. It was only then he realised that Helen's mother was in the room, hovering and flitting almost as anxiously as her daughter; Nora had been a staunch supporter of the match and the hopeful suitor had grown fond of her. Nora poured tea in a slightly cracked mug and put it before Barry as if tending to the sick.

'Well?' asked Nora, as Helen was struck dumb by anxiety, 'What happened?'

'He knows.' Barry looked at his intended and squeezed her hand, 'he knows, I told him. We're to get married as soon as we can. He'd nothing more to say after that.'

All three jumped slightly as the kitchen door wobbled open half-heartedly as if pushed by a sickly child; Sam Wilson was framed in the doorway, gaunt and white, the very model of a man who'd seen a ghost, and without crossing the threshold or looking at Helen and Barry he said in a low voice, 'Nora, come to the front room. You and I have things to discuss.'

2012

'Oh I remember his face, I remember it so well, pop-eyed, mouth going wah-wah like a tropical fish, as if I'd fetched him an open-hander!' Uncle Barry was a fine raconteur and he had Francine weeping with laughter; Jeff Clayton was purple-faced and half-choking even though he must have heard the story uncountable times before.

'One moment he was so composed, so bloody *complacent*, the English gentleman in his seat of power, the next he was like a broken puppet! But I never felt sorry for the old sod, not for a moment, for he'd have broken *me*, aye then jumped on the pieces, if I'd not had that little hand-grenade to drop on him! Soon as I'd told him, he shut up tight as a clam, not another word, and I had to work out for meself that my interview was over, the marriage was on and he could stick it up his weskit if he didn't like it!'

Barry broke off into hysterical whoops that sounded dangerously unhealthy for a man of his age. 'If only we could've waited another year!' he gasped, 'I could've saved myself the worry, the old bugger wouldn't even have been there!'

'A good year, 1945.' observed Jeff Clayton, 'you got shut of ole Hitler and Sambo Wilson within months of one another.'

The Articles

1936

Dr. Dyedd said nothing, but privately he feared for Mrs. Wilson's reason. He had superintended the birth himself and all had seemed well when he left the family behind, the exhausted mother taking some much-needed sleep while poor Sam Wilson tried, with the help of a neighbour, to control the noisily over-excited Wilson girls as well as her own eleven-year-old as they celebrated the long-awaited arrival of a boy. It would be Sam's turn to tumble into the rebirth of sleep before long, the Doctor had pondered to himself, looking at the man's already shadowed face. When he was called back fewer then ninety minutes later he feared he would be too late to do anything, that the tiny life had flared briefly and then snuffed itself out. But the baby was in the care of the neighbour-lady, the girls gathered around the kitchen table, silent and solemn, and Sam Wilson sitting at his wife's bedside, gripping her as much as he was holding her; there was more tension and even possibly rage in his face than tenderness or concern, as if he were angry at the poor woman for making a spectacle of herself.

Nora Wilson's eyes were reddened, swollen and aflood with tears, and her voice had pitched to a despairing howl, a bitterly off-key soprano that tore at the air with every jagged, jarring note. 'I don't want him, I don't want him!' she yelled, trying to throw her arms around her husband but unable to move properly, so rigidly did he pinion her. 'I don't want him, I don't want him!' she shrieked again, 'I don't want him!'—this time she looked at the approaching medical man rather than her husband.

Wilson loosed his grip on Nora as Doctor Dyedd took his place on the edge of the bed; the doctor caught a look in Sam Wilson's eyes, a look that neither he nor, he suspected, anyone else was accustomed to seeing; Samuel Wilson, that stern ramrod of certainty, was bemused and frightened as he flittered about behind the doctor, hovering over his shoulder as if using the other man as a shield against his own wife.

'Now then Mrs. Wilson—Nora—what on earth is all this about?' Dyedd attempted to be comforting, but the woman's eyes grew wilder at his lulling tone and she raised her fists and attempted to beat them against his chest.

'I don't want him, I don't want him, take him away from here, I never want to see him again!' The doctor was concerned by the intensity of her hysteria. 'I don't want him, he's a changeling, he's not mine, he's not ours, he's a changeling!' Her voice reached a hoarse, painful climax and then broke, shivering into silence, and although she eventually returned to her panic-stricken chant, it settled under her breath, shuddering in and out as she sucked hard at the air, as if the atmosphere in the room was dissipating into nothingness.

It took many minutes of patient, low-voiced persuasion for Nora to take something to calm her, and even as she slipped into sleep she jerked awake, cried 'I don't want him!' this time drawn-out and tearfully before she subsided into silence and deep, regular breathing. Shaken, Dr. Dyedd motioned Sam Wilson to follow him out of the room, and they padded downstairs into the front room before either spoke another word.

'She wanted to look at the baby and Mrs. Davies and young Peggy brought him to her—she—Nora—smiled, reached out, but then she prodded at the child as if he were rotten fruit, her face changed, and... *that* business began.'

'So suddenly?'

'Indeed. One moment she was triumphing at having given me a son, she'd reached out for my hand and asked me if I was proud of her, as if she'd completed some Herculean task, then next she was yelling at the woman to get the child out of her sight. I don't understand it.'

'It isn't unknown for a woman's mind to be a little... softened by childbirth, and for her to reject the baby, at least at first.'

'It's never happened before.' Wilson sulked, as if his wife invented this jape to try his patience.

'Give her time, rest, I'll come back later today. I think it best to let nature take its course for a spell; she may well have changed entirely by the time I return.'

'And if she hasn't?'

'Let's decide that if and when we need to.'

'But if she doesn't change, if she doesn't want him?'

'Let her rest. You rest, if you can. Ask your neighbour to stay and mind the children. Time may mend.'

2014

'Did it?' asked Francine.

'Oh yes, it took longer than the doctor said, but Nonna recovered, and Alex became quite her favourite—his father's too, the only one they agreed on. And competed over.'

'What was wrong with her?'

'We were never told, we had to keep our noses out of it. Postnatal depression, I suppose it was, but I have no idea if such a thing was recognised or treated back then. My sister Minnie went through it as well, she rejected her first son on sight, bellowed loud enough to demolish the hospital, just like Nonna did. I suppose it happens. Happily it never happened to me.'

'But Alex became her favourite?'

'Yes, and as usual with Nonna, she took the whole thing to excess. I think her initial distress was at the realisation that at her age, having given birth to seven children already, Alex was the last. Some of the girls were already quite grown up, she could see they were growing away from her: so she found her bond with Alex, she clung to him, became almost obsessed with him, she couldn't let go of him. Had he lived he would have been a real mummy's boy, maybe one who would never have left home, because she would never have allowed it. All of which made it so much harder for her when he died so young.'

'It must have been hard for Grampa Sam too.'

'Oh terribly, but he would never admit that, never show it to us. But I always thought that Alex's dying was as important to the ending of Mother and Father's marriage.'

'Not Mrs. Ellis?'

'No, she was symptom, not cause. There was plenty else going on between Mother and Father for a long time before Mirabelle Ellis came along, but losing Alex put the tin hat on it, at least that's what I think. In fact I sometimes think that Mum's childbed rejection of Alex was caused by her realisation of what a responsibility she now had: she had produced the Wilson son and heir, so to speak, but in a way that was the easiest part, giving birth to him. Now she had to bring him up, and bring him up to be the type of son and heir that his father demanded. And it was the realisation of that burden that caused her to turn against him at first.'

'And when she made a favourite out of him?'

'Nonna Nora couldn't reject a child, not in the end, it wasn't in her nature. But she still knew the scale of the task that faced her, and it terrified her. She had been trusted with her husband's most precious possession, and he would never forgive her if she failed to protect that child. I think she never lost the conviction that had Alex lived, so would her marriage.'

1939

'You don't care about your children!'

Sam set his face for stoic patience and answered Nora's shrill allegation with studied calm.

'I uphold the simple faith that my children are not fools, and that they will obey me.' Much as he was trying to be measured and resisting the temptation to make easy mock of his wife, Sam could taste the tang of sarcasm on his lips.

'He'll drown!' Nora yelled with as much urgency as if the imagined event was taking place.

Sam's tone hardened as he gave up the effort of trying to treat this shrieking thing as an adult. 'Are you raising your son to be an imbecile?' he demanded. 'Is he stupid enough to run from under your skirts, to flee pell-mell across the road and jump headlong into Knype Pool for no reason?'

'Sammy he's only three years old…' Nora pleaded.

'And yet he shows a deal more sense than his mother! He is old enough, woman, to understand the word "no"! He is old enough to listen to what I tell him, to know that if he answers me back I shall warm his trousers and that if he disobeys me I shall part him from his breath!'

Nora, more distressed, was crying. 'I know that if we stay in this place he'll die, I *know* it!'

Sam heaved the sigh of a man attempting, with strained patience, to achieve the impossible. 'Listen to me. That park over there has heavy iron gates and railings all around it to keep out trespassers.' His voice rose almost as if he were preaching.

'They're going to take them all away for scrap metal, for the War effort, I heard they were, what happens then? There'll be nothing to stop him…'

'Nora!' Sam, bellowed, seeing no other way to get through to her. 'Alex has been told not to cross that road, never mind go into that park alone, and he has been specifically forbidden to go near that pool. He has heard my words and by God he will *obey* me! And if he then goes and perishes through disobedience and damn foolishness it won't be for want of trying on *my* part!'

'We must leave here, we must!' she wailed, stepping towards her husband with her arms open, but he put up a stiff arm to rebuff her, leaving her gesticulating feebly as she continued to plead. 'This house is marked with death, I've seen it, I've had visions, I've got a power you know, an old gypsy woman told me I had it when I was a young girl, I…'

Sam cut her off with an impatient swipe of his hand through the air. 'Powers? Balderdash! Such things are against common sense and against God! Talk sense if you must talk at all!'

'If anyone in this house has to die then let it be me, Sammy! I swear I'll do away with myself if it'll save the little ones!'

'Be quiet you stupid woman, be quiet now!'

1942

Ole Hickler was a horrid monster who lived in a filthy-dirty cave in a cold land far away. He had awful greasy black hair and little jagged teeth like dirty, broken knives. He sat all day on the jerry because he was so dirty, and his breath was so stinky he had been made to go and live on his own. Because of this he hated everybody in the whole wide world; the only things he liked were other monsters called the Huns, who all had square heads and ate sausage all the time; there were the Germ-Huns, who were dirty like him and if you so much as looked at them you could catch their germs, and the Hairy-Huns who were covered all over with thick fur and grunted like pigs.

One day, after brooding on his jerry, Ole Hickler called the Germ-Huns and the Hairy-Huns to his cave and told them that he was fed up with living there and wanted a house of his own. Now although they were monsters, none of them wanted Ole Hickler living anywhere near them, and so they told him that they would help him find somewhere far away, providing he promised that he would never come back. They brought him a map of the world, and Ole Hickler looked at it, choosing where to build his house. In the end he pointed at a place called England and he said that was where he wanted to live.

Now England was a long way away from Hun-Land and the Germ-Huns and the Hairy-Huns were delighted that Ole Hickler should choose to go so far distant. But one Germ-Hun was a little cleverer than the rest—although none of the Huns were really very clever—and he put his hand up and told Ole Hickler that although England was a lovely place full of sunshine and sweet flowers, Ole Hickler could not live there because England was looked after by the King and Mr. Churchill, who would seize him by his greasy hair and throw him into the sea if he tried to build a house in their land.

Now Ole Hickler had a terrible temper and when he got angry he would shout loudly so that the hills would shake: when the Hun told him about the King and Mr. Churchill he became very angry indeed, and he shouted and shouted for nearly a day, and the Huns all ran and hid. After that nobody dared tell Ole Hickler he had chosen the wrong place to go, and the Huns all decided to help him to go to England, because at least he would be far away from them.

When Ole Hickler came out of his cave he was very, very hungry, and because he was such a monster he didn't eat proper food, didn't even eat the sausages and stinky rotten cabbage the Huns ate, and so he set off towards England, sitting on his jerry which the Huns carried between them, and as he went he would eat up countries, scaring the people away with his loud shouts and bad breath, and killing and eating them if they didn't run away.

Every night he and the Huns would hold what they called a Nasty Party as he chewed up his victims. He ate up the whole of the land of the Sprouts but that dish wasn't enough for him, he wanted to eat England and Englishmen. He ate up a million-million Dutch cheeses, but that dish wasn't enough for him, he wanted to eat England and Englishmen. He ate Danish pastry until he was sick, but that dish wasn't enough for him, he wanted to eat England and Englishmen. He ate up all the frogs in Frog Land, but that dish wasn't enough for him, he wanted to eat England and Englishmen.

And finally Ole Hickler and his Huns came to the sea, and he sniffed the air and cried out, 'I can smell bully beef! Put me to sea now so I may reach England as soon as possible! I want to eat England and Englishmen!' And the Huns pushed Ole Hickler out to sea on his jerry, but he did not float; instead he sank to the bottom, and when he crawled out again he was so angry that he wanted a fight. He wanted a fight so badly that he tried to pick on Uncle Joe, the Russian Bear. Uncle Joe roared and struck Ole Hickler with his great sharp claws, so hard that Ole Hickler nearly fell off his jerry.

And now Ole Hickler's days are numbered, for the whole world is against him and the King of England, Mr. Churchill and Uncle Joe and all their many friends have sworn that they will fix him, him and all his Huns. And soon Ole Hickler shall never, ever be heard of again.

1941

The sirens had again mourned the long-lost peace and the

Wilson family was gathered close. The youngest children crowded in on Nora, competing to place their heads in her lap or on her breast while their elders sat hunched and uncomfortable, unmoving almost as if they had been starched, shaped, pulled in on themselves, determined to occupy as little of this horrible cramped space as possible. There was no light and they were hemmed in by a ceiling of heavy wood and white cloth walls; the family's dining table was as good a protection as any Anderson Shelter should the windows shatter or the walls come down under the force of a blast, Sam had decreed, and so whenever the raids shattered family life, they were driven into this temple of protection, the Wilson Shelter. Sam sat cross-legged in the darkness like some little pagan god engaged in obscure, glowering meditation, disdaining the enforced company of his loved ones even though Helen was jammed up so close to him that they were practically fighting for the same air.

Sam never spoke when there was an air raid and he killed with the sharpest shush even the lightest hiss of a whisper from Nora or one of the children. Was he afraid the Germ-huns would overhear? Nora for her part could scarcely contain her fear of the invasion everyone said was coming, it seemed as if the enemy were going to sweep into Woolsend and take whatever they wanted, she wondered how Sam could fight them, what she should do with herself, what to do with the children: should they kill them to prevent them falling into Nazi hands, before Ole Hickler could do those terrible things the ladies in the Avenue talked about day in day out...

'Surely they'll never come here,' she said for comfort as they hustled the children under the outfolded leaves of the heavy old table, 'after all what would they come here for, what could they possibly *want?*' For all that Nora craved his answer, Sam never replied, but she never gave up asking the question. Nora listened fearfully for the deceptive gentleness of the whuff and fluff of parachutes descending through the air, the muffled thud of feet landing on the soft ground, the solid, unstoppable *jack-crunch* of boots, the beasts, the Hairy-Huns, closing in on the town—*their* town, *their* house. She feared that the whole family would be caught taking shelter under the dining table in the middle room and that she would be pulled out from this suddenly feeble haven by an impossibly strong, almost clawed hand, its dirty fingernails digging into her arm, its palm as cold as that of a dead man; it would be Ole Hickler himself who took her, face white with hatred and flecked with spittle from shouting and screaming at his men. What would they do to her, to her girls? Sam they would surely shoot, even though he was not a soldier, Ole Hickler would have no mercy, he made no distinctions between soldiers and civilians. The horrible things they would do to her and her little girls! There would be troops billeted in their house, lying in their beds, treating them as servants, as slaves, and demanding food and fags and god knows what other awful things. Nora remembered the things that the Huns did in The Great War; they even violated nuns, for they knew neither shame nor mercy, they had no conception of sanctity. Those the Germans left alive would have to serve as whores to their smelly soldiers. Shouldn't Sam keep a gun in the house? How else were they to defend themselves? But Nora Wilson was determined not to surrender. If those filthy foreigners threatened her children she would fight with screams and spit and fingernails, even if these were all the feeble weapons available to her.

Later, when the all-clear had sounded and everyone struggled out to straighten cramped limbs and fight pins and needles. Flora emerged from under the table stretching and yawning as carelessly as if she had been camping in a field of daisies under a protecting, loving Sun. She looked aloft, as if she could see the clearing of the sky, and her face smoothed, furrowed and smoothed again with the passage of a significant thought.

'God kept the bombs away,' she concluded sagely: Sam smiled at her and ruffled her hair. Nora felt as she did every time a raid came to an end, still filled with apprehension, the pins and needles were in her gut and gullet and they would not go away as she worried and worried, was it really over, wouldn't it be just like Ole Hickler to cheat, to sneap his enemies and come to earth to commit his beastly acts just when everyone says it's safe at last?

2014

'The story finally had an end, I'm glad to say.' Flora smiled, finishing her mother's long-ago thoughts for her, 'There was no invasion and we all lived—through the bombs anyway.'

'And the story?' Francine prompted her.

'The what?' the old lady had slipped into a momentary glazed vagueness.

'The *story*!' said Francine, in a tone that should have been accompanied by a foot stamp. 'Can you remember the end of Nonna's fairy tale?'

'Oooooh yes—let me see now, how did Nonna tell it when it was all over? The King of England, Mr. Churchill, Uncle Joe and their new friend Uncle Sam all together gave a mighty shout that sent the Germ Huns and the Hairy Huns scurrying home in fright, then together they seized Ole Hickler, toppled him from his jerry and threw him high in the air, so high and so far he fell hard back into his old, smelly cave. Ole Hickler was so angry at this terrible defeat that he stamped around his cave until he was so hot that he caught fire, and then with a mighty bang he exploded like a horrid bomb, and that was his well-deserved end.'

'That's a good story.' Francine laughed.

'Funny; we'd ask her to tell it quite often—even when we were all quite grown up. It was a comfort to hear it.'

The Beauty of Chell Street

2016

Francine had closed her curtains with meticulous care and the room became darkness without dimensions. She struck her way through this nightfall, misjudged her stride and collided with her dressing-table; her hand fell on the box of matches she'd left there and in a moment light flared in her hand and she lit the wick of a little tea-light placed in front of her mirror. The flickering, bending flame tossed her shadow playfully around the room and lent her reflection an uneven, shifting and fickle illumination. She seated herself and faced her own image framed in glass and those of two other women, framed in photographs. They were her two best friends and closest rivals, Shayla Mattu and Nora Wilson. The face of Francine Latimer danced in living light, that of Nora Wilson was locked in a tiny, time-dulled scrap of paper, and Shayla's shifted and altered as the images changed in a digital frame.

Francine gave herself a coolly serious appraisal: her eyes, cheeks, neck. Her features had at last achieved the sculpted elegance she had craved; the little packets of fat she had been storing against her will gone, and she was free—free as anyone could be—of the spots, blackheads, whiteheads, blemishes and other imperfections that had caused her embarrassment and frustration for so long. Yes, without the aid of an airbrush or dishonest pixel-twiddling, this was as good a face as anyone could expect, a real living woman, not some characterless android from the glossy mags, not some polymerised illusion. She examined herself as if for a self-portrait, she held her own breasts like a man might do if he were embracing her from behind. Oh, she knew she was desirable, there had been enough ogling eyes and shouts and wolf-whistles in her direction lately, she used to find such things alarming but now she took them in her stride, almost as if they were her due. She knew that men young and old were looking at her; even when she was with a gaggle of friends she sensed that the male gazes were passing through the others and they were seeking out, centring upon her.

The pictures of Shayla continued to shift in their frame. In most of them she was bathed in natural brilliance, she was beaming, shouting, laughing, but Francine locked the frame when the shadow picture came up. In this Shayla was at rest, calm and serious, but for the nascence of a wicked grin; her olive skin-tones blended with a dark background. In this picture, Shayla Mattu was nothing less than a goddess. Whenever she listened too closely to flattery, whenever she started to call herself the most beautiful woman who ever… she looked at this picture, and the century-old portrait that stood with it. Francine Latimer was beautiful, but her good looks failed alongside these women, one living and one long dead.

Francine and her mirror-other smiled broadly, counterpointing the seriousness of Nora and Shayla. Her hands moved with celerity but care; twirling, pushing, patting and pinning, sculpting her hair. It was hard work, it would have been useful to have someone there to help her with the task, but they would have interfered and asked stupid questions, she had no time for that. Taking artist's glances at the photograph of the young Nora, Francine was modelling her hair as closely as she could on the complicated loops and twirls belonging to the woman in the picture.

When her attention returned from the fixed image to her own face, Francine could not suppress a shudder: there was vanishingly little difference now between the living woman at the mirror and the dead one preserved in captured light and half-lost stories.

'To the life!' she whispered to herself, and her nerves strummed again. It was as if she had opened some mystical door and the past had emerged to swallow the now, as if Francine Latimer had surrendered her existence so that Nora Wilson could live again.

'You talk too much about that ole lady. And when you're not doing that you're thinking about her, I know you are.'

Shayla had accused her without malice or rancour, but Francine had felt an upsurge of annoyance, a desire to slap down this stupid-headed suggestion.

'Too much her and too little you, like. It's a bad idea. You're becoming her ghost.'

Francine could no longer contain herself, and the row that followed was as short as it was unexpected and as bitter as it was brief; it spread a poison-cloud over their friendship that took days to die down. There had been a great deal of unexplained tension between them lately, 'needle', Shayla called it, silly mutual antagonism arising from nowhere. Neither of them could understand it, nor articulate its cause, much less stop it. It just—happened.

Francine looked at herself again: she felt no ghostly presence, no otherworldly compulsions, and there were no ectoplasmic, supernatural fingers attempting to shape her face, still less steal it. It was all just stupid, stupid fancy. What she was doing was just a laugh, a little experiment; one shake of the head, a hail of pins and a flurry of loose locks, and all spooks are exorcised. So not a very powerful ghost then, and not the least bit scary. Shayla could be such an idiot.

She and Shayla had been talking a lot about boys lately, which increasingly meant talking about sex. Time was, Francine would simply sit and listen as her friend spilled the beans about 'my latest whorings', but things had changed, Francine had her own adventures to disclose, about Mart Payton especially, and her coy confessional tone had soon been superseded by one of firm confidence. Francine noticed that as her confirmed experience grew, so Shayla's love life became ever more complicated and spectacular. The cow, she was keeping ahead, it was becoming a competition. Shayla was different from all the other young women in Francine's circle; she was utterly unafraid of the opposite sex, evincing no girlish awe of men. She was always the one in control, and blokes were there for her disposal and amusement.

'Check me out, I'm a Maaaaaaaaaaaaaaan Traaaaaap!' she carolled; that song was tearing up dance-floors and passing round the college like a kissing-disease. She shook and gyrated, running her hands lovingly over her own body then stopped in a frozen pose, as if making a present of herself to Francine.

'There's power in here, child. But it's like electric. Handle it properly or it'll kill you.'

'You should think of the future and not so much about

the past.'

This was the other subject Shayla couldn't leave alone.

'Who says I don't?' Francine's gorge was already rising.

'Oh come on. You're positively fucking backward, your head's in the past. Get out in the woods with that buff bloke and forget all the stinking old stuff.'

That triggered another row; Shayla was wrong. Again. Start to finish. Even here at the mirror, thought Francine, I'm in the presence of the past, but my mind's on what's to come, not what's gone. She thought about Mart: if he invites me for another 'walk in the woods', what do I do? Perhaps I should do what Nonna would tell me, refuse, send him away, he's just a typical man, he wants just one thing and I'll get a slut's reputation. God knows what he tells his mates. But fucking hell I want him, and I want him to want me, and if I lose control I'll let him strip me naked and lay me down and reputations and rumours and old-fashioned morals can go to hell, I want today's pleasures, now. I've got a gift and I should use it before it's too late.

She caressed herself again, the way Mart should have done but he got too excited and fumbly and in his excessive eagerness he could hurt her with his big hands. Maybe I should not share it with Mart Payton, maybe an older man with a surer touch. Maybe I should try to find a good man, like Mum and Gran would want me to, fall in love, forget what I've said before and get married, have kids, defy the Wilson curse. If I have kids, at least there'll be someone who will carry the stories forward once I'm gone.

Oh, but you are beautiful, girl; it was as if the mirror was encouraging her. Wasn't that the sort of thing mirrors were supposed to do? She cast a glance at Nora, then

Shayla, who were framed as if caged, and her self-confidence grew. I'm not done improving yet, I'll be prettier still and outdo you both—one of you is dead and the other, well, she's getting past her sell-by-date I reckon. I can be greater than either of you, both of you. I have the gift, the only question is how best to share it. I should have a portrait done, she thought, I should be painted and I should pose nude. God. Girls were doing that all the time and from time immemorial, it was nothing new, all that changes is how it is done. For art, for the papers, for magazines both glossy and grotty, slutting it on the internet, there are thousands doing it; millions. But I can blow them all away. I want to be seen and people are entitled to see me.

And I won't have to run after some stupid bloke and break my heart over him. Not with this face. And I'm no Nonna Nora, I'm cleverer. The men will come to me and offer themselves up; all I have to do is choose well. *There's* power for you Shayla Mattu, that's what I'll say as she trails off in her stained white dress. I don't need to pass exams, I don't need College, I don't need University, no matter how much Gran and Mum nag me to go. I've got all I'll ever need: what could go wrong? What matters is beauty. Beauty is earthly power, Beauty can outlive eternity.

There was a sound of movement in the house; Francine flushed hot red, burning all over as if her mother had caught her posing bareskin in the eye of some lecherous camera. God, what was she thinking? All that stuff in her head: if I did it it'd kill Gran off for sure, probably Mum too. She dressed hastily, her good sense returning almost as if her mother had delivered fresh supplies in bulging shopping bags. It was all crazy thoughts, vanity. *Whooof*, out went the candle-flame, the curtains were swept open, window wide letting in fresh air. What for, Francine scolded herself, do I want to be some passive bimbo, some dumb eye-candy? I can do better, better by far. I've made a mess and a waste of things so far, but I can do better. I'm not like Shayla, not just some leg-spreading tart. I can have what none of the women in my family had; but it won't come just through the power of beauty. Beauty fades, dies. Nonna never thought it would. But it did.

2013

'I was thirteen years old when our Dad left. I thought it had killed Mum. My sisters got me out of the way speedily enough, but I was there the day he left and nothing could shield me from that. Dad had gone, never to return, and Mum took to her bed, once she'd worn herself out sitting up day and night waiting for him to come back and say he was sorry and that he loved her. It's all a bit of a blur now but I remember being bundled off to one of Mum's relatives who ran a farm, then returning like an evacuee at the end of a war. Helen and Minnie sat me down and told me Mum was ill, that I wasn't to expect her to be like her old self and that I wasn't to bother her. Worse, when Helen and Phylly weren't about, Minnie told me Mum had "aged overnight", "a shadow of herself, a ghost". I damn near broke my heart over it and demanded to see her, yelling that they shouldn't keep me away from her. So much for me not being a bother.

'Well I burst out crying again when Phylly took me to

Mum's room; she was pale in the face and she'd clearly been crying again, but she was the same, so warm, so loving. She held me close and took away all that desolate hopelessness our Minnie had managed to plant in me. I sat with her as she did her hair, and yes I could see streaks of grey that intruded since Dad went away, but she teased them out and sang "Silver Threads Among The Gold" as she did. My sisters, I resolved, had been dead wrong. Mum was alive, and as young and beautiful as she'd ever been. She remained young even when all the women her own age were lined, withered and shrivelled. She didn't seem to age, hardly a day. But this miracle couldn't last; she eventually slipped into a truncated middle age and by and by was much the same as the rest of them—petulant, sad and ill. Mum always said it was "that bloody man" who'd done it, but it wasn't him alone. I think the decline set in when she gave herself up to the neighbouring.'

'What?' asked Francine.

'Something people, women, did in those days. Dropping in on the other ladies in the avenue for a cup of tea and a chat; it could have, should have been a comforting, friendly thing to do, but there was poison lurking in it, these old biddies coming through the back door without knocking, and usually with a horrible, shrill cry of *Yoo-Hoo!*'

'How did they get in? Weren't the doors locked?'

'Goodness me no, girl, not in those days. It's taken decades of progress to shut us in behind electronic locks and video-spyholes. Mind you, there'd been some way of keeping that creepy gang away from our home. Dad wouldn't let them near when he was there and they knew better than to try; but once he'd taken his hook they were quick enough to come "sympathise". *Yoo-Hoo!*'

1946

Mrs. Saviour's house was a mausoleum, quiet, still and dark, but for the kitchen where she and the other ladies sat sipping tea and chattering. Flora had thought her own home dingy and cheerless, but at home there was at least life and noise and an enlivening family spirit: here only the gloom thrived. She had wandered from the gathering in the kitchen, and nobody had noticed. She had intended to explore a little, but was restrained by a blood-pulse of fear and the feeling that here was the last resting place of dead air, dead light and dead things. The house was not dirty so much as exhausted, expiring, and Flora feared something would sap her vitality, as it apparently had that of dusty, rumpled Mrs. Saviour. Flora had intended to find and use the WC, but the little brick outhouse was too forbidding, it was bitter chill and filled with unfriendly shadows; she would have to wait until her mother agreed to go home, for although home was a mere few doors away, Nora forbade her to return alone. Voices from the kitchen, keen and piercing, reached her ears as she padded cautiously around the downstairs rooms; Mrs. Saviour lived here with her husband, but there were rooms enough for a Wilson family and a half. Flora peeped round the door of one vast, slumbering space, but saw nothing but a near-void, a chair swaddled in dust-sheets and a birdcage on a tall stand, untenanted and soundless.

Flora had wondered why Mrs. Saviour and her friends

had headed straight for the kitchen when there was so much available space in this place, but a short adventure inside the front parlour, surely the natural gathering-point of the house, was sufficient to settle the matter. It was dingier than any of the other rooms. It took a short while for Flora to make out shapes within the artificial, curtained night that hung eternally within these four walls. At first there appeared to be living creatures, great lumpen beasts slumbering in the unbearable darkness; Flora froze, affrighted, but gradually her eyes adjusted and she made out the shapes of tables, settees, armchairs, dining chairs, but not ranged in placid groups around the fireplace or the window to catch the morning's light. They were piled higgledy-piggledy, some chairs in dizzying stacks that would surely tumble if touched, some of the bigger pieces mounted awkwardly on each other's backs like animals rutting on the farm thought the girl with a burning in her cheeks. There was something piled uneasily and crazily on practically everything else, as if the contents of the house were performing acrobatics. Through the curtain-stifled windows came an unrelenting gust of cold air, which sometimes stirred itself into small swirls that lifted up a smell of neglect and stirred it further into the room's musty air. Intimidated and puzzled, Flora stepped backwards over the threshold to the safety and relative brightness of the hallway, keeping an eye on the unstirring gloom lest something leap out to attack.

Mrs. Saviour's house was by far the worst, but in recent months Flora had been dragged around the homes of all the ladies in the Avenue, and it had been a seemingly unending succession of cold, dark, oversized houses that echoed with the absence of children's voices, dead husbands' footsteps, the barks and yelps of family pets long since gone. Sometimes she had been obliged to sit with the women gathered in a gang as they were today, sometimes she and her mother attended on lone, lonely old ladies propped up in their beds or whose fragile bones were wrapped in antique shawls, struggling in and out of hard and nasty chairs, trying to bear along a tea-tray and behave like a hostess when they had scarce energy to draw breath, never mind wait on visitors. But everywhere they went the conversation, as well as the tone in which it was held, was the same. Sad and bitter tales of tragic deaths or marriages gone awry; hand-me-down sagas of family rows and village vendettas that had their origins deep in the last century when even the oldest of the gossips was unborn; doomed romances and convoluted intrigues. But the favourite topic of every one of them was the iniquities of over-sexed youngsters, or even better the fall of their self-righteous elders.

The ladies were still in session in the kitchen, sipping tea from floral-patterned cups, massaging fruit cake in their busy jaws and spraying crumbs and secrets, some fresh, some stale. 'Satan's Harpies' Samuel Wilson labelled them, and that he had done so to his wife's face in the presence of their children was the measure of his contempt. Their mode of reference to themselves as a body was the delicate 'We Ladies'. Flora had her own name: 'The Tut-Tut Club'.

The lady of the house was not sitting at the head of the solid, oblong table; she had ceded pride of place to Marjorie Batten, the group's mutely-acknowledged leader.

Mrs. Batten occupied a good deal of space; she would never have fitted in the cluttered front parlour, thought Flora, although her size and shape matched the occupants of that room. Her mouth was a red, bowed smirk that glowed eerily against her china-white face and horribly against her yellowed, shark-like teeth. To Flora, this woman typified age and decay, and yet there was a defiant, undying cruelty in her brilliant eyes, and her ever-raised eyebrows communicated her disdain for the failings and foibles of the world. She was talking with lip-smacking delight, leading the group in their ritual.

'Betty Middleton and Celia Whitrow, husbands away on business, and what do they do but go jittering and bugging at the palais de danse. *Married women,*' Mrs. Batten heaved both her breath and breasts, her rolling eyes signalling disgust. 'Yes, off they trot to the Adulte—or should I say the *Adultery?*'

A quiet schoolgirl giggle fluttered around the room.

'They say they just wanted taking out of themselves, but we ladies know better, I rather think.'

Tut-tut-tut-tut-tut!

Mrs. Saviour, keen as a terrier and rather resembling one, sat at Mrs. Batten's elbow, taking as high a place as she could while still deferring to the Club's boss. At a benign nod from her chief she offered her titbit to the table.

'Has anyone spied Jeannie Moffat lately? Remember how our hearts went out to her when her Ian went away to serve in Palestine and she wept a torrent? Near broke my heart never mind her own, so she did; I feared she'd not live for him to come back and marry her, but she seems to have recovered her spirits—a little too well, one might say. I saw her just this Monday, parading around like the Queen of the May, all bright smiles and new clothes, nothing but the gayest of colours. Where's she get them from, eh, and what's she got to grin about so much while that poor boy's hundreds of miles away from her?'

Tut-tut-tut-tut-tut!

Next to take up the baton was Miss Dean. She was six feet and even had she been a foot shorter she would have been painfully thin. She had perpetually feverish eyes set in her perished face, and smelt to Flora of mothballs and damp. Miss Dean had, reputedly, been disappointed in love many years before, so long ago the truth of the tale had been lost. She sported a tragic, hurt look, thought Flora, who wondered how such a half-remembered heartbreak could fuel this woman's ever-ready malice and plain enjoyment of the suffering of others.

'I had a chat to Bertha Orme the other day,' she began lightly as if discussing the weather, 'her Edith is to go on a boat trip next week, come over terrible poorly says Bertha, needs to go away for the sake of her nerves. Well, I never said a tittle to her but *really*. Nerves! Anyone who's been watching the swell of that girl's belly knows that it isn't nerves troubling her!'

Tut-tut-tut-tut-tut—huff! The last was the signature sound of Mrs. Saviour's imagination discharging sewage.

Mrs. Critchwell was appallingly over-eager to have her say; she had a better tale to tell, but she knew she must wait her turn. She was a relatively new addition to this circle, a pleasant-looking woman with greying hair, but also greying skin and a little moustache that darkened as she faded, and that she seemed bent on demonstrating to all via her habit of running her finger along it as if massaging her mouth in preparation to speak.

'Perhaps it's little wonder some of the flock are straying, for I have to tell that their shepherd may hardly be any better. Now I make a point of dropping in on old Mrs. Peace, she's sinking fast poor soul, she knows it too, and she's been waiting for that wretch from St. Anselm's to show his face and offer her a little of God's comfort, but he comes but rarely and seems keen to dash as soon as he's muttered a few words snatched at random from a child's Bible.

'I contrast this shocking state of affairs with his *assiduous* attention to young Martha Hopkins, whose husband skipped so sudden with his boss's takings—you know of that of course—where our vicar cannot bring himself to cool the brow of a dying woman, he has bags of time to lavish on a young and pretty parishioner, who though she is to be pitied is scarcely in danger of losing either her life or soul! It's a scandalous shame, and not the first time there's been high-jinks at that church!'

The assembly tut-tutted dutifully, but sensitive Flora realised at once that some of their disapprobation was reserved for the tale-teller herself. Mrs. Critchwell had offended, Flora fancied, on a multitude of counts. Her little vignette of sin and debauchery was more exciting, more appalling, more authoritative and credible than those of the other ladies. All in all, Mrs. Critchwell had forgotten her place; it was not for her to outshine her new friends, and it was simply the poorest form that she should eclipse Marjorie Batten.

To Flora's relief, the one woman who had nothing to say

for herself was Nora Wilson. A real newcomer to this gathering, she was not required to do anything but nibble, sip and tut as the situation required. The child shot her mother a longing, pleading glance—can we not go yet? But Nora was accepting more tea, her face filled with sour enjoyment as Mrs. Batten led the table once again, broadcasting local scandals to her hushed, attentive audience.

2013

Rapt in her remembering, Flora tutted and clicked her own disapprobation and age-old sorrow.

'A group of very, very lonely and unhappy women,' she murmured, 'with nothing truly in common but the emptiness of their lives. All of them looking to get horrid thrills, a kick from the scandal-drug. I complained bitterly about being dragged along, but Mum never listened. I hoped she'd end up as bored with these women, as sick of their tiny world and tinier minds, but to my horror she thrived on their bile, blossomed once again, grew brighter and cheerier than she had been since Dad left; she even put on a little weight and regained that lovely youthful roundness in her face. She seemed younger and more beautiful than ever. But then again, perhaps that was only by contrast with her chosen company.

'And of course it showed, it had to. To forget her own sorrows, she cracked her face at the misfortunes and misdeeds of others, and those cracks stayed. The wind changed and she got stuck like that. Lingering with that gang of hags was her initiation into old age. Sad decline.'

The Book of Fire

1944

'I know what you do with that woman!'

'You know nothing of the sort; truly my dear you know nothing. How many times, Nora? I tell you we sit together in tranquillity, we read the Bible and then we discuss its meaning, its relevance to our existence and the guidance it offers. The rest is simply your imagination.'

'We could do that Sammy, read and talk together, what for d'you need *her*?'

'I explain the Good Book to you, Nora. I discuss it with Mrs. Ellis. There is a plain difference.'

'I know a sight more about that dratted book than you'd credit, Sam Wilson! I know that what you get up to is forbidden in every verse and line!'

Sam rolled his eyes. He had tried, truly, to communicate to his wife the longing he felt, his profound spiritual need, but she had evinced no understanding: there was scarcely a whit of the spiritual about this fleshly woman.

'I ought to tell that precious vicar of yours about your shenanigans!'

'Perhaps you should. He is after all a man of God, and witness to my absolute innocence.'

'I know what a so-called man of God can stoop to an all!' Nora slunk, almost shuffled, away, round-shouldered, deflated and defeated.

1947

I am a moral woman. I have more claim to that title than do some. I was taught what was right and wrong and heeded my lessons, so I did. I fell in love, so wildly in love, and yet I waited till I was wed before I surrendered my inner secrets, yes. Not that I was without desire, not without the urge to give myself to my lover before the bond between us could be sanctified, but I controlled my mind and body and behaved as I'd been told. But what is this morality they preach, this queer scheme to which Sam Wilson tethers his soul? Commandments that can be slithered round by use of his quick, clever tongue. Talks as his belly guides him, that man, always did. If morality springs from that book of his then Sam Wilson is one of the damned, so he is. If morals come from the human spirit he's still a sinner. He cannot escape, no, not that way.

Is 'morality' Sammy Wilson bellowing and booming because his eldest girl has got with child before a slip of cheap gold can sheathe her finger? Then morality is a footling fart of a thing. Our Helen and her Barry, they love each other and what does it matter whether they're wed or not? Their babies will grow up healthy and happy and loved, what else matters? Is morality to preach from the lectern and then sin without shame once without the church's doors? Then morality is a dead thing, dead and rotten.

I know what *immorality* is. It is a worm in the guts of a man who'd spurn his wedded wife and his begotten babies. An old dry-bones who'd take his own pleasure but deny the same to others. He can talk morals—parrot them more like—but practice them? Pish! What wickedness there must be in such a soul, touched by evil, yes, from when he first saw the day's light!

1910

'You must learn the love of God, Samuel, aye, and the fear of him too. It is the beginning of wisdom.'

Sam said nothing, but it was not the Almighty who stirred his fears. It was not, after all, Our Father who came into the room without warning, bearing a stout stick to punish thoughts not had, deeds neither committed nor contemplated, sins the nature of which he could not even conceive, purposeless wickedness of which he was surely not guilty. No, it was his Aunt Laura who would intrude even into his quietest moments with a fevered eye and a deep-furrowed brow, speaking an ancient, incomprehensible language of accusation and retribution before bending his body like a sapling to receive divine punishment.

'Boy, be quiet!' she would bellow. She was an Israelite in battle; her sword, her armour, her limbs and her face were bespattered with the sacrificial blood of the twenty-thousand slain at Gidom. She smote with the edge of the sword—the men, the beasts and everything that came to hand—she sought revenge against the Midianites and would never commit trespass against her Lord by saving anyone alive: oh obedient, she would kill every male among the little ones, every woman who had known a man by lying with him. For she lived in accordance with what the

Lord her God commanded.

Sam Wilson could never, in his thoughts, conjure the face of the Almighty. The only features he could see amongst the high hosts of heaven were those not of a redeemer but a destroyer, not a fatherly man but an enraged, turbulent woman. Even later, in his manhood years, his tranquil contemplations of the divine could be shattered by a noise or movement within the house; the crash of a door would make him jolt with a spasmodic echo of antique violence. Without volition, he would fearfully scan his surroundings to see if she was there, rod in hand, the angel of wrath who had arrogated the Lord's face and form.

1912

Aunt Laura sat beside Sam as he exerted himself to stop weeping; he was attempting to drag the tears back inside himself with huge, painful sniffs that made him curve his back with effort. She sat close, far more intimately than she had ever done in his life, her arm extended as if to encompass his shivering shoulders and yet nowhere was she touching him. His aunt sat patiently beside him until he was completely still and quiet.

'It is very difficult to divine what is decreed for us Samuel. It is hard to see what is intended for our lives. And as that is the case when man tries to read God's plans for him, so it is when a child tries to understand what is in the minds of his elders and betters. What may appear to be harshness may in the fullness of time reveal its true nature—as kindness. Blow.'

With a conjurer's suddenness she pressed a handkerchief to his nose. He blew.

'There. Now go away and read; sit alone and read The Book. It will help you. Then we shall take some supper. Yes?'

He nodded obediently; an empty, meaningless bob of the head.

Sam sought out his dark old Bible and opened it with a careless flick of the wrist that was the sole outward sign of the corrosive, insubordinate rage that had taken possession of his soul. He flicked the pages over and over as if wishing to tear them, but perhaps hoping faintly to happen on a piece of text, *the* piece of text that could bring him comfort, relieve him—deliver him. It was in the book, he was certain, and yet it avoided his wet, reddened eyes. How she had yelled, what unnatural strength she had shown!

'There isn't an ounce of you that the Lord would save! Show me one occasion when an unrepentant sinner did not feel the wrath of the Almighty!' Her cries were louder than his own shrieks as she beat him without mercy: she was a fury, a demon. Yes, a demon. It was no blasphemy to offer his prayer.

'Make it stop, Lord.' Sam Wilson sobbed a whisper. 'Protect me, protect me and save me. Take her God, kill her. I want her to die.'

1937

Dressed in uncomfortable mourning attire, Sam nevertheless felt a lightness of spirit such that he could barely refrain from smiling. It took effort for him to behave as he knew he should—he realised he was almost dissembling—and to accept the sincere sorrows and good-hearted pieties tossed in his direction like change into a collection plate, the tribute of the believers who were at a loss to know what else to do.

'She was a good Christian.'

'She was strong in herself, and in her belief.'

'She held this church up as surely as the stoutest wall.'

'Thank you,' he answered each, gravely.

And yet his mood continued joyful and triumphant. Today was the day of his freedom, the day he could throw off his past. She was gone, there was to be no more Book of Fire; and he craved to bury along with her the memory of a tear-stained child praying impiously for divine vengeance against that Bible-dark old lady. There, boy, you have your wish, wicked as it was. Can you be satisfied now?

And to crown his joy, today was when he regained his daughter; Helen was coming home. The girl, sixteen years old now, blossoming and handsome, stood by his side and received the commiserations of the parishioners with a gravity and composure that impressed Sam: not a tear had escaped her eyes during the service, and not even when the tiny wooden boat of a coffin had finally sunk out of sight. Once the black-dress observances were done, Helen packed her bags and prepared to exchange the place that had been home to her since infancy for a house that had never been her home. And still she betrayed nothing of her feelings, if indeed she felt anything at all. Helen had found Aunt Laura slumped across her bed, face-down as if she had flopped there at the end of an orgy of secret, overpowering sin. She was not yet dead but she could barely stir, and one side of her face was puckered and immobile as if it had sustained a terrible blow. Her breathing was shallow and she understood not a word said to her; in the time it took for Sam to receive word and make the train journey, divine mercy had relieved the old woman's sufferings and only Helen awaited him, her face unchanged from its customary prim, serious set.

There was little said between father and daughter on the way home. Helen sat opposite Sam and the scene was a mirror's image of that long-ago journey, the silent infant who had been delivered to her great aunt with the howls of her mother still resounding in her ears was now making the return journey in the same equable silence. Sam spent the journey in a furtive study of his rescued child; furtive because her expression, close, closed and sober, forbade intrusions, and reminded him unpleasantly of the woman they had left behind in her grave.

It had been Sam's duty and labour to shape the minds and manners of his children, not least to compensate for their over-indulgent mother's tendency to spoil them, and he flattered himself he had done as good a job as could any man. But this child, who was now so near to womanhood, had been the work of another and, in spite of his visits to her over the years, he did not know her. Here is a deep one, Sam mused: how he wished to quiz and test her—what are you girl, what has been forged out of you these dozen years? Has your young life been as mine, were you treated as I? Has that barren creature that never bore a child of her own made of you what she tried to make of me? Did she count you as one of the blessed or damned? Looking into Helen's dry, cold eyes, Sam could not suppress a shudder.

'You are not just some Tom, Dick or Harry, you are one of a *better* breed, a member of one of the best sorts of family, and that makes you special, privileged. But it also means you have duties as well. You must be worthy of your station in life.' Had Helen heard these words? And were they accompanied by a loving touch or the whistle and burning pain of a stout stick? Aloof, tight-lipped, stern of face, haughty of bearing and unswaying in her piety, Helen seemed to have become Aunt Laura's ideal, a polished and perfected Wilson, purged of her father's defects and of the consequences of his commingling with inferior blood. Even the simple manner in which she wore her hair and her plain, no, antique manner of dress marked the girl as the product of that hymn-roarer, that vile wilderness prophet of a woman.

When Sam dared venture a sequel to that brief examination of his child, the prospect before him had changed somehow. He saw now how youthful and soft was her small face, there was a sweetness of countenance that she had inherited from Nora, a loveliness that could not be suppressed with sermons and that should be made complete with a smile; he yearned for the girl to put aside her puritan garb and adopt some gay, girlish colours while youth remained in her. Perhaps her return to her true family would summon up a new force of life within her.

'Your mother is very much looking forward to seeing you,' Sam ventured, awkwardly.

Helen inclined her head; expressing agreement, acquiescence, without joy or sorrow.

'And your sisters and little brother, they are all in a ferment; I shall struggle to control them, I'm sure.'

If there was a change in her expression, it was to admit of distaste, but Helen quickly mastered herself and her face resumed its inscrutable calm. In spite of his ache to speak to her and hear her reply, in spite of the many questions he longed to hear answered, Sam did not attempt conversation again, and not another word was said until the train reached its destination.

Gathering the Family

1939

'Oh thank you Sammy, this is wonderful darling, thank you, thank you! Oh you *do* look after us don't you!'

Nora was as intemperate in her gratitude as she had been in her relentless pestering to move from their previous home; she had sighted this house and learned it was for rent, and from that moment set her heart upon it almost as if it were promised to her by God. She swept towards the door, the lady of the manor taking possession of the ancestral home, thought Sam dourly, but then spun, twirling like a child at play, pirouetting neatly into his arms.

'Sam, Sammy, it's lovely, this is our home, this is where we shall spend the rest of our lives, I just know it.'

She slipped forward and surprised him with a kiss, mouth to mouth, her tongue alive and wet, a bedroom kiss full of lust hot as raw spirits: Sam had to push her away, the children were watching, the little ones laughing, but he could see a look of disgust haunting Helen's ethereal features, and Minnie had flushed up like a beacon. Could Nora never behave in a seemly way?

'Will you give me some peace?' Sam had intended to sound gruffly fond of his wife as he held her by the elbows and looked into her still-ecstatic face, but even to his own ears he was peevish. Peace, he thought, that is all I desire, is it so much to ask of the world? Attempting to break his overly reflective mood, he took Nora's arm and led her, her smile undented and her adoring eyes fixed on him, across the threshold of 88 Woolsend Avenue.

Peace: for some time Sam had been lobbying his bosses to put an end to the peripatetic existence he and his family had been obliged to lead. From house to house, town to town as business demanded, it was no longer appropriate, argued Sam; he was a long-serving and senior man who deserved a settled life. 'I'm a respectable man, not a blessed gypsy!' was his more pithy assessment to Nora. Entering his new home, Sam felt a mood of satisfaction, bordering on exultation, descend on him, but it was not long before his wife put paid to it by scampering around the broad, empty rooms, shrieking almost as excitedly as Flora and little Alex.

'Sammy, Sammy, this house is beautiful! Oh if only we could make it ours, ours absolutely!'

Sam's rising irritation was clouded with confusion—bless my soul, she has just stolen my own thought and blurted it out. Perhaps after their wanderings they had now come to rest.

The house was fronted by a tall, broad bay window and a stolid wooden door that looked as if it could withstand a thousand winter storms; it was a door that would have done well on a church, dark and oaken, inlaid with strips of blackened iron in raised, squared studs and a knocker wrought in the shape of a hand. It only admitted light through a small, diamond-shaped and frosted window, and no busy-body or intruder, no matter how hard they peered, could determine what was within. The hallway was consequently starved of light, and along with the deep, muddy brown of the paintwork gave the impression of entering into a warren rather than a house. The main room was on the right, and the twilit hallway then executed a sharp right turn, with doors abutting one another. The first, lurking in still deeper shadow, led into a narrow and cold but bright room looking out to the rear garden, and the second led into the well-lit square of the back kitchen and scullery. The children were already in every room, he could hear them thumping about upstairs, even the older ones were now exploring excitedly, making claims on bedrooms and arguing about who must share with whom.

Sam supervised the arrival of the family's furniture, taking care to direct the placing of the pieces he had selected for his sanctum, the large, cool front room looking out on to the shaded avenue. That done, he left Nora busily colonising the back kitchen and turning it into her own fiefdom; he put on his hat and coat, disengaged from his squealing, over-excited infant son and set about quartering the locality. He intended to identify the best shops, reconnoitre his new place of worship and possibly find an agreeable hostelry for an occasional quiet drink, but he was also determined to map this territory in his mind, resolved that within two days he would be capable of directing a stranger to any point in the village. And Sam Wilson himself was not going to be caught asking the way like a fool.

Woolsend was referred to by its denizens as 'the Village', as if there were no other in the world, never mind along the narrow windings of the long road between the two large manufactory towns that lay to the north and south. Woolsend may have been a village standing proud and alone, but it was now a small spot on an increasingly busy thoroughfare and in mounting danger of being claimed body and soul by one expanding town or the other. The village was a stacking of houses on the lip of a pit; the winding-gear of the colliery clearly visible from the crest of the hill that rolled away into semi-distant, smoky Hanston. The galleries of the coal mine wormed under every road, shop, home, and in some ways Woolsend was a village on stilts, propped by matchwood and perpetually vulnerable to being sucked into the earth; yes, the lightest of blows from the hand of God would have sent the entire place to its grave.

The largest street, the Parade, was lined with shops: those will keep Nora and the girls busy and my pockets empty, thought Sam. The Parade, curved along the brow of a small slope, spilling sidestreets away like rivulets, and it was bookended by churches, the sharp spire of St Anselms to the west, and to the east the solid square battlements of the Congregational church, as if the people were protected on one point of the compass by a lance and at the other by a bastion. Sam passed by the latter with a frown; he would certainly not be seen worshipping in that fortified haven of heretical Lollards.

He made his way back downhill, descending through the short terrace of labourers' houses that was Lion Street, which gave off at a sharp left to the tree-lined row of larger dwellings where his new home stood on the corner. Number 88's tall garden walls screened it from prying eyes in Lion Street, but they fell away to waist-height as they took the corner and faced the neat houses of more respectable people. Sam continued downhill, to where the slope lost its energy and flattened peaceably: here, some way beyond his new home, lay an oasis of ancient prosperity, houses of the old sort, large and dignified structures discreetly concealed by screens of tall trees, with wide gateways and shaded drives that curved inwards to deny passing strangers all but the least glimpse of the house. These were places where not so long ago coachmen had driven their masters and mistresses to their private, pillared thresholds. The Wilson women had been thrilled at the roominess of number 88, but the place was dwarfed and made ugly by the palatial dwellings that Sam could—with little effort—see.

These had been the dwellings of the wealthy and the powerful among the factory towns. They were surely possessed of everything from large, elegant receptions and bedrooms to great old-fashioned kitchens and smaller quarters for the servants. Some of the houses may still have been occupied, but many appeared empty, neglected and dreaming of better days. No doubt they had been emptied of money and then voided of people by the process of grinding, unstoppable, unhappy change—the Great War, the market crash, the simple march of time, had all conspired to humble the local nobility that had once lived so well there. Their time had come and gone, mused Sam as he passed them by. So near to those ghosts of greatness, he allowed himself a small flicker of a dream: might he head the family table in such a place one day? Perhaps, when the shadow of coming war had passed and England was great again, the fortunes of the Wilson family could rise as it deserved. Why, Sam Wilson told himself as his step lightened, even at Woolsend Avenue the little bedroom above the front door could serve as a place where a maid might rest her head in the dark hours before rising to make the fires and attend to the needs of the household.

Towards its end, the road was so heavily shrouded by tall trees that daylight almost lost itself; Sam Wilson huffed in quiet relief as he broke free of that darkness and emerged on a narrow pavement at the far end of the village. He turned right, heading for the village boundary as marked by St Margaret's church, striding confidently and noting landmarks as he went. He had already passed a beer-house and two taverns, too small and too tatty, but not far from the church he spied a more acceptable building, almost in the shadow of the spire, which styled itself the Royal Oak. Not too far from home and, importantly, not too close either. Sam decided to explore its possibilities further—later that day perhaps.

1945

Minnie said that father had left carrying his old suitcase and that he and mother had high words before he left. Mother slapped his face but then fell to the ground and clung to his trouser cuffs as she tried to step away; she was screaming, begging him to stay. Helen said that was nonsense and Minnie should stop inventing tales—nobody but Mother and Father knew what had happened. All Flora knew was that by the time she had come home from school her father was gone and her sisters were flocking around her mother, carrying unwanted cups of tea, food that went untasted and words of comfort and advice that clacked emptily upon their tongues.

Mother was sitting in her chair by the fire in the back

kitchen, wrapped in blankets as if she had a bad cold, and for a time she did sniff and choke as if she really was unwell, but nobody called the doctor.

'She's gone so quiet,' whispered Petra to Helen, 'so quiet I'm frightened.'

'Better than all that bally noise we had earlier,' Minnie grumbled, as if she resented Nora's being so much the centre of attention.

Helen shushed them imperiously, but Nora, wide-eyed, wakeful and tremulous, gave no sign of having overheard. She also took not a scrap of notice of Phyllida, who sat by her holding her small hand. Petra had even attempted to sing to her earlier on, but the nursery-rhyme crooning had unsettled Nora and so descended the fragile, nervous silence that now prevailed.

It was Mona Welkins who first realised something was wrong: she was on her way to drop in on Nora when she heard a commotion from the house. She had been too late to see the fugitive depart—though she had nearly stopped a passing stranger thinking he was Sam, but the man was far too old—and she found Nora making sufficient racket to wake the dead and make them dance too. The carry-on had continued long after Helen and Minnie had come to help out. Flora, at Helen's orders, had been intercepted on her way home from school and had not been allowed in until the distressing noise declined, and had not been permitted near her mother until she had been made to understand the situation and the need not to upset her further.

The sisters took it in turns to sit with Nora; Flora was only permitted to be at her side with Helen or Phyl superintending. They stood by like jailers; Flora at once resented their high-handedness and was comforted by it. Nora remained stiffly in her chair, blanketed in silence. Once or twice there came sounds from the street, once there even seemed to be a scuffling at the door, and Nora's eyes gleamed with a half-drowned hope that grew dull and lost within moments. Still her daughters attended her side or gathered in the chilly middle room to talk in hushed, agonised tones. Not one of them suggested they transfer to the front room; that was still their father's domain. Flora ventured in there on a whim, finding herself searching the room carefully in case her father had been there the whole time.

As the evening grew old, Helen sent Flora and then Petra to bed. There was nothing to be done, either to comfort their mother or summon back their father. Flora, troubled and sleepless, looked up at Petra as she came to bed.

'Where d'you think he is?'

'Gone to the devil. And that Mrs. Ellis too, for all I care. Bag and baggage.' Petra's voice was a venomous hiss. 'And should you ever see him again, tell him I said so.'

'D'you think he'll come back?' Flora asked tremulously.

'Do you *want* him to?' Petra shot back.

The only remaining sound in the back kitchen was the steady, muted ticking of a clock. Nora, who had neither moved nor spoken in a long time, was nevertheless still awake. The clock whirred and cracked twelve shrill notes, but still Nora did not stir.

'Mother?' Helen spoke gently; Nora did not look at her, but nor did she turn her face away when Helen knelt in front of her.

'Mum, where are the house keys? It's time to lock up now.'

'Lock?' Nora's throat clicked as the word forced its way out of her.

'Yes, it's gone midnight now. You can't stay here all night, you must go to bed, lie down a little while at least.'

Nora stretched and groaned in agitation. 'No, no, don't lock the doors, leave them, he might... I must wait, wait for him.'

'Mother, he is not coming back.' Helen's bluntness drew a gasp from Minnie, who was hovering behind her.

'Don't lock him out,' Nora half-commanded, half-begged. 'You want me to go up? If you leave the doors I shall lie down for a while. Just don't lock him out.'

'Oh very well Mum; Min will go with you.'

Nora unwound herself from the blanket with painful slowness and shuffled out of the room stooping, as if she had become an old woman in the course of a few hours.

Minnie returned within a short time, spreading her hands helplessly in reply to a questioning look from Helen. 'She says she won't sleep with someone stood over her. Practically shoved me out she did.' She sagged into her mother's chair, helpless and empty-eyed. 'What on earth do we do now?'

There was no reply. When Helen padded up the stairs an hour later to look in on her mother, she was panic-stricken to find her bedroom empty; she was about to bellow down the stairs to rouse Minnie, but instinct turned her step to the small front bedroom, Alex's room. Nora was there, seated on the edge of its tiny single bed, staring out of the window into the dark, empty avenue below.

The Dark Angel

1940

A queer lull had fallen at the Royal Oak; George Shenton had spent some time lamenting the fact that, 'Ah may never see a proper game o football ever again if what they say is true—they'll stop the big games an'all the players'll be humpin packs and flyin planes an what ave you before long an what's left o the teams'll all be smooth-faced lads or crocked-up owd uns like me.'

'As good a reason for someone to put a good bullet through Hitler bloody soon.' Jack nodded.

'Football is good for people's morale,' Sam Wilson chipped in. 'We should keep things as normal as possible to show the damn Bosche. Perhaps they should make soccer a reserved occupation.'

Jack and George were astonished at the man's easy good humour and the fact they agreed with him.

Contrary to their custom, the Trappers were reluctant to bait Sam, as if something had told them that this was a day on which he deserved respite from the traditional knockabout fun. Jack had just refreshed the vital fluids and was about to sit again when he stopped, crouching, then straightened again at the unusual sight of a child, a little girl, in the doorway.

'Now then Miss,' said Jack, having caught her eye. 'What are you doing here?' The child was frowning, looking for someone, and then Sam Wilson's voice cut across the suppressed muttering in the bar.

'Petra! You are not supposed to come here!' His authoritative tone was undermined by a quizzical note, which in turn was counterpointed by a discord of incipient panic: his thoughts whirled even as he spoke and a terrible realisation dawned—the children would never come here, Nora would never send them, unless... the girl was breathless, her face flushed with the effort of running, and as the puffing of her breathing slowed it became clear that her eyes were red and swollen too, and her cheeks dirty channels for recent tears. Sam stood in one swift movement, a violent momentum that threatened to propel him through the ceiling. 'What is it?' he commanded his daughter to speak.

'He touched it!' she stammered. 'We'd all told him not to but he touched it! He's just lying there; Minnie's gone for Dr. Wallace and they said for me to come fetch you as I was quickest and...' the words Petra wanted had raced away somewhere into the distance and she gave up the chase. Jack and George watched soberly as Sam, without a look at them or anyone in the bar, abandoned his drink, snatched his hat and coat and stalked out, nearly leaving Petra behind in his rush then recovering his wits and placing a shepherding hand against her shoulders. Out on the street she stumbled and fell behind him, still panting, and he picked her up and carried her all the way home, the overwrought girl weeping and gabbling over and over again, 'He touched it, we'd all told him not to!' She continued until they reached the front door of 88 Woolsend Avenue.

Sam and Petra arrived a few moments before Dr. Wallace; the house still, and for a moment it seemed empty, as if this were some morbid prank being played on Sam. But, tugging at his hand, Petra led her father to the long, thin middle room, the heart of that stillness; the tableau within resembled the family gathering for a child's piano recital, but the focus of their attention was on the other side of the room and the piano was closed up and silent. Nora was sitting in the room's only armchair, her face frozen in an ugly gaping expression as if she had been struck by an apoplexy, while little Flora clung to her, face in her lap. Helen was kneeling over the small figure in the corner of the room while Minnie, having returned ahead of the doctor, was at her sister's shoulder, and she was the one to catch her father's glance as he strode into the room.

Minnie pointed, hand shaking, to Alex's body, face-down on the floor, and to the gunmetal grey electric fire beside it, as if she was simultaneously telling tales on her little brother and yet standing between him and Sam's wrath. Just as Petra had before her, she began with a stammer, then managed to say, 'It was cold, it was very cold and we said we should have the fire on, we told him not to touch, he knew not to touch but the moment he wasn't watched, he...'

She flinched as Sam stepped forward, but he was restrained, whatever he had intended at that moment, by a large hand on his shoulder.

'Best let me, Sam,' said the newly-arrived Wallace, moving Sam gently aside, then with equal tact and care prising Minnie and then Helen from their charge.

In a thin, shaking voice Sam ordered the girls to leave the room; they took long moments to obey and he felt his temper rising at their reluctance, but then Dr. Wallace repeated and supported the demand and the family shuffled out, Nora practically lifted out between Helen and Minnie, Flora and Petra following like mournful bridesmaids, all silent but for the faint beginnings of sobs. As the door to the kitchen closed, the doctor gently turned over Alex's tiny, unmoving body. Sam stared down at his son and knew what he was supposed to see—peace, angelic tranquillity, a small boy asleep through the ages to come, a small life returned to God. He tried for a desperate moment to hope, to summon the belief from somewhere within himself that Wallace could do something, pull the boy back, that this sleep was not endless and that his son would at any moment give out long, breathy yawns and be on his feet again, out in the garden playing and singing. But within one heartbeat Sam Wilson looked down without illusion on the face of a dead child; he could see, believe, nothing else. The face was not composed entirely to peace, it retained something of the grimace that must have been Alex's last, spasmodic muscular movement; he could see the scar on the child's lip, a reminder of the day he had run into the kitchen too fast, too excited over some silly thing and had sailed straight into the edge of the table, folded out for Nora's baking. There was a shocked moment in which a stunned Alex, pitched on his hindquarters, touched his lip as ribbons of blood started out; Alex's face had started to twist in pain and Nora had stepped towards him, but with a whip-crack snap of his fingers Sam had halted both of them. 'Don't you *dare* to cry!' he had ordered the boy. 'That was your own fault, so don't you dare to cry! Be *quiet* boy!' and so the blood had bubbled but the tears miraculously had not. And there would be no tears now, not from Alex, not from Sam Wilson. He knew his own nature well enough to be aware that such an outburst would not overtake him, not yet awhile; only when he could achieve absolute solitude could he give way to a shock that was potentially as fatal as the one that had destroyed his infant son.

Dr. Wallace examined the child's burnt hands, folded them on his still chest and stood, trying but unable to look at Sam. 'He died instantly; electric shock, it went right through him. It was the work of a moment, nobody could have stopped him. I suggest you go and join Nora and the girls—I'll do... I'll do what's needed.'

Cold and numb still, Sam obeyed, but he hovered in the cold, dark hallway between the kitchen and middle room doors, hearing strained, wailing voices from the kitchen that made him unwilling to join his family even at this time: lacking the courage to return to the doctor and his work, he stood there, paced the hallway, then stood again, waiting for the physician to emerge almost as if he were impatiently awaiting the news of a birth. The noise from the kitchen became too much to bear and a moment later he found himself facing Nora, who, crumple-faced and high-voiced, was telling one and all, 'I saw this, I knew this, I tried to prevent it but still it happened. You can't cheat the Angel, it'll come no matter what you do.'

'Nora.'

Sam's entry to the room had silenced the girls in an instant, but his wife wailed on, 'We should never of come here.' Her voice gathered force, 'There's been the devil's curse on us since we came to this house, we should never of...' Even Sam's angry, determined stride towards her, which cleared his way of daughters, didn't stop her, nor did his scarcely gentle seizing of her hands. 'I saw it and I couldn't stop it!' she shouted out, then her head sagged on to her breast.

'Look after her.' Sam dropped Nora's hand that fell as if dead, and blazed his eyes at the two oldest girls. 'Just look after her.' He left the room silently, and stood again outside the middle room; a miracle, he thought, perhaps a miracle may still mend all, for I do believe that they happen. With a jolt, he realised he should pray.

For some time Nora said nothing more to Sam of that day's events and he was grateful for her self-restraint. Her nonsense had nearly caused him to lose all composure in the presence of their children, both dead and alive. But some weeks after the funeral, she started again with her mumbo-jumbo.

Clinging to him she shuddered and spoke in a hideous, hysterical whisper, 'I had foreknowledge of his death, I knew it was to be, and yet I couldn't... why, Sammy, why? What is it I've done, what offence have I given to God?' And it wasn't just his wife's words that made Sam seethe, it was her failure to understand that his stoic silence was all the reply he wished to give, and that her repetition of these empty, childish questions could only make him angry.

'Nora, *enough!* Our son is dead, d'you want *me* punished for it now? Your keening is making me half-mad! You tell me over and over that you foresaw Alex's death but I remind you that only God possesses such knowledge—God alone, not you or I!'

'But I saw it...'

'You saw nothing, woman! I have to remind you that

you "saw" his death in Knype Pool, and gave me no peace day or night until I had removed the entire family, lock, stock and barrel, to this place! And what happens? It comes to be that *here* is where our son dies, not at Knype or in any other place you supposedly saw in your silly muddle-headed daydreams!'

'You blame me for bringing us here? You think I killed him?' Nora jabbered, and Sam had great difficulty in not screaming in her face or striking her.

He managed a restrained response in a marble-cold expository tone, the voice he would use to explain life's basic rules to a simpleton. 'I said nothing of the kind. Alex died by accident, he died because he was curious about the fire, because he didn't listen—he died because he didn't understand. I blame nobody; now do *not* tax me with witch-visions and stupid imaginings. If you truly have them then they are poisoned gifts from the devil and they should be cast out of you! What good is it, forever foreseeing disaster as you do, of course such "visions" will come true eventually, how can they fail to?'

'I was told that I had the power...' She wouldn't let go, either of the subject or him, and Sam's blood heated again.

'By the gypsy, yes, yes, yes, I've heard this hoary tale so often, Nora! You were told a flattering lie by some stupid hag, riddled with superstitions and pagan filth! You saw no image of the future, you never see the future, all you do is draw on your fantasies of disaster and death, the mirror of your own overworked imagination, your own anxieties! Now I shall have no more of this. The proper way is to pray, and not to be further steeped in this nonsense!'

'You're a hard man, Sam Wilson!' Nora fell away from

him, falling also to weeping, but at least that stopped her words.

Sam was minded to say more, to remind her that their son was dead through disobedience and that she, not he, had charge of the children at the moment of the death; that Alex was dead because she had spoiled him; that if anyone had predicted this situation it was himself, Sam Wilson, who had fought against her febrile imaginings at Knype. Mastering himself, Sam buried these recriminations and knelt in front of Nora, taking her hands and looking at her drained, sad face with compassion and the remains of his love.

'The proper way is to pray, Nora. Come, hold my hands and we'll pray together.'

1943

The evening meal was done with; Sam rose from the table at once and, bidding as ever that the house should remain completely silent, made his way to the front room. He made a disciplined effort not to hurry. Closing the door firmly behind him Sam let out a long, slow breath and sank into his favourite armchair with the cautious dignity of a man who craves to be alone but fancies himself watched. Closing his eyes again he offered a simple, silent prayer. He had commanded silence, and silence he had obtained. But that alone did not amount to the peace he sought.

In solitude in this room or at worship at church, for so very long these had been his only sanctuaries from a restless mind and an unquiet conscience: now both failed him. Every step he took up to the lectern used to make him feel a better and more worthy man, but nowadays each step diminished him and he was again the boy whose wicked inner core was known, who would not be saved. Now here in his last haven, Sam found only discomfort and discontent.

Standing alone on the mantelpiece was a solid old clock; its ticking calmed and eased Sam, its sound so firm and solemn, it was as if the mere counting of seconds was the least of its concerns. Aristocratically generous, it shared with Sam just a little of its stolid, measured serenity. A small fire glowing in the grate warmed him, and yet the comforts of warmth and the orderly progress of time were insufficient on this night. How dark this room is, Sam thought, why is it that I had never noticed it before?

Behind the polished bulk of the clock was a partly obscured oval mirror. Sam, without ever knowing why, had always shuddered at the sight of that mirror and placed the timepiece in front of it deliberately, to mask much of the silvered surface as possible. The mirror was old and dulled, in some places now completely black, as if fingers of decay had stroked it and left their etched traces, obscuring and then killing reflections. Sam didn't care to regard his image in that mirror; it was the source of a spreading darkness, and gathered to itself the dust and dirt of advancing age. He hated to see his face so imperfectly reflected, dirtied, as if he were staring at himself though a shifting veil, or through the material of a shroud.

The mirror was surrounded by the same light-draining wood that made the mantelpiece, and around the oval's curves the stuff was worked into raised patterns of plant leaves and tendrils that touched the mirror's edges and then curled away to form dark, tight flowers at the four corners of the wooden backing. Who could have found such a thing lovely or decorative, Sam Wilson wondered; this lightlessness, this suffocating colourlessness? There was something gloomily foreboding, almost frightening, about the whole fireplace. The coal's bright flames always under attack from the thick wooden surround of the fireplace and confined by the lustreless grey tiles and stonework of the hearth. The fire was a sprig of cheer threatened by heavy clouds, a good spirit besieged by melancholy. Hearth and home, home fires; was this not the place where a man should feel most at rest? And yet Sam, in the quiet of this room, felt like a frightened child who had been left alone in the dark for the first time in his life.

Sam made no move either to close the heavy, gloomy curtains or to put on a light; his thoughts, along with his surroundings, slipped further into uncertain gloom.

What was it that Nora had said? 'This is our home, this is where we shall spend the rest of our lives, I just know it.'

Sam restrained himself from speaking his thoughts aloud: I do not belong here any longer; I believe I have never belonged here.

I cannot, I shall not wait here until the household empties out and only Nora and I are left. I cannot, I shall not bear such emptiness.

I cannot, I shall not sit passively until that creature, Nora's pet angel, comes to claim my soul.

Peace and salvation lie in another place. If I wait here, all I shall do is die slowly.

1940

'He's a hard man, Jack.'

'How d'you mean?'

'What sort of a father sits in't pub suppin a half, leaving his wife and kiddies at home when he's not long lost his youngest?'

'There's plenty come in here as would behave like that, George.'

'They're not supposed to be holy men. You'd expect him to act more...'

'He wasn't turning cartwheels just now, old lad, just sat there grave and serious as ever. He just shows nowt, that's all.'

'Christ above, it's a miracle, Jack Carthmain is defending Sammy Wilson!'

'Even Sammy hasn't got a heart of flint. Concrete, mebbe, but not flint. He was just keepin up appearances George, being normal. P'raps he finds comfort in that—life goes on.'

'If I was im I know what I'd find comfort in.'

'Now then, don't you get excited owd, it'll start that cough of yours again.'

Nora clung to Sam in the darkness, her body warm but her face wrung and wrinkled with her grieving. Her grip on him was tenacious, insistent, and for a moment he broiled in a horrible half-dream that he was being smothered in his sleep by some life-destroying succubus, but the creature holding to him so tightly wanted not his breath, not his blood, but comfort, comfort in her wretchedness.

'I feel so miserable about it Sammy, miserable in my heart and soul. But I swear before God there was nothing I could do, you know that. There's no rest for me and I shall curse myself forever, but you could at least show me that you admonish me of all blame.'

'Absolve.'

'Come again?' she asked in a gasp, taken by surprise.

'Absolve, I would absolve you of all blame. "Admonish" is quite the wrong word.'

'But you knew what I *meant*! Sammy!'

Sam lost interest in the conversation.

The Trappers

1940

'Hast heard Sammy Wilson holdin forth?' George asked over the top of his glass.

'Holding forth? It's bloody hard to get a civil word out of him sometimes, what d'you mean "holding forth", about what?'

'Not about what—about *owt*, owt and all. Nearly talked me ears off the other bloody night when you decided you were too laid up to come along, it were like someone ad cranked is andle and set im off! He were standin right where you are now, pontificatin about...'

'"Pontificating"? You been stealing dictionaries from the WEA again ole lad?'

George sighed, displeased by the interruption. 'I'm not a bloody ignoramus Jack, leave that alone will yer and listen! I know full well old Wilson's scarcely said bugger all since he started comin here but t'other night he *did*. And you know how I reckoned he thought he was somethin special, a cut above like? Well now I know.'

'What d'you mean?'

Jack gestured 'tell on' and signalled Netta for more drinks; George was about to go on one of his famous tirades and these were always better if he had some oil for his engine.

'I decided not ter be so frit of im and his high-handed ways, get chattin like, so I was reelin off tales o the ole days. Like how after the Great War Billy Clewlow come back wi just one leg an set up as an odd-job man...'

'Ah; now that's a right noble old tale.' Jack sniffed as if at a classic vintage.

'Jus so Jack, so I tells Is Nibs about ow Billy goes from ouse to ouse fixin an mendin an also puttin a smile on many a housewife's tired little face...'

'So he did, so he did, a public servant that lad.'

'Any road, too late I sees the thunderclouds gather over Sammy Wilson's ead, an I realise I've gone an done it again. "I didn't realise that such immorality was rife in this small place, Mr. Shenton," says e, and then, well, e's off, innee? Half an hour on God's opinion o people what misbehave, the sanctity o marriage an where Billy and is peg-leg are burnin right this minute. And oh did he make it clear that e's from a better class o person what doesn't get up to party tricks like that. God elp us.'

'Yes,' Jack concurred heavily. 'Fancies himself does that man, as...'

'As, and take this how yer want mate, a *nob*.'

A little lubrication later, George expanded on his theme. 'Good day, mey name is Sammyoowel Wilson,' began the slighted old miner, issuing a frothy, beery sigh. 'I tork hout of my harse and look dine my nose. Some folk call me a snob, but they is just common scum and I never, never listen to such creechas.'

Jack settled back to listen.

1945

Jack Carthmain was about to go too far; too far for George Shenton's taste, and that was *far* too far. They had been baiting Sammy in a bits-and-pieces, none-too-satisfactory way and the humourless old sod had been at his perceptive best in avoiding all their tricks and traps, but it was plain Jack wasn't going to be content until he'd drawn blood, and he seemed ready to sacrifice even the inviolable brotherhood of the Trappers to pursue and obtain his kill.

George felt uncomfortable: due propriety was being abused; was it not he who usually led the most reckless charges against the foe, allowing himself to be guided by Jack's restraining influence if the assaults on Sammy edged too near the knuckle? Tonight, however their roles were reversed and it was Jack who was becoming reckless—not to mention legless. George reminded himself of the time of year—it was the anniversary of Peg's death, five years this time, and every year so far between the anniversaries of his wife's death and the date of her funeral Jack had lost control, wallowing in booze as if determined to follow his beloved into eternity. Netta and Fred were accustomed to it now, and they had even conspired with George to water down Jack's drinks to fend off the worst effects of the bender, but Jack's current state was as much an effort of will as an alcoholic achievement, it was almost as if he would have achieved this royally pie-eyed state even through bibbing water alone, never mind the small-beer he had been served.

And so, booze-warmed but quite in control of his faculties, George was trying to keep his boon companion under nominal control, but at last the restraints could hold no more and Jack, frustrated by Sammy's failure to be pious, foolish, pompous or the least bit entertaining, was over the top and running headlong for the enemy guns.

'Sammy—Shamuel. Lemmy talk to you—as a friend, yesh, a friend.' Jack leaned too close to his quarry and Sam winced; for once George could feel sympathy for the fastidious holy man, Jack was already stinking like the outside jakes at a brewery; he was not, at this moment, a man you wanted exhaling on you. The modulation of Jack's voice slipped from mock-emollient to simply mocking, the drunk's attempt to play best-pal utterly unconvincing and Sammy's defences, raised already, reinforced even as they conversed.

'Samuel, I have need of your guidance and your goodnesh. Not for myself, I want you to know, but on the behalf of a very verrrry good friend of mine. He needs—he needs what you are best at, Samuel. He needsh—shall we call it moral guidance?'

Sitting as he was, elbow-to-elbow with Jack, George was unable to properly read his friend's expression, and this disadvantage, allied with the stage-voice that his fellow-Trapper was affecting, meant George was dangerously uncertain about the direction his friend's little spiel was taking, but already he had butterfly suspicions fluttering inside his guts.

'He's a good mate, a close mate, and he has a problem; a *moral* problem. See, he's innan un'appy marriage like, and e's all enam-emman-*enamoured* of this woman. And a fine woman she is, radiantly beautiful and not in any way your common sort at all, oh no, special this one is. But the problem is that she's married, an so's he, see, just to add spice—erm, complication—to the prob... belem. Any road, he needs your advice as a good sound man of the church, as he can't take his eyes off this skirt—tart-woman—and he never stops fuckin talking about her—sorry to swear, Sammyuel—now, as I say, she's married but her old man, he isn't up to much, a man who takes his Misshus for granted, thinks of little as her as she might be a sack o spuds in the scullery. So there's all that lovely stuff—so sorry, all that loveliness going to waste, and there's my old pal, pining away, an it's not asiff e's so young as e can *wait* too long. See now?

'Now, Sammy-ule, as a manna God, as a *moral* man, can you tell me if it is ever right for a married man to woo an win another woman, even in a case when both marriages are as dead as stone and the other man and the other woman probably wouldn't even bloody well notice—sorry to swear, our Sam? Would it be susha a bad thing to do even if the "wronged" parties wouldn't care a monkey's? Tell me, Sammyhool, tell me.'

In the past, Wilson had donned his hat and coat, made his apologies and fled at lesser provocations, but tonight he was indomitable under fire. He looked unflappably thoughtful, which was not at all how George felt as he twitched with barely suppressed anxiety at Jack's side. The hound, how could he, this was no fair way of baiting Sammy, Jack was practically *telling* the man that George Shenton would fill the space in his marriage bed given half a chance: it was nothing but a betrayal. Granted Jack was drunk, granted also that Jack was deep within his soul trying to cope with heartbroken thoughts of his beloved Peg, but this was just not on. Like as not, Jack wouldn't remember any of this tomorrow so he would be hard to remonstrate with; Netta and George would drag him into the back room to sleep it off and that way Jack would bury the memory of his unspoken mourning along with the memory of all else from that night.

Sammy composed himself to reply to Jack, his face calm and serious. It was perfectly possible that he hadn't the foggiest notion that Jack was aiming a shaft at the state of the Wilsons' own marriage, still less that it was George who was the wicked would-be fornicator tortured by adulterous lust: George could only hope that Sammy remained as stolidly unimaginative as ever.

'The Bible is perfectly clear on the subject; the bonds of matrimony are quite indissoluble until death.'

'Aye, death—do you part,' Jack echoed, deflating as his thoughts turned still further inwards. Damn Sammy, what a howler to commit even if Jack had more or less asked for it, he knew what night this was, why was he never the least bit sensitive to other people's feelings? George was tempted to intervene, but then Jack recovered from his brief, befuddled ruminations on mortality. 'In the normal wotsit of events, Sammy, yes,' Jack picked up the thread again, 'But ever since King Enry the Hathe people ave bin divorcing, not counting Catholics. Yer norra Catholic are yer Sam?'

'Of course not!' Wilson was still playing up and playing the game.

'So.' Jack paused, his face relaxing to a reddish blank and his eyes misting over before he recovered himself with a jolt. 'If two people are parted in all ways except by... one... then there have to be times when it's allowable-like, for them to, you know, be separated legal and proper, and to get spliced to someone else. In a situation like that everyone's happier that way Sammy, everyone, now can that really and truly be wrong?'

'Marriage is a solemn sacrament,' Wilson continued to play a straight bat, but at least he'd been lured into pontificating; George hoped Jack would still be sufficiently conscious to appreciate these late fruits of his dangerous labours.

'I really don't think any man or woman should so casually think of betraying their solemn vows; those vows were taken in the sight and hearing of God.'

'Well in this case pr'aps he were lookin t'other way at the time.' Jack had begun to gargle on his own words and his eyes were now under constant half-cloud. Surreptitiously George nodded to Netta: more water next time.

'God listens and God hears,' Sam Wilson assured his companions. 'His attention never strays and His judgement cannot be avoided.'

'But wouldn't even He see it as *wrong*? A man and woman could find happiness, another man and woman don't care either way, so why can't they just mebbe... swap?' Jack extended his fingers and crossed them, jabbing them at Sam. 'Whass immoral bout that? That, Samyool, is the nob... nub of what I'd like to know.'

'I really don't think that any such behaviour would receive the divine sanction of the Lord.' Sam was like a blast of sobering wind, and he slipped his chair a little from the table; there was a mere mouthful left in his glass and he was clearly intent on beating a retreat as soon as he could daintily drink up, but Jack had more to say, and he was now becoming not just loud but bellicose.

'How can a God of Love be a God that's against people's appiness?' He sank the last of his own drink. 'What sort of a fuckin God of Love is *that*?' he added in a roar, 'Netta! Another! An this time save the watter for yer fuckin pansies!'

It was a devil of a job getting Jack's huge recumbent carcass into the back room that night. It took the combined efforts of George, Netta and Fred to land their fish. He was unresisting; his jaw moved spasmodically but otherwise he was deadweight. Sounds came out of him: groans, snatches of songs, nonsense, chunter—and, just once, his dead wife's name. They laid him down on a pile of sacks, and his face resumed a flickering of life, grinning wickedly.

'Sammy, Sammy, moral guidance Sammy!' slurred Carthmain.

'He's gone, Jack!' Netta shouted, as if he was half a mile away.

'Juss think what he's thinkin rightnow. Juss think.' Netta folded some more sacks and placed them under his head, then spread yet more on top of him.

'Night Jack,' she said heavily, stepping away with her helpmeet to go and tidy the bar.

George remained with her, standing over his friend, just as Jack's eyes rolled open horribly as if he were the dead come back to life; he fixed George with an unsteady gaze but spoke with a surprisingly clear voice. 'Take the wise words of Sammy Wilson, may they be hewn in stone, every one of them, and let them be set up on a mountain top for all to see, where the birds may fly over them, and shit on them forever more. Amen.' He rumbled into sleep at last.

'You bastard Jack,' George whispered it, angry and hurt. 'You bastard.'

The Book of Fire

1947

'She's a witch,' moaned Nora, 'she's a witch, she killed him, her own husband, that's as plain as a pikestaff, did away with him so as she could fornicate with your dratted father; oh, she did it but they are both steeped in guilt.'

'Don't talk such tripe mother!' Helen was tired and testy and had heard this litany far too many times. 'You know full well that Bill Ellis killed himself, shot himself in the mouth when he was drunk. People who want to be polite say he "died of his wounds", but those who say "blow politeness" also say good riddance, so I'm told. And, Mum, the man died before we even came to live here! How could our Dad have a single thing to do with it? You're just being silly.'

'She drove im to it,' Nora insisted doggedly. 'I see her hand in it. Doing away with that man then weaving her spell round your father. Witchcraft.'

1945

'They say Bill Ellis laid out the bottle and gun before him like they were prizes he'd won at Woolsend Wakes. Then in an instant he sucked down half that Scotch and took a gulp at the gun.'

'That's what I call a chaser!' cackled George darkly. Jack echoed his humourless laughter.

'If he'd only waited a while he could've let the Germans

do the job for him. But he couldn't even wait for a war!'

George pondered for a moment. 'Dost think it was heavenly work?'

'Say what, George?'

'Y'know, powers above, helpin Sammy Wilson get what e wanted by clearin ole Bill out the way?'

'Come off it, owd!'

'Aaah, it's just a thought. But for reasons that onna clear to me, someone up there seems to like Sammy an it wouldn't be the first time the Almighty as elped one of is own—David and Bathsheba is the story as comes to mind.'

'Don't get all fevered now George. Bill Ellis did away with himself because, one day, he looked in the mirror and at long last saw the same worthless, drunken wife-beater that the rest of us saw day by day. Best piece o work the man ever did, that one tug of the finger.'

'Seekin peace I reckon e was, driven spare by livin with Joan o Bloody Arc.'

'Possibly.'

'An I reckon it'll be Sammy's turn ter seek peace next.'

'George, now then!'

1942

'What is it that you want from this book, Samuel? What is it that you're looking for?'

Mirabelle Ellis's eyes were small torches of heavenly fire, beacons of holy light. Only she could have asked such a question, only she could display such insight and understanding. Such acuity, compassion! She could guide him: surely she could aid him to the deeper comprehension he sought, and the peace that dwelt only in eternal love, the certainty that, come his end, whenever that should be, he would be received by fatherly, forgiving arms. Yes, save the good Lord himself only Mirabelle Ellis knew his mind, and her open, benevolent enquiries were free of malice and judgement.

'I ask,' she continued in a girlishly playful voice, 'because when you read to us in church you seem to *know* this book; you are so strong, you never falter or hesitate. But sitting with you here I feel that you have never seen, not in any passage, the truth you are looking for.'

This woman was by no means beautiful and yet she possessed a soul filled with the sort of radiance that had stunned and subdued Saul. Could she be the saving of the sinner that was Sam Wilson, this angel of light? He had to be close to her, he yearned to keep her with him.

'Have you never asked yourself the same question Samuel?'

Her tone, so gentle; he wanted to lay his head in her lap, to sleep, to weep, to confess, but instead he held her gaze, his hands resting on the thin pages of the book on the table before him.

'I look to this book... for law, for strength, for guidance.' Sam knew that his voice sounded unusual, strained.

'I think we all do that. But that is not really what I asked you.' She had laid a loving snare and she would not let him free.

'Perhaps I have never been able to think the matter through properly. Perhaps you can help me in my search for an answer.'

He looked at her in a frank appeal; she will accept my

challenge, he told himself, and until that answer is found she will never leave me, she is bound to me. Shepherds and lost sheep: what Christian woman could refuse him? She was not alarmed by the uncertainty she had discovered, it had quickened her concern for him. Through this innocent pursuit they could continue to spend time in one another's company, and that of a greater love.

1908

Sam dipped his head toward the close-printed page as if ducking a blow, but his aunt's hand came to rest gently on the back of his neck; her palm soft and warm.

'That's right,' she almost cooed, 'read the book, learn it, absorb it.'

She stepped away from him, but moments later retraced her steps, placing her index finger on the page as if pointing out an especially significant verse.

'But don't try searching for ways out of your fate. There is mercy and compassion and goodness in this book, but your deserts were decided in creation's first days.'

That night, as ever, Aunt Laura bade him to his prayers. Eyes closed, head bowed, Samuel Wilson wondered incoherently how prayer could be of any assistance, since he was a lost soul. But when left alone he took hope and offered up his lonely, impious entreaties to his God.

1941

Nora froze like an animal that has scented a predator bearing down upon it, but her composure returned and she peeled off her gloves and placed them daintily on the hall table before carefully removing her hat and settling it on a peg.

Before she could turn, Sam spoke. 'Where have you been?'

'Visiting.'

'Gossiping with some silly old women in the Avenue?'

'Talking. To someone important. Sammy, I have been in church.'

'Without me?'

'All alone. At the church in Hencaster.'

'There is no church there.'

'Sammy I went to the Spiritualist service and they helped me, they really helped me; they told me where my children are, they gave me messages Sammy, messages that could only...'

'That is not a proper place to go. It is not a church. What foolishness put this notion in your head?'

'The medium, he told me things, spoke things, knew things that could only have been about my boy, my girls...'

'Stuff and nonsense!'

'But he knew darling, he knew my children...'

'Our children Nora, *our* children!'

'How could he have known unless it was them who told him?'

'It was the devil, Nora, the same devil that tempted you to go there in the first place! You would call yourself a Christian but defy the Bible! You have been lending an over-eager ear to the voice of a demon!'

'Sam, Sam, it can't have been...'

'Nora, I am out of all patience with you! You have been

tricked by cheap charlatanry and parlour games at best, and at worst you have been willingly communing with the blackest darkness. Now *be quiet* woman!'

'It can't be as you say Sammy, it can't, that Bible of yours, it's too dark and too cruel, and you make it say what you *want* it to say! It was our children, it was!'

'It was the devil Nora, and sometimes I feel he has a fast hold upon you. He may lure you into Hell, but the children are most assuredly not there. Hell is not for children, it is for foolish and disobedient adults. Now dry your eyes, attend to your children who are still on this earth—and give me some *peace!*'

1949

'Dig deeper in thee pocket an get another pint Jack, ere comes Sammy Wilson to see is ole pals!'

'Never in a million bloody years.' Jack Carthmain didn't even turn his head in response to George's silliness.

'Dost think e ever would visit ere?' asked the older man as Jack sat again.

'I hope and pray the idea never enters his head.'

'Dost ever think about im?'

'I try not to waste my time on such things, owd.'

'I wonder about im, where e's bound, like. I could never reconcile—is that a right word?'

'It is, old lad.'

'Good. I dursn't use a wrong word in front o Sammy, he never offered me any mercy on that, e'd jus step on me.'

'George...'

'Awrate, I were tryin to *reconcile* Sammy's b'haviur with

is preachin.'

'That was always a waste of time, ole feller.'

'Well, aye. I've tried an tried, it dunner work. I reckon e must o'bin a very *troubled* man.'

'There's no peace for the wicked, so they say.' Jack was implacable.

'Wot about God an sinners reconciled?'

'Surely not in his case, George? What brought that bugger to mind anyway?'

'Oh, e visits me thoughts from time to time. There was summat about im, summat as tells me that e would've loved to be an ordinary bloke like us; bad diction, slang, lack of *propah ennanciaishun* an all o that, but somehow e couldn't. Like there was summat took away from im, part of im as was cut off.'

'I know which part of Sammy Wilson should've been cut off,' pronounced Jack Carthmain.

2014

Another series of stories safely in her protection, Francine had one more question for her grandmother.

'What *did* Grampa Sam want?'

Flora sat still, thumbing at her lip, furrowing and smoothing her brow for a long time.

'He didn't want arguing with. That's what.'

Wedding Bands

2014

'Well,' Flora pronounced flatly on the flimsy sheet spread before her; she had spent an inordinately long time peering at it through her tinted spectacles, blinking frequently as if expecting the thing to vanish. 'Well. I never truly believed it until now, not in my heart. How could he behave like that, how? Oh I tell you, if our Minnie were here now, wittering about what a wonderful man he was and how we didn't appreciate him, I'd give her such a mouthful!'

The certificate would never have surfaced had it not been for the loss of yet another witness to the past: Francine had been attempting for nearly two years to negotiate another meeting with Cousin Jeanette, but it had never come to be, and instead her first visit to Jeanette's tiny home had been as part of a small gang of family members who came to clear the cluttered and dirty house after Jeanette's funeral.

'It wasn't much use talking to her anyway,' explained Terry, who had tried hard to broker the desired interview. 'She believed what she believed and that was that, there was no telling her otherwise. Besides, she generally hadn't much to say, when you spoke to her at Aunty Flo's party she'd got a positive case of verbal diarrhoea, she never chattered so much before or since. I think she'd got a point to make, eh? No surprise either that she didn't want to see you after that, it got hard enough for me to get in here, especially later on. She was ill, of course, even when you met her, but it got worse, and fast too. She couldn't think clearly, couldn't remember, you had to work like a navvy to get her to grasp the simplest things. Then she was gone; simply gone.'

Jeanette had begun to respond to any statement, question or call with 'Hah?': at first it was a sharp, querulous sound, a moment of irritation while she fought to focus her thoughts, but in time it lengthened to a strained and then increasingly helpless and then placid 'Haaaah?' Her head began to nod and her body to fold in on itself, as if she was attempting to hide, at first within four walls, then in one room, then in the small space of her favourite armchair, and finally within the confines of her own head. She comprehended less and less, became less articulate until 'Haaaah?' became her only question, her only answer, her sole sound.

'Always the quiet one, that lass. A sight different from her mother, I can tell you.' Terry winked at Francine, but his face was filled with sadness. The disease stole away Cousin Jeanette's recall, emptied her mind and then extirpated her personality, leaving her feeble and immobile, unknowingly alive for a cruelly long time before a merciful but belated dark angel descended to bring her pitiful nonexistence to an end. She had been taken by the Place of Lost Stories.

The house was comfortless, filthy and littered; its occupant's death had frozen its interior in a state of rampant chaos. Terry assembled his team to clear the place of its archaeological accumulation of bric-a-brac, photographs, documents, ornaments and oddments that lay all around, some apparently obsessively hidden and others scattered and abandoned where they fell from numbed fingers. There were some unpalatable finds, and some surprises too. Terry began to find small, tight slabs of cash tucked in queer places—behind loose bricks, inside a broken-down commode, stuffed into holes and cracks, slipped behind broken skirting; it amounted to several thousands of pounds. The ancient, purposeless money had been as friendless as its owner and though the windfall cheered the company, it was not this miser's fortune that impressed Francine Latimer. Cousin Jeanette may have been lost to the Place, but she had left a legacy.

'She was a listener more than a talker—and a bit of a hoarder too,' observed Terry as he and Francine piled box after box of papers and photographs. Francine busied herself sorting them, and was soon absorbed in the task. Some of the photographs were so old and ill-kept they bordered on disintegration, but it became clear that here was an archive that charted, however erratically, Sam Wilson's entire residence upon the Earth. There were time-eaten sepias of a serious-faced but handsome child, creased black-and-white portraits of a sapling of a youth, and then a growing man with the trace of a roguish smile that never fully dimmed even when he stood posed in the formidable presence of a solid-stone gargoyle who could only have been the dreaded Aunt Laura, an intimidating icon from a long-lost time.

Francine also discovered buried snaps of a youngster who could only have been Sam's abhorred brother, smiling unabashedly, slim and very pretty. Francine judged at once that Sam had rejected his brother for no better reason than jealousy; Sam Wilson may have been handsome, but his sibling was angelically beautiful. So, it wasn't only Nonna who paid too much attention to the message from the looking-glass. Present too were a few small snaps of a striking Wilson woman; their sister, for sure. She looked ill-at-ease in every shot, entirely lacking her brothers' obvious self-assurance.

The vast majority of the pictures were, however, of her great-grandfather. A youthful Sam Wilson in his Sunday best, the word 'confirmation' scribbled on the back of the print, Sam in uniform, scowly and commanding, dashing Sam arm-in-arm with his bride to be, the photo dated '1919' in firm handwriting. They both looked so happy. Nora was represented in the collection: up came what Francine thought of as *the* photograph, The Beauty Of Chell Street, but this time the image was not clinging tenaciously to that of her lost husband. In every frame, Nora lent colour to drabness with her sunrise beauty and guileless smile: in pictures of their wedding, Sam exuded an air of unruffled authority, poker-faced with awareness of a solemn duty, while Nora oozed an almost salacious joy, contemplating what was perhaps, to her, the true beginning of her life. She looked to Francine like a lottery winner preparing to enjoy her prize: triumphant. There were even a few letters from Nora to Sam, none dated later than 1922, presumably written when he was away from home on business. *My darling Sammy, you have only been away for two days and already my heart is lonely.* Teenagers always write bad poetry, thought Francine loftily.

Evidence of Nora's existence petered out as Francine deepened her search. The narrative was firmly that of Mr. Samuel Wilson. Awkwardly-posed portraits of an old couple—Sam and his second wife, neither comfortable with the camera as if they had something to hide; Sam receiving some sort of award at the office; Sam on holiday; Sam outside a church; Sam inside a church; Sam at ease at Minnie's house. It was odd, Francine reflected, that Jeanette had haphazardly documented this man's life and yet there were few papers relating to, and yet fewer images of, Jeanette herself. It was as if she had chosen to efface her own existence to worship at the altar of Saint Sam. Damn, hissed the girl to herself, she would have been *so interesting* to talk to...

It was at the last that Francine fingered a water-stained envelope and extracted a long, folded piece of paper; she took one glance and pocketed it, quick and guilty as a thief, but she knew that she could not leave it behind. The wads of money were nothing: this was a treasure-trove.

And so the stolen paper lay before Flora.

'I wonder why Jeanette had *this*? Was she hiding it, to protect his memory? I wonder if he offered her his silver teapot in return for keeping it safe.'

'His what?'

'We'll talk about that another time.'

The paper told a plain and simple story: there was the date, the church, the name of Yvette Parsons, spinster, and then the words from which Flora could not tear her gaze.

Samuel Wilson Bachelor

'I always wanted to believe that this was one of mother's tales, a thing of hurt and spite. But haven't I been deceiving myself. I thought he must have... I thought there must have been some arrangement made… Good God, I'm more disgusted now than I was at the time! A divorced man with eight children, he swore his whole past life away in a hallowed place! Oh God, Mum, I'm so sorry. It's as if there's nothing she couldn't dream up in her overheated imagination that he couldn't actually outdo. Mother, I am so sorry!'

Flora was heavily silent for a long time, and Francine began to regret flourishing her find.

'I'll be all right soon darling,' her grandmother read her thoughts, 'and it's better to *know*, isn't it?'

1972

Mona Welkins' hearing aid played a burst of manic birdsong, twittering up and down the scale as she struggled to adjust the small box clipped to her breast pocket, then on suppressing the electronic squawk she fiddled with the clumsy plastic earpiece to recover the mood of slightly somnolent afternoon comfort that the unwanted shriek of feedback had just ruined. Nora was still talking, Mona realised with a sprig of relief, and hadn't noticed a thing; she had become peevish lately if she thought that you weren't paying attention. Keeping her eyes on Nora's moving mouth, Mona settled back into her interrupted reverie.

From when they first met, Nora had talked incessantly about her husband: all that had changed were the words describing him. 'Handsome', 'dashing', 'gallant' and 'wonderful' had become 'cruel', 'immoral', 'selfish' and 'insane'. Sam Wilson did this, Sam Wilson did that, did you know he was from a noble family, was a more Christian man than that silly vicar, was sick in the head, thought he could deceive God; all the stories Mona had heard over the span of years.

Sealed within her thoughts, Mona meditated on her own husband. Derek Welkins had an eye for the future, after a fashion; he had a knack for sighting where money could be made. Even when it seemed to be nothing but the plaything of the wealthy he had recognised the potential of the motor car, had been able to envisage it becoming the common possession of the common man and when the wind did blow that way he had very smartly established himself as one of the first and best-known driving instructors in the area. They'd done well out of that, very well, but they'd have done better had Derek's minor genius for making money extended to retaining it. 'No sense of proportion Derek Welkins, that's the problem with you! You'd give your shirt to any Tom, Dick or Harry who spun you a sad story!' How many times had she said it?

Ah, but Derek had been a better husband and man altogether than you-know-who. Sam Wilson had treated Derek with a little respect, but Mona had always believed it was Derek's bank book to which Sam deferred rather than the man himself; there was ever a condescending air to his friendliness, for there was no real room for a self-made man in Sam Wilson's world. That man thought of himself as a toff, and whether you were richer or poorer, he was better than you and that was flat. Derek, being the man he was, had never even noticed Sam's hauteur, and if Wilson was ever rude to him he gave as good as he got instead of treating him with the slapped-face deference everyone else offered when he made his nasty, snobbish little sallies. Derek knew how to deal with old man Wilson, and Derek had stayed at home, he had remained true and faithful, he hadn't made a laughing-stock of himself with some neighbour-woman, and hadn't upped and gone leaving his wife with the near-impossible task of feeding a family of *that* size.

Derek had left a profit-and-loss account in place of a will, and once the finances had been disentangled and lawyers paid, Mona was lucky to hang on to the house and a precipitously tiny private income. She was eternally grateful that their sons had inherited Derek's business flair, but balanced with her common savvy and prudence, they never diced with bankruptcy like their dad.

Nora was still talking. Mona wasn't listening, but knew very well what was being said.

1970

The tears were running into her mouth; hot and appalling, they tasted—she was sure in her unhappy shivering—like blood. Damn, damn, damn, I'm no teenager so why can't I stop this? She cursed herself, tried to summon a stern inner voice to call herself to sense again, but found that the voice had long since been drowned in the raw torrent. Cough-choke-sigh-gasp, then start it all anew, Flora was weeping like a child and it was only the realisation Kara was standing behind her that pulled her out of her dark, despairing spiral. Her daughter slid her arm over Flora's shoulder; Flora took her hand but that just started the tears again.

'I'm sorry, I'm sorry darling, I'm so sorry.' Flora could barely squeeze a breath between the words and tears. Kara, touched and yet angry, spoke in a low tone.

'Don't Mum, don't say sorry. Sorry what for?' Flora subsided a little but then jerked as if roused violently from sleep when the young girl blurted, 'He's a bastard anyway, Mum, he's a bastard and I'm glad he's gone, and I never want to see him again, you shouldn't neither.'

Odd, contradictory, strange and inappropriate emotions washed around in Flora's head as she absorbed her daughter's bitter words. Kara was only eight; she should wash the child's mouth with soap for using language like that, not to mention reprimanding her for showing such disrespect. 'He's your father, after all, no matter what he may have done!' Who was that speaking in her mind—her mother and then her father. But damn it, the girl was *right!* Trevor Latimer was a bastard, polite words couldn't conceal the fact, and all that she had to apologise for was limping along, surviving from day to day in the hope he would change. What did it matter how it was said? He was a bounder, they may have said years ago, a cad, a swine, a blackguard: but *bastard* was better, more honest, more expressive, more profound—more modern. A fucking bastard, a cheating fucking bastard; a lying, selfish, cheating fucking bastard. That was even better. And so Flora did not scold or strike the child, and instead meekly nodded her head.

Kara came round the chair and knelt, kissing her mother and then laying her head in her lap, and the two of them sat silently as Flora's sobs became regular, even breaths and she dropped the hand that had been holding a soaking tissue to her eyes. Kara offered to make tea, but Flora refused, saying she needed just to sit quietly and let everything fall into place, this new life into which they had so suddenly been pitched. Kara seemed reluctant to step even a few feet away from her, but slowly Flora convinced her that she was fine, getting better anyway, and that what she needed was thinking time—alone.

'I'll pop over and see Nonna,' Kara offered, slightly reluctantly, 'I promised I would, and you know what she's like if you break a promise to visit.'

Flora nodded, but called her daughter back as she collected her coat. 'You know what to expect…' she said unhappily.

'Yes Mum.'

Nora was already aware that her son-in-law had been thrown out after one final drunken tantrum, taking an ill-packed case with him, and Kara knew she was unlikely to hold her peace on the matter. Nonna was well-behaved, at first. She chatted to Kara about school, asked her what she and her friends did for fun, talked to her about her favourite TV shows, but eventually the old lady fell silent, spent of small-talk. For a few moments she stared ahead of herself, soundless, and then emitted a series of urgent clicks from her throat as if struggling to hold something down.

'I always warned her that he was—' she began, and Kara sat bolt upright, waving both hands in front of herself as if shielding her body.

'Nonna no, please don't, please, please don't!'

Nora's face puckered with a truculent, angry frustration. 'I only wanted to say it just shows what happens if y'give em a second chance…'

'*Please* Nonna!'

'Well, it's come to a pretty pass when I can't talk to my own granddaughter.'

'We can talk about anything, anything at all Nonna, but not that.'

'People never want to hear what I've got to say,' the old lady growled. 'But if people had listened to me before there'd have been a lot less trouble. I told your mother that.'

'Nonna!' Kara scolded.

'It really is something when a grandmother is told off by a damn girl child! And all I'm doing is speaking God's honest truth!'

'Let's talk about something else—I'll make tea. Mum didn't want any.'

'*You'd* be well advised to pay heed to me too!' Nora had to shout, as Kara was on her feet in an instant and out into the scullery, clattering the kettle and teapot with exaggerated force.

'Past, present or future, men will always be the same,' Nora muttered, not caring that she was alone and unheard. 'And women will never listen, never learn.'

1950

I am the perfect wife. I married my handsome man and surrendered my name for his, I gave up thoughts of my childhood home, left my friends behind and relinquished my life and devotion to my husband. Each day when he set off for work he was fed and watered and when he came home again his meal was ready and his room prepared, aired and warmed so that he could take his ease and forget the strains of the day. If ever he felt passion come on him I never refused him, I always gave him his satisfaction and pleasure. I gave him children and I never asked him to trouble himself with them unless a man's authority was needed; he said that children should be seen and not heard and I tried to give him that, no matter how hard it was to convince the loud and lively little ones that they should be still and quiet in their father's presence.

I cleaned for him and shopped and skivvied; I felt this keenly, a woman with my background should have had someone to do such work for me, but two great wars did away with such things, more's the pity—but I still retained my dignity. I was polite and cheerful but not over-friendly with the neighbours and local traders, I was my husband's representative, his ambassador, and I did everything I could to make him proud. I stood at his shoulder in church, hung on his arm and adorned him when we stepped out. I was beautiful, the most beautiful woman in the avenue, in the village, even in the big towns; that was something to bring a warm glow to a man's heart. A beautiful wife, devoted to him and his children, desired by many a man, but who never let on that she'd noticed, who never encouraged anyone's attentions, nor allowed her husband to be eaten by jealousy because he could know, with a flood of pleasure through his frame and loins, that although others wanted her, craved her, she was his, wholly his. I was the perfect wife.

1931

Nora stroked Sam's cheek but he turned sharply away as if she had brushed him with a razor claw or a stinging-nettle. 'Bad temper!' she cooed, trying to turn his face to hers, catching his chin between her thumb and forefinger. Sam resisted, scowling, as if he was a child whose face was about to be cleaned with handkerchief and spit. 'Bad temper!' Nora repeated, this time pettishly, her eyes watchful and filled with potential hurt. 'Sammy, what's the matter?' hers was now a little girl's voice.

'Never mind,' snapped her husband, leaving Nora feeling as if her guts had dropped away from the hollow shell of her body.

She ran her finger around his collar and whispered silkily, 'But it's my job to make you happy, Sammy darling.'

Sam swallowed hard, his adam's apple bobbing violently, but made no reply until he pulled away from her embrace. 'Nora, you can't even attend adequately to your own happiness, how in God's name are you going to attend to mine?'

1945

Sam found it hard not to extend his hand to reach out and touch her, to caress her, and his words were transported by a sigh.

'You wouldn't know the sheer relief of being understood. I mean truly, fully understood.'

'The good Lord understands us all.' Mirabelle's eyes were on the page and would not engage his; it was impossible to tell if she was being ingenuous, or had understood his barely-hidden meaning and was being evasive. Sam felt a momentary shaft of irritation at the thought that she was playing games with him. He was too old to be indulging in the emotional hide-and-seek beloved of callow youth.

'The Lord understand us yes,' he ventured again. 'But I'm talking about the understanding between a man and a woman. One sanctioned and blessed by God.'

She made no reply. 'I have long lacked that sort of understanding—with my wife. I have come to the conclusion that it was never there.'

'Oh Samuel, that's a terrible thing for you both.' She shook her head and tutted lightly.

'I need that understanding, I need it to go on. I *need* it Mirabelle, and I know I shall never have it from her, it's a quality that is beyond her.'

'But she has many others?' her voice was serious, and again he felt that irritation—it was as if she was trying to pick holes in what he was saying, why could she not help him along?

'I have come to a very serious decision, after much thought, much prayer, much agony.'

No response but a level gaze.

'I have decided to leave my wife.'

Mirabelle Ellis seemed profoundly shocked, but she must surely have known it was coming. Had they not spent all this time together, growing closer and closer in mutuality and understanding—in love?

'That's very serious indeed Samuel—are you very sure? You know what the Bible says of marriage—'

'It is over, I am sure of it, it is irreparable, at an end. And there is something else...' He quailed, even though he was so sure of her, she was gazing straight into his eyes, and where they should be soft, bathed in inner light, her eyes were dry, shuttered windows. Sam pressed on, for his life, his future, depended on this.

'I have not loved my wife for a long, long time. I have stayed with her for the sake of our children, she would never have coped with them alone, she could never have given them what they needed, the guidance, the discipline... but now they are all old enough to find their own way, even little Flora. I can do no more good there, it is at an end. I intend to leave home within the week, find lodgings, start again. I have no choice.'

'I'm sorry Samuel.' Mirabelle inserted these words, spoken softly, into a half-pause as he strove for breath.

'And to start again, to be the man I could be, I need someone who can give me that understanding of which I have been deprived, someone who understands my mind, my soul. I have been blessed with someone who possesses that, and such a blessing can only come from one source and it mustn't be scorned. I want you to come with me, Mirabelle, away from here, in time, of course, not right away like runaways, but I can never be a whole man, spiritually, unless you are with me. I think you know my mind already, that's why I say you understand me. Will you do it? Will you come away with me?'

Gathering The Family

1965

Jack Carthmain hadn't heard of old George Shenton in God's own age, and he had vaguely assumed that the daft drunken owd gimmer had died off, hopefully in peace after one last night in the snug bar of some familiar pub back home. He was therefore surprised but profoundly delighted when he received a phone call from George's daughter, who had spent unknown time and trouble in tracking him down. This call was an invitation to George's eightieth birthday party; Christ, not dead after all, then, he'd made it this far in spite of that unpronounceable disease he'd got, the coal-dust one.

Jack was delivered to the party by his own son, who then got on disturbingly well with the twice-divorced former Miss Shenton, who took him on a tour of her three-bed council house with the air of an unprofessionally flirtatious guide to a stately home. Jack shook off his worries of an inappropriate liaison—bloody hell, the lad was over thirty and it was his own damn business—the quicker to reacquaint himself with his own 'inappropriate' friend, the Trapper-in-Chief, the drunkard, the arch-lech, the teller of the dirtiest jokes in the Midlands, the man who had kept the makers of Woodbines solvent.

On seeing George, Jack reverted momentarily to his previous belief: he was face to face with a dead man who had somehow counterfeited the faint aura of passing life and breath. George's chest heaved at the tiniest exertion, his breath sang high-voiced arias as it squeezed in and out of his neck; he was skinny, nay, skeletal, hairless and helpless, sitting on an overstuffed sofa, propped up on lacy cushions, looking uncomfortable, out of place and impatient as if he was awaiting a merciful blow to his fragile skull. But, Jack soon discovered, the appearance deceived: the old man's eyes flickered with the same excitement as they had when the towels came off the taps in the good old days at the Royal Oak.

'By the roast—Jack Carthmain; you owd bugger!'

'George.' Moved, Jack found himself unable to say more as he drew a chair up.

'Want a beer?'

The old sod had got his own supply down the side of the sofa, placed where he could easily slide his slender hand down to seize his prey; Jack did the honours and the bottles hissed and bubbled, the beer didn't taste half as good as the brew Netta used to serve up at the Oak, but what did that matter? George raised his bottle—no glass—in salute.

'I'll be pissing and farting till a week next Michaelmas, but I don't fuckin care,' George announced with the confidence of a man who had postponed his obsequies until further notice. 'Normally they'd be saying, "Dad, no beer, Dad no fags, Dad no nothin." But just this once they've left off. A man deserves a pint on his birthday. Mebbe more'n one if they turn their bloody backs long enuff.'

'Good on you George. Happy Birthday.' Jack raised his drinking-arm in salute.

'Old times,' said George, clinking glass.

'Old times.'

'Old timers!'

'Old timers.'

'Me more than you, owd mate, but still...' George laughed at himself.

They each took another healthy draught, then a playful, if not downright wicked grin lit George's face.

'Did anybody invite *him?*' he asked archly.

'Him?'

'You know! *Him!*'

'Sweet Jesus George, how would I know? Couldn't find him even if I wanted to; I dunno if that Sherlock Holmes of a daughter of yours has tried. I've no idea if he's even still *in* this world!'

'Oh, e will be.' George was sourly confident. 'And wherever e is, e'll not be far from a church an even less far from someone else's wife, that's what I reckon. Any road I'm only jokin, I don't want to see that holy fool, I'd much rather see you, owd. And anyway I never did quite know what to *say* to Sammy.'

'That never stopped yer, you said loads—and not much o fit was it to say in front of such a godly man!'

They laughed heartily, but briefly. George couldn't do that pub-laugh of his anymore, he hadn't nearly enough wind. For all George's fierce determination to hang on to the breath of life, it seemed as the party was a sort of anticipatory wake. While their conversation managed to rekindle the spirit of the Royal Oak, underscoring it, Jack noted gloomily, was an all-pervading smell of air freshener and disinfectant rather than beer and wartime cigarettes. George's grandchildren, initially curious at the arrival of the silver-haired giant, had already grown bored and sneaked away into another room to watch the television, but George didn't mind; kiddies weren't welcome in the bar anyway, and for the moment, like an embassy of days past, this room was on the home soil of the Royal Oak.

'What did we do before we had TV then eh?' he asked Jack good-naturedly.

'We laughed at Tommy Handley on the radio?' Jack offered.

'And what did we do before—and after—we laughed at Tommy Handley on the radio?' George pressed on: Jack twigged, and they boomed in unison. 'We took the fuckin rise out of Sammy Wilson!'

'I surely ope an pray Sammy inner dead anywees. I'd like to be a fly on the wall when e pegs out.'

'Steady on George old son!'

'No-no, tha mistakes me. It's not as I want to see im *die* as such—but e converted didn't e? To a Left-Footer?

'So they say.'

'That's why I want fer be there fer, when e confesses. It'll take *hours!* Poor fuckin priest, e'll be avin to say, "Owd up, Sammy, go back a ways, what was that un you said just now?"' George was almost carried out of this life by the cackle that escaped his withered chest; he fair keeled over, but straightened after a few moments and wiped a tear. Eager to save the old man's breath, Jack took the lead in unleashing a torrent of reminiscences; of the pub, the beer, of Netta and her old man Fred, of the seemingly endless evenings of chatting and of trapping Sammy Wilson, of the end of the war and the slow dawn of something new. Jack's throat was sore with talking when he saw George's near-toothless mouth working away, lips peeled back, apparently sucking desperately for breath: what was this, a fit, a stroke, a final failure of his done-in heart?

But then he cut across Jack's fulsome flow of words in a borrowed voice. 'You, my lad, have got too much of what the cat licks its bottom with!'

He was Sammy Wilson to the life, and this precipitated more life-stealing laughter, so much so it attracted concerned glances from George's family, which the old man ignored as he recovered, sucking at an inhaler, puffing at it with the devotion he had once shown to his fag packet. The sound Jack heard was a hollow, shallow rasp, as if the drug hadn't penetrated where it needed to go, and never would.

'We had some good times,' said George at last.

'We had good times, yeah.' Jack regretted his tone, it was as if he was patronising the old man, too keen to show agreement with him.

'Had I not had such good times I suppose I could well have been lookin forward to seeing next week.' George nodded to himself, grimly serious.

'George, I...' Jack again felt compelled to reassure his old friend, but his flow of words was stemmed by a wave of the older man's hand.

'I'd have done nowt different. Ceptin I wouldn't've gone so easy on Sammy. Christ, I'd love a fag. Won't let me ave em they won't; do yours tell yer what to do, and what you can an can't ave, move you away from ouse an ome and tell yer it's fer yer own good?' He kindled a not-very-angry stare at his children, who were talking together quietly, as if once again plotting his future.

'More or less,' Jack agreed dolefully. 'And doubtless it'll

get worse as I get older.'

'Depend on it,' George accorded with a wise nod. 'By seventy-five your brain's gone, your mouth's drooling and your bowels are permanently out o kilter—that's what they think. I'm amazed not to be in a nappy and bib. Silly beggars.'

The conversation went into remission, but only to allow two more bottles to be opened; George didn't check if his drinking-mate wanted more, he just attacked the bottles and handed one over.

'What about *her*?' George asked, much to Jack's puzzlement.

'Who?'

'*Her*. That wife of his.'

'He's still with her, amazingly. He married again, I heard, about four year ago.'

'Naaahhh, I'm not interested in some ole lady tryin to make an honest man of im at the end of is days, I mean *her*. Remember her?'

'Oh, Nora.'

'Nora, aye.' George rolled his eyes at Jack's foolishness. 'How old would she be now, Jack?' the retired coal merchant tried to tot up the figures in his resisting head.

'Sixty-five by my reckoning,' he finally announced, embarrassed at his slowness: a faint ember of lust, a sort of twilight of lechery, animated George's time-nipped features.

'Sixty-five and I'll bet she's still a fuckin knock-out. Women in that town were fading flowers by thirty and old hags by forty, but not her. If only I'd had the courage...'

You old sod, thought Jack in wonder and admiration, in

all these years you've never forgotten. 'D'you ever see her?' It sounded like George would have been made just a little jealous by a yes.

'Not since fifty-nine, I'd say, old mate. She's still there in that same house, or anyway she was when I left town. Don't think she'll ever move.'

'No, nor do I.' George looked momentarily like a relieved hunter; his quarry would be easy to find, but then a sad realisation dawned. 'No mate, she'll never move. But it's all for him.'

'Eh? You've lost me again George.'

'Only for him, for Sammy. She wants to be there, waiting, when he finally decides to come home. She wants to make it easy for him.'

George was breathing with increasing difficulty and Jack could hear now, louder than anything in the house, the seams of coal dust that were torturing the old miner's lungs.

'Take it easy now George, eh?'

'It's been grand t'see you again Jack.'

'And you, old lad.'

'No, really. Just like old times. *They* wouldn't understand.' He jerked his head at his family, still deep in their conference but again there was little anger in him; then in a moment his demeanour changed and he was damp-eyed and maudlin, a state he had rarely achieved at the Royal Oak. 'Good times, Jack. Wouldn't have missed them for the whole wide world.'

'Nor me.' Jack was forced back into uneasy reassurance, but he was sincere.

'If I had a farthing to leave to anyone it'd be you old son, not to *these*.' This time when he looked at his children there was a careworn spite in his face. 'Kept me a prisoner, they have. Sometimes I think I'd rather be dead—an I'll soon enough achieve *that*. And don't tell me not to be fuckin morbid, mate.'

'Wasn't going to.' Jack was a practical man, and there was little point in denying the obvious. 'No George, no, I was just thinking about what you said and wondering in the back of me mind if you'd got something to leave for old Sammy.'

'Sammy?' the old man's eyes rose momentarily out of their state of slow death. 'For Sammy, yeah, a packet o French letters, and idiot-proof instructions on how to fuckin use em!'

And the burst of laughter that followed nearly carried them *both* away.

1960

Helen stopped the car outside the compact bungalow, and an eerie silence obtained, undercut by a low, mournful wind. Flora did not move from the passenger seat; she did not move at all.

'Come along Flo,' chivvied her sister, clambering out of the car in a flurry. 'Let's get this done. And remember it's not *we* who should be nervous. Our consciences are clear—yes?'

There was a puritan tang to her voice. She slammed the car door then strutted over and opened Flora's door too. 'Come *along*!' she snapped with customary Wilson éclat. Helen stepping out, Flora trailing reluctantly, the two women walked towards the gate. This moment had been sooner in coming than they had anticipated; Sam Wilson had summoned his offspring to meet his new wife. For his own reasons he had only invited two of them on this first occasion, the oldest and youngest. Predictably this had been the cause of a spat among the sisters; Minnie was angry and jealous not to be first, and she had been nothing but trouble from the moment she had heard about the arrangement. Sam could not be prevailed on to vary the terms of his summons and so Minnie was left to stew.

The building could not have stood in greater contrast to the enormous, dark family home at Woolsend Avenue. It was neat, square and featureless, fronted by a big, generous window that should have admitted floods of light but for the mean, Sam-like touch that was the blinds: venetian blinds that looked like prison bars, tilted with care to exclude as much as possible of that sweet daylight, their multiple jaws set to snap fully shut. Within, the house proved prissily tidy, a dwelling, thought Flora, that had never seen children, decorated with a proliferation of shiny mirrors and equally shiny silver crosses on the walls, a scrupulously over-clean environment in which Flora knew should one speck of dirt appear, it would be considered a disaster. She felt a sense of violation, that as she stepped over the threshold she was bringing uncleanliness into this sterile chapel; she had to quash the physical desire to stop dead and check she was not trailing slime behind her. Sunlight strained through the sieve of the near-closed blinds, spreading fingers of light into the living room; in any other house, gnat-clouds of dust would be visible tumbling and dancing in these searching rays, but here not an atom stirred, not a mote.

Tea and cake were served after smiles and welcomes, but it seemed to Flora that her father's new wife believed herself to be hosting a chimps' tea-party, as her eyes seemed to follow every stray crumb, her face tensed every time a tea-cup clanked or someone spoke with even the merest fragment of food in their mouth. Neither Helen nor Flora could decide who in that room was the most uncomfortable. Conversation came uneasily too, it did not flow so much as bleed, painfully. The new Mrs. Wilson was concerned only with Sam and their new life together, and she sat still and expressionless when the sisters attempted to tell Sam of events at home, about the lives of his grandchildren. Mention of the family seemed painful and distasteful to Yvette Wilson, reminders that Sam could never be entirely, wholly hers.

Yvette—nee Parsons—was pretty, judged Flora, though her looks were fading. She was an unused but patched and fragile specimen of womanhood, as if she had been built enthusiastically but inexpertly from a kit, pieced section by section in accordance with Sam's tastes. Her hair was an indeterminate brown-blonde, it seemed to dither and shift shades as if desperate to please. She was slim and slight, a woman who had never carried an ounce of excess weight. She was childless; but of course. The strain of even the easiest of births would surely have broken her apart; as far as being a mother eight times over—well! The way in which Yvette carried herself spoke eloquently that she was inviolable, untouchable to all, even to her husband. Perhaps that lack of physicality, the evident rigid sexlessness, was also in tune with Sam's desires: he was done with the business of the bedroom, he was sixty years old and his concerns were ethereal.

Yvette spoke with faultless discipline, affecting an English correctness: when she spoke it was in neat boxes, clean-cut, and always with a glance in Sam's direction as if seeking a nod of his head as cue and approval. But when she spoke on her pet subject, both that discipline and her lofty, aristocratic bearing ceased to serve her: she spoke of her husband, the flesh-wrapped saint at her side, and the words spilled out.

'As soon as I saw Samuel I knew at once of his great goodness. I mean it was apparent right away, but you must know that of course.'

The words carried on; she gushed and twittered about his piety, charity, deep and inspiring Christian faith, his ability to navigate the Bible with an abiding confidence, this great man, so kind, forbearing and wise. Flora cast a desperate glance at Helen, who seemed to be verging on rage at witnessing such idolatry; this woman has surely confounded her husband with none other than the gentle Jesus.

The act of misdirected worship rattled on: what did this woman intend, wondered Flora; did she believe that she could win over her husband's children by convincing them of her earnest love for him? Or was she lost in reciting a catechism that she would, given the chance, spout off to anyone whom she felt needed to be informed of her ecstasy? Yvette's voice, a tone of high-strung brightness, was as fragile as her physical frame, and as likely to break at any moment. Her reliance on her Samuel completed that; were he to desert her as he had his first wife, she would surely wink out of existence with only a dry cry of amazed despair. As she persisted with her air-portrait of the moral colossus at her side, Sam smiled shyly, only slightly abashed at her fulsomeness, perhaps happy at last that there was someone who appreciated him as he deserved.

To Helen's clearly mounting irritation, Yvette prattled unstoppably about the church, about the coming of Lent and what she and her Sam might give up for forty days, and she giggled childishly as she waved about a plate of fancy cakes as she anticipated the glorious abstinence to come. What on earth could there be for this joyless pair to deny themselves, wondered Flora sourly; it must be a very, very short list of pleasures.

Neither Sam nor Yvette made any reference whatsoever to her own past, tempting Flora still further into the suspicion that her father had plucked this woman from the void. Nowhere in sight were there pictures of a younger Yvette, no sign of brothers, sisters, parents, friends, of any independent existence whatsoever. Flora also noticed quickly that when flittering in and out of the room to replenish the tea or fetch another cake, Yvette was forever checking her appearance in one or other of the mirrors, patting her hair, running a finger down her cheek or, with quick, precise gestures, amending some invisible flaw in her face or dress. So: Sam Wilson, a forest of crucifixes and a hall of mirrors. This place was full of objects of worship.

At the end of his wife's panegyric, Sam sang her praises in return, as if he was making formal response to a toast. Yvette withdrew to the kitchen again, blushing and fluttering under the ticklish burden of compliments; she glanced at a mirror as she pattered by it, smiling, happy; absorbed.

Alone with his daughters, Sam treated them to a heavy-browed and forbidding expression. 'You'd not deny me my happiness?' he asked softly. Both Helen and Flora understood him; the question was nothing of the sort and the gentle tone was an imposture. Their father had made his pronouncement, and did not intend to be defied or opposed in this matter. A still quiet fell between them and Flora let her eyes wander the fussy little room, occupying her mind by comparing it to the room where Nora sat, surrounded by photographs new and old, the framed histories of her children and grandchildren, always waiting for the much-loved company of the real thing. Her lost husband, by contrast, sat at the empty heart of cold denial, there remained no acknowledgment of anything but the here and now, of himself and Yvette.

Yvette's return brought lighter chatter, but neither Helen nor Flora found comfort in the new conversation.

'This is a *terribly* respectable area,' commented Yvette, having invited her visitors to admire her home. 'There are some *very* good people here. I have lived here for, oooh, many years...'

There was a momentary pause, a flinch, as if at the realisation that she had made a tiny, accidental reference to the pre-Samuel past, but the moment of awkwardness was gone in a trice and the bright tone continued untarnished. 'I know everyone hereabouts of course, but we are very careful about being too *familiar* with certain people. The man over the way, for instance, he is a jolly nice person, you understand, but he is a taxi driver. We pass the time of day with him, but we don't encourage anything more. Not the sort—you know.'

A click-click noise started deep within Helen's throat. Flora dropped her eyes to the floor as if smitten with the carpet. Sam Wilson's representative on Earth did not seem to notice their reactions.

'We had hoped to live out our days here, dear Sam and I, but we hear tell that there are Indian families getting in not ten miles away; we should have to up sticks should they come much closer, isn't that so Samuel?'

Neither of the sisters spoke until they had been driving for about ten minutes. Eyes resolutely on the road.

Helen was matter-of-fact. 'You know what our dad's gone and done, don't you?'

'Married the same woman. Yes.' Flora had no hesitation.

'Pretty, vain, shallow and lost in admiration of Saint Bloody Samuel,' growled Helen. 'Did you not have the temptation to step up and just slap her? I did until I realised that much of the sound I was hearing was the wind whistling between her ears.'

As they neared home, Flora fell to thinking; he may have married the same woman, but Yvette-nee-Parsons is a poor counterfeit of the first Mrs. Wilson. She owns all her poor qualities, but all her earthiness is extirpated, and what is left is a colourless, odourless imitation, a ventriloquist's doll, a creature controlled by Sam Wilson.

'I spent a good deal of the time wondering where her off-switch was.'

'So—how d'you like your new mother?'

Nora was hunched in her chair, refusing to look at anyone.

'Oh it's no use pretending, your father may have trained you to think me a fool, but it's not so. A little bird told me where you were bound.'

'And would that little bird be named Minnie, by any chance?' enquired Helen tartly.

'*Bum'ole!*' Nora exploded. 'At least your father told me to my face that he thought me a fool. You pair don't even show me *that* courtesy. Oh Lord what have I done, my daughters not only side with that bloody man, they prefer his new, false wife an all!'

'Oh come on Mum, it's not like that, you know it's not...' Helen began, but Nora was not mollified. Helen and Flora had smelt out the fraud and theatre in Nora, and yet they both felt the taut pull of guilt, and within moments were competing to cheer their mother with their unfavourable impressions of wittering, twittering, snobbish Yvette.

'Lady Muck—I bloody well thought so. And I'd heard somewhere she was soft in the head. Yes.' Nora smiled, satisfied, appeased.

1945

'If the good Lord were to bless me with another daughter, I should certainly call her Enola Gay.' The firm, decisive voice was familiar, but lurking within its tones Jack and George detected something they had never previously encountered: there was a wandering quality to the diction, as if the speaker knew what he intended to say, but that his tongue had grown too fat and lumpy for his mouth and was scraping against its roof, jamming against the teeth. The name 'Enola Gay' came out as intended, but the experienced topers knew it had come close to disaster; the thick tongue had nearly slurred and mangled it into 'Egola Nay'. Saints preserve us, Sammy Wilson was one over the eight! He had never indulged in more than his customary pint and a half in all the time they had known him, not enough ale to sozzle a church mouse. 'Not even enuff t'cheer the bugger up a touch,' George lamented. Sammy had even remained abstemious amid the wild revelries of VE Day, so why had he now chosen the defeat of the yellow peril to suddenly let go?

'Is, er, the good lord *likely* to bless you with another daughter?' George, sloshed and grinning out of a beetroot face, couldn't resist prodding his prey. But Sam did not answer, his eyes were wide and his whole body still; was he about to fall on his face or had he been momentarily paralysed by some holy epiphany?

'It is at an end,' said Sam, distinctly. He stood, his stool tottered and so for a moment did the man, but then he regained fluid movement and within a moment was gone from the bar.

1945

George Shenton was pie-eyed again: what was wrong with the man these days? How did he get pissed so easily on that war-watered beer? His bladder was getting bloody unreliable too; first sign of old age, decided Jack Carthmain as he sat next to his mate, who was guiding a battered fag, one that he appeared to have sat down upon at some point, to and from his mouth.

'Awrate, George?' Jack enquired with a touch of the

bedside manner.

'Aye, awrate. You?'

'Can't complain.'

For a time it seemed as if there was nothing either man could think of to say, and each realised that his eyes were wandering over to the door.

'He's finally gone, mate,' said George, too loudly.

'How's that?' Jack blinked, momentarily confused.

'Sammy. He's finally fucked off. I passed by is front gate this afternoon and could hear is missus from there, keenin like a bloody banshee she was.'

'How d'you know it was cos of Sammy?'

'Heard her calling for im I did, shouting, "what am I going to do without him?" Calling his name. She sounded heartbroken one moment, angry the next. But always... helpless.' The glass wobbled towards George's face as the last words bubbled uncertainly off his lips. Just how many had he had?

'Didn't just pass by that gate did you George, by the sound of it; you stopped and listened a good while too!'

'Only to light a fag, I swear! Anyway, you could ear er down the whole length of the avenue, no trouble. I reckon Joe Stalin in Moscow would ave bin sendin out to know what all the palaver was.'

Jack took a moment to light his own gasper and collect his thoughts. 'So where is he?'

'No one knows to the best of my ken. Tell you something, though, Sammy's not within bloody miles of here and yet Mirabelle Ellis has been seen at the butcher's and the baker's today, behaving as if nothing's happened, same cold good mornings, same prissy expression. She inna weepin.'

'Ah.' Jack took this in with a lungful of smoke. 'Reckon Sammy saw the light before it were too late?'

'Who knows? Them two are better off without one another anyway,' Jack began to agree, but then paused, realising that there was more than one way of understanding what George had just said.

'I wonder...' George was lost in thought, or beer, or both, and Jack had to cough pointedly to prompt him. 'I wonder;' George started again, but once more the dreaminess palsied his face for a long time. 'How long should I leave it?'

'Leave what?'

'Till I can move in on Sammy's missus.'

'Oh for crying out loud George, be your age! And what would *Mrs.* Shenton say?'

George's expression became concentrated, face furrowed. 'That sort o'thing never stopped Sammy, and *I* am just a humble fuckin sinner, not one of God's chosen! What's good enough for Sammy's good enough for me, and Monica would never notice anyway, not if Mrs. Sammy was right there in bed with us she wouldn't!'

Jack decided to leave the silly old fool to his fantasies and endeavoured to change the subject, but the latest news retook the conversation shortly afterwards and it was Jack's own doing.

'Huh. He's had two women on the go for how many years and then dumps them both on the same day. A real moral trail-blazer is our Sammy!'

'What am I going to do without hiiiiiiim?' George burst out in a piercing falsetto. 'S what it sounded like. You'd think the air-raids were back on, up and down like Wailing Willie.'

There followed another long pause in the conversation, and Jack and George realised that they both had their eyes on the door yet again.

'Come to think of it,' mused Jack quietly, 'What are *we* going to do without him?'

1986

'Wicked old sinner,' Nora said to silence. 'Wicked, wicked, discussting. A bigamist, if you like. He wasn't married to her, not in any way I would recognise, not in any way the Lord would recognise neither, so what does that make him eh? Absolutely discussting.'

The fire was dying, just glowing orange-red cracks between the fused coals. A half-full teacup was at Nora's elbow and the TV glowed and chattered as her head nodded, taken by surprise by sleep. 'Wicked ole sinner.' She struggled out of her chair and seized the poker, closing the damper with a clank. Painfully, she turned, took faltering steps into the corner of the room to turn the television off, straightened herself by pushing against the set's flat top, and then rubbed at the pain in her hips as she shuffled off to bed. The dishes, her dirty ashtray, they would have to wait until morning.

How curious the house was, a place once full of children's noises and smells, empty and silent. When the kiddies had been there, Sam Wilson had tried to impose unchildlike hush on them, a thing against nature so it was. Now all that remained of Sam was the silence. Nora made her aching way upstairs: steeper every day they were, her path to bed longer and more arduous every night. The air on the stairs and the landing was chilly, indeed the whole upstairs was cold, and three of its rooms had stood empty for many a year. The girls had shared two, but always in changing formations as they fell out and formed alliances in a seemingly endless cycle. Nora could still hear their hissed confidences and irrepressible giggles leaking out of the walls and through the doors. The third room had been hers and Sam's; she never even looked at it as she passed by, it was only ever used when one of her daughters stayed, perhaps for one of their measly, fleeting Christmas visits. Other than to air the room and change the sheets, Nora never went in there. In her nostrils it retained a musk, the odour of warm bodies, of love and arousal, and that juxtaposed with the room's emptiness was more than she could bear. She made do with her tiny, tiny room, the boy's it once was; she could tuck herself in the single bed with just a small table to hold her glass of water and false teeth in their night-time fluid. The four, close walls were easy to make and keep warm, and being squeezed in by them had advantages, she might more easily save herself should she take one of her falls. This was the room in which one night, probably soon, Nora Wilson would turn her face to the wall and forget her suffering.

The youngest of the great-grandchildren, they didn't like the upstairs, they quailed and said it was spooky, and even if Nonna could persuade them to stay they would never settle no matter how cheerful and welcoming she made the old rooms. There had been nightmares and tears and Nonna had sat up with the little ones many a time, sometimes all night, no doubt contributing to the ruination of her health. Ah, there were no ghosts here, not wicked ones at any rate, just the sad memories of lost children and herself, the ghost-to-be. The only malignant spirit pervading hearth and home was the unsmiling, undead spectre of Sammy Wilson. Perhaps he caused all the trouble, still going from room to room forbidding and crushing childish joy and exuberance, ever commanding silence with his dark-browed glower.

'Why don't you give up the house, Mum?' those girls of hers, always going on at her. 'You can't cope with it any more, you know you can't, you're only really living in two rooms, you'd never keep anywhere properly clean if we didn't come over and help you. We can't always be there, we've lives of our own, you know, and some day it will be too much for any of us. Sell up, mum, get a bungalow or something, a little place you can manage...'

Bum'ole. I shall die here. I have known it as a fact ever since I came here.

Besides, I fought hard for this house, wiped the self-satisfied smirk off of Sammy Wilson's face when I outmanoeuvred him, so I did. If I give up this house I shall have lost everything: the souls of my poor dead children will have to bide with strangers and I shall never hear my erring husband's footsteps as he comes home at last.

Money and Fine Words

1944

George Shenton's shoulders were slumped, his eyes flickered back and forth, aimed always at the floor as if scratching for scraps like a nervous hen in a farmyard. His hands were darting in and out of his pockets, ferreting and patting, but whatever he was seeking was not there, and his discomfiture grew. Finally, with a sigh, he approached Sam Wilson, hands rubbing together slowly as if about to join in prayer, and addressed the man in respectful, embarrassed tones.

'Er, Sammy now,' he almost stuttered, 'I needs must confess a slight problem.' He was even making an effort to enunciate; a schoolboy trying to discipline his lazy tongue to please a difficult master. 'Sammy, I gorra... got a... problem... changed me trousers afore I came out... left all me money at wom... home... I don't suppose you could... borrow us a tanner, owd?'

'Lend.' Wilson hadn't even looked at his supplicant.

'Beg pardon?'

'I lend,' Wilson turned a dignified gaze upon him, 'you borrow.'

'Erm, well yes, that was the general idea, old son.'

'You know the wise words Mr. Shenton, neither a borrower nor a lender be.'

'Ooever said that wasn't peggin for a pint, Sammy!'

Sam said no more, finished his own drink, found his hat and left. George's face was akin to that of a superlatively depressed bloodhound.

'Never mind owd,' came Jack Carthmain's cheery, breezy voice, 'I'll stand yer a pint. That performance was worth a whole evening's worth of beer!' Jack jingled his hand at Netta, smirking.

'No Jack, by my reckoning it's my shout.' The near-broken old miner straightened. 'Oddly enough I've *just realised* I had me money with me the ole time…'

The Trappers guffawed until they were breathless.

1947

Something had changed about Mrs. Murchison's shop, something Flora could not define. Change, change, change, it was all around, the whole world had changed, the war over, Ole Hickler was dead and Sam Wilson had left home—but what had shifted in this tiny place had nothing of the obvious about it.

There was a great deal that had changed about Flora, too—she was no longer a little girl, the shop's counter no longer loomed above her small, wondering head like a cliff face; she could now see all the wares on their shelves and baskets rather than them appearing from a great height as if the shopkeeper were a benevolent goddess dishing out sustenance from atop that flat-sided wooden mountain; the bacon-slicer was simply a tool used to cut fine strips of meat, a spinning disc of metal to be operated with care and skill lest its user's flesh add to the meat falling into the greaseproof paper. Years before Flora could spy its metallic flash and spin, hear the light grinding, slitting noise it made, but she was unable to work out if Mrs. Murchison was working a mundane act or a miracle, and her childish mind tended towards the latter. She once believed that the Wilsons would die without Mrs. Murchison and that even if their father or God himself failed them, then the shopkeeper would still provide.

The shop certainly looked different—smaller, more drawn-in; the whole square space colder and with a bare, starved look as if the years of rationing had perished and withered it, and the promised new years of plenty would not arrive soon enough to make it bloom again.

Mrs. Murchison herself was altered: she was a large lady, kindly and smiling, always willing to lean over the counter to let the children share that generous beam, sometimes pulling up the flap of the counter to come out on to the floor and make a fuss of the little ones and give them treats she 'just happened' to have in her apron pockets, but now she no longer looked so large, Flora was sure she was a good few inches taller than the shopkeeper, and that while her own body was filling out the older woman was shrinking in length and breadth, as if the decline in the shop's dimensions was reflected, or even sparked, by its owner. Mrs. Murchison always used to be laughing, all the time, thunderous and jolly peals Flora found herself unwittingly imitating, so much so that one of her sisters used to say 'Hello Mrs. Murchison!' if a joke or jape found its target, but now there seemed scant chance of that resonant boom making a return—the chest from which it had come had shrunk, the face no longer wore the smile that was the precursor to the laugh, and there was a pinched look about that expression behind the counter.

Mrs. Murchison was always nattering to Mother about

this, that, the other—gossip that was frequently the cause of that laugh—but now she was taciturn, not impolite, not cussing quietly under her breath, nor spiteful or sarcastic as some shopkeepers could be, but there was no more chatter or banter. Flora had enjoyed listening to Mother and Mrs. Murchison chatting, it had always been a sunny event, cheerful and positive, of course we'll win the war, have you heard who's getting married, aren't you *happy* for them; the antithesis of the sour carping that went on behind closed doors with those dried-up crones in the Avenue. But now no more chat and no more cheer; Mrs. Murchison was not exactly miserable, not hostile, but she was unforthcoming. The change, above all changes, of which Flora was aware was in the shopkeeper's mien, in the way in which friendly loquacity had been superseded by a form of dourly amused watchfulness.

Another great change for Flora was that she was alone; her mother had not set foot in the shop since Father left them all, she had begun to ask Flora to 'go to Murchisons' on a regular basis from that day, and although the girl had obeyed without demur she had not found the shop or its keeper to be the same since; am I, she wondered, a disappointment to Mrs. Murchison, less worthy of her friendship than my mother? Or have they fallen out, is that why Mother won't come here? Does she think her old friend will now look down on her because Father went away? Of all the people in Woolsend, Mrs. Murchison would have been the one whom Flora would have guaranteed to be sympathetic and not to sit in judgement, and yet Mother now avoided her.

As she stepped into the shop Flora almost fancied that

a welcoming smile had been switched off—put that light out—doused the moment the woman behind the counter realised who was there. Is it something about me, she wondered, something I've done or said, or not done, not said, am I not as good as my mother, does Mrs. Murchison think she's wasting her time talking to a fifteen year old? She shook aside such silliness and yet still was troubled by the sense of change all about her, subtle and silent but all-pervading change.

That watchful, sardonic look, almost teetering into a sneer, hovered around the familiar face the time that Flora was in the shop, but it deepened as she placed her order, almost as if Mrs. Murchison was ticking off the choices the child made and talking to herself. 'Silly thing to choose, only a fool would buy that, do you know nothing girl?' The bacon-slicer spun, greaseproof paper crinkled, other cuts and pieces were wrapped in rustling paper and Mrs. Murchison placed each one into Flora's small wicker basket with careful hands that had begun to show the first effects of age's gnarling, as if they were turning into tree limbs.

'There you are my darling,' said Mrs. Murchison in a quiet voice, reaching out over the counter with an open palm she then flipped over, patting Flora's hand and at last liberating that old smile. And the girl went away reassured, although somehow felt eyes following her from the shop, as if making sure she was not going to make a grab at the little bits and pieces on display in the wide, cold window.

2011

'And it took me a while to work out what was going on.'

Flora sighed into a cup of steaming tea, warming her memories and ruing her girlish foolishness. 'For I'd go to that shop so often, I'd tell Mrs. Murchison what we needed and she would drop it into my basket and off I'd go—but there was one step missing, wasn't there, a little something one normally did before leaving a shop?'

'Saying goodbye?' Francine floundered, and felt a rush of red heat to her face when her grandmother laughed.

'Paying, child, *paying*! Oh I shouldn't laugh: you not thinking of it makes me feel better for myself age fifteen! No, I was never asked to pay, not once, and when I finally woke up to the fact that other people would go into that shop and hand over their coupons and pennies and the till would go ting-clank, I realised that the normal thing to do was to *pay*.

'Well; I thought about this. From what my father used to say about other families being common and so forth, thinking too about the airs and graces my mother often allowed herself, at least before he took himself off, I decided perhaps I had made a mistake about our position in the world, that Father *was* right, that there was something *special* about our family, and that special people, toffs like us, did not have to mess about with money.' Flora blew a mist of steam off her cup. 'But of course I was wrong; that's what the silences were about, the death of the smiles. Mother sent me up to that shop because she couldn't face it, going in there knowing she had nothing in her purse and no idea of when anything would materialise. Old Ma Murchison was bitterly unhappy about Mother's never-never bill, as there seemed to be more "never" to hers than to anyone else's. She was too kindly to let us starve but too human not to be peeved at what Mother was doing. Never-never. Never again, I'll tell you.'

1938

Sam had treated himself and treated himself finely; there was an expression of indulgent pride on even his ascetic face as he examined the little metal object nestling in the palm of his hand, and his index finger wound gently round the fine-linked chain, coiling it up and then letting it go again so that it clanked, almost hissed, against the side of the pocket-watch. He sat by the fire in the kitchen, and Flora sat opposite, watching quietly. Mother was supposed to be there, they were supposed to be baking, but something else had captured Nora's attention for the time. It was uncertain if Sam even knew that his little girl was in the room as he toyed gently with the watch, winding it up with slow, almost reverent care, pressing at its catch to make its shiny lid spring, staring at the flawless glass and the digits and hands behind it, then pressing the lid shut again as if secretively closing a shell in which he had discovered a pearl. Open-shut, open-shut, he did it again and again, silently fascinated, his expression absorbed and boyish.

Flora saw the way the flicking of the lid caught the light and followed the progress of the small stars that it threw out, hoping every time daddy would do it just once again so she could see the lights. This thing must be precious, she thought, it's not gold but it must be silver, awesome, shining silver. She slipped from her chair and crept closer to her father, who still showed no sign of realising she was there.

'Daddy, that's beautiful,' she half-whispered; the watch-face snapped loudly and Sam looked up, inexplicably frightened, but recovered his composure and settled the watch into the pocket of his waistcoat. Flora followed its path, regretting it should now be hidden.

'It's very beautiful,' she said again, 'how much did it cost?'

She had thought her question innocuous but her father looked at her with a fiery-eyed glare that made her realise once again she had said the wrong thing. She took two steps back, involuntarily, and felt her stomach do that collapsing thing it did whenever she had made her father angry.

'How much did it cost?' He threw the question back at her, but at least he did not shout, she couldn't bear it when he shouted. 'Money and fine words my girl, money and fine words.'

Sam fell silent and Flora, shaking with relief, realised she could go now. She set off to find her mother, acutely aware that she had just been very lucky.

1958

'I got a letter from slissiters.'

'Slissiters?' Petra was puzzled , but her mother produced a paper from among the clutter on the small table beside her chair, and the ludicrous multiple name of the firm made it clear what sort of creature they were dealing with.

'Slissiters,' Nora waved the letter, 'working for your father.'

Her voice rose and fell over the course of these few words, but it was impossible to divine if she was inclining towards crying or crowing. A fragile smile settled on her lips, so dainty and ambivalent it might fade or crack and flop downwards, or ratchet up and widen to become knowing, even malicious.

'What do they want?' asked Petra.

'What does *he* want, that's the point.' There was a lurking triumphalism in Nora's voice. 'A divorce, that's what he wants. Found a new wife, I suppose.'

'Oh Mum ...' Petra began, uncertain whether to smother her mum in sympathy or to be businesslike and aloof. Nora's normally open, telltale face was a mask of emotional ambiguity.

'What are you going to say to him?' Petra asked, mastering herself and managing a neutral tone, and at that question Nora's smile became firmer, a forceful and quite unpleasant grin.

'Oh he can have what he wants,' Nora's eyes flashed, but with a metallic defiance in place of her habitual tears. 'I'm fed up of the bloody man pestering. But he's going to pay for it. Oh but he's going to pay.'

'How, Mum?' Petra sat beside her, intrigued at this harsh new aspect of her mother's character.

'This house. That's the price, he must make this house mine, give up any claim he has on it, and then he can have his divorce and go to the devil—he can *marry* the perishin devil if he wants to for that matter. No doubt that Mirabelle Ellis will be putting on her best frock and trying to tidy her hair ready to join him.'

'Mum...' Petra warned.

'Oh very well, but he's got some damn floozy in mind, some old maid with a face like the back of a bus and the heart of a slut.'

'Mum!'

'Oh *bum'ole* girl, I can say what I like! This house: he can well afford to give it up, he got it for a song from old man Thorndyke in any case. I'll rest better, safer, when this house is mine and mine alone and Sam Wilson has no right to set foot in it.' The look of vulpine cunning deepened and spread over Nora's face. 'And when I die I shall have to decide who gets this house, which of my daughters. Perhaps the one who doesn't treat me like I'm some sort of...'

'Don't start those games mother, I'm not impressed.'

'*Bum'ole*! You're too serious missy, that's your problem, always has been, there's no sense of fun in you, there's a poker up your backside, just like your wretched father. He can have his divorce. He can have it an choke on it. What do I care, what do I care eh? *Bum'ole*.'

1944

'Borrow us some cash Sammy, oh my lord...' Jack was still cackling.

'Next time I'm goin ter tell im I've used up me copper ration or summat,' mused George.

'Why didn't e just take pity an offer to stand you a pint?' asked Netta, pushing another two brimming glasses towards her best customers.

'Sammy?' George was aghast. 'Dearest landlady, have you *ever* seen Sammy Wilson buy another man a drink?'

Netta had to think, but eventually shook her head over the bar.

'Course not,' George pontificated. 'E's bin comin ere five year now and he's *never* put is hand in is pocket. I dunno if it's because he's just a mean ole sod, or e's Lord Muck with the seat out of his pants for all his airs and graces.'

'I reckon he's a patriot,' offered Jack, at which obscurity George furrowed his brow.

'A wha?'

'A patriot, owd feller, a true and sincere one. See, he loves his King so much, he can't bear to be parted from him; so in Sammy's pocket His Majesty stays!'

'One o these days,' George Shenton drew himself up to his full height, hand at his breast, taking a solemn pledge. 'One o these days I hereby swear I shall achieve the impossible—and get a drink out o Sammy Wilson!'

1958

This house will be mine. I can lock the doors and know he can never return. I'm done with Sammy Wilson, done mithering, done mourning. I shall forget him and die content.

Wedding Bands

1982

The car lurched into graceless, uneven motion as if clinging to the road, digging in, unwilling to undertake the chore being demanded of it; Flora cursed herself for crunching the gears and shot a warning glare at Minnie, who, unabashed, gave vent to a great exhalation and then uttered a loud, disapproving tut from the back seat. Very well, thought Flora, my clever-dick sister can show off her superior driving skills on the way home—that's the arrangement—and I'll make damn sure Minnie gets her share of tongue-clicks, rolling eyes and weary gasps *then*, oh yes.

Flora dismissed such infantile pettiness from her mind and redoubled her concentration, swearing to herself she would keep her attention strictly on the road in spite of all temptation; but she couldn't help it, something distracted her and her gaze kept sliding to her left; she snatched guilty snapshot looks before hastily redirecting her eyes, as if furtively sizing up a potential lover: but the figure in the passenger seat, the person who fascinated her so greatly, was no eligible handsome stranger but the most familiar face she could ever wish to see.

It was the mode of her mother's dress, not to mention how she smelt, that was exercising Flora's mind. There was an air-clogging scent tickling her nose and curling noxiously down her throat, an oily, cloying fragrance: Nora had gone to town on her perfume, presumably because she couldn't smell just how heavily she had doused herself. Hopefully the invisible but overpowering gas cloud would dissipate before they reached their destination; the man they were visiting may have considered himself the acme of elegance and good manners, but he was perfectly capable of ruining the occasion within moments with vulgar complaints such as, 'Someone smells like a tart's boudoir.'

Mother had insisted on the outfit too, and again Flora felt it was a terrible mistake. For years Nora had denied herself pretty clothes and gewgaws, what good were all such silly things to a woman soon to wear a shroud? She would always say in that hideous, defeated moan of hers, but now she was attempting to blaze like the sun—it was all too bright, too keen, too eager-to-please. She probably hadn't dressed like this since she paraded proudly in her Sunday best when Dad was still at home. Both Flora and Minnie quietly feared what their father would make of Nora's appearance and aroma. And as for the pink fluffy slippers that adorned her feet—well, they would just confuse matters further. 'They're too swollen!' Nora had winced as her daughters tried to fit her best shoes for her, 'Too swollen, I'll not get two yards in those.' And, dressed up more as a pantomime dame than a femme fatale, she pointed firmly, decisively at the ancient, saggy-sided slippers.

The set of her mother's face also intrigued Flora. It was the selfsame expression she adopted watching the 'plays' on television in the evening; her eyes were glazed, gauzy, and fixed on some infinitely distant point, she smiled in a disturbing semi-rictus and all expression was otherwise absent. It was as if she was adrift in another world, the disembodied witness of some joy that belonged to a remote stranger. Had Minnie slipped her one of those dratted tranquillisers before they got into the car? Her sister had always been one for rash, ill-considered decisions and never favoured canvassing others' opinions.

Flora shivered. She was not looking forward to this. At a mirror's glance she saw Minnie's expression was guarded, serious, verging on disapprobation of all around her, but little could be inferred from this steely self-importance, it was an inheritance from their father that masked and nothing more. So much for attempts to read my passengers' minds, thought Flora ruefully.

Beside Minnie in the back seat was Flora's handbag, within which she had stashed the letter that caused this dubious, probably doomed venture. Flora had brought it along as—what?—an insurance policy? Something to wave in her father's face should he deny its existence? The words ran through her mind, and she fought again to concentrate on the road.

My Beloved Children,

I have the sad duty to inform you that my dearest Yvette passed away recently. This was a terrible blow for me, but I have learned to master my grieving and to be serene in the knowledge that she is now with God, which is ultimately The Place where we would all wish to be.

She was an inspirational Christian and a good and dutiful wife to me in the twilight years of our lives, and I believe all of us can draw beneficial lessons from her goodness and improve ourselves by seeking to emulate her piety and devotion.

I have been obliged to deal with her private affairs, and I have found the process exhausting, emotionally and spiritually. I would deeply appreciate it if my children would think of me and make an effort to come along to ease my new loneliness, and perhaps to share a quiet private prayer with me in Yvette's name; her real name, by the way, was Ethel. She preferred the name of her own choosing rather than that of her baptism, but such an affectation is surely a minor blot on the character of such a woman.

I have been given to thinking very much about the past, of my life and yours, of the need to make amends and ensure that we as Christian people seek to exercise the best of human virtues, that of forgiveness. With that in mind I also extend an invitation to your dear mother, should she wish to accept it. For there is much forgiving to be done.

I look forward to seeing you very soon.

With much love,

Father

Flora couldn't help but wince. She had never warmed to Yvette, the task had been an impossible one, and yet she still felt humiliated on Yvette's behalf; why could her husband not guard the simple, snobbish secret of an old woman? Such tactless, self-centred bluntness: he may have been more maladroit than malicious, but still Flora was pained and embarrassed. It was ample warning, too, that for all his advanced years, her father remained unchanged. By mulling over the letter, Flora nearly missed the motorway exit and had to maintain a teeth-clenched, determined silence in the face of Minnie's driving-instructor humphs and ahems. I'll pay you back later, lady, she vowed once again.

Flora and her sisters had rarely agreed on anything, and when they gathered to discuss the letter and what to do about their father's request, predictable sparks had flown. Helen was dead against the whole idea, regarding it as a transparent ploy. 'To return to the home and family he turned his back on. He's my father and I'll never let him suffer or go hungry, but he's not to be forgiven, no, not ever. Can none of you recall the day he left, the state our Mum was in, and the way he pushed past her as if she were some sort of filthy beggar? Have you for some reason forgotten the last forty-odd years? He destroyed her, and he didn't give a damn. Now you want to deliver her up to him when she's too old and foolish to know what's best for her?'

Flora was filled with doubts and unable to decide. 'You always were wishy-washy, girl,' snarled Helen, 'always wanting to please everyone and so making no one happy!' Flora wilted before this blast, afraid that the discussion would deteriorate into another fight over long-cold grievances, but Phyllida, usually sharp-tongued but this time a peace-maker, reminded her sisters why they were there gathered around the kitchen table at 88 Woolsend Avenue, laying arguments on the table before them as if they were cards in a high-stakes game.

Having seized the initiative, Phylly made her own views clear. 'Dad is an old man and at long last seeing the end of his life coming. Maybe he wants to make amends: perhaps for once in his life he's prepared to admit he's been wrong. Now we've all got reasons to dislike him, maybe to hate him if you girls remember treatment such as I remember, and of course Helen, we all remember the day Dad went, how Mum broke before our eyes and never mended again.

But what if this can mend her? I don't picture Dad coming home to unquestioning love and forgiveness, in fact I don't see him coming home at all, but I think if our Mum could see him, just once... I think that would help her, cure her of this... this *madness* she has suffered for so long; Sammy Wilson this, Sammy Wilson that, tortured memories, all those sad songs, bilious tirades and Bible quotes stuck in her head like poison barbs, it might—just might—free her of all that, and she could be herself again, a proper Mum, and proper grandma to the kids, a *person* again, not just this old, sick, broken little thing that parrots that man's name over and over...'

Flora felt persuaded by Phylly's words, but her thoughts swung again when Helen countered. 'Sam Wilson wouldn't admit he was wrong, not to St Peter at the gates, not in front of the Judgement Seat he wouldn't then! He's no more going to apologise and make amends than he give us all a million pounds! That man wants something, though I very much doubt it's anything Mum can give—not anymore!'

'But whatever he wants, set that aside, suppose it helps Mum if she sees him,' Phylly was almost pleading before her stern sister. 'We have to think of what's good for her!'

'And you think I do *not?*' Helen roared, a fresh family row seemingly imminent.

Minnie, usually incoherent and self-contradictory, swept the others aside with a simple but effective argument. 'You're all sitting here arguing about what's right for Mum and she's sitting in the other room not even knowing she's being talked of: have you bothered asking her? I did, and she wants to go. I think that's enough, don't you?' There was a lengthy chagrined silence, which Minnie ended by pressing home her rare advantage. 'She's not an idiot and she's not dead,' she scolded. 'We should never speak of her as if she's not all there or a baby. If Mum wants to go, there's an end to it.'

Flora attempted once again to clear her mind and devote her thoughts to getting to their destination. Bah; some hope. What on earth, she wondered—her thoughts coiling, constricting her mind—awaited them at his small bungalow? What, more to the point, awaited their mother?

Nora made slow, awkward progress from the car to the open doorway where her lost husband stood waiting; Sam seemed restless, unable to conceal a rising, gnawing impatience. Minnie had brought along Nora's walking-stick, an ugly metal and rubber tripod that put Flora in mind of hospital sounds and smells, but their mother had refused to use it in Sam's sight and as a consequence she wavered and wobbled, more sideways than forwards, with her daughters sculling anxiously around her like attentive tugboats. Flora feared they would be busy the day long with the labour of guiding her indoors and settling her into the largest, highest chair.

The day had dawned dull and moody, light had leached away with every passing minute and by midday it seemed to be the Friday when the sky turned black. Sam closed the blinds as if shutting out the dark of night and the little front room was made cosy by the modest yellow light of two standard lamps. It was only once she had made her mother comfortable and settled herself that Flora could note the simple but telling changes that had taken place in the room. The crosses were gone, as were the mirrors large and small, only discoloured patches on the walls betraying their removal. The paraphernalia of worship had gone, along with the worshipper; the last living soul in this house had no need of such devices.

Conversation had been difficult when Yvette was alive, but in these circumstances it was well-nigh impossible until Sam broke the tongue-tie, and although he shot out his words as if declaiming from the pulpit, at least the silence was no more, and for that Flora was grateful. As he spoke, his eyes strayed to and from his daughters' faces but never stayed on them, but his gaze seemed to avoid his former wife, as if having asked for her, he was now pretending she was not there.

'It is kind of you to visit. It has been a terrible, terrible time, of course. I am humbled to say that the ladies of the church have been exceedingly good to me since... in the last few weeks.' He paused as if awaiting congratulations. 'I have been telephoned regularly and received some very gracious visits, and each time they have brought along a little...'

A surge of cynicism made Flora wonder what he meant to say—'tribute', 'offerings'?

'Let us say that I have been neither friendless nor hungry.'

Silence threatened again. Sam suggested a cup of tea, and Minnie scrambled out of her chair, eager to oblige. Was she being helpful or seeking refuge—Flora's inner cynic kept up its commentary. As Minnie abandoned her, Flora took up the task of making desultory conversation with their father, but her attention was now almost wholly absorbed in Nora, who sat bent like a bow in her chair, rocking as if trying to build momentum to launch herself across the room. The eerie smile remained plastered on her face like bad makeup and his head nodded and bobbed. She reacted in the same dead-set way whether offered tea, or asked if she was warm enough, or if she was nudged to agree what a shame it was that the weather was so poor, and after such a nice spell too: she nodded yes-yes-yes, eagerly assenting to anything and everything, but with no sign of having heard or understood a whit of what had been said. And Nora Wilson's eyes were fixed unwaveringly on the still-handsome, still-proud features of her Sam, her gallant Sam, the man she had not seen since the guns fell silent one summer in the middle of her life.

Oh Mother, I should never have brought you here. God forgive me, why did I agree to this idiocy? As Minnie returned with a tray, Flora poured tea and dispensed milk, sugar and small-talk like an automaton.

Sam Wilson had made a brief examination of his one-time wife, but there had been little to detain his curiosity. For a short time his thoughts dwelt in the penultimate year of the Great War, no, not just his thoughts but entire being; he was momentarily transported so that he experienced rather than recalled how knowing-shy Nora had dazzled his young eye, making a redundancy of the dying ember that was the Sun; she was the mother of rainbows, banishing all shadow. How he had wanted her then, even if in his innocence he would hardly have known what to do had she offered herself, he wanted her and that was all there was to know, all he could know. He wanted her. He had wanted her. He had once wanted her. With a shudder he was drawn back to a later, darker point, and stole another glance, filled with pain and distaste, at the faded thing he had admitted to his home. Gone was the pure effulgence of departed days, what sat before him, empty-headed and nodding like a child's toy on a spring, was a creature of paint and plaster, perfumed and highly coloured but broken by time. How could the girls have allowed their mother to lower herself in this way? It was against nature: light had been lost to corrupted nightfall. The Angel of Light was no more.

Nod-nod-nod went that head, and those smooth, unnatural teeth were fixed in smiles. Sam wondered if this was some nervous compulsion in the old woman, an outward sign of the inner foolishness, a symptom that had broken through the surface. But how very beautiful she was in those times of light, a prize to be won, no man could ever deny that. He recalled her hair, that long brunette cascade—how he regretted it when she cut it to a more 'practical' length; that was the first loss to Sam Wilson, the loss of his erotic girl-child; the first sign that she would not remain the creature he had first encountered, and that beyond her looks there was a vacancy, a nothingness. She had remained physically lovely in spite of the years, there could be no doubt, but appearance was just a hollow shell that enclosed nothing but vanity and vapidity. He could never have remained with this woman, this fallen, dying star. All those years ago, he had done the right thing; at least this encounter assured him of that.

Flora was once again trying and failing to read minds; Dad looked at Mum, two or three times he stopped averting his eyes and looked straight at her, see, just there, he did it again, what is he thinking? Was he sincere in what he wrote in that appalling letter, has he brought her here to seek her forgiveness for his ancient misdeeds? Is he even, of all things, considering granting that inconceivable miracle, his return home? Is he picturing the old house now, preparing to shuck off this one and re-establish himself in his old domain? What on earth would Mum say if he... Stupid question: yes, yes, yes she would say, head, body and soul, all in accord, nod-nod-nod. Flora made an effort to unearth herself from her thoughts as she felt a profound melancholy drape over her; what have I come here for? When can I leave? The gloom refused to depart from her mind.

Sam offered more tea and yet more anodyne conversation, carefully, if over-elaborately avoiding the mention of his late wife as he spoke of church, church goers, small items of uninteresting parish business and anything to fend off silence and its unwelcome echoes. Driven by the same need, Flora and Minnie talked eagerly of their children, their sisters' children, the esoteric doings of tribes of far-away creatures Sam barely knew, though he seemed suddenly interested in their histories. And for the whole of this uneasy time, Nora nodded and smiled her metronomic and uncomprehending approval, eyes fixed, never on her daughters, always on Samuel Wilson.

At last, at last; they could depart. Taking shameful, expedient advantage of Nora's time-measuring tic, Flora chirped up, 'Well Mum, you must be tired and it's a bit of a drive home. D'you want to get going now?' She and Minnie were helping their mother out of the chair and

Sam was standing politely at the door even before Nora could fully nod this motion through. Nora was slower on her feet than ever and slumped against first one, then the other of her daughters as they ushered her out of the little bungalow. Was she reluctant to leave? Sam closed the door behind them, and he did not appear at the window to see them off.

Minnie was about to start the car when Nora seized her left hand as it grasped at the gear stick. Momentarily alarmed, she turned to look at her mother and saw in her face an expression that had been absent for a long time: Nora's features were firm, defined, her eyes clear and hard, no longer watery, and her jaw was tight and had shed that smile.

'He doesn't want me,' she said decisively. 'He got you to bring me here to see if I could be any use to im, if I could look after him: now he knows I'm a cripple he's not bloody interested. He thinks there's nothing left for him, and I s'pose he's right. I shall die alone. Now you watch out, you and all of your sisters, for he'll come to you next, testing you, looking for somewhere to live out his days. And he'll be full of promises, whoever puts him up and looks after him will come first in his will, that's what he'll say. Watch out, each and every one of you—or this will be another silver teapot. You mark my words—and make sure you tell him to stick it up his weskit, or somewhere else for preference.'

The old lady slumped back into the passenger seat, exhausted, and Flora had to reach over to help her to click her seatbelt into place. The expression on her face had fogged back into a languid, unfocused look; the corners of her eyes damp and her jaw began to move as her throat made that click-click-click noise that was only drowned out when Minnie started the car. As she pulled away, Minnie looked in the mirror and caught her sister's eye.

'Were we right to do that?' Minnie asked, as if awaking on the sudden to the thoughts that had tormented Flora so long prior to the visit; Flora shook her head helplessly. She simply didn't know.

1985

'Grampa Sam was a horrid rapscallion, an old man long before his time, yes he was, the hair on his head was white as snow even before he was five-and-twenty years old, which is much older than you are, but it's a very young age really, when a man's hair should be jet black, yes it should. Why was Grampa Sam an old man before his time? Well, that was because he was all eaten up inside with nastiness; he was chock-a-block with hate, but also filled to the brim with something else even more horrible, something called lust. His hate made him a nasty, nasty old man, he hated everyone, but most of all, and most shocking of all, hated children, all children. He even hated his own children, and frightened them with his rages and shouting and wicked ways. His lust was an even worse sin, and he lusted after an ugly old lady called Mrs. Ellis, a lady who was not his wife, and for a man to do such a thing is very, very wrong, it says so in the Bible, yes it does. But so nasty was Grampa Sam, so full of his hate and lust and another terrible thing called pride, he wouldn't listen to anyone who begged him to mend his ways.

'He wouldn't listen to his children when they pleaded with him not to leave them and their poor mamma, or to the vicar who came down from the church to tell him that what he was doing was evil, he even refused to pay heed to his own doctor who told him that he was sick and needed medicine. Grampa Sam closed his ears to all of them, shut himself off from all things good and one day finally ran away with that awful Mrs. Ellis; they went far, far away and no one knows to this day where they are. But everyone knows that it was his hate, lust and pride that turned him shrivelled inside and made him old.'

As Nora began this tale, Flora took a firm step towards her, intending to pluck the spellbound, wide-eyed child from the comfort of her lap and tell the old woman to stop filling the kiddies' heads with nonsense, but to her surprise she found herself gently but effectively restrained by Helen, who stood close to her, gripping her arm and whispering earnestly.

'No,' hissed Helen, 'let her tell her fairy tales. If we stop her she'll only wait till we're not listening and then tell the poor little buggers something ten times worse.'

Flora relaxed and stepped back slightly; her sister's hand stayed on her arm, but she was now not in a grip but a light but tender embrace.

'It's the same story, Sam the monster, Sam the sinner, Sam the sick man. The same story she's fed to the kids since the old rogue ran off. And she never, ever mentions that she saw him again. Not to me anyway, and it's never part of her stories. Has she ever spoken of it to you?'

'No,' replied Flora, her eyes on her tale-telling mother, 'not to me, and not to the other girls. It's as if it never happened.'

'It never should have.' Helen being Helen just had to get that keenly-honed knife in between Flora's ribs. The two sisters remained standing and watching as Nonna's story ended in the inevitable crooning of a sad, sad song.

Gathering the Family

2012

Flora Latimer had waved off all but the last hard-core of her party guests, wondering, in practically every case, if she would see them again. The party remained alive, however, while Jeff Clayton and Barry Fenton were still entertaining Kara, Eileen and Francine with their yarns of old times. The only other straggler was Nina, who sat close to her father, hissing to him to drink less and talk more quietly, advice he resolutely ignored. She laughed at the two raconteurs only in the thin, nervous manner of someone who didn't get the joke.

'Tell y'what about old Nora, *burppardon*,' Barry was beginning to slur and Nina frowned. 'Sammy Wilson may have claimed she needed to put er foot to er head to think, but she had him dotted right enough when she warned her girls about him coming round with a face full o teeth and lips bubbling wi promises. Bloody spot-on, she was.'

Jeff cackled wickedly. 'Sammy did a-wooing go! Sam Wilson's 1983 tour! Oh Lord, I can't bear it—you tell em Baz!'

1983

Barry Fenton sat opposite Sam Wilson and their exchange was riddled with unspoken, seething tensions. Time had moved on, they were on his territory, the room more cheerful and even the chairs a million times more comfortable, but Barry was unavoidably reminded of their confrontation in Sam's lair forty years before. Another vital difference, he strained to remind himself, was that this time Sammy Wilson was the applicant and Barry Fenton the one disinclined to give his consent. I'm the boss, mused Barry, so why doesn't it feel like that? For a kick-off, because although we both know what he's after, nobody has admitted it, he won't say the words: to all appearances this is just a social call, the old man coming to see his family—making up for lost time like he'd said he would: Bosh.

Things had not started well. Three of Helen and Barry's youngest grandchildren were there, delighting them with their spirited play, and their mum was late collecting them. When Helen answered the stout, confident knock on the door she found herself admitting not her daughter but Minnie, chauffeuring Sam and apparently acting as his general support, factotum and lieutenant. The old man had made his stiff, arthritic way into the Fentons' living room, plying his walking-stick as if dowsing for something, and he pulled up short at the sight of the little ones, dashing in and out of the bright sunshine through the open French windows.

Sam said nothing but his frown did him eloquent service. 'What are *these* little buggers doing here?' it asked. Helen caught his glance and for a moment Barry thought there was going to be a father-daughter set-to, but Helen, with an effort, resumed her play-time smile and lined the children. 'All meet Grampa Sam!' she chirped. Sam looked down at the children, inspected them as if they were at a military parade, and with due solemnity was told their names as he nodded gravely, serious-faced as if determined to commit this new knowledge to memory.

'Now.' Helen clapped her hands. 'Let's give Grampa Sam some peace and go and play outside! Come on, hop like frogs, one, two, three!'

Barry ushered Sam to a seat and Minnie lowered herself next to him, the picture of filial solicitude. Having made his guests a pot of tea, Barry sat to face his father-in-law and to play out the undeclared contest.

'This is a lovely cosy room,' declared Sam as his opening move.

'It is, yes. It does well. For the two of us,' countered Barry.

'The two... You brought up children here.' Sam probed for weaknesses.

'You don't notice when it's your own kids, you just get on with it.' Barry brushed him off.

'A lovely house nevertheless.' Sam seemed keen to offer praise; Minnie nodded reluctantly. Stalemate so far, thought Barry.

'A very comfortable chair, this, I'm bound to say.' Sam wriggled his shoulders appreciatively in the padded depths of Barry's swivel armchair while swinging it almost gaily on its metal pivot.

'Yes,' replied Barry flatly. 'It's my favourite.'

'I can quite see why. It must be very cosy right by the fire here on the winter evenings.'

'Yes, we pull our chairs right up, Helen and me...'

'Helen and I,' Sam interrupted sharply.

Stunned, Barry uttered a 'Wha'?' before the sound died horribly in his throat. Minnie, the silent spectator, grinned at him horribly, meaningfully.

'Still,' Sam sniffed, 'as I say, you have a very nicely-appointed little home here. For a Council place, you understand.'

Helen had come back in; her eyes flashed fire as she guessed the nature of the game. She rebuffed Sam's next few sallies with barely-concealed impatience and Barry read her face without difficulty, 'they shall not pass.'

'Do you know, in all the times I've been here I have never seen the upstairs?' Sam ventured after a truce of nothingness chitchat.

'I'll take you Dad, so you can see it.' Minnie gave Helen a cursory glance, assuming, bypassing her permission.

'*In all the times I've been here?*' hissed Barry in his wife's ear. 'How many times has he blessed us with his presence? Once before this? Twice?'

Helen waved a hand in front of her face as if to brush away a cobweb; Barry knew this gesture, she was losing her temper, enraged by her father's shameless effrontery. The two of them followed Minnie and Sam only to find them at the foot of the stairs, Sam gazing up uneasily as if unsure of making the ascent without sherpas.

'Very *steep*, these stairs,' he said critically, then struggled up with Minnie's help.

'This spare room, Helen, with a little work this could be a very snug bivouac,' Sam called down from aloft. Helen looked fit to explode, and the inspection went on.

'Very small bathroom,' they heard an echoing grunt; 'can barely turn round in here.' And after a little more shuffling and muttering, a stage whisper, '*Their* bedroom's good and spacious...'

The householders stood at the foot of the stairs, silent and thunderstruck. The children yelled and laughed outside and Barry yearned to join them.

2012

'They finally left, without bloodshed, and Helen and I celebrated the fact we'd been tested and found wanting.' Barry raised a toast to the memory of that backhanded triumph.

'As we came back from seeing em off, I overheard the kiddies talking.

'"Who was that man?" lisped the smallest.

'"Was it the King?" said her sister.

'"Naaaahhh, don't be stupid!" Their older brother sneered. "That was *God*!"'

1983

'Hmmm.' This noise, this slight growl, could have been the hum-haw of a non-committal man or, perforce, a faint whisper of appreciation, and yet Phyllida heard within it an inflexion of scepticism and more than a slight reminder of far-off times. She told herself to be steady and strong, but first her resolve failed and her nerve followed; within moments her insides had become jelly, and the consequent quaking rattled into her legs. She felt obliged to speak, and loathed herself when she heard the jittery, quailing squeak that was her voice.

'I painted it myself,' she told her father as his gaze bored into the framed canvas as if he were a keen-eyed connoisseur searching a valuable under-piece, obliterated by these inept modern daubings. 'Percy encouraged me to paint,' fluted Phyllida, 'he said I had a talent.'

That Percy had been an indulgent idiot and that no talent was here on display was expressed by Sam as 'Humph' as he turned from the picture above the mantelpiece and, with the ever-present help of Minnie, seated himself in Phyllida's most comfortable armchair.

'I was sorry about Percy,' added Sam, ambiguously; was he commiserating on her husband's death or existence?

Phyllida had been braced for this meeting, and told herself in steely terms she was receiving a visitor to her home, her own father, and was not to be nervous, put upon or afraid. But Sam Wilson had always had this effect on her, and within a moment of his arrival she had shed twoscore years and ten, and her adult bravado collapsed. Minnie's presence didn't help; she was saying little but her eyes were glittering with a mean-spirited enjoyment as she accompanied their father on his wrecking-ball mission around Phyllida's home. Sam had demolished the painting without the need for words; he had glowered at the living room as if something in there had offended him, and uttered sharp, critical clicks, clacks, sniffs and humphs around the premises as his second-oldest daughter guided him around her home on a tour of inspection Sam himself had commenced with a confident step, Minnie on his arm and Phyllida trailing after them explaining and apologising in that damnably weak voice as they moved from room to room.

Phyllida hated being alone, would have given anything for company, but as for these visitors, she just wanted them to depart. When the ordeal came, at last, to an end, a wretched, spent Phyllida saw her father and sister out of the door; Sam gave her a peck on the cheek and stepped off for the car as if he was late for a vital appointment. Minnie trailed him and shot her sister a smile which, like her eyes, was filled with a sort of venomous triumph, as if witnessing Phyllida's humiliation had somehow, for Minnie, righted an ancient and obscure wrong.

1983

'We have visitors coming.'

'Yes Mum.'

'Your grandfather has invited himself at his own convenience…'

'Yes Mum. Can I go out?'

'I'd prefer some help. Please.'

'Yes Mum.'

'D'you know what "stand by to repel boarders" means?'

'Of course Mum. I took the call from Aunty Phyl, remember.'

'You should get changed before they arrive. Why don't you wear that t-shirt of yours, the new one?'

'But you said it made me look like a street urchin.'

'Maybe I did.'

'But it's vomit green, and it says Maggie-Maggie-Maggie Out–Out-Out.'

'Perhaps it is a bit… what's that music I don't like?'

'Punk rock.'

'Have some ready. The noisiest. And how about a couple of your badges?'

'Mum!'

'Penny dropped has it, darling? Oh and Kara—some house rules now you know what I'm about. Follow my lead, don't overdo it, do not laugh, mention your boyfriend all you want but under no circumstances mention you're considering moving out to live with him. If you do that you shall never receive my silver teapot. Clear?'

'Yes Mum.'

Grampa Sam, white-haired and smiling, kissed Flora on the cheek but hesitated before the figure of Kara, who stepped forward, seized his hand and shook it. Minnie smiled a tight, minimal smile as she brought up the rear; her eyes were narrow, her mien wary, as if she was cautious of trip-wires and snares. Once the guests were seated and offered refreshment, conversation was as desultory and difficult as ever, and Sam's eyes pinned on Kara's t-shirt. Consumed with curiosity, he pointed a sharp-nailed finger at a small badge on her chest, a black-white swirl bearing contrasting black/white, white/black capital As.

'What does that represent? Alcoholics Anonymous?' A self-satisfied chuckle played low within his chest.

'It's the Anti-Apartheid Movement, Grampa.' Kara piped up, 'Against what's happening in South Africa.'

'What on earth is wrong with South Africa?' demanded Sam importantly.

Kara did not wait for her mother's permission: she went straight ahead and answered the question, clearly and passionately. The old man was visibly unsettled; he had gambled that the girl would um and ahh and falter in the face of his question.

'I don't know what all the fuss is about,' Minnie

intervened. 'Our Ralphie's working out there now and he says it's a beautiful country.'

'It is, but that's scarcely the…' Kara curbed her zeal at a signal from Flora, and Minnie ploughed on.

'Ralphie says that he sees the blackies who work at the airport, sees them playing leap-frog he does. People who're so unhappy as you say would never play leap-frog would they?' She sat back smartly with a so-there look on her face.

Flora shot a look at her daughter—*do not laugh!* was its unmistakable message.

2012

'And it got worse. They asked if Kara had a young man and we told the truth—including that he stopped over at weekends. Dad said our sofa looked too small for a man to sleep comfortably, Kara told him where Brian really slept, and well, that knocked the stuffing out of him, and within ten minutes, they were gone. Our Minnie told me later Dad had confided to her—*confided!*—that he could never accept an invitation to live in my home. "He could never countenance being under the same roof as such a *slut*," that's what he said!' Hearty laughter swept through the gathering; Nina sputtered with faint, dutiful amusement.

'Mum, Gran, you were just *cruel!*' chided Francine, a little appalled even as she gathered the story in gratefully.

'Oh fiddlesticks child!' Flora responded stoutly. 'He deserved a damn good teasing, and so did our Minnie; sorry Jeff.'

'Nowt to be sorry about, I wish I'd been there only I could never have kept a straight face. No point being ticklestomached about it girlie,' Jeff turned to Francine. 'There was something about Sambo Wilson, made you want to pull his whatnot without mercy.'

Barry, still laughing, nodded in agreement. 'Our Helen always said that the one thing Sammy feared more than the wrath of his God was the sound of disrespectful laughter.'

2012

'How did he come to live with you?' Francine asked Jeff, searching for the next thread.

'By changing his bloody tactics. He'd blown his chances with Philly cos he couldn't resist crushing her underfoot just one more time, he'd treated the Fentons like he was doing em a favour by even considering living with em, and—bless you Flora Latimer for your stroke of evil genius—he fell into a bloody great elephant trap on *her* leg of his little trip. So it was time for the onion in the hanky and the scratchy recording of Hearts and Flowers. He kept on telling us how he'd fallen to thinking he'd never seen enough of his grandchildren and great-grandchildren and that he had realised that this was a mistake and he should be more a part of their lives. Minnie howled at that, said he was a desperate and lonely old man pleading to come back to his family. Decided he must be dying, she did, it all became a great big tear-stained melodrama.'

1983

The mild, quiet old man who shuffled diffidently into the living room bore frighteningly little resemblance to the

Sam Wilson of erst. Although stooped, he was no little old man, his former stature still clear, enhanced by his painful thinness; he looked a gentle, frail elderly man who would benefit from lavish and loving care and attention. He moved slowly and carefully across the carpet, even his gait showed he was changed by old age and the debilitating effects of repeated surgery on his heart, and when he sat he looked around for a few moments as if to make sure he was not exalting himself unduly in taking the best seat or someone's favourite place. He then sat quiet and meek, like a child once again, only able to converse when instructed.

His face was still sharp and eagle-proud, but it too was altered: far too thin and paper-skinned, and his too-white, too-even dentures forced him into beaming an unending small smile that gave him a slightly foolish look even when his brow furrowed with secret thoughts and his eyes worked watchfully, appraisingly, across the room and the people in it. This was a Sam who surprised everyone by making small-talk when encouraged; a man who asked after his children and grandchildren with the calm politeness he had always preached to his family as a social perfection, but yet he had never quite mastered, but even as he did so he demonstrated a slightly halting uncertainty as if surreptitiously consulting a script or being prompted through the earpiece of his hearing aid.

2012

'Nice as pie he was; *nice-as-pie*. And that Oscar-winning performance just about settled it. Minnie decided the old man should live with us and be looked after, waited on and idolised as Saint Bloody Sambo.' Jeff crumpled his face.

'What did you say to that?' prompted the eager story-collector.

'Gave her me mind—said he was more of a hungry tiger than a feeble old codger, that he'd had ample opportunity to see his kids, their kids, and *their* kids too, but never had a mind to. What I loved about it was his sheer cunning, the way he "confessed" his own fault in showing such neglect, and yet always managed to make it seem like...'

'...ours.' finished Barry feelingly.

'Aye. And he got his way , Minnie wouldn't be put off. But there was one obstacle in Sambo's way. This is the best bit...'

1983

If Jeff Clayton was afflicted with the sin of pride, it was a small and perhaps justifiable sin on his part, for his pride lay in his vision of himself as easy-going, a bloke who could get on with anyone, providing the other person was willing to observe a minimum of civility. This outlook helped him to get through life tolerably, and he congratulated himself on being a man with many good friends, even more comfortable acquaintances and few enemies. But even laid-back Jeff had his limits, and these were tested daily by his step-son Paul. Paul had been lodging with Jeff and Minnie noisily, untidily, expensively and interminably since the collapse of his marriage into a rancorous exchange of drunken threats and angry phone calls months earlier. Jeff's private, and carefully unspoken, sympathies were with the poor girl who had tolerated this impecunious, bookie-addicted sot for ten years before giving him a long overdue heave-ho, and his regard for Paul was diminished further by the young man's search for 'a place and a job' that became more desultory with every day that dragged by, and invariably terminated in a lengthy soak at the boozer.

So Jeff Clayton prided himself also on being a patient, tolerant man, but this vaunted patience was burning away like a notched candle; and what irked him, no, *narked* him, apart from Paul's sullen and loutish presence, was the way Minnie flared at a teeny-weeny sideways criticism of the creature she called 'my big lad', as if he were no 'big lad' but the angel-faced, delicate budding genius whose childhood photographs were dotted round every room, accompanying every step of the stairs, greeting visitors in the hallway, balancing on shelves and sweeping nearly everything of everyday use off the top of the sideboard. Minnie would simply shout Jeff down or feign deafness if he ventured to suggest her big lad put his back into his search for a home, not to mention meaningful employment. 'You're just selfish Jeff Clayton! You want me to turn my boy out! You can't understand what it's like, you've never had children!' He only had to clear his throat in a certain way and the ructions started; he had blasphemed and that was that.

But all of this aside—and in between bouts of disbelieving, tummy-tickling laughter that were heard more at his local than home, Jeff had to express some small sympathy with Paul on the day his extended tenancy came to its unexpected end. Jeff bumped into Paul as, with an expression appropriate for a man who had been slapped in the face and kicked in the arse simultaneously, the troubled lad stumbled past him, having just laid the telephone down after taking a short call.

'What's the matter sunbeam?' Jeff tried to be friendly. 'The other half got the legal-eagles on you or something?'

'Nah. It was granddad... Grampa Sam.'

'You what? Is it your birthday or summat?' Jeff was bemused; as far as he knew, the old man hadn't addressed so much as a glance at Paul since before the Beatles broke up. Or was it before they formed? 'What on earth was *he* calling for?'

Paul's hang-dog expression became more of a 'long-since hanged dog expression', as Jeff put it later, as he began to explain what had just been said to him.

'I'm speaking out of concern for your mother, you understand,' said the grave, commanding and pompous voice. 'I understand that you have been rooming with her and her husband for six months or more now and never once have you put your hand in your pocket to offer to pay for your keep. Your mother, she's too indulgent of you, she won't say a word, but I know what's what and I'm determined to see fair play for her. Now I suggest you pull your socks up and either pay up or push off: do I make myself clear, boy?'

Paul had stumped and clattered around the house a few days more, bereft of even the modest vocabulary that was at his command, before he had announced in wounded tones he was moving out 'to doss at a mate's'. Minnie would have taken pity on his slumped posture and saucer eyes, but she was now driven by an even greater imperative; she watched with sadness, and Jeff with suspicion easing into relief, as Paul and all his odds and sods disappeared off to another estate in said mate's battered old van.

2012

'Nobody could shift that great lump, not for yonks, yet with one call, *one call* mark you, he's put to flight! And the cunning old sod, the crafty, scheming, bugger up the back who made that call, within two weeks moved in and took the lad's place, he'd just allowed enough time for Paul's sweaty bloody smell to be aired out of the house!' Tears of mirth ran down's Barry's face. Jeff tried to stop laughing for a moment, eager to round off the tale.

'Even if they'd wanted him, the sisters would never have got Sammy to live with em. Minnie, she took im round everywhere and stayed close, and when her sisters weren't there she'd let her dad know what unfeeling, disloyal little cats they were, how he'd be better off with her. And so the favour, fortune and silver teapot of Sammy Wilson went to our Minnie. And to be fair to her she never regretted it. *She* didn't...'

1946

Helen, reflected Sam, had always been a disappointment: an awkward, self-important girl, overly keen to take the lead and unshakeably convinced of her own rectitude. He bristled with indignation as he sat in the parlour of his diggings and was read a damn moral lecture by a girl who, he felt tempted to remind her, had recently married in a humiliating hurry, with a suspiciously thickening middle.

Yes, the keenest of disappointments. He recalled with

sadness the day he recovered her from the aegis of Aunt Laura, the return of his precious girl; it had begun with the disdainful curl of her lip as she faced her noisy siblings—the mirror of her mentor—and the way her tolerant courtesy to her older sisters had deteriorated into ill-disguised distaste the moment she realised that she had no choice but to share their cold and draughty bedroom. He had been pained by the way her mother's effusive emotionality had so plainly repelled the girl. Nora had predicted that Aunt Laura would school the child to scorn her; perhaps for once she had been correct, although it was scarcely a sign of that wretched foresight to which she so often laid claim.

His disappointment had deepened thereafter: aware of Helen's discomfort and desiring to offer her respite from the clamour of the household, Sam had relaxed his iron rules and invited her to join him in the front room, his den, so that they might talk like sensible people. But even here Helen had proved ill at ease, lofty and remote, unwilling to take a comfortable seat or to take tea with him, or to talk of anything bar the most formal observances of politeness. Sam, to his mounting annoyance, found himself fidgeting and twitching in his chair, denied the peace and comfort that were his right, here in his own territory. He was never to extend the offer again, after the girl had fled the room with his blessing.

Sitting in silent contemplation, Sam upbraided himself; what had I hoped for, what was I expecting from her? But he knew well what he had wanted, what she had failed to deliver. They had the same upbringing, in the same place with the same person; he had wanted to know if her life had been as his, had she suffered at the hands of the virgin-harridan and her Book of Fire, had she suffered the same pain and fear, felt the hot pulses or shame and rage and confusion, did she now yearn for peace and yet fear destruction every moment of her life and with every thread of her being? He had wanted to take a weeping Helen into his arms and tell her that he knew, understood, all she had suffered, all that she was, and desired to offer understanding and receive it. But all that his lost girl offered to him was a mirror of his past.

The passage of time had served only to add dimension to Helen's sententious piety and increase her physical resemblance to Aunt Laura, that vengeful demon. It was as if the child's being had been scooped out of her frame and replaced with the essence of the older woman: Aunt Laura had not trusted the Lord to raise her into a new life beyond death, and she had made her own arrangements. Only traces of Helen's native gentleness gave any hint to Sam that his firstborn was still present upon this earth.

Why had Helen taken it on herself to track him down, write to him in such a peremptory tone and demand that he see her? Why did it have to be Helen? He wished earnestly that if he had to see anyone it should be Petra, or Phyllida, even Minnie, had there not been a special bond between him and Minnie? Surely he could have explained himself to one of the other girls, they may have understood; but instead he faced Helen, and felt as if he were a young boy once again, awaiting fiery condemnation for his sins.

'I could not remain at home, my girl; that was as plain as a pikestaff. And so it was agreed between your mother and I...'

'Between your mother and *me*,' interjected Helen pointedly. Sam's eyebrows arched in *I beg your pardon* and his mouth flapped open slightly as if suspended in the act of being force-fed with foul medicine.

Helen pressed home her advantage. 'Agreed? Mother agreed to nothing of the sort! And if you bullied her into mouthing the words that you wanted to hear, that doesn't mean it was right for you to do so, or that she meant a word of what she said! It's destroyed her, Dad, what you have done to her, it has destroyed her completely. Now I'm not here to ask you to come home, I'm certainly not here to beg on Mother's behalf, but it was agreed between the older girls and me...' She hesitated, expecting a cavil that never came. 'Between the older girls and me—Flora is too young of course—that I should point out to you the effect of what you have done, upon us all, but especially upon Mother. Her heart is broken, none of us has seen its like and not one of us can do anything for her relief. You *must* help her.'

'So you *are* her agent after all. You and the other girls, you decided to hunt me down like a damn criminal and make me feel guilty. How can I help her; by returning and spending the rest of my days with her? No, the best thing I can so is to stay away, let her come to terms with matters. And she will find someone else, someone more suited to her, you'll see.'

'Fiddle-faddle! That is rubbish and you know it sir!'

Sam cowered, in reflex at another echo of his boyhood; that voice, that angry voice. He rallied and roused his ire. 'Kindly remember who you are Helen Wilson, and who you are speaking to!'

'To whom I'm speaking, surely?' snapped his daughter. 'And my name, Father, is Helen Fenton. Kindly remember I am a grown woman with my own mind and that unlike the other girls I have always been proof against your bullying ways! That is why I told the others not to come, lest they wilt before your stony gaze and weep quietly when you so much as raise your voice!'

'What is it you want from me?' Sam was desperate to be alone.

'That is a matter for you and your conscience. These are the facts: Mother is sitting at home half-mad with grief notwithstanding that nearly a year has gone by; she bursts into tears at the drop of a pin, her only pleasure smoking and gossiping with those awful crones in the Avenue, but most of the time she sits there in that back kitchen, doing nothing, thinking nothing—waiting, Dad, just waiting. And you know what for.'

'Helen, I cannot...'

'And she hasn't two brass farthings to rub together. That is one thing that you could remedy. And don't tell me you can't help her with that, you can't be paying much for your room and board in this tatty old place.' She stopped talking, stared at him. 'So aren't you going to ask?' Helen ended the long silence that had fallen between them.

'Ask?'

'About the latest news from home, about your other daughters, how Flora is doing at school, perhaps? Or about your old friends and neighbours, your drinking pals from the Royal Oak? You aren't going to ask are you? Mother isn't the only one that you have left behind.'

Sam, bemused, kept his counsel.

'Aren't you even going to ask after Mrs. Ellis?' Helen enquired with sugary spite, allowing the wince to pass from his face before finishing, in a softer tone, 'Will you write to Mother? Write to her at least?'

'But what good would that do?' he asked helplessly.

'For you or for her?'

Oh but he had sired a ruthless hussy. 'She knows my mind perfectly well; besides, she may misinterpret a letter, she may entertain hopes of me changing my mind…'

'And it just *might* grant her a little peace. Or do you think you are the only one entitled to that?'

Father and daughter parted soon thereafter with a cold kiss on the cheek. Helen was rigid with fury and chagrin; Sam felt invaded, betrayed. Yes, Helen had been a terrible disappointment to him.

Money And Fine Words

1964

Sam Wilson was alive with a suppressed glee, and unusually eager to extract himself from the cloying presence of Yvette. He had offered—with some sudden haste—to make a cup of tea, and had made excessive play of inviting Flora to come with him to assist. His wife chirped away to Phyllida, and neither of them seemed to notice anything amiss, but Sam Wilson's youngest daughter was alerted to an aspect of her father that she had not seen before, a magnesium-flash of an excited and almost boyish nature that had conceived an idea and could brook no delay putting it into action.

As soon as he had put the kettle on, Sam gestured furtively to Flora and opened the back door, which led out on to a neat square of lawn, trimmed by a richly brown-black but oddly empty flower bed; along its side ran a ruthlessly-weeded and swept crazy path, one so short a tall man could cross it in three strides. Sam, in his near-agitation, almost hopped and skipped across it, and within moments fumbled at the latch of the garden shed, a neat and clean structure that smelt new, freshly-planed wood and varnish. Even its one large window pane was clinically free of dust and unvisited by spiders; Sam pulled open the door and stepped inside, where Flora could see that the interior was as spotless as everything else in that odd residence, as if Yvette spent as much time dusting and mopping the garden shed as she did her tiny, pristine home. There was scarcely any room for a second person, but Sam beckoned his daughter to his side with a muffled hist; what was to be done here was plainly to be transacted hugger-mugger and out of sight. Flora could hear the kettle building up to an uneasy whistle, as if trying nervously to cover for them, as Sam rustled at the back of a small pile of bags and extracted with a look of satisfaction a canvas knapsack, a small thing that bulged with its secret load.

'Here,' he said, smiling naughtily, as if Flora should be instantly fascinated and grateful to be shown this mysterious object.

'What?' she responded in a laryngitic hiss, finding herself almost mocking her father's conspiratorial whisper.

'It's something I'm keeping.' Sam was not deflated by her unimpressed manner. 'Something for the future. For my children. I've always said that the daughter who brought me the most pleasure in my life should have this.' He opened the flap of the knapsack and tussled briefly with some astonishingly loud, hissing tissue paper before he retrieved his prize; a teapot with a black handle and dulled finish—a treasure wrapped up and kept out of the light for a long time.

'Needs polishing,' Sam was momentarily apologetic, 'but it's a real beauty—silver, see?'

He pressed it into Flora's hands: her first thought was that for all that her father deemed it precious it was an ugly old thing, fat and lumpish where it should be sculpted and curved. Her second thought was a mother's thought—she couldn't use such a thing for her family, you could get no more than four or five cups of tea out of it, small ones, they'd be up and down refilling it during their dinner, not that she would abandon her trusty old earthenware pot for this thing in the first place. The thought that took its place was how light the object was—as her father had placed it in her hands she had braced herself to feel it tug at her grip, but the pot had rested inert in her hands as if weightless. Then there was something about the sound it made as she turned it around and the feel of the metal against her hands, oily and somewhat unpleasant—Sam's voice interrupted her thoughts.

'This shall go to my most precious daughter—when I'm gone,' he added this rider with clumsy haste, as if to head that precious daughter off from cutting and running at once with the precious heirloom. Flora wondered what to do, what to say, some trite emptiness such as, 'Oh how nice—where did you get it—how long have you had it?' But the need to chatter was obviated by the urgent warning of the kettle; Flora led the short way back to the kitchen and Sam followed, having wrapped up the pot again, and he looked proud and pleased—smug, even—as if he had been glad to share glorious tidings. As they assembled the tea things, Sam whispered that perhaps it was best that she tell no one about what she had seen, for the time being, adding, to her surprise, 'Yvette doesn't know about it.' Flora nodded, but she didn't consider herself to be bound by her father's injunction, she had simply acknowledged that she had heard him; she told her sister about the odd encounter before the car had turned the corner on their way home.

'Pewter!' exploded Flora. 'He really seemed to think I wouldn't be able to tell the difference between solid silver and bloody pewter!'

'Perhaps that's a sign,' Phyllida ruminated gloomily, 'of

the measure of his regard for us. Pewter for silver, that's how "precious" we are to him. And what's all this about the daughter who gives him the greatest pleasure, what is this, a competition?'

'It's possible. It's a little thing that says a lot about our dad. Do we tell the others?'

'Why protect him? If he wants to behave like an old fool, let the world know.'

'What about Mum?'

'Not Mum.'

'Why not? She'd enjoy the story.'

'Yes; too much.'

'What's the matter? Don't you like the fact that it proves her right?'

'Proves her right?'

'Proves the kind of man he is.'

'Humph.' Phyllida closed down the discussion inarticulately.

"That's Sam Wilson.' Nora smacked her lips at the titbit. 'Chapter and verse, so it is. Meanest man as ever walked the earth. Skinflint, that's the word then. Discussting skinflint.'

1946

'End-end-end-end-end-end-end-end-end-end-end-end-end!'

Flora beat her heels against the wall as she chanted, right foot first, then left, swinging, impacting with a scuff, swinging again, 'End-end-end-end!' When she wanted to increase the impact and vehemence she would drum with both feet together, and then to vary the beat she would go right-left; right-left; right-left close together to help her with 'Finish! Finish! Finish! Finish!' She felt a mildly trance-like effect from the repetition, but it brought her little comfort and there was no magic in her spell, her mother remained in the shop. 'I want to go *home!*' the girl said, louder, pettishly, with a slow-burning tail of anger to her words. Home was almost in sight, just two street corners away, but Mother had insisted Flora could not stay there on her own, she had to remain in sight at all times. Flora wouldn't have minded so much if she could have sat in the shop, but Mother claimed that this would be against the law; it was the local outdoor, selling beers and spirits, and it was forbidden for someone as young as her even to step inside. Flora muttered and growled rebelliously; she wasn't *that* young, and wasn't stupid either, why couldn't she be at home? Why couldn't this end-end-end-end?

Flora had hated the dingy little shop the moment that Nora had announced, not a little shamefacedly, that she had the job, and she hated it yet more passionately when she realised that it was her fate to wait on that blessed wall until Mother was done, mollified by occasional bottles of pop and perhaps two penn'orth of chips from Thrakes Fishery on the way home. *Why* couldn't she be at home? In case Mother came home to find her lying there dead, like Alex? She wasn't a baby, it wasn't as if she didn't know how to look after herself.

She glared angrily at the shop, almost as if it had consumed her mother, gulped her down whole. It was a fly-blown, stinky little shack of a place standing alone is if in shame and disgrace, kept at arm's length by respectable premises: you couldn't even see into it—though Mother claimed she could see out perfectly well to check if Flora was still there—that ugly little pile of ill-assorted bricks shrouded with street dirt with its filthy windows, muddy lights, brown glass, brown ale, brown paper. Flora watched the customers come and go, and judged them to be a shifty, guilty lot as they sidled through the gloomy door into the smelly darkness and then shot out again minutes later clutching their faintly clinking parcels. What a beastly horrid place, why would anyone want to go in there? Flora fretted about her mother, alone in that ugly place with all those strangers. And there was another thing—although most of them scuttled off as furtively as they had come, there were some men who seemed to remain within for a worryingly long time, and Flora had to suppress her urge to burst in and see what was going on, to throw herself at these men, biting and scratching to defend her poor mother from whatever they were doing to her. She knew what those chattering neighbours in the Avenue would say if they caught one breath of such a thing; those old harpies could see sin and adultery in a stray glance, how their tongues would wag. Flora, for she really was not a child any longer, knew what those men were really doing; they were dawdling, deliberately drawing out their visits and taking lingering looks, staring at the still-beautiful woman behind the counter, it was a little treat for them, gratis. Mother declared herself disgusted by this lechery and Flora believed her when she said that she didn't encourage them and *certainly* did not flirt, but the girl couldn't help thinking that Mother was at least a little flattered by even such grubby attentions.

'End-end-end!'

Mother came out to smoke a cigarette on the front step of the shop when there were no customers and smiled at Flora, came over to her, took her hand, patted her hair and kissed her.

'How much longer, Mum?' the girl pleaded.

'A while.' Nora often looked peaky in this place, and always uncomfortable, out of place. Flora wanted to beg her to quit this job and never, ever return here; the shop was changing her, she had begun to behave differently, was almost coarse in her manner sometimes, forever dealing with people off the street rather than her own family, and her voice had shifted from its customary tuneful sweetness to a more guttural tone, punctuated by irritating clicking in her throat and an increasingly troublesome cough. She had even begun to smell differently, the enlivening motherly aroma Flora remembered from her childhood had been displaced by a miasma of stale ciggies and boozy fumes, as if her beautiful mother had degenerated into a helpless tippler. Nora, who was all things bright and beautiful, who radiated light and the most gorgeous colours, did not belong in that dowdy hatch; wallowing in that toxic semi-darkness had aged her, her looks draining away, there were tight lines around her eyes, which in their turn had lost much of their warm glow.

What would Father say if he knew? He never tired of saying how the Wilsons were one of the finest families in the neighbourhood, how had things come to this? It was demeaning. One sunset as they dragged reluctantly towards another evening's labour, Flora could contain herself no longer.

'Daddy wouldn't like it if he knew you were working—especially working *there*.' She jabbed a scornful finger in the direction of the outdoor. To the girl's profound shock, her mother's face became chalk-white and tears rolled down her cheeks from eyes that had reddened and swollen in a moment; her voice rasped bitterly like a match scraping hard against brimstone.

'It's because of your blessed father that I'm stuck doing this! He's got money, yes he has, but he's too busy spending it on some cheap…' she had almost begun to wail, but with a shudder and a gulp mastered herself. 'So… I have to work.' Shaking and tearful, Flora clung to her mother and then sat patiently waiting for her that night.

On the way home, Nora had recovered the bloom in her cheeks and the light in her smile and she threw her arm around her daughter's shoulder, pulling her close as they walked.

'You're a good girl. Good to your mother. You're the one who looks after me, aren't you?'

1944

'That Clement Attlee is such a *vulgar* little man! He looks like an office clerk with ideas above his station, a hairless little busybody hell-bent on telling every man and his dog what to do!'

Mr. Thorndyke had firm ideas about the would-be tenant of Downing Street, as did all the denizens of the Conservative Club: but Billy Thorndyke was the angriest, the most vociferous.

'Vulgar little man! A nothing! How would anyone

choose him over the voice, the mind, the sheer *bulldog* spirit that Churchill has got! Common little upstart! The war is not yet won and yet they speak of an election! The presumption!'

Sam hastened to agree, watching Thorndydke's doglike jowls wobble with the earthquake power of his righteous fury; across the spacious room a rumble of 'hear hears' greeted Thorndyke's outburst.

It was a fine thing to be here in this noble room with its huge fireplace, wood-panelled walls bearing Union flags and a portrait of the King and Queen. The parquet floor scattered with thick rugs and welcoming, comfortable armchairs. Sam belonged here, not amongst the hoi-polloi at the Royal Oak with their Woodbine stink and sniggering insinuations. Mr. Thorndyke behaved like an old, if rather condescending friend rather than Sam's landlord, and Sam had been honoured to accept his invitation to the Club. He held Mr. Thorndyke in appropriate respect, and always impatiently shushed Nora when she complained of 'Old man Thorndyke and his ever-rising rent!'

'It comes to something when we have to give a share of power to Attlee and his cabal of Communists! Perhaps they should be allowed to do their bit while the war goes on, but thereafter they should be taken off and shot, before they betray the nation!'

'Surely even they would not betray us to Hitler?' a hesitant voice cavilled.

'No, not to Hitler, but to the other bugger, that's what they're waiting for. To hand us, land, people and empire, to him.'

For all the luxury of the surroundings, Sam was acutely aware of the delicacy of his mission and unable to take his ease. There was a job of diplomacy to be done, and Sam had to hang on to every word; not out of sycophancy, he had too much pride, but diligence and dedication to his task. Thorndyke was an aged, shrivelled creature, diminishing daily; he also appeared cognisant of his decline and was making appropriate provisions, disposing of his worldly goods: as recompense for what, Sam neither knew nor cared. The house at Woolsend Avenue was in his gift and it did not seem close to his failing heart; it was a piece of bricks and mortar, and at the present he seemed inclined to grant Sam the boon of selling him the house at a very advantageous price.

Bobbing his head in agreement with yet another assault on that *vulgar* little man, Sam knew well he was blacking the old man's boots, but it was a largely painless process, passing his time in a salubrious location, in superior company.

1944

'Weer's Sammy?' asked George Shenton. 'As e bannered off wi' Mirabelle Ellis at long last?'

'Think not such unworthy thoughts, owd.' Jack expelled smoke through his nostrils. 'I'll have you know Samuel Wilson esquire has been spending his recent evenings at the Con Club in town, rubbin shoulders with a better class of person than one might meet in *this* den of iniquity.'

'And wot might ee be *doin* with this better clahhhhss o'person eh?'

'Now that I don't know George. I have my, ah, informants, working on the matter and I expect to get the gen soon enough.'

'Breakin free o the lower orders, so e is. They'll be measurin im up for the ermine next. And I reckon the King is sittin uneasy on is throne tonight.'

1945

Sam was beginning to tire of being summoned to the club to hear the Thorndyke coterie clear its chest of stale smoke and the ire of impotent men whose world was dying. It was time for his labours to offer up their reward. But the prize remained worth the investment; he had saved his money as much as any prudent family man could, but it would be better for some of his capital to be secured within four walls. His mind wandered to Nora's rhapsodies as they moved in. 'This is where we shall spend the rest of our lives. I just know it.' Could that really still be so?

He laughed again at one of Thorndyke's tobacco-stale witticisms and prayed for an end to come soon. This extended process was stinking of charity; to salve his conscience, the aged landlord was doing one last, extended favour to the poor of the parish. He swallowed his rising pride; for the moment it was necessary to remain a faithful courtier. The prize was surely within his grasp; Sam Wilson's legacy was all but secure.

1971

'I can pay you if that's your mither.' Nora was offended and peevish; Flora sighed here-we-go-again.

'Mother, I can't take money for looking after my own family! It's just that I've got children to care for too, you know what that's like, I can't very well split myself in two!'

'If you'd bin capable of keepin your husband, he could of helped.' Nora glowered over the red warning-signal of her cigarette.

'I'm not going into that nonsense again Mother, I'll come as often as I can and help as much as I can. There's still plenty you can do for yourself.'

'But I've got athritis!'

'...And I've got *how* many sisters? Surely one of them can come round when I'm busy?'

'They're always "busy" too,' countered Nora sourly. 'You girls forget where your loyalties should lie. Time was a girl would stay at home an look after her mother; it was the job of the youngest or the unwed.'

Receiving no response, Nora changed tack and her voice became high-pitched and pleading. 'Flora, you're the only one who's good to me—'

But the youngest daughter was ruthless. 'The only one who's *any* good to you, maybe.'

'Don't know what you mean.' Nora fell sulkily silent and Flora drew a breath through gritted teeth. 'Yes,' she could only manage a heavy, weary tone. 'Well, I'll be back round tomorrow.'

'Your visits *are* short.'

Flora didn't release the rest of that tightly-drawn breath until she had closed the back door behind her.

'Our Flora's a wonderful help around the house now I can't do so much. She comes here *every* day.'

Helen was wiping down the kitchen table; she did not look up from her task and her tone was studiedly neutral.

'That's wonderful for you, Mum, and it's easier for her no doubt because she lives so nearby.'

'She thinks I need someone here more often. Thinks her sisters could do a sight more, so she does. She talks to her mother, see, shares her worries with me. She thinks that just cos she got rid of her hubby that's no reason as she should do all my work, life's hard for her on her own with two kiddies. But she's worried about me, see?'

'You'll be fine, Mother.'

'But Flora's worried…'

'Perhaps she shouldn't be; you can look after yourself.'

'So *you* say. I can't manage this house on my own. It's all I've got in the world, but it's a weight on me.'

'Then sell it, Mum.'

'Where would I go then? Don't be daft.'

'You're fine here Mother, and you're perfectly well looked after.'

'So *you* say madam. I ought to show you girls what I think of your b'aviour, I ought to leave this house to the dogs' home when I cash in me cheques…'

'You do that then.'

'It's all I've got! I shall leave this house to the daughter as looks after me best.'

'Mum, I'm not listening.'

'You'll be sorry when I'm dead. Every one of you hussies will be sorry.'

The Dark Angel

1952

For as long as she could remember, Flora had never welcomed the coming of night. As a child she had regarded the darkness as an implacable enemy, ill-intentioned, spiteful and angry; she feared the harm that may come to her during the hours of helpless paralysis, and her slumbers were rarely restful. Her sisters were ever complaining of her endless turning, groaning and whining as she protested feebly against her dreams. And when she awoke she could hear the blood pounding in her head, fast and fearful, like coarse wings beating, swooping and threatening. Even now, not far from her twentieth birthday, Flora slept poorly.

To be wished sweet dreams was usually a vain thing, but on this particular night she lay at peace, afloat on warm, tideless waters. She was aware of some indefinable presence, but on this occasion was comforted by its nearness, lulled into deeper and deeper, warmer and warmer stillness.

For a while she wondered if she had finally made her peace with the old ghosts of the night; she felt a profound happiness, exhaled a wordless joy, curling into herself, bathing in the sweetness of the night. But that peace was not long-lived, she sensed the return of that predatory pulse, the wing-beat: a nightmare creature had found her out at last. Still she welcomed its coming, and in its turn it would never refuse or reject her. She let the slow warmth flood over her, into her.

They carried out the body of Nora Wilson's youngest daughter on a stretcher: her third dead daughter—the fourth of her beloved children to be taken. What sort of a mother could fail so miserably to protect her brood? Nora watched her girl depart the house and this life, yet somehow failed to feel grief, the self-destructive mourning suffered at the loss of Jocelyn, Vanessa and, worst of them all, Alex. Was it possible to grow hardened to such a thing? She realised how echoingly empty the house was these days. Phyllida and Helen were wed and living in their own homes, Minnie too was married but she and her man were lodging at Woolsend Avenue, yet there was the whiff of discord from the old bedroom where they hid away. And now Flora's bed would be empty and the house quieter still. One by one her girls were leaving her.

The family was now gathering, eager to fill the void. Helen was taking charge, as ever. Nora decided that she should attend to the little ones, before she was battered by the realisation that there were no little ones requiring her attention any more. She heard the girls talking about contacting their father: oh fetch Sammy Wilson if you must, what is he going to do, call on some tame miracle-monger and make all better? Silly nonsense! This child needs her mother, and yet even her mother is helpless. Nora could only watch as the body was loaded into the ambulance.

'My baby's gone,' she sobbed.

'Mother! She is not dead and you know full well she is not!'

'Oh she's dead. It's that mennygitis, just like the other

girls, and could they be saved? I've lost her, I know I have.'

Faintly aware of her mother's far-away mourning, Flora now knew in whose arms she lay, and at last she was afraid. And yet death's bird—Nora sometimes gave that name to the angel persecuting the Wilson family—had a gentle and warm touch, and Flora was unresisting, dream-soaked and weightless. She was not pinioned in hard, cold talons as she had been taught to expect. She stirred and found that she could move just a little, but she did not test the limits of that freedom for fear of falling; who could tell how high into the heavens this angel had already flown? In moving her limbs she became aware of their weakness, there was no prospect of breaking free even if she should wish it. She hoped her brother and sisters had been borne away thus gently; there would be comfort in that. Black fog rolled across her eyes and she shuddered, wondering if the moment had now come for her to account to her father's angry, vengeful God.

No light broke upon her, the flight through unending night went on and Flora slipped deeper still into the hot, clinging, dirty state of sleep that was a physical substance, an oily, viscous quicksand that writhed around her. Profoundly frightened now, she tried to snap herself into wakefulness, an old trick for escaping nightmares, she forced open her eyes, sure she had broken free into the good daylight, but each awakening was a falsehood, a dream in itself, and she remained mired in the pulsing darkness.

Now something was stirring and sounding outside of her isolated state: there were noises, movements, flashes of light, they came and went as the dead-alive slumber coiled itself closer around her, growing thicker, hotter. Voices penetrated the veil of blackness, familiar but faceless and somehow lacking names.

'So much for *you* saying she'd fallen pregnant,' snapped one of the disembodied voices, angry and accusing.'And any road you're a fine one to come over all holier-than-thou on *that* score…'

Its sound-sister was equally enraged, alive with desire to vindicate itself. 'It was *not* just me, we all said it! Fainting the whole time she was, white as a sheet, "only one cause for that, she's up the stick from that beastly Terry Cauldon!" And those are *your* words madam, not mine!'

Time passed, it must have been passing, as Flora floated still in dreams. Events passed, clocks ticked, people moved around her in a procession of days, or weeks, or months. Flora was aware that she was not in her home, knew that she was at a hospital, a sanatorium rather, and knew also that her long, foul sleep had been a dangerous journey along the margins of life and death. She had awareness of being moved about, examined, washed by gentle hands; she heard cheerful, determined voices chivvying her to 'buck yourself up now young lady'; she was dimly aware of the sporadic presence of her mother and sisters, and unwelcome memories of the intrusion of cold needle pain into her body, moments that made her wish to continue to hide away in sleep.

'There. Those blue eyes are open again at last.'

Phyllida was smiling down at Flora, rearranging her bedclothes then gently running a damp flannel over her face. She would have made a good nurse. Mother was there too, but she looked anguished, and she was dressed as if for the graveside.

'So the Lord saved you.' Nora breathed as she stepped up to the bedside. 'God is good.'

At that moment a snake-pit hiss sounded from behind her, and Nora turned away to shush the two disputing voices bickering in loud whispers over some curiosity.

'What on earth is the matter with you?' Nora asked whoever was behind her.

'She's being foolish Mother, don't you bother.' Helen's unmistakably schoolmarmish tone sounded out, then was drowned by renewed outraged hissing from Minnie.

'It's obscene, Mother, obscene! Have they no sense of propriety in this place? Philly, can't you get more covers and make her decent? What if a man walked in here?'

Flora was at a loss to understand the exchange, and was then mortified when she realised that she was its subject.

'You can see *everything*, she's so thin and the blankets are even thinner, you can see her... her... *pubic bones*!' her voice was constricted with censorious horror.

'Minnie, this is a hospital, not a cathouse!' sensible Helen tried again.

'It is indecent!' the protester spat back, 'It isn't right and I shan't stay here a moment longer!'

The sound of clattering footsteps indicated that she had acted on her threat.

Nora tutted and shook her head. 'There goes Sam Wilson's daughter.'

Helen drew nearer to join Nora and Phyllida, and they tried to offer comforting smiles and a pretence that the embarrassing incident had not just happened.

1970

I am seventy years old—threescore years and ten, count them, they are spread out before you—my time is up, but what has happened? Another of my daughters has been spirited away in my stead. What cruelty! My Petra, my sweet girl, not even forty years of age and you stop her heart with your cold hand, not allowing her even to bid us farewell. You vulture angel, my children are supposed to lay me in my grave not the other way round, will you make me live unnaturally long so I must see each one to her rest? Stop this game, I beg of you, it is against nature and surely it is against the will of any God. Why do you attack and torment me so, what have I done to wrong you? Now there is one out there who truly deserves punishment, you must surely know where he is hiding, seek him out, why don't you, and spare my children! His heart stopped long ago, so it did, and yet you failed to gather him up. Take him, and then take me for God's sake! What are you about? Who directs your way?

1975

'Mum? Now listen to me Mum, it's about Dad.'

For a moment Nora's face flickered with an unpleasant, hopeful tic, but then tears sprang into her eyes.

'No, no Mum, it's not that.' Flora was hasty and flustered in delivering the news. 'But he has had a heart attack and he's in hospital, very ill.'

Nora said nothing. Flora was not even sure she had heard.

Fighting back a reluctance to enter a hospital atmosphere, Flora then had to practice another sort of self-control as Yvette emerged from the ward. Sam was out of danger, and Yvette's confidence had returned and strengthened alongside her husband's pulse.

'I was so frightened for a while. But I prayed and prayed, and the Lord answered me!' Yvette's voice still betrayed the scars of her distress, and yet Flora still found her daintily smug, as if she had whistled up the deity, who had hopped to it and attended neatly to the job at her bidding.

'I must thank the doctor too. Samuel says he has been wonderful, a life-saver quite literally.' She paused, momentarily uncertain. 'He's a *coloured* doctor, don't you know? Perhaps they aren't all such bad fellows after all.'

She tripped away, perhaps, mused Flora, to give the *coloured* doctor a pat on the head.

Sam Wilson was gaunt and greatly aged, but alive and alert. He offered his own praises to his mortal deliverer. 'And of course I regard it as a prime example of the great power of prayer, as well as the clearest sign of Yvette's devotion and goodness. She saved me as surely as did the dar… the doctor.'

'Dad, Yvette was not the only one who was praying for you.'

'No-no, of course not. We've had our differences, but my girls came to my aid too.'

'It wasn't just us girls either Dad.'

'*We* girls,' said Sam Wilson crisply, and the discussion was at an end.

1979

So he lives on, notwithstanding that was his third—or was it fourth?—do with his heart. Sammy Wilson; protected by Old Nick, so he is. Is that why you have failed to take him, Angel, were your outmatched by a greater power? Then tell me also why you have failed to claim me, though I'm here, defenceless and ready for my end? Tell me why others have died in my place, tell me why you came for our Flora but lost your grip on her? Are you truly tormenting me, or are you a cack-handed killer? What are you, Angel, a trickster or a fool?

Gathering The Family

1952

As Flora floated from her near-fatal slumber she heard more voices, ones that talked as if they were at the end of a long, echoing subterranean tunnel, of her need to convalesce.

'We should send her to Switzerland,' enthused the first. 'They say it's ideal for invalids to recover; it's the air, you know, the clean mountain air!'

'And what, pray, are we to use for money to send her there?' asked the second voice crushingly, after which Flora, still not free of that clinging sleep, knew no more.

On waking, a bemused Flora at first thought she really was in Switzerland, magically transported across the seas in the night. The cold, refreshing breeze that wafted and then slapped around her face could only, surely have come from a snowy peak on a clear day: why there was the mountain itself, tall and craggy with a five-pointed sun balancing precariously on its summit... and yet she had never really moved. Her bed, along with those of five other young women, had been rolled out through the enormous French windows of the sanatorium. It was as if the whole wall of the ward had been cut away like that of a doll's house, and they were taking the air and light in a large patio garden with the nurses standing close, ready to decide when the cool air would become more of a threat than a tonic to their delicate charges. Flora's eyes focussed a little more and she saw her majestic Swiss peaks resolve themselves into the tops of tall trees and, in the distance, some gently rolling and very English hills, all under a rain-cleansed blue-pink sky that sent the wonderful cool breeze to wash her bed-smell away.

'Carry your bags, miss?' said a sharp, jovial voice to her left, and Flora's head jerked around painfully; it was another bedridden patient, a woman of perhaps Flora's age with straggly reddish hair, a thin face that pined after the memory of being a full one, and a playful, attractive, even smile.

'Pardon?' in her puzzlement, Flora remembered her manners at least, 'pardon', you had to say, not 'what' or 'eh'.

'Carry your bags, Miss?' repeated the girl, dotting her fingers under her eyes. 'You look like you haven't slept for a month.'

Flora rewarded her sally with a wan smile; from her own point of view she seemed to have been sleeping forever, and she had never truly expected the return of earthly wakefulness.

'First time I've seen you sit up and take notice anyway,' the girl continued cheerfully, 'p'raps we can have a chat soon, when...'

'No talking now,' a nurse gently commanded. The nameless girl grinned at Flora and rolled her eyes at such foolish rules. Flora smiled back: and the next thing she knew, she was opening her eyes to find she was back indoors, the sun had gone and the great windows were tight shut.

Flora had been ordered firmly that she should still stay in bed but, driven by skin-prickling embarrassment at having to use bed-pans, she decided at last to rouse her piffling strength and get up to answer the call of nature. Alone and fuzzy-headed, she half-fancied herself to be at home, creeping through the dark upstairs passageway so as not to disturb her sleeping sisters, or worse her father, and yet a common-sense Flora was present in that half-dead mind too, placing her steps around the geography of the ward, and not that of her far-away home. She was coldly shocked out of her confused inattention when a figure approached out of the semi-darkness and, appalled and affrighted, she wondered at it—it was a skeletal, stooping creature with a ghost-white bony face and untidy, dirty-brown hair, it shuffled along like an ancient crone on matchstick legs and, on seeing her, attempted, in a remarkably childish act, to hide itself behind its own stick-thin arm.

For a moment she believed herself to be face to face once again with the Dark Angel of which her mother so often spoke with gloomy enjoyment. Regaining her self-possession she thought again, it must be another patient from the ward, some ruined old lady shuffling towards her: I feel I can barely walk, thought Flora, but she seems ready to drop, poor soul. She stood slightly aside to allow the frail creature past, but at the same moment the shrivelled figure also stopped and stood aside for her. Unsettled by the rapidity of its movement, almost as if the other woman were making fun of her, Flora dithered a moment, raised her hand as if to greet the oncomer, seeing at once her gesture echoed before her. She dropped her hand in surprise, and so did her emaciated shadow. No, not her shadow, her reflection, she realised, putting her hands to her head as if berating herself for her foolishness, and sure enough the phantom in the glass mimicked her; her eyes being now slightly better adjusted to the darkness, Flora realised that she was facing one of the great plate-glass windows of the ward, and that she had indeed been playing after-you-Cecil with her own image. Without the breath to chuckle, for walking was such an effort and any noise may have attracted attention and a scolding from the nurses, Flora turned from the ghost in the pane and found her way out of the ward and to the WC down a harshly-lit corridor.

She made a brave effort to go step-by-step back to the ward but found herself dizzy, it was not just her head but her whole body spinning within, and somewhere in her hazy mind she prepared herself to hit the tiled floor with a sickening smack. She seemed to fall, tumbling over and over, but then she stopped with a jerk, straightened, no, she was *being* caught, *being* straightened, held from behind by two strong arms, a warm body braced against her back.

'Looking at your eyes, I was about to say "carry your bags, miss?" again. Didn't realise that I was about to be carrying *you*. Lucky there's s'little of yer.'

For a moment Flora feared she had been captured by the ward sister and that a dressing-down would inevitably follow, but none of the nurses spoke with such a pronounced north-country accent. Her rescuer released her and turned her around gently, and Flora, still a little mole-like, peered at her face. It was the girl who had spoken to her on the terrace; she seemed to be much better; she was mobile, agile and strong, at least in comparison to Flora, and in this light it was plain she had the cheerful, rounder face of a patient who had defeated the disease and was growing stronger, perhaps even beginning to dream of returning home.

Flora moved her lips with an effort, wanting to thank the girl, but she was shushed with finality. 'Let's not chat, neither of us is supposed to be up and about, I'll be bound. Tell y'what, let me help you back to bed, you won't never make it alone, an then I'll come see you tomorrow, see how you are. And prove I'm not a dream.'

She flashed a smile that made her face momentarily beautiful indeed, then slung her gentle arms around Flora once more and more than half-carried her to her bed. 'Nighty-night princess,' whispered the stranger, vanishing into the same nocturnal void that had swallowed Flora's mirror-self.

Flora's head played at carousels once again and dreams rushed to meet her descending mind, but before sleep claimed her one last thought crossed behind her eyes; I've never heard anyone speak like that before, such a curious accent. What would my father call it? Lower class. Yes, lower class.

True to her word, Flora's dream-time saviour paid her a visit, sitting by her bedside full of cheer and a surprising vim, as if she were soon to exchange her hospital outfit for civvies and make the transition from being an inmate to a visitor. Her name was Liza; she was the product of another large family, of six sisters and four brothers, three of whom had been 'lost in the war', which left Flora momentarily picturing these boys wandering dazedly round some distant battlefield. Liza's mother was bed-ridden and 'always very ill', her father worked on ships, was forever joking and playing pranks on his daughters. 'He's a shocking tease', and, 'Drinks more than he oughtter, but even in his cups all he wants to do is laugh and laugh and laugh'. Flora was instantly lost in her own mind again, trying to picture her own father tiddly, her father playing pranks and seeking to fill the house with hilarity. The effort made her head perform cartwheels.

Liza came to play visitor at Flora's bedside regularly, and Flora could not help herself, she liked this girl. The harsh-sounding accent and suspiciously over-ready smile made the daughter of the staidly serious Wilson household fear that she was being made fun of, but a reassuring instinct told Flora that her new friend was simply not that sort of person. She enjoyed the companionship and liveliness Liza brought, but stirring within her was an inner voice, the conscience of the Wilson creed, that told her to recoil from this brash, noisy, common creature: *What will your mother think? What will your sisters think? And most of all, whatever might your father say of this misbegotten association?*

Although still weakened by her own abortive flight with the Dark Angel, Liza was gaining strength, and the one thing she could do with little difficulty was to talk. Gradually as she listened to that coarse voice, Flora heard loveliness in it, gentle and girlish tones and an acute, comical knowingness that no longer struck her as mocking or cruel. Liza was unschooled, or at the very least, less schooled than was Flora, and yet her every word was underscored with an innate intelligence and vitality Flora came to admire, and then, silently, guiltily, covet. She observed with mounting envy the easy way in which Liza made friends with the other patients, with the nurses and the ward sister, even with the otherwise aloof, impersonal doctors on their rounds. 'Why can't I do that?' Flora asked herself enviously, knowing that an answer would come from within herself; *Because you would never lower yourself in such a way. You are a Wilson, and Wilsons do not canvass for approbation like a beggar seeking a penny here and there.*

At first, all Flora had to do was listen, and she did so with a growing delight that began to win through, however slowly, against the ice-cold Wilson voice that still stirred inside, condemning this loquacious, presumptuous child who, because they were levelled by hospital gowns, dared to pretend that she was the equal—perhaps even the better—of a Wilson. As Flora smiled, nodded and clapped at Liza's stories of her home and family, the creature that lived inside her carped and sniped. *Talk, talk, talk, it's like listening to foreign jabber on the wireless. Mouth Almighty Chops Everlasting, does she never pause for breath?* As Flora listened, so she fought the creature within.

Although she was cordial with practically everybody on the ward and quite thick with not a few, Liza had clearly, irrefutably taken the strongest fancy to Flora. Even when her family visited, that warm, funny, loving family Liza had depicted with such animation, she led them over to Flora's bed and they spent quite as much time with her as they did together. Flora battled back her embarrassment at such attention and found herself growing fond of Liza's energetic, unruly tribe. Watching them leave one day, and returning their departing waves with almost as much vigour as Liza, Flora found herself in a tumult of speculation: it is as if I am being invited into another life, a new life, I am being transplanted to a new family. It was with shock and guilt that she recognised her own pleasure at that thought—and with that introspection came once again the Wilson voice. *Invited away? Lured and seduced more like. You just try it, just see what will happen to you; you'll be sorry, so you will!*

Sleep was no longer a powerful death-bird that could bear Flora away bodily, nor an unbearable weight that pressed her to her bed like an insect under glass, or a filthy mire in which she boiled and burned. It was, however, still the most frequent visitor at her bedside and it still made nonsense of all that she knew about day and night, but its touch had become light and benign, it smoothed her brow and brought comfort; it was by this time a gentle, unseen nurse, coaxing her into being whole once more.

Voices seemed always to be disturbing Flora's rest, and one day two voices encountered one another—one warm and friendly, the other grave and self-regarding—a few feet from her bed.

'Why hello there!' chirped the friendly voice, that now-familiar 'common' tone of her gentle friend, 'You're Mr. Wilson!'

Flora snapped into instant, frightened wakefulness as she heard the sharp intake of breath that was the well-known precursor to one of her father's vitriolic sarcasms, the ones that came when he felt himself faced with a fool. He snapped, 'Are you a nurse?'

Liza's back was turned to Flora, but she imagined the girl flinching. 'No I'm not. I'm your girl's friend. I'm Liza.'

Sam paused then clicked his tongue, the sound carrying across the ward like the cocking of a gun. 'Lee-za,' he repeated, as if chewing over the jaw-crackingly primitive name of a savage. 'Well, Lee-za, I am not here to see you but Flora. So you may run along, mayn't you?'

He stepped past the girl as if brushing off a ragamuffin who had obstructed him in the street. Flora could not see either his or Liza's face, for she had her own crumpled into her pillows; she was afire with humiliation and throughout the conversation that followed, all she could think about was finding the first chance available to apologise to her friend and make whatever amends she could. By contrast, Sam Wilson, in the few moments it took him to reach his daughter's bedside, had clearly forgotten the encounter.

Flora feigned a slow and muzzy awakening, giving a wan response to her father's tight-lipped smile as he looked down upon her.

'I *have* been here before,' he said somewhat hastily, as if to parry some expected accusation, 'but I think that you were never properly awake, and you may not recall.'

Flora shook her head; 'I can't remember much even now.' Her voice was filled with strained notes, it was run down by disuse; hearing it she was cross with herself, for it also made her sound nervous and fearful, a little girl dreading another scolding from Papa.

'You seem much better,' Sam asserted briskly, commandingly. 'Your sister Helen wrote to me and said I should come back quickly, she was worried about you. Perhaps she shares the family talent for exaggeration.'

Flora could simply think of nothing to say.

'Your mother no doubt pestered her into it. That was her habit,' Sam finished off-handedly.

Flora began to count the times she had seen her father since he had left the family seven years before, but sleep clawed at her like a playful cat seeking attention.

'I'm glad you're so much better.' Sam touched her pale,

thin hand as it lay like a snowdrop on the bedcovers. 'I have prayed for you daily. And God is good.' Dismissing the unworthy thought that daily prayer was of less value to her than more regular visits, Flora smiled. Shortly thereafter, Sam ran short of words, and Flora did not dare to venture any, still preoccupied with planning how to make her apologies to Liza. Sam stood, touched his daughter's hair and leaned to kiss her brow. He smelt of rain.

'I shall continue to pray. Goodbye my dear.'

Flora watched him as he went, hoping, hoping that he would not cross paths with Liza again. How odd, came a thought, he said goodbye but didn't mention coming again.

'No offence, sweet, but when you first came here, I mean when you first started to make any sense, I thought you was a bit, well, la-di-dah, y'know, airs and graces, lady of the manor. It was like you was wondering why I had the *heffrontery* to talk to someone so fine, why didn't I just serve the tea and then clear off back to the servants' quarters. But if *that's* who brought yer up, I can see it was no fault o yours. And compared to im you're a barrel o laughs.'

'I'm sorry,' Flora heard herself whimpering, 'I'm so...'

'Me too if I've offended yer.' Liza touched her lightly on the arm.

'No, no, no!' Flora pondered. 'He's my father, Liza, I can't help but love him, but he...'

'No need, no need, no need to say it.' Liza waved a placating hand. 'I'll stay outta his way in future, but I'll tell yer for free, it ent just me. The nurses have had a basin-full of him as well, just ask Jeannie when she comes back on duty. Takes over the place does, like he's a bloody VIP. Jeannie wants to slip im some syrup of figs and see how he likes imself then!'

'Oh. Lord.' Flora was mortified.

'Some folks are like that.' Liza ignored her blushes. 'I gorran uncle, street-sweeper he is, but after hours he dresses up an makes out e's a toff. Talks like a dictionary. We just think he's queer in the head an let him to it.'

'D'y'mind if I risk causing more offence?' Liza had stopped laughing now, and was looking straight into Flora's eyes. 'I've watched yer mam and yer sisters too. They're much better than *im*, but there's still something up… listen princess, I always take the view that there's a bright side to everything, even to coming to a place like this and going through what you an me have gone through. I think someone up there—y'know, the powers that be—did this to get you away… away from all of em. And when you get your strength back, you ought to think about that, about how you might keep it that way. If you go back home to them, it's a pound to a penny that you'll never get away again.'

Flora ventured no reply, but didn't turn away from her friend's gaze.

'Have yer took offence yet?'

'No,' whispered Flora Wilson. 'No.'

Offence was almost impossible. Liza by her very nature was warm of soul, good-hearted: if Nora called somebody 'good hearted', the compliment was fragile, usually a scarcely-sugared drop of acid, a damnation of a person's entire character with faintest, flimsiest praise, but Flora had adopted these words to describe Liza as a heartfelt and sincere compliment. As Flora recovered, Liza led the way, and she was beginning to blossom once more, she was putting on weight and regaining the colour in her face; there were times she seemed to be willing Flora to catch her up, as if she were attempting to share the benefits of her recovery with her friend. But that was Liza: generous and kind.

She was generous with her time too, even when she would legitimately have demanded privacy. As she recovered from her illness and was allowed more visitors, a young man began to call on her; his name was Tom Peterson and he was a handsome, cheerful nineteen year old who, too thin and tall for his military uniform, was doing his national service at a base a few miles from the sanatorium. He had been Liza's sweetheart back home, and the two of them seemed to regard his posting as both a gift and good omen. All around the ward there was good-natured envy, and persistent whispers that Tom would walk Liza down the aisle just as soon as her legs were strong enough to hold her up for the duration of the service. They were clearly, inspiringly in love, and yet as with her family, Liza insisted on bringing her man to sit with her at Flora's bedside, neither of the couple seeming to resent sharing their moments; 'I know I've got him forever, princess, an there's plenty of forever to share around.' It was Liza's reply to any attempt at thanks. She even gave Flora a little, slightly tattered photograph of the married-couple-to-be; a smoother, glossier version of the same picture was propped up by Liza's bedside.

'I've noticed that you ent had no visits from a sweetheart,' Liza said one day after waving her Tom off. 'Now that's wrong that is, a flamin crime that there's no lad sittin by your bedside waiting for you to get better.'

Flora laughed and embraced her friend, then made an excuse, claiming she was suddenly tired and dizzy. Unaware of the thoughts that she had stirred up, Liza slipped away to her own bed. No sweetheart; no visits. But there should have been, there *should*. Terry Cauldon had written a couple of times, he would come along and see her as soon as he was allowed, he swore it, she could almost hear his earnest, still-boyish voice as she read his letters, she could *see* him, breezing into the ward, carrying that pale raincoat always folded over his arm… and yet he had never once shown his face, and the letters had ceased. Flora was baffled and hurt, and an empty feeling spread across her insides even as her body grew stronger. She prayed in vain that her mother or sisters would bring news of him: she was, naturally, not such a fool as to ask questions of them. She had no illusions about their opinion of Terry Cauldon.

She decided to keep her troubles from Liza; what could a fellow-patient do except sympathise quite uselessly—and yet her ever-acute friend seemed to understand that Flora was suffering a new kind of pain. 'Of course there'll *be* sweethearts, course there will,' she would repeat time without number, keen to reassure Flora and make up for any inadvertent hurt that she had caused. 'Oh there'll be sweethearts for you, plenty of em too, I should say, specially now that pretty face of yours is filling out. Chase em off, you'll have to.' Liza held Flora's hand palm-up, as if reading her future. 'Word of advice though, princess, real honest advice: for God's sake don't go grabbing the first one who looks and sounds good and make off with im just because I said to get away from…' Liza paused, looked into

Flora's face as if expecting anger, and continued more circumspectly, 'I mean don't make a hasty choice just to feel a lady, all grown-up like. You deserve better; you deserve the best, you do.'

'Thank you Liza.' Flora was formal and prim, covering up for the fact that she was unsure how to interpret this sagacity from her friend.

'And I hope you'll still have time for pals too.' Liza smiled, but by now her eyes were lowered.

Flora sat up in bed, still propped by pillows but pink of face, stronger of voice and making animated gestures with her thin hands as she told her mother about her new friend.

'I've never known anyone like her, Mum, she's so lovely. She's the best friend I ever had.'

Nora's face puckered as if she had been slapped.

'Salt of the earth she is, I'm sure,' her tone was sour and unhappy, 'but you just remember, your mother is your best friend. And it's your mother who's seen you through this terrible time and who'll look after you from now on.'

The day came for Liza to leave—it had to come, Flora told herself, angrily attempting to rein in her emotions; why be so childish, she tried to tell herself, why make a carry-on when *of course* this day would arrive? Liza would leave the sanatorium and she, Flora, would do the same not long afterwards, and they would resume their normal lives and this brush with death's bird would be forgotten. Tom Peterson collected his girl, and their departure down the aisle of the ward was nothing less than a foretaste of the coming wedding; nurses and patients lined the way, grinning like children, clapping, cheering, some even singing. Some patients had attempted to create their own confetti, but 'that mess' had been vetoed by the ward sister, not that this stopped her from being one of the merriest celebrants on the day. The young couple, Liza, now looking robust, dazzlingly happy, and Tom shy but immensely proud, took their leave and accepted with gratitude and grace the good wishes and small presents that were thrust upon them.

Of course this day has been coming Flora Wilson, why are you behaving like such a baby? Grow up, grow up, act like a mature woman! It was odd, though, that although they had continued to chatter all day every day, neither she nor Liza had acknowledged the fact head-on. There was daily talk of 'when I go home' from them both, but it was fuzzy, imprecise, referring to a never-to-come future, as if they were small girls telling stories to pass a long evening. Flora, standing stiffly by her bed as if preparing for military inspection, watched the joyous procession come towards her: and she was afraid for a moment that the bride-escapee, in her excitement and ecstasy, would pass her by without a word or glance, sweeping out to freedom and normality. I know, thought Flora Wilson to herself, that if she does so I will not, *cannot* step forward, I cannot go to her. I know that I will let her go, I will let her ignore me. For that is what I am to expect.

But Liza, solid, reliable Liza, showed that she was not the slave of Flora's darker imaginings, and a moment later she had broken from her man and fastened on to Flora with her joy momentarily abated. She sobbed wordlessly a few moments and Flora, alarmed by pangs of contempt deep within herself, clung to her friend and matched her tear for tear. Finally recovering a little of her dry, droll tone, Liza attempted to wink, propelling another large tear from her right eye.

'Do stay in touch princess, you and yer bags. Come to the wedding if yer can, make it your first step away from that queer, closed world of yours.' She held Flora close and whispered, 'But I'll understand if... honest I will.' She paused, heaved a breath, then finished, 'I'll understand if y'don't.' Unseen by anyone else, Liza pressed a small piece of paper into Flora's hand, with a frisson that was almost guilty, as if they were engaged in bribery or espionage. 'Me address,' she whispered. '*Do* stay in touch.'

As the hullaballoo died and Liza and Tom were gone, Flora lay on her bed toying with the slip of paper, imagining herself attending the wedding, choosing and wearing a lovely dress, dancing at the promised party afterwards, meeting a lad as handsome and stout as Tom Peterson and never going back to Woolsend or the faithless Terry Cauldon again. But before long the Wilson voice resumed: *Stop being so silly, Flora Wilson, stop being so childish. You'll no more go to that wedding than fly to the Moon.* She sat up and pressed the note into a pocket of her purse; she had Liza's address. She would write, yes, write, as soon as possible; *that* at least wasn't beyond her.

Flora was, in her turn, finally discharged from the ward, and once again she dreaded the night-time. To begin, her old bedroom at Woolsend Avenue now seemed empty and chilly, distressingly silent and unwelcoming. The walls were drab, cheerless and drained of colour, the floor a sheet of thin ice, and the fireplace gaped emptily, belching cold air; flowers, intended to brighten and cheer the room, sagged in a cracked vase, crushed by the impossibility of their responsibilities.

Huddled in a mound of blankets, Flora was also afraid she had already put her room-mate's nose terribly out of joint: Minnie had been dragooned into sharing. 'We can't leave the poor sick girl alone,' Nora had insisted. Minnie might perhaps have been glad of temporary relief from the ever more voluble and shrill rows shaking the walls of her own room, but she showed nothing but bad temper and irritation.

In spite of her awareness that silence would have suited Minnie far better than a young girl's prattling, Flora found herself possessed of a reckless spirit, quite unable to keep quiet; she was chattering about her weeks of absence, of the sanatorium, of her fantasy trip to Switzerland, of the other girls—especially Liza. 'She's nearly twenty-one and she fell ill just a week or two before I did and she lives in Liverpool somewhere, and she's got six sisters and a brother...'

'But she had more brothers than that till nasty Ole Hickler did for them,' Minnie picked up the story in a sarcastic, dead tone. 'I know I know, if you've told me this bally tale once you've told me a thousand times—Liza this, Liza that, it's as if you've gone funny on her. And you've walked off with her bloody accent, easy as you'd slip on her coat. You sound like a blessed shop girl. Now I'm sick to the back teeth of hearing about Lee-za or any of the others. Go to sleep. And in the morning try to act like a Wilson, not some street arab. You're back home now, where you belong.'

There was a long lull, until Flora's quiet thoughts turned

themselves into words, which then crammed themselves into her mouth, and she was quite unable to resist letting them free. 'Liza says I'm not a child anymore; I should consider myself grown up, that I should move away from home and live my own life.'

'Where would *you* go?' Minnie snarled after a disbelieving pause, turning over, thumping her pillow, then settling to sleep.

'I'm glad to be home,' whispered Flora into the unresponsive darkness.

2015

'Did you ever see her again?'

There was no reply; Flora was lost in unhappy thought.

'Gran?' Francine abandoned her questioning in response to a gentle, silent gesture from Kara, but it was clear not one visit had taken place, not one letter sent; the Wilson voice had triumphed. The friendship was another lost story, another broken thread.

1953

Nora sat in her favourite chair, frowning heavily and blowing smoke towards Mona Welkins while retailing her woes in her familiar disconsolate tone.

'Soon I shall be alone, all alone. Even my Flora, my little one, not up from her sick bed for five minutes but she's on the arm of that Latimer lad. There's only one thing in his mind, I know that. And only one thing in hers—to leave her home and her mother, even though I nursed her through her sickness and fretted and worried all those long months. Even she can't wait to get away, even with a worthless so-and-so like him.'

Mona knew better than to argue or interject.

'One by one my girls are leaving me. It's not what I call gratitude.'

The Place of Lost Stories

2015

Gran was very frail now; she had lost a little stature every time Francine saw her and she was moving ever more slowly, as if she would grind to a halt any day. Francine, Kara and Eileen knew well that she felt frail too, that she was assailed old age's aches and pains, breathed with increasing difficulty and that coughs and colds clung to her dangerously, refusing, like rude, impertinent guests, to leave when their time was done. But all the time Flora was doing her failing best to conceal it all, and she never, ever complained.

'She's trying hard not to be Nonna.' Eileen judged, 'trying not to let history repeat itself through her: and trying too hard, for my money.'

Gran rarely mentioned illness, still less did she broach death; all in pursuit of the negative imperative that underscored the course of her life. For her daughters and granddaughter, this silence was painful and did nothing to protect them; mortality was, to vary the cliché, the skeleton in the room. How long had Flora left? Both of her parents had lived into their nineties, perhaps she would too, but who could tell? There was not long to go until the ending of yet another thread of the Wilson story. And all around, threads of the tale were finishing.

'If you've got any more of your questions you'd better ask em quick, girlie.' Jeff Clayton described slow, disconsolate semi-circles as he swung in Barry Fenton's favourite chair. 'History is disposing of the witnesses, one by one.'

Nobody laughed. Flora winced. Jeff, his umpteenth whisky dancing with soda water, continued to swing unhappily to and fro. He was in a strange, combative mood, a man who had lost a close and beloved comrade and didn't know whether to send him off with tears or cheers.

The funeral had been uncomfortable, and now so was the sparse gathering back at the house. Rachel and Nina were in the throes of an ill-tempered, undeclared sibling war and the conflict was palpable even in the eulogies to Barry that each insisted on delivering. Rachel, whose laughter tonic had somehow failed her, made repeated, pointed references to '*my* dad' while her sister had presented a range of sentimental happy memories of Barry, Helen and herself, with her sister going unmentioned, expelled from the family portrait. At the house they left the mourners largely to themselves, moving in complicated orbits that focused on avoidance of one another.

'Damned Wilsons.' Jeff swung and swigged. 'Time and progress have done nothing to water down the family inheritance: spite, war and conflict. Whenever two or more of this blasted family are gathered, lo shall there be ructions. The old man and the old lady were always promising their daughters a legacy, and here it bloody well is.'

Yet more of that legacy was apparent through the absence of anyone bar Jeff from Minnie's side of the family.

'Yesssss,' Jeff was very well on now, but nobody tried to stop him drinking or talking. 'Playing our Min's game, as ever, staying away because of some old, silly, stupid grudge that's none of their business and neither they nor Minnie understood in the first place. Does anyone recall how Min demanded to be *invited* to poor Phylly's funeral? I told her, they don't send you a damned card, RSVP and all that, you just *go*, for crying out loud! But she wouldn't without an invite! It turned out she only wanted one so that she could publicly tear it up! All to get revenge over god knows what from the ancient, buried past! Damn spitfire! What a woman!'

'Goodness me Jeffrey, you sound almost fond of her,' teased Flora.

'She was wilful, unreasonable, stroppy and exasperating. She and logic were oil and water. Yet I loved her true as any man could. Queer isn't it?'

Everyone laughed, for the first time that day.

So love was spoken of, but death was not to be denied. 'Does anyone remember being here after Aunty Helen's funeral? Uncle Barry was plastered, talking complete rubbish.' Flora did not look at Jeff but he raised his glass in salute. 'But you realised at that moment, even if you'd been deaf and blind to it before, he loved her dear and true.'

'Ahhh, anyone who didn't know that was either a damn fool or Sambo Wilson,' breathed Jeff, taking another swig from his tumbler. He paused, musing, then added, 'I always feel sorry for Phyllida. Now Helen and our Min, at least they died loved and knowing they were loved. Phylly, she died alone and lonely. Makes me sad to think of it.'

Nobody spoke for a time. In the mind of everyone was the question; how and when shall I die? And shall I die alone and lonely? Francine found her gaze locking to her gran's thin, lined face, and when Flora noticed her scrutiny the youngster had to tear her eyes away in embarrassment, as if she had been staring at a stranger.

'There's a story in *how* they died too; even death has a tale to tell in this family.'

'Now Jeff…' Flora began warningly, but he was whisky-fuelled.

'Old Baz now, he wouldn't be embarrassed to hear it said that the light went out of his life when our Helen died, and that for the last ten years and more he's been waiting, just waiting, to be joined with his girl again. He hit the booze a bit to ease the finger-drumming delay, but who am I to criticise on that score?' Jeff grinned at his audience and took another large gulp of amber eloquence.

'Now Nora, she was waiting too, spent half her bloody life at it, waiting for the second bloody coming of you-know-who. Time all wasted too. Anyhow: Helen, our Helen, she died of a stroke, just the same as that wretched old bat as brought her up…'

'Jeff, please, some respect!' Flora was demanding, but not angry.

'For our Helen yes, but not for the other creature. It's too late to pay false respects to them as don't deserve.' Jeff was unabashed. 'Helen had time to know what had happened to her, a short time to live on when perhaps she didn't care to. But God she was brave about it, a stoic, a fighter. You might even call her a martyr. You taking notes, girlie?'

Francine squirmed in her seat, but Jeff emanated an avuncular beam. 'This is for you so get it all down, soon as you can. The family story you wanted. So… What now, ah yes, Phyllida, Phylly, poor old puss... found she was, by a neighbour I think. Heart had packed up, just like Petra before her: sitting up in her chair, though, smiling all warm and sunny; like she was greeting a very welcome guest. Food for thought, that. And Minnie—no Flo, I will talk about her—well, what was she to the very last but a stubborn, contrary pepperpot of a creature? There she was, eighty-one and supposedly ailing and housebound, storming headlong across the road to "have it out with Margaret Beecher" over some silly sodding grudge our girl had suddenly remembered out of nowhere. Too keen to get to grips with the unfortunate Mrs. Beecher, she didn't look if anything was coming at her—*bump*—didn't stand a chance. But she died fighting, and that's how she would have wanted it says I. So there you go, girlie, the fallen of the Wilson family; and in their various ways, all nobly fallen too. May we have the good fortune to die as well as em.' Jeff raised his glass in tribute then tottered to the door, looking up the stairs and crying, 'These stairs are too steep!' before clumping slowly up to the bathroom.

Kara, Eileen and Francine all looked to Flora, fearing Jeff's outbursts had distressed her, but instead she was chuckling indulgently.

'He could always say the unsayable, that man. And *Lord* wasn't he fond of our Barry then?'

Rachel threaded between the chairs in the long, narrow sitting-room, offering plates of snacks and asking, with a resurgence of her natural cheer, if anyone would like another drink. She exempted the newly-returned Jeff from the latter query but he, equally cheerily, continued to serve himself from Barry's cabinet, handily positioned at his elbow. Nina came through a short time later, plainly determined to perform the same office; she was peeved at the various polite refusals, and clearly angry at being outmanoeuvred by her sister.

'The service was nice, wasn't it?' she tossed into the air, satisfying herself with nods and inarticulate noises of agreement before disappearing to the kitchen, presumably to plot how to outdo Rachel on the next pass. Kara, Eileen and Francine exchanged meaningful looks but said nothing; the religious content of Barry's farewell had been another area of bitter contention between his daughters, each of whom cleaved strongly and unbendingly to opposing churches that scorned and damned all rivals. The tepid and inoffensive tone of prayer that had filled the air at the crematorium was the result of reluctant compromise. 'Nice' was about all it was. Jeff Clayton was not in a fit state to keep his thoughts within his head, and so he broke the fragile silence.

'Stupid sluts. Squabbling to claim their old dad's body for their different cults. Well he didn't care for god-bothering, not a bit, and wouldn't have thanked them for that tug-of-war, so *there*.'

With a frisson of horror, Francine realised that this trenchancy had been overheard by a returning Nina, who hovered uncertainly in the kitchen doorway as if fearing that bar-room fisticuffs might break out.

'*Father* used to talk like that when he was in his cups,' sniffed Nina to Francine, 'when he was old and losing control I mean. He sometimes used old age as an excuse to be just bally *rude*.'

She disappeared from sight once again; Jeff laughed

loudly. 'So he did, so he did the old beggar! Ha! And now I'm an owd mon too, that's what I'm going to do!'

Flora looked at him with a glittering eye; was she about to scold him for his boorishness on this day of sadness? 'Have you decided to "tell the truth", Jeff? Just like Mother did when she grew old?'

Now the two of them were laughing.

'Oh Lor,' breathed Jeff, 'yes, when Nora decided to tell the truth and nothing but the *untrampled* truth to one and all! Now *there* was a time...'

To the relief of all, the spirit of death retreated from the room and stories of the past claimed its place.

1979

'Mum, we'd like to invite the family, as many as we can, to have a little party to celebrate your eightieth birthday. Would you like that?'

Nora appeared not to have heard, so Helen repeated, bellowing like a jolly Guide leader. Nora turned slowly to meet her eyes, as if waking from a dream; there was a lost, almost fearful expression as if she were returning to a now unfamiliar home after a long journey. She didn't speak for a few more moments, then a clicking erupted in her throat and her face cleared.

'Yes,' she said almost as a whisper. 'I'd like that. Who's coming?'

'Well, we haven't asked anyone yet, we wanted you to...'

'Not him.'

'What?'

'Not *him*.'

'No Mum.'

'No, not him.' Nora's face readopted that lost look. 'Not him,' she repeated in a husky, low breath.

'We'll do a list, start contacting people. Would you like that?'

'Yes. I'd like that. I'd like everyone to be together. One last time.'

'Mother, not that again, it doesn't have to be the last t...' Helen began rather aggressively, but Flora, standing nearby, waved hush at her, looking at their mother with quiet concern. Nora's eyes were glinting again with distance and dream.

1980

'Are you all right?' Flora slid down on the settee next to Kara, who had been engaged in earnest conversation with Nonna Nora. Nonna had been guided off to the loo by Phyllida, and Kara looked glad.

'I'm fine, but Nonna's cutting up a bit. I think she's got hold of more sherry than anyone planned. She was just saying her daughters are wicked—too mean to take her out to dinner on her birthday.'

'More dratted romancing! She turned us down flat on that and insisted we have her party at home! *I can't walk, you can't make me go outdoors!*'

'Mum, I know. Oh, and you're all too tight to allow her a decent drink. Sherry's not an alcoholic drink, it's *good* for you, see; her doctor has recommended she takes a glass or two a day but her horrid daughters are too cruel to allow that.'

'I'll take over the Nonna-sitting duties now.' Flora patted her hand. 'You've done your stint.'

'Thanks Mum, it was getting a bit—what's that sound?'

It was a voice, one that lectured and hectored in a tone of great self-certitude and boomed with sonorous self-importance. It was the sort of voice that had once dominated the house but which had not been heard since Ole Hickler had taken a powder.

'It's Aunty Peggy.' Flora giggled. 'I think she's found the other half of Nonna's bottle of sherry, but Peggy's found the *happy* half. She's got quite a talent there, whoever would have known it? I just hope Nonna doesn't overhear...'

As Kara came to investigate, Peggy was entertaining a gaggle of partygoers sat round her in the back kitchen as she dispensed sarcasms and condemnations in her eerily accurate borrowed voice.

'What is this *vulgar gathering?*' scowled Peggy-Sam, 'what are such *low characters* doing in my home, making merry with *my* food and drink, eh? Making free with the fruits of my labour! And don't you dare to laugh at me, you heathen mob! Don't you know that you should respect your elders and betters?

'Well, I never did think much of this family but when I see the *articles* gathered before me today, I despair! Jesus wept and well he might! Look at you all, anyone would think you were a cageful of blessed monkeys! Oh, but this family has gone downhill since I was last here; you, the young un sniggering over there, you're a student, I hear, at some high-flown university: student? Parasite more like, drawing your unearned income like blood from the veins of decent hard-working men! How dare you try to claim you are cleverer than I, sir! Get out and get a job, earn your crust like a decent human being!

'And you young lady, you can quit that silly smirking right now, you are just as bad! I hear tell you're a "career woman"; in other words a dratted shop-girl with ideas above her station! At least your sister had the decency to get wed and stay at home to look after her children, but why in God's name did she lower herself to marry... *a bus driver*?

'A parcel of degenerate heathens, that's what you are! A shame and a disgrace to the noble name of *Wilson*! To think I am related to a single one of you: I am *mortified*!'

'Oh c'mon gramps!' a voice played along. 'Be a bit more Christian! Love thy neighbour and all that!'

'Now *there* is a teaching I have taken very much to heart...' The rest of Peggy-Sam's next sally was lost in a roar of ribald laughter. Aunty Peggy broke character, took a sip of sherry and tottered slightly. 'Ooooh, I've gone all *wobbly!*' she cried, flopping with undignified haste into Nora's favourite chair, while her adoring public applauded her performance.

Kara returned to the living room just before her grandmother. Nora was swaying and bending like a flag in a breeze, alternately sinking against and swinging away from Phyllida, who was evincing no little panic as she attempted to steady the old woman.

'She's *drunk!*' roared Minnie, breaking from a small knot of cousins to trumpet her disapproval. 'Phylly, you were supposed to be *watching* her!'

Phyllida opened and closed her mouth like a creature

unaccustomed to breathing air.

'And you sat there, Kara, and let her get away with it!' bellowed Minnie, pointing accusingly.

'Oh hush then!' interceded Helen. 'She's only a kid, how can you expect her to—'

'Kid my backside! She's old enough to help *herself* to a drink or two!'

'Mind your damn tongue, Minnie Wilson!'

'Minnie *Clayton*, you stuck-up madam!'

The room fell into an expectant silence as the spirit of family conflict stirred once more.

Antie Mary ad a canary
Down the leg of er drawers—

Nora, seated once again, cut through the tense quiet with a bawling, lusty voice.

'Mother!' Helen cried, horrified. 'Don't be embarrassing!'

'Ohhhh, *bum'ole* girl! I thought this was meant to be a party—*my* party, yet here y'all are so gloomy-faced you'd think ole Sammy Wilson was preachin one of his dratted lessons at you! Now stop spoiling things you prissy missy, I wanna sing-song!'

Antie Mary ad a canary
Down the leg of er drawers
An when she farted
Down it darted
Down the leg of er drawers!

'Mother, please! It's indecent!' Helen was outraged.

'You all sang it happily enough when you were kids—when you thought the old bugger wasn't listening!'

'*I* never did!' insisted Helen primly.

'Well that was your loss from living with that damn old hag of an aunt of yours,' Nora slurred. 'You'd of bin far better off at home with your mother.'

'Oh Mum, not again...'

'I'm saying it as it needs saying! There's a lotto things as need saying, a lotto things as you girls need to hear before it's too late, and I'm not going to my grave without telling you! I'm talking to you *all!* I've felt the touch of the Dark Angel, it's coming for me soon but the good Lord has allowed me just one last chance to reckon with you little lot and I'm damned if I don't take it!'

'I *knew* there'd be ructions,' whispered Barry Fenton to Minnie's new husband. 'Strap yourself in sunbeam, and enjoy the ride.' Barry opened a couple of beers, handed one to Jeff and made himself comfortable.

'This is my chance to tell every last one o'you the truth, the untrampled truth of things! You've not treated me right, not one of you, not since your father went queer in the head and abandoned us all. You all took his side, yes you did, not one of you supported me, you all fled home fast as you could go, and y'only came back to hurt and treat me like a dam fool! You're no good to me, not none of you, you're Sam Wilson's brood and that's that... all this family's good for is to make children an live a long, long, empty life...'

Nora, exhausted, broke off to find Aunty Peggy, who had been sobered and summoned by the her angry voice, plucking at her sleeve, and the old woman allowed herself to be guided away.

'See Peggy here?' she croaked at her children, 'She's been more of a daughter to me over the years than any one of you! She's a better girl and a better Christian and she's more love for me in her little finger than you've got in your big fat Wilson arses! *Bum'ole* to y'all!'

She flopped against Peggy, breathing heavily, and was removed from the scene with effort.

Helen turned to rally her sisters, and found to her astonishment that Minnie's eyes were reddened. 'What if she's right? What if poor Mother's time has come at last?' she snuffled. 'I feel terrible, how cruel we've been to her, how we've hurt her! We must try to do better by her!'

'Oh for crying out loud!' Helen cut her sister dead, 'Don't be so soft in the head! She'll be here in ten years' time, playing the same old tune. We all know that.'

Minnie's lachrymose moment was over and the harsh, glittering light of battle reentered her eyes. 'No, I shouldn't upset myself!' she snapped at Helen. '*My* conscience is clear even if no one else's is. Mother is right, the way you all treat her is terrible, you're an ungrateful pack of hussies...'

The new row broke over the room as Peggy took Nora up the stairs and put her to bed.

2015

'I haven't much time left meself,' announced Jeff Clayton to the gathering, 'and I wish to say one last thing. I wish to pay tribute to Barry Fenton; a great brother-in-law, a great mate, a fine drinker, a loving father and husband and a craftsman of skill. And most of all, a man who knocked the wind out of Sambo Wilson's sails: to Barry!'

He tipped his last drink down the hatch and collapsed backwards into the padded comfort of his departed friend's old chair.

'Shall we go home?' Flora asked her daughters. 'We'd best drop Jeff off too…'

Money and Fine Words

1945

'Jus lately, Himself as bin even more pleased with hissen than usual. Any tickler reason for that is there then Jack?'

George Shenton, seasoned trapper that he was, sniffed the air and was aware of a change in the behaviour of his prey. He had noted that Jack Carthmain too evinced an inordinately smug air, although his manner was more furtive than Wilson's recent positively expansive and cheerful mien.

'Jack, you know summat. Tell us,' demanded the old miner.

'Now George; I know full well you despise Madge Batten and all her raddled gang of tattletales—*your* description, I might remind you, though I've always thought it odd coming from a feller who gossips like an ole woman—but there are occasions when you should lend the dear lady an ear...'

'Quit goin round the ouses Jack! Tell!'

'I shall do better than that old lad, for here comes Sammy in person. Watch what unfolds—and rejoice.' Jack stood to receive the oncoming, and decidedly self-satisfied, Sam Wilson.

'Evenin Sammy, nice o you to drop by. I rather thought this humble house had lost you to the opulent allure of the Con Club.'

Jack, as if currying favour, escorted Sam to his seat: so far unsuspecting, the victim plonked his bottom down but then paused, suspended in space, as Jack spoke again while directing a crooked finger at his head.

'Owd up Sammy, what's that there? It… it could almost be a bitta shoe polish or something…'

Sam was bemused, as was George who, although he was interested in the sporting display, could not fathom what his partner in the hunt was up to. He noticed, however, that although Jack was pointing at the centre of his victim's dial, Wilson's hand had strayed, momentarily, as if to touch his hair. Unable to hover over his seat any longer, the disconcerted Sam plopped down into his place while Jack yanked a large, ancient handkerchief out of his pocket and gestured with it as if offering to remove some mote or blemish.

'Shoe polish?' Sam Wilson's new confidence was in sudden abeyance.

'Aye.' Jack leaned in for a closer look. 'Shoe polish or… summat else brown…'

With a fluid movement Jack slithered from his floundering victim, as if he had expected to be struck a blow. He winked at George playfully and made a quick gesture of playing a fish on a line.

'Any road Sammy.' Jack was all bonhomie once again. 'Not ter worry; let's ave that smile o yours back Sammy, for you've a little somethin to celebrate, ave yer not?'

'Celebrate!' Wilson's smile resurged.

'Aye, celebrate! And you'll be buying, will yer not Sammy, bein a man of property, no less!'

To George's astonishment, Wilson's confusion ebbed, replaced with a stout, complacent happiness, a spreading and slightly alarming tombstone beam. To George's further astonishment, a feeling so great it nearly struck the breath from his body, he witnessed Sammy Wilson digging deep into his pockets, beckoning Netta over and ordering three pints of the Oak's finest. A witness to a miracle, he later declared, awestruck and amazed.

'Good health now Sammy.' Jack matched Wilson's cheerful smile and added a bit. 'And here's to a happy home, eh?'

George merely grunted assent: he could not trust himself to attempt speech.

As the door closed, slowly and reluctantly as ever, behind Sam, Jack Carthmain sighed like the satisfied soul that he was. 'Back to his castle e goes!'

'Now that e's off Jack—answer uz some questions!' George was agitated, eager to know.

'Anythin for you, old son.'

'Firstly, ow did Sammy ever resist the temptation t smack you in the chops for the way you just pulled is leg?'

'You know Sammy, owd, he's a man who's proof against all temptation.'

'And, I get it, Sammy's bought that house o'his. But how did e get the brass to do *that?* Sellin is body or summat?'

'Not quite George, but, tell you what, I'd venture to say e could tell you in detail what Billy Thorndyke has had for breakfast...'

Those idiots, they were just a couple of performing monkeys, Sam told himself as he strode purposefully home. They were men without a scrap of dignity and simply could not cope with a man who placed a premium on respectable behaviour, but their infantile sallies could not discomfit him. They were envious, plain and simple, and why should they not be? 'A man of property', it was nothing less than a fact, for all Carthmain's jeering. That jabbering pair could prod at him all they liked; Sam Wilson was their better, and they could put *that* in their pipes and smoke it.

1959

Had Nora been standing there before him, Sam would have struck her and done it full hard across her face, he was in such a passion. He was animated by a barely controllable desire to dash his hand across something, *anything*, even if it meant battering his own hot brow. In the end he revenged himself on the piece of paper in his hand in the stead of a living being, screwing it up into a tight ball before hurling it towards the fireplace, where it bounced half-dead into a cold corner of the unlit grate.

Yvette had retreated to the kitchen and he had not seen her for nearly an hour; he knew that she would not emerge now until he deigned to fetch her, the room was his. He was supposedly only visiting, he still lived in his small flat nearby, but she did not balk at being restricted in her home, she had learned to cede space and solitude to him when he needed it. She had, at first, tried to ask him what was wrong, but she soon fled from his angry glare, only once unwisely returning to ask if he 'wanted anything'. As if a cup of tea and a sympathetic word could ameliorate this disaster! He shook his head so violently in refusal he rendered himself dizzy. He was almost unable to hold back a bellow of 'peace!'—an imprecation aimed at his wife-to-be, also at the heavens themselves and above all at the unquiet forces resolved to torment him unendingly and ensure the tranquillity he needed and craved eluded him even here. He had built a new life with the aim of claiming the prize of peace, of rest from strife, of housing tranquillity safe in his breast. And yet, his mind was agitated and afire.

'How?' he strode around the room asking himself over and again, each time with an agony and fury that burnt ever more greatly. How had she the wicked gall to demand this of him? How did she have the *brain?* How was he to deal with the matter, short of returning to his former home and parting the scheming hag from her breath? She must have had help, he concluded unhappily, some sharp-nosed pen-pusher of a lawyer had suggested this ploy; she had the brass neck but not the intelligence to extort this thing from him, to commit this blackmail.

The demand was set out in a letter from his own lawyers: '*We are advised that your estranged wife Mrs. Nora Wilson has now agreed to your request that she seek a divorce, but she will do so subject strictly to the following conditions…*' Divorce; that it should come to this. Yet it was necessary. He had not blundered into matrimony blind to the possibility of its failure, what dolt would behave so, but neither had he schemed for it, what swine would do such a thing? He had surely loved Nora, yet it was a love that had not proved true or enduring. He had been lost in idolatrous worship of a false angel who, conjuring and beguiling with sunbeams, had made herself irresistible. They had been wed before he could master his passions—and before his senses were repaired he and Nora were responsible for a hungry, quarrelsome brood, yet the uneven match had to be ended. Woman had never been the equal of man, not even in the blessed groves of Eden, but the hideous inequity in his marriage was plain once he was free of the obscuring infatuation. He had bound himself to a woman his inferior in every conceivable way.

Aware of the terrible mistake he had made he was however trapped, it would have been dishonourable simply to walk away from small children, and so he had trained himself to endure. Twenty years he had borne it, was that not of some account, had he not earned remission? He had seen the girls through the puzzles and perils of childhood, held his hand until the good God smote down the Hun monster, was that insufficient? Even after their parting he had not requested Nora divorce him; when he first came to suggest such a thing he did so purely with Nora's interests in mind, not for his own sake. She was still young and attractive in face and figure—that no man could deny—and had she sought her freedom she would surely have found a new husband with ease, someone more of her kind and class, better suited to her. He was prepared to bear the stigma; all he asked of his wife was that she should exercise discretion. He had ventured the suggestion via the girls, though not Helen, who scorned him with a hard-face and Bible quotations, but Nora was not to be moved. As was ever the case with the woman, she could not perceive her own true interests, blinded by bitterness and hysteria. It was for Nora—legally and morally—to seek the remedy. He could not charge her with desertion, nor yet with infidelity; in truth she suffered not from a lack of fidelity but a morbid excess of it and clung tenaciously to the dead hope that he would return to her side and bed.

When final mental rest and contentment in wedlock with Yvette had become a real prospect, Sam tried his embassies to Nora once again, but with no hope or expectation of success, for she would surely wish to choke his new joy, to do all in her power to poison it. And yet word came back that, at long last, she would consent to his suit: at first he had wondered at the perversity of her mind, why had she resisted so stubbornly when it was she alone who stood to benefit and then conceded when it was his gain? Ah, but there was an answer to that conundrum and it was a cruel one. Nora would stand out of Sam's way if and only if he would sign over *'sole and undisputed ownership the dwellinghouse and land comprising 88 Woolsend Avenue in the County of…'* Rage almost took him to the Devil once again.

'How?'

Oh, he had been sorely mistaken to dismiss her as a feeble thing without an organised thought of her own; such pride of mind had brought him to this pass. She had displayed an untrained but undeniable intelligence, low cunning more like, and picked his pocket clean and whole. The house he had worked for, the home in which he had invested his money and the sheer, awful effort of tolerating that fool Thorndyke and his appalling coterie, men who believed themselves of a superior breed but who were simply snobbish, boorish and spoiled by money; that house was his by every legal and moral right. And yet his former wife was to take it from him and he was not to resist, not if he wanted his new life, his deserved repose. How had she done this to him?

'How?' he screamed in renewed agony, not caring who

might hear him.

Sam sat for a moment but then was on his feet as if a marionette, jerked into life all unwilling. He crossed the room and scrabbled in the fireplace for the paper pellet that was the letter; so hastily did he unroll it that he tore a gash through its middle, and the paper sagged open like a jeering mouth. And again the rage almost took absolute possession of his soul.

'*How?*' he howled once more, as if he were a wolf in the moonlight. How had he, Samuel Wilson, been so comprehensively outmanoeuvred by a woman with such a petty, piffling mind?

1982

Mum had been on the phone for half the afternoon, it seemed to Kara; it had started with a call from Aunty Helen during which Mum's grasp of language appeared to have slipped, and 'Hmm', 'Ahhh' and 'Oh dear' to be her pet and only phrases. Then calls from the other aunts came in, and Mum called them back with afterthoughts and they called her back again with their further musings and latest news. Kara paid little attention to the to-ing and fro-ing, assuming some new front was opening in the Wilsons' unending sibling war; minding her business was always best in these circumstances, she had found. Over dinner that night, however, the tale unfolded.

'Another little secret of Grampa Sam's has wormed its way into the light,' said Flora. 'Another revelation concerning Yvette.'

'Not more bedroom stuff, pleeeease!' shuddered Kara.

For some reason Grampa Sam had let it be known he had never, in the twenty or more years of their marriage, seen his second wife naked; why tell us that, Gramps, why not let that sordid fact die with the woman and her assumed name?

'No,' her mother reassured her. 'It's about the house.'

'Sold it at last has he, and offering the proceeds to the daughter who'll look after him for the rest of his life, along with his silver teapot?'

'Well I'm sure that was his intention, but he can't. Turns out it's not his house.'

'You what?'

'He thought it was Yvette's, but she, ah, misled him more than a bit. She owned a share in it, but that was jointly with her two sisters.'

'I never met them.'

'Lucky you, girl. The three demons we called them: the other two made Yvette look positively loveable, and God knows that took a lot. They were vile, self-righteous and snotty bitches—that's giving them the best of it—and Grampa Sam despised them royally. They reminded him horribly of Aunt Laura, he admitted that himself. And Grampa being Grampa, he showed his feelings openly. He regarded them as puffed-up prigs.'

'Huh, did he now!'

'And he was right, even though he was pretty much looking in a mirror. Anyway, he thought he was beholden to them for nothing, so he didn't spare them his contempt, and now it's all come back to bite him. He thought that he was safe to give them the length of his tongue, but he was terribly mistaken. Yvette may have asked them to let him stay in the house if she predeceased him, but even if she did, they've disregarded her wishes.'

'Oh God. I can see what's coming.'

Flora nodded with a grim smile. 'Grampa's only just found out. He's threatening to go to law but I think he will lose. And so…'

'We'll all be hearing from Grampa Sam and his silver teapot, very soon.'

'Precisely. Oh, and on an unrelated subject darling—have you locked the doors yet?'

1959

'Money and fine words, Sammy Wilson, money and fine bloody words.' Nora laughed to herself, a screeching, unhappy sound like some night hunter. Slowly she took a tour of the house, looking at it as if for the first time; it was her home, hers alone and entirely. If Sam Wilson wanted to come home now he would have to beg her leave. Now there was a turn-up for the bally books.

The Beauty of Chell Street

1966

I was in love, so in love, with a handsome man; but what in truth did I love? A face, a frame, a body; not a soul: I was in love with handsomeness, and not a man. Yet I was too young and too foolish to know what awaited me, I believed myself so happy, I thought I had fulfilled my every dream. I recall hugging myself as I sat up in my bed, thinking of Sammy Wilson and his so-lovely, so-stern features—yes, stern even then with the soft down of youth still upon them. I felt a special warm sensation, a tickling over my body, for I was to marry this man, this beautiful, beautiful man; I truly believed a benevolent God had smiled on me.

I remember how I would stand at my window thinking of him, hoping that for some reason he would appear at the door calling my name, then I would look out over the neighbourhood, the roofs and down the tight, winding streets. I could see the sloping roofs of the homes of my friends, my rivals—and my body, my whole being tingled again. 'I've beaten you Betty Crace, for Tom Stanton may have a little silver in his pockets but a thousand pounds wouldn't make me content with *that* homely, silly face! You too Elizabeth Ballington, for I shall be married and away from this place long before your backward Charlie Simms has blurted out the vital question and fumbled his way to the altar! And as for you, Hilda Montgomery, so proud you were of Steven Motley, your talk was forever of his golden hair and titan's body. Well he's come back to you at least, but war broke that body and turned his ripe-corn hair a powder-grey and now an old man stoops where youth stood. What he was, you have lost. All of you and a dozen more, I have outdone you, I have my man and he is better in every way than any of yours. Soon I shall shed my name and take up *his,* I shall leave this house, this town, I shall forsake this family for a better one. I cannot wait. Oh let him come to my door and take me away now, now!'

Triumphant, yes I was. Little fool.

2016

Lanwell Woods ho—why u not stick 2 suckin Mart Paytons dick? Uain no frend ur a bich. Home crowd r gonna no about this an they will hate u. Im takin all yr contax off my gear. Pis of bichslut.

Francine offed her handheld and blew a mouth-fart. She rubbed and slapped at her face, irritated with herself as tears tried to break through the backs of her eyes and her breath caught on a knot inside her neck. Shayla could 'pis of' herself, it had been a fair contest, and Shayla was just 'pised of' that she was the loser. Anyway, Francine had got rid of Mart Payton long ago; at first he had looked good, smelt good, tasted good, but after only a short time she'd found him to be an over-eager, sweaty, stinky-breathed little boy who lived inside an adult like a crab in a shell. He'd cried when she told him there was to be no more, which had made it hard, but she hadn't allowed him to draw tears from her. It was more honest to show that she wasn't sorry. And the same harsh but necessary rule applied to this business with Shayla.

2016

'Mum, we need to talk.'

'Plainly: you have your council-of-war face on. Am I right to assume that the subject of this little chat will be my beloved granddaughter?'

'Oh Mum don't turn it into a game: I have to do something. *This* time. It feels as if I'm losing her.'

'Isn't that putting things a mite strongly?'

'I just can't sit and watch her do this! She hardly tells me a thing these days, I'm lucky if I can get a cave-girl grunt out of her in place of a conversation, she won't touch me, won't even come near me, her college work is suffering, she thinks nothing about the mess she's making of her life, the sole-thought in her head is boys-boys-boys, no, worse still it's men-men-men, there's nothing else in her whole life!'

'She *is* seventeen, Kara. I grant she's a handful at the moment but things will calm down; she's a sensible girl underneath it all.'

'She *was*. *Used* to be. She's changed so, Mum.'

'That's normal too.'

'But you know what's happening, you know what she's turning into: who she's turning into...'

'Come on now Kara, life doesn't work like that and nor does heredity. You've been watching too many silly films darling. Are you trying to say that our girl is... what, turning into a throwback, a new version of Nonna?'

'She keeps that picture close by her you know, the one that started it all off. She's deeply proud of the resemblance.'

'So what are you saying?'

'And did you know that she spends some of her evenings shut in her room dressing her hair and making up her face so that you wouldn't be able to tell her and Nonna apart?'

'How do you know that she does?'

'The same way that you always knew what I was up to. Plus although she's secretive about it, she hasn't put sufficient security on her little look-at-me web-site and I'm not the dummy she thinks I am. I worry about what it all means, Mum. She's striving so hard to look like Nonna, she's studied her so closely, it's as if she were trying to become her.'

'Oh nonsense child! You'll accuse her of conjuring up spirits and ghosts next!'

'In a way, that's what she *is* doing! Look at her behaviour Mum, look at how she's changed! The Francine I brought up is vanishing, and another woman is taking her place.'

'It's a phase, that's all. She'll grow out of...'

'She broke up with her best friend you know, all over boys.'

'Young girls do. You fell out enough times even with your closest pals.'

'Not like this; this was nasty, utterly venomous. She's lost every last one of her friends over it and doesn't care a bloody damn. It's just not *her*.'

1966

How did she feel, that Mirabelle Ellis, as she took him

away, my handsome man? And what, tell me, did she fall in love with, the sour-faced old cowbag? With his 'spiritual nature' she'd doubtless say, and I'd say you can keep his spiritual nature and whizz it all up the s-hole missus, oh yes I would. The dour preacher, the sermon-maker, the hypocrite, take them all if you please, but leave me the man I had. Did she feel that triumph as she passed me in the street, did she smile at my back, a foul smile of victory, glorying in the way she pinched him from me, my jewel, my prize? Did she mock me for that unfaded and yet useless beauty that failed to bind my Sam to me? I loved the boy, the man, the real Sam. She loved a phantom and a fraud: that is if she really loved at all.

2016

It had been coming for a long while. Shayla had long become a prize pain and there was no sense pretending otherwise. The two still met from time to time, but each meeting pushed them further apart. They had ceased to share intimacies and instead nursed secrets and grudges. Not that Shayla held back from describing her man-eating exploits: but she was no longer whispering a sisterly confession, she was fucking *bragging*, making it clear she was as ever one move ahead of Francine, of everyone.

'You did *that?*' she would spit with condescending scorn at Francine. 'That's kid's stuff, I did that *ages* ago!'

It wasn't a game anymore, and certainly wasn't a joke. Things had changed, Francine knew it and wasn't sorry. She herself was altered, no longer Shayla's awe-struck, timid little shadow, the follower in her perfume and sweat-scented wake; now she had her own way, her own style. And that was what Shayla didn't like.

When Shayla met Jem she turned from a fuck em and forget em happy harlot into just an annoying, pitiable prat, and from there things went to shit. She was 'in love', moon-eyed and soppy; the way she looked as the two of them held hands or snogged or turned themselves into a tangle of interlocked limbs, always as a fucking public spectacle, God it was disgusting. No matter how intense the clinch she was in, Shayla's eyes always managed to find Francine's. 'See,' they said in a code of malicious glints, 'I got *him*, I got there first. I won.' The way she acted the sweet-innocent was sick-making. Anyone would think she was the virgin bride awaiting her big bloodstained moment, not some used old boot who'd been done a thousand times over in every hole she possessed.

Home Crowd all said that the Jem and Shayla Show was 'sweet', even if one or two regretted the taming of someone who had once been an elemental force. Home Crowd were dead wrong. Shayla needed slapping down. It was too much to bear to sit there and say nothing, do nothing.

1989

They jut out sharply and then close to an edge like a diamond, the little windowpanes of this elevated birdcage where these days I make my bed. If I sit here and crane just a little I can see practically the whole of the Avenue. If someone spies me they will think nothing of it; perhaps they will think they are being watched over by a ghost. By

God they won't be far wrong. This old avenue; I see it here and now, but just as clearly I see it as it was. I belong more to that past time than I do to now.

I have watched the cars gather outside Mona Welkins' home: I watched them carry her out to that long black hearse. They asked me to go to the funeral but I said no, I'm fit to follow her soon, what for do I want a rehearsal?

Like me, Mona never married again once her man was gone. But once Derek was gone at least all the heartache was over for her, and she ever knew where he was, held firm in place with a stone until the good God sees fit to release him. At least she can go to him now, rejoin him body and soul.

2016

'All she seems to have learned from those old family stories is how to fight with bare claws and grab what she wants regardless of the cost.'

'That's certainly a trait of the Wilson women; they know what they want.'

'They *think* they know. And then they spend half a lifetime regretting their damned stupidity.'

'Ah yes. That's *very* Wilson.'

'I'm afraid, Mum, afraid for her, afraid of her and for the future. I've spent the last two years trying to drum it into Francine that life isn't a blasted competition, but she just isn't listening.'

'Because she's winning.'

'*Believes* she is. For the moment.'

'Indeed. She can't conceive that her luck will ever

change.'

'Mum, what can I do?'

'Watch helplessly from the sidelines as I was compelled, offer her advice and support when any intervention won't cause World War Three—and catch her when she falls.'

'Is that your special motherly recipe?'

'Kara darling, it's all I know.'

1989

Those ladies of the Avenue, tongues wagging nineteen to the dozen, still I see them, hurrying pell-mell, in and out from door to door, chattering, whispering—spreading their poison, busy as a nest of ants. Doubtless they picked the meat off my bones soon as I turnt my back, but nothing they could say could hurt me. In spite of all, I had something that they did not, for all that it was taken from me it was still better than anything they ever could boast. I could never of borne the burdens of the other wives in the Avenue.

Derek Welkins was a lovely man, but a waster when all's said and done. Kind, gentle, but feckless. I couldn't of bin with a husband like that. Marge Batten now: her old man was a nothing, a stain on the wall, we rarely saw him, she never spoke of him, never spoke *to* him far as I know. He was like a little fish that swims in the shadow of a shark. She paid him no mind and did him no harm, but that was all. Old Ma Saviour too, she had a husband, so she claimed, but he was forever 'at work', whatever the time, whatever the day. Well, they should of lived like bloody royalty if he'd truly laboured all those hours, but I never saw anything but bread and spit in their kitchen, I can say. I used to imagine he was locked away in the cellar, sitting on a pile of coal, or maybe up aloft in a room like the one I'm in now, peeping out, watching a world he was no longer a part of. Mildred Critchwell, how she use to wear us out with her everlasting hymns to her husband, while all the time he was pleasuring any dizzy bitch in the neighbourhood who'd open her door to him. I would of never remarried, not like Paulette Kerslake, one after another she took, each one more worthless than the last, as if she had to prove to herself that there were worse men in this world than her first.

And as for that dreadful Dean woman—'Miss' Dean, always that hissy 'Miss', so proud she was of being unmarriageable and barren. She cared for nothing and no one; that song made me think of her, *I hate men and women I don't like too*—but there never was and never would be anyone of whom she could say *I do, do, do like you*. The only one I ever had any respect for was Mrs. Truss: how the other ladies would snigger at her name, and I, naive girl, had to have the joke explained to me. Mrs. Truss now, she was a widow-woman, she'd been alone so long no one could remember her man. She was dignified, quiet, more than a mite frightening, but a better woman than the silly chatterers around her. She was a rock of faith in her lost love. She devoted the remainder of her life to his memory. I could of worn widowhood, I could of worn it well. Better by far than what I've had to live with.

They're all buried now, men and wives, good and bad alike. I wouldn't of had their marriages, not one of em. What love did they have, those worn-out women, what love given or got? Though it went awry, what I had was a hundred, a thousand, a million times better than all their matches put together. My husband was better by far than all of them; the handsomest, the cleverest. We had love and passion once, once we did, even Sammy Wilson could never deny that. What for did he have to rob me of such happiness?

2016

Men were dead simple; you just pulled on the right bit and they'd follow you anywhere.

She did nothing to attack Shayla, never slagged her off, never even uttered an indirect criticism, in fact she said absolutely *nothing* about her. She let her own face and form do the work, and let Jem make his choice, fair and square.

Jem and Shayla had started spending a little time untangled and apart, just for show—'Look at us, we're so great we don't need to be together the whole time'—and it was this overconfident flourish that had both provoked Francine and provided her with an opportunity.

No dirty tricks, no lies, no badmouthing then; it was a straight contest.

Jem was friendly but nervous, distant, at least at first. But he was good at taking hints and so was Francine: he wanted her, that was plain: so much for his icky declarations of undying love for Shayla.

Francine concealed nothing from Shayla, she didn't cheat or anything: Shayla saw herself beaten and that was that. Francine did not crow, only kids did that. Beauty was put to the test, Beauty won out.

1989

When did he cease to love me, my Sam, my Sam? I know he loved me once and loved me true so he did, and Lord knows I only ever saw good in him. When did I hear from him his first harsh word, first scorn, first curse? When did he first speak to me in front of the children as if I were the smallest and the least of them? When did he cease to smile at me, when did his heart turn from me? Even when he had stopped loving me I could of stayed with him, even if it was with only the faintest hope of winning him back. I could of borne his disdain, cruelty, if only he hadn't gone away, if only he'd come back. It was her, she was to blame, that black witch from the shadows of the church. If it hadn't been for her I could of kept my Sam.

2016

Jem was not Francine's type; God, no. He was enough on the eye but his prettiness was that of a doll, glossy and painted. Francine could not imagine him ageing; his skin would stay olive-rose and hair jet black, stiff and coiffed, and yet his artificiality would look increasingly absurd as the lacquer cracked but the surface remained unchanged. He was pleasant enough too, but like so many of Francine's contemporaries displayed little interest in anything beyond the curl of his hair, the sheen of his skin, the tone of his muscles. He had no idea of what he wanted from the future, he just expected good things to be heaped on him as a matter of course and right; he had no grasp at all of the value of the past. He was, along with nine tenths and more of those Francine knew, a beautiful nothing, the walking dead whose smell of decay was smothered with a nose-tickling scent.

As she grew to know him better, Francine found Jem worse than that: vapid, flaccid and self-obsessed, he even sought to look at himself as he made love, searching, craning for a mirror throughout the unsatisfactory process, collapsing quickly and totally, exhausted by his quest. Jem had never been someone Francine had wanted to keep, but she jettisoned him quicker than planned. She arrived at his house for a date only to be received by his mother, who said he was 'busy'. She waited twenty humiliating minutes, crept towards his room when she was unobserved, and sneaked a look through the crack of the door; Jem was there, naked bar his boxers, making shapes and stretching sinew in the mirror. His face was blissful, his mind wholly absorbed. Christ, thought Francine, shivering with self-mockery, Shayla should be grateful, I've saved the bitch from this, though I never meant to.

Jem looked blank when Francine told him she didn't want him anymore, he was like an innocent being taught his first foul language. He was still working on the word-puzzle she had set before him long after she had walked away, no doubt, and no doubt too he was hurt once the unbelievable message sunk in, but she comforted herself he would soon recover, with the friendly help of his best mate in the glass. Shayla never took him back; though she was welcome to him.

2016

A message flashed up on Francine's handheld.

I hate u hoar

That was it. So; you haven't wiped my details off your system at all. Dumb slut.

Little hate-bites like that kept coming through, short and bitter like the sobs and chokes that come after the main crying is done.

Jem, Mart and others, they proved to Francine she could manage men, no problem. There would be no Sam Wilsons, no Trevor Latimers in her life, no way. No self-righteous prigs, no cheating, lying bastards, she would never be found defending the name of some scumbag who'd hurt her, hanging on in desperation for a worthless bloke. Men were easy, she had them sussed. Now Nonna Nora, she never got it. She was beautiful, and had understood that this meant she was powerful, but beyond that she had misunderstood the whole thing. She had seen beauty as a lure, had waited for it to have its effect, was passive and suffered for that. Beauty was a weapon; allied with the intelligence Nonna never had, it was deadly, a winner. Francine had uncovered a secret Nonna never knew. Now she intended to use it to the full.

The Trappers

1987

The Royal Oak was an oasis of darkness in an over-bright world. When the visitor stepped inside it took an exquisitely long time for his eyes to adapt to the less-than-half light, but at last his gaze settled on a time-honoured bar, beer-stained and brass-railed. The dim bulbs above sucked up as much light as they gave out, and a trapped, malted fug descended on the visitor, who realised he must learn to fall in love with this place or flee to the clean air without. That which was not brown within the Oak was a deep, dirty red; the walls, tables and bar must once have been deep-tanned, polished and handsome but now bore the dust, stains and scars of the ages. There was a carpet stretched like a dead skin over the rough wooden floor, ragged and in an advanced state of alopecia. It vied for the visitor's sympathy with the sighing, sagging chairs and shredded, threadbare curtains. Everything was mauled, stained and abused by time and men.

The Oak, mused the visitor, had probably not altered much since before old Hitler did the world a belated favour with a gun at his temple. It was once part of a huddle of buildings close by the church, but the developers were active and gradually the ground was cleared so that the pub stood alone; doubtless it would now remain in its wonderful, shattered and time-locked state until bulldozers attended to it.

Jeff Clayton was, in a word, knackered. He had pulled up at this glorious old survivor of a local for a breath of its curiously refreshing, alien air and a pint and fag or two before the last leg of his journey home. He didn't mean disrespect, but sometimes simply needed fortifying before he got home to Minnie. He was already feeling more himself when he spied Barry Fenton through a frame of daylight that cut off behind him slowly as the door dragged itself to. He knew Barry had spotted him too, but each man affected ignorance of the other's presence, recalling that their wives were not speaking, although the feud defied explanation. The sisters did that sort of thing, and seemed somehow to enjoy it, so Jeff left them to it.

He decided on another drink, determining also to stroll over to stand by Barry, who was perched none too gracefully on a tall bar stool, making idle chit-chat with the landlady. Barry Fenton nodded in greeting and bobbed his head again as Jeff tapped his empty glass and mimed the obvious question.

'I won't tell if you don't,' Jeff encouraged his brother-in-law. Barry had always been a good bloke, ready to laugh and joke and, if you let him, enthuse at length about the deepest, dirtiest guts of engines of all sorts. Neither man was one to bear a grudge, especially ancient and obscure ones from the perpetually warring distaff side, but even so each had to take care, there were subjects probably best not raised even by non-combatants.

'How's your lodger then?' Barry opened with a chancy one, but the query awakened a light of mischief in Jeff and he grinned.

'Under my bloody feet and in my bloody way. And

besides, I wonder who's the lodger and who's master of the house.'

Firmly on common ground, they laughed together.

1947

'Now Jack; when that there door swings open behind us, dost ever wonder if it might be Sammy comin back for a half?'

'I can safely say George, hardly ever. No: simply categorically never.'

'I do. I miss pullin is leg, so I do. But also I'm not finished with im, e's still got questions ter answer.'

'What sort of questions, in God's name?'

'All sorts. F'rinstance, ow does a man's air get darker as e gets older—and the like. All the unsolved mysteries o Sammy.'

1987

'Got the feeling that your home's not your own Jeff? I know I do even when he just comes visiting, I feel we should scrub the house top to bottom so he doesn't wrinkle up his nose the moment he puts a foot through the door. He can demolish buildings with one sour look. I've never known such a—'

'So and so.'

'That'll do. Any road, he's got microscopes for eyes, I swear it, he can see dirt anywhere, makes me feel I live in a coal-hole. Say, if he does that at yours, doesn't your missus give im an earful for casting nasturtiums on her housekeeping?'

'Oh lord have mercy... our Minnie? Far as she's concerned, the old man is God's emissary on earth, he's right about everything and there's nothing she won't do for him. No matter how overbearing, pompous and flatulent the old beggar is, daddy is right and that is that. Father bloody Christmas he is, with all the brass knobs and sugar coating you want. It's pitiful to see the Spitfire reduced to such a state. Remarkable woman, she is: sees and hears what she wants, in the dustbin with facts and useless stuff like that. I thought she'd inherited her flibbertigibbitness from her mother, but there's something else too: the tendency to treat that man as a... dratted icon.'

1947

'I bet is wife does.'

'What?'

'Wonders if Sammy will ever slip back through er door.'

'Not if she's got the slightest sense, owd. Her place should be locked and bolted safe and tight, with "bugger off" written on the door. And underneath, ole lad, in smaller letters, it should say "this means you too, George Shenton".'

1987

'I wonder what the old cuss would make of this beautiful dive.' Jeff blew a trail of smoke and sipped another beer; he would get a cab, pick the car up tomorrow.

'Didn't you know? It was his regular.'

'Good God, Sammy Wilson—*here?*' Jeff Clayton was flabbergasted.

Barry nodded. 'The same Sammy Wilson who now lives in a council house—oh, he can slum it with the best of em when it suits him.'

Jeff peered with renewed interest into the deepest shadows of the old room, as if searching its bibulous spectres.

'If walls could speak, I wonder what tales they'd tell of Sambo Wilson in his palmier days?'

'I'd rather not recall. He used to make me quake in my boots, so what he did to his drinking pals I don't know. He'd play with you like a cat with a half-dead rat, carrying on for his own amusement long past when you were done for. Bloody cruel it was.'

'Ever feel like getting revenge?'

'Every time I see him.'

'Me too, and he's never had a chance to treat me like that! I just can't resist it, I do something, say something, knowing it'll get up his nose, and I want to take a photo of his mush every time I score a bullseye! I call im Sam and watch him wince. Not respectful enough, y'see!'

'Try calling him dad—oh he hates that!'

'Sir.'

'Your worship.'

'Your Holiness.'

'Sometimes I leave the room walking backwards and bowing. He doesn't get it.'

'Ever feel sorry for him?'

'When I see a feeble old man taking short steps to his grave, I think, well, he's scarcely the old devil Nora paints; but then I remember just how he was, everything the girls say about him, and I wonder how a man could be that way and still regard himself as some sort of superior being. Mind you, I reckon doubt is creeping up on him. Sometimes he looks troubled, as if he's fretting about how he's going to explain himself in the hereafter.'

'Our Min says his every action can be justified with reference to the gospels.'

'Good God!' It was Barry's turn to be astonished.

'Exactly. Says she's reading the Bible, a bit every day, and in all the good men she finds in there, she sees something of her father.'

'In King David especially.'

'She says she's seeking for the truth; and for his salvation.'

'And she's persuaded herself that everything he did was right? What about leaving his wife and kiddies in the lurch?'

'He had to do it, Nora was unbearable, drinking and smoking, she was quite out of control.'

'I know the ole lady hit the sherry but I thought that was years after...'

'Facts, Barry, facts,' admonished Jeff playfully, 'what use are they here?'

'What about him telling bare-faced lies in church to get wed again?'

'Tittle-tattle, not true,' said Jeff Clayton for his wife.

'Dallying with Mrs. Ellis?' Barry fired off another round.

'Mirabelle Ellis was a sad and lonely woman whom he helped in troubled times.' Jeff had achieved a mellow, holy tone in his second-hand defence of Sam.

'Hum. Hows about the way he'd thrash the children?

How saintly was that?'

'He never did it. Gentle as a lamb, that man.'

'But I've seen young Flora barely able to stand after he'd larraped her with that damn strap...'

'She provoked him.'

1947

It's no good owd, Sammy's long gone an not comin back. Leave the pining to his missus, hang your hunting cap and dream of past glories while you sup, then let's look to the future for God's sake.'

George drank up as ordered, and a long silence descended on the Oak. Jack threw his hands in the air, exasperated, laughing.

'Oh very well Mr. Shenton, if Sammy *was* to grace this place again...'

'If he *were* to grace this place, surely.'

'Shut your neck! If Sammy *was* to grace this bloody place again, what *would* you be askin him?'

George composed himself as if greeting an arrival in the bar and cheerfully addressed the empty air. 'Ey up now Sammy, tell me, is divorce still an offence agin the laws o'God? Izzat so now? While we're about it then, ow's yourn goin?'

Jack wished Sammy Wilson was there. He had almost forgotten what fun the hunt was.

1987

'Does he clank on about religion these days Jeff? Time was

it was hard to stop im, unless you'd got a gun…'

'Not so much; he makes excuses for getting out of going to church too, you know, he's suddenly got a chest pain or his leg's playing up: Minnie sometimes drags him there like he's a reluctant five year old on the way to Sunday School. I reckon he's done with religion mate, he's shot his bolt and knows it. It's too late for good deeds, for knee-bending and all that mercy-me stuff. He's sort of resigned to getting what he gets when the time comes.'

'And can we hear the sound of pitchforks being sharpened, old man?'

1947

'Dost think e come out o the womb preachin?' mused George lazily.

'I find it hard to imagine him as a child,' Jack confessed. 'Can you see him as a little lad, George?'

The old miner pondered a moment, ran his open palm through the air as if caressing the soft hair of a small child, then flipped his hand over and with a sweeping gesture delivered an almighty cuff to that head. Jack remonstrated with him, but was chuckling all the same.

'Bear with me owd, I have it now; picture im, do, as a little mite without a wicked thought in is head, filled with playfulness and the love of his mother…'

'I'm strugglin, Jack.'

'Come now, what *made* him, George? What changed him? He weren't born like that, no bugger is.'

'P'raps it's just that Sammy's different to us, like. Just not in the way he thought—the hoity-toit sod.'

'No-no mate, something happened, something made him what he was: something that hard is *forged*.'

'Forged you say now? It were a bad job then; he's not just hard, he's *brittle*.'

1987

'I'd love to know the truth about the old beggar, but he'll never tell it.'

'I feel the same Jeff mate, but the truth about Sambo Wilson is lost. He wouldn't tell even under torture, the girls all recall different things and Nora, well, she don't know the difference between true life and her fairy tales. It's hopeless. The only un as knows Sammy's true story is Old Nick—and he won't split.'

'It's hopeless, but it's fun, Barry mate. Now go on, tell me again about the day you told Sammy that your Helen was up the stick, describe that look on his face...'

The Dark Angel

1990

'What's it like outside?'

'Fine, Mum: a fine day like summer.'

'I don't like too much sun. Makes me frown, makes me forehead wrinkled and makes me look old.'

There was a draught; Phyllida had opened a small top window 'to freshen the room a bit', but for Nora the air was not so much fresh as deathly cold. What did that matter? She felt as if she had been picked up like an autumn leaf by the intruder breeze and was floating off to another place. Is my long wait at an end, she wondered.

For some time Nora had been sleeping in the front room, unable to face the long climb to her tiny bedroom. She had told none of her daughters, and made herself perfectly cosy in the biggest of the armchairs: large enough to accommodate a giant, never mind her tiny frame. One morning, however, she had found herself unable to stir a limb, not even to open her eyes properly; she was a prisoner in the deep, cushioned luxury of that chair. And so they had discovered her, Helen and Flora had arrived more or less simultaneously, as if pushing and shoving to be first at her side, and there had been the very devil of a fuss: they couldn't have screeched more if they had found her dead and cold, so they couldn't.

Once they had finished making a racket they set their mother aside, ignored her, as telephone calls were made, other girls arrived, and that hideous little doctor came to tut and growl.

'I can't even die proper for Speakman, the pig.'

'Mum!'

'Oh *bumole!*'

Having called in that antiseptic prig to pronounce over her, the dizzy wenches inundated her with unwanted advice, and, unable to agree as ever, bickered, then rowed. Nora should make the effort to get up the stairs—no-no-no, they should bring her bed down here and make this her room—rubbish, that was nothing but surrender to silly aches and pains and imaginary illnesses—don't be stupid, she might have a fall, she's ninety you know, it's safer this way—let Dr. Speakman decide—no, silly, this is family business alone—and on and on they went. Minnie was especially vociferous, no-no-no, Mother should *not* make her bed here: but she was not defending her mother or trying to make what was left of her life easier, not at all, she was protecting the room from sacrilegious invasion, Daddy's girl was defending his territory. He's not *here*, girl, can you not see, can you not stop flapping your lips?

Flora sided with Minnie, but she was arguing that to abandon the upstairs was a shameful retreat in the face of... she meant *death* but was too mealy-mouthed to say it. So, thought Nora, at least one of my girls at long last agrees with me that the end is coming. Does she fear the Dark Angel will find me more easily here than in that little box up there?

Helen and Phyllida bossed and bullied everyone to their own way of thinking, calling in evidence the fact Nora had already suffered two falls, nastily twisting her wrist in one of them. The madams, suddenly they were no longer claiming she took a tumble deliberately like she was some blessed clown or acrobat. That blinking doctor, he almost took me serious too, she thought—first blasted time ever, mind. And so her bedchamber was arranged and Nora felt a distinct pleasure, she was a newly-validated invalid in her very own sickroom. Thank you all so much, it has only taken you, what, thirty years to admit I am breakable after all.

Flora continued to complain, she never was a good loser even as a little one. 'That room, it's become her world, it's just not right!' Nora no longer sat in the back kitchen, and her chair, her little table, the little life-counting clock and medicines, all moved in with her. She didn't move over to the chair much even though it was hard by her bed, just getting her legs out of bed was making her feel dizzy and spent. The girls, who had made excuse after excuse to get out of looking after her in the years before, were now there practically round the clock, taking it in turns. They want to be close now I'm going—what queer consolation that is after a lifetime of neglect.

Was the vigil over? She could feel a presence: perhaps it was time, and Phylly's opening of the window had let the creature in. Locks and barriers; prayers, pleas and curses; they hadn't deterred it before when it had been an unstoppable, greedy thief in her home. So why was it so coy now? Perhaps the Angel too was older and less able than it had been.

'There you are at last, where have you been?' Nora chided as if to a child that had stayed out too long at play, but she felt no anger, only an exhausted disappointment at having been kept waiting. With the deepest, most profound relief she surrendered thought and feeling: she simply surrendered.

'Dad? Dad listen, I've some news, it's about Mum.'

Muzzily, Sam sat up in his chair and made an effort to straighten his clothing as if preparing hastily to receive an unexpected visit.

'What is it?' His speech was slurred and half-asleep still. 'Your Mother? What does she want?'

'No Dad, nothing like that.' Minnie sighed, wondering if Sam was making this difficult on purpose. 'Mum... she died, a few hours ago. I've just come back from the house.'

Sam was consumed in a long and thoughtful silence, but managed to whisper, 'How?'

'Natural causes, the doctor says.'

'What in God's name does *that* mean?' the old man snapped and Minnie flinched as if before a childhood scolding from a man who wanted *proper answers*.

'She was old, Dad, maybe sicker than we believed, and anyway she was unhappy.' Minnie struggled to remain calm, she was already fighting her raw instinct to raise her voice to him, to fight back. 'And she was sort of... worn out. She didn't want to hang on any more.'

Sam grunted but said nothing more. Minnie stood over him, finding herself exploring his face searching for traces of tears, a flicker of expression, a mistiness in his eyes, but truth to tell she could detect no emotion.

'I'm sorry.' he said huskily. The words Mum had always wanted to hear; no good to her now. 'I can't go to the funeral,' Sam added quickly, 'too ill myself.'

Minnie bit her lip: she had never imagined in her wildest dreams he *would* go, how would Nora ever rest easily if Sam Wilson was there to hymn her to heaven?

'It'll be my funeral soon enough anyhow,' Sam added gloomily. Oh Jerusalem, now he was starting to talk like her. He sank into his chair, a thin, white-haired and fragile figure.

Something had come to an end, something Sam had somehow believed impossible for all that we are every one of us mortal. Nora, the vital force, the life-giver eight times over, was gone. If such an elemental could be extinguished, what prospect was there for him? But no, he rallied, she and I are different, I am stronger and shall fight the Angel. Nora, she fell in love with the shade of death long ago, was embittered and broken, unable to change. The physical corruption of old age destroyed her body but her spirit had failed long before, but not me, such a fate is not for me. Nora called down the Angel's cold embrace, but I shall resist it, for all the pain in my heart, for all the failing of my sight and stiffness of my limbs, I choose life, the Angel of Light.

And yes, I fear death and what lies beyond it, the inescapable Hell of the Book of Fire, the fate that awaits me because I was weak. Oh Lord have mercy.

Minnie flitted about the house dusting and tidying, but always passing by the living room door to look in on her father as he sat lost in thought—in grief?

'D'you want anything Dad? A cup of tea?'

'No.' He scarcely made a sound.

'I'll come back in a short while. Perhaps you'll want company when you've taken it all in.'

If that crazy priestess, my aunt, was right, I shall have company enough in the flames that scorch but give no light: I cannot think of a single soul I have known who might escape that fire, we are all bound for it, not one of us sufficiently free of taint to be spared the searing heat. Even Nora in her innocence, her childlike simplicity, is she to go there too? Can the innocent be condemned when they do not, cannot know that they have offended Heaven? And what, then, of a man who had read that book, and declaimed its words before the people, who knew well how he should live his life but fell into the ways of sin in spite of all?

Samuel Wilson realised how much he dreaded death; he was afraid of the sensation of life leaving his body; afraid of pain, of opening his eyes once again on the other side. Oh, to hope that it was different, that Nora was now reunited with Petra, Jocelyn, Vanessa, Alex, and that they were in a state of bliss. Oh to hope he too would be embraced by this blessing.

'Nora,' he said, plainly. Minnie did not hear.

Nora, that child, that golden erotic faerie for whom he would in his passion have committed any sin, risked any damnation. Oh, he was hopelessly steeped in sin, doomed to burn. Perhaps he would be granted a small respite, an innocent smile from his lost babies before his doom took him. But after there was surely nothing. He suppressed an instinct to pray; hopeless, hopeless.

On their first night alone, he and Nora took a small rented cottage for a few precious days, it was all they could afford, and at last there was no one nearby, no sharp-eared busybodies, no children; not yet. How determined Nora had been to transform that dirty tumbledown into a home; even stronger had been her determination to pleasure her husband; oh, her coarse, dirty passion as they performed the business of man and wife, great God the *noise* she made. But it was no sin, surely, and the Lord had blessed them, granted them their children. Nora cared for them well. Yes, even with her whore's mouth, her lewd love of the flesh, Nora had been an innocent. Surely she would sit at the right hand of the Lord.

'Nora and her gallant Sam,' someone had once called them, and for many a year their friends had used that phrase. He could not now remember who had coined it; nor could he recall quite when it fell out of use, but it was long before the coming of peace.

The pews looked small and squashed, as if they had been cut and planed for an ancestor race of diminutive and delicate stature. The arrivals at St Anselm's squeezed in, unable to find comfort in its bare primitivism. The organist was weaving gentle sounds that filled every crack in the walls, the notes shifting and dipping in a low, funerary moan, but the trance was broken on and off by fumbling discords and jarring, piping intruder sounds.

Helen leaned across to Flora, hand on her forearm.

'What's the matter with the organist—is he wearing boxing gloves?'

Flora smiled wanly; would their mother have complained or just laughed?

The play of light and sound in the church had always fascinated Flora. The old building was now at a busy crossroads that roared with traffic day and night, and yet the alien noise stopped at the fortress-like doors, unable to penetrate even when open to receive the solemn congregation. In the church proper, a majestic serenity was paramount; the light from the stained glass windows scattered everywhere in colourful confetti pieces that shifted slowly, swept along by the unseen sun. Flora was entranced; the thought was irresistible, inevitable, she was a child once again and she and her sisters sitting silent and obedient, waiting for their father to emerge, dressed in his simple dark robes, to deliver the day's lesson in that familiar, feared tone, his face tight as he concentrated on his work, his brow deeply lined as if scowling at the gathered faithful.

Helen's thoughts were distracted also, it seemed; she leaned over to Flora, *hist*. 'He's not going to show up, is he?'

Flora floundered, puzzled. 'Who?' she mouthed; she was still in her childhood, it was wrong to talk in church.

'*Him*!' Helen was impatient with the slow-witted. 'He wouldn't dare—would he?'

Flora spread her hands, confounded.

'Our Dad!' Helen had raised her voice too far; her whisper ran around the old stone walls in hissing echoes.

'Don't be silly!' Flora performed more dumb-show than speech. 'He'd never!'

Helen subsided, but again and again during the service she would look over her shoulder to the church door as if expecting a tall, proud frame to fill it, silhouetted against the afternoon's brightness. Flora patted Helen's arm in both remonstrance and sympathy; soon enough she would find herself unable to resist aping her sister's new tic; had Sam Wilson really the sheer brass neck to do such an inconceivable thing?

'I'd put nothing past him,' cautioned Phyllida, who up till then had given no indication that she had heard their exchanges.

The casket was so small, small enough to be that of a child. Surely, thought Flora in alarm, our mother was not quite so diminished by old age; or am I beginning even now to forget this old woman and recall only what Mother would want, the youngster, the brown-haired beauty? Nora Wilson was returning to St Anselm's, the church she had rejected, where her hypocrite husband had extolled the word of the Lord, where it required but little fancy to detect the echo of his voice. The family's decision, after yet another white-hot disagreement, that Nora should depart from this place to her grave struck Flora, as Nora might have said, as 'ridickleous', but they had clung for some reason to a ruined and disgraced tradition.

Flora was unsettled, cold and uncomfortable, and more strange thoughts assailed her. She remembered coat-tailing her mother to the other church, where they promised her converse with the spirits of her lost children. It had all been a nonsense, but there perhaps had begun Nora's long, cold entanglement with the romance of her own death. What is she finding out now, thought Flora, ashamed but unable to stop her transported mind, about death and what lies beyond? Let us hope she is content at last.

'All those silly imaginings—dear me.' Flora giggled over her drink as she stood in the kitchen at Woolsend Avenue.

'We were all the same, that place fills your head with dreams.' Phyllida comforted her. 'I'm still not convinced that the old man won't poke his nose through the door just to get a free glass of sherry and check the house is ready for his return.'

The three sisters laughed together, but a fourth voice made an angry, inarticulate noise and all eyes turned to

Minnie, her face stern and pious.

'You are all stupid, disrespectful bitches, you never understood our Dad, never! He's a good man and if he came here you should make him welcome, not make fun of him like a gang of bar-flies! It's our business to honour him, not to mock him!'

Helen bridled and it seemed that the modest wake was about to deteriorate into a classic Wilson row, but Flora interposed and apologised quietly and Minnie withdrew, apparently satisfied with her victory.

'There goes a lucky woman,' muttered Helen. 'She has the privilege, it seems, of living with one of the martyrs.'

1992

There was something squatting on Sam's chest, leaden-heavy, and he had no strength to even attempt to shift it. It was a demon, a succubus risen from a shadowy hell to feed on the last fadings of his vitality. Sam stirred under the deadening weight, wakening slightly and clearing his mind a little. Perhaps it was one of Minnie's dogs flopping on his bed and pinning him down, the silly mutts did this often, she was far too soft with them, treated them like children, so she did, and like children they took dumb advantage of any weakness they were shown.

Another degree awake, Sam tried to stir again but the weight would not relent and for long moments he tried to call out, but could only manage a thin, keening wail. Still that weight pressed, compressing him as if determined to drive him down, ever down into the softness of the mattress. A split second's further thought and he knew the identity of his visitor.

'Lord have mercy,' Sam heard himself croak in an old and broken voice, betraying no confidence that there was any mercy to be had. 'Nora,' said the same voice. Only she would intercede for him, only she. 'Lord have mercy.' The words drifted out of him as if he were a small child nagging a parent in hopeless reminder of a broken promise.

1946

'Ahhhh, there'll be no hell for Sammy Wilson.'

'What makes you say that, George?'

'There's been no retribution for im in life, why should the life hereafter be different? God's too good Jack, too forgiving. No, there'll be no eternal punishment for Sammy: he'll get told off, mebbe, an made to stand at the back so e don't embarrass no one, but that'll be all.'

The Place of Lost Stories

2079

'Play Nonna for us Gramma Frankie, be Nonna!'

'Tell us the story—Nonna Nora and Grampa Sam!'

Four of her youngest grandchildren sat in a semi-circle at Francine's feet; their sister, a clear ten years older than the oldest of them, sat apart from the group, pulling sulky faces and looking ostentatiously bored. She wanted it to be clear that she had heard it all before. She was forgetting—deliberately—that was the point.

They had lived a good while, these stories; survived far beyond Francine's most optimistic, no, crazy expectations. Now she nursed hopes they would abide still longer, outliving her as they had her mother and grandmother. If the stubborn Wilson habit of longevity proved as effective in her as it had in them, she would remain to carry on the telling and retelling for, oh, a comfortable while yet. The children, even the very youngest, loved to hear the tales of the old-old times, and she was happy to retell them for as long as she continued to draw breath.

'Grampa Sam was a horrid ole piker, twisted an ugly an wasted away he was, his face was all pruney wrinkles and his hair like dirty snow, even before he was five-an-twenty years old. Why was he so old and ruined before his time? That was because he was all eaten up inside with rottenness and hate and something else truly terrible...'

'What's a piker?' asked the youngest.

'Shuttup, spoiling it!' shouted her brother.

'Leaving your babies is a *horrid* thing to do!' she interrupted again a little later.

'Shuttup, we want to hear the finish!' the boy shoved her, argy-bargy broke out and Francine had to use her Sam-like glare to restore order.

'And when the story's done, sing for us, one of those old songs!' the youngsters demanded; they always did.

'Oh no, they're too sad!' protested the youngest.

'Shuttup, spoiling it!' bellowed her brother.

The tale was told at last and the little ones had rushed out into the garden, disputing noisily over who was in the right, Nonna or Sam. The oldest girl remained, still looking displeased and rebellious. Much had changed over the course of Francine's life, but the love of small children for stories had not, and nor had the surliness of teenagers. She was nearly seventeen; although the Wilson features were blurred and altered, they were present for those who cared to look for them, and by anybody's standards she was radiantly beautiful. She was perfectly, and at this point sometimes quite painfully, aware of her looks. From some storehouse of heredity she had been granted straight blonde hair, which she wore long, and the most shapely, perhaps over-large bosom, awareness of which made her unable to decide whether to flaunt it in the most daring and incomprehensible modern fashions, or hide it in baggy, shapeless, colourless clothes. Her parents were worried. Francine, however, felt confident in her ability to navigate the future.

'They think you were there and that you saw it all,' said the oldest girl, indicating the yelling children and smiling at her grandmother. She was always more tractable when the little ones were not under her feet.

'They think I had to dodge dinosaurs as I went to school; they have no sense of time, not yet. They think *you're* old, as old as me you are to them. They'll get the hang of things by and by, just like you did.'

'Did it really happen?' asked the oldest girl. 'Did any of it, or did we just grow up on a lot of fairy tales?'

'You should know that Ole Hickler was real enough.'

'Yes, but Grampa Sam and Mrs. Whassname and all of that, did it really happen, and does it matter anyway?' She may have pretended to object to the told-again stories in front of her siblings, but she was now engaging in her own ritual; these questions were oft-asked and answered.

'Yes it did and yes it does—to me. What you lot do with all my old romancing later on is up to you.'

'When you're dead and gone and we're all sorry?' The smile was still there.

'I wasn't going to say that.' Francine grinned in reply.

'Good. I want you to stick around a while yet, specially for your birthday party. And I don't want you to be like Nonna Nora. Have you never been afraid of just turning into her?'

'No, never.'

'Nonna's life was just stories. Yours isn't.'

'I'm glad of that, but stories have their place. They always have for me.'

'Why *did* she turn it all into stories—Grampa Sam, Ole Hickler?'

'Nonna was like most people—she loved stories to have a moral. It was her way, I think, of dealing with what she found to be… unimaginable evil.'

The Beauty of Chell Street

1987

I was never going to grow old: such a thing was simply not going to happen to me. And I was so successful in this aim that eventually I quite forgot I could ever be anything but youthful and lovely. But I had started to age from within, from a place I couldn't see it happening, as if I were nursing a canker in my guts, an invisible worm making a slow meal of me. Yes, it turned me withered inside and yet it couldn't destroy the Beauty, not until it found a way to break out on my skin; and I resisted it, how I resisted it. But it was a clever enemy, cunning and subtle, it changed its tack, ceasing to eat up my innards and turning its vile attention to my soul. It gave me bitter thoughts and supped on my unhappiness. Misery, misery, it grew and I shrank, my strength drained by the leech and gradually the struggle lost and that blight, old age came creeping out of my within, spreading, spreading, and my face and body became as I was inside.

I remained beautiful, more beautiful than any other woman in this tiny world, for so long I thought I had won. But even for me the bloom was lost at last, lost to the worm I nursed.

1916

Nora settled on the photographer's tall stool and composed her face. A smile kept trying to break out of her, but the man had demanded she remain still and serious. He took forever to organise himself, interfering with, rearranging and adjusting the clumsy equipment pointed at her head, but finally there was an almighty flash and he told her, in a kinder voice, to relax, that it was done. Nora stepped down from the stool, pulling her skirt away from the leg, it had become wrapped around it; finally that smile escaped her lips and her face lit up anew. The portrait was taken, she could hardly wait to see what it was like; perfect, she hoped, something that would confirm her, now and forever, as the Beauty of Chell Street.

Lightning Source UK Ltd.
Milton Keynes UK
UKHW010012220822
407609UK00002B/435

9 781788 649421